SPACE CITY

by

Jared Austin

Huntsville, Alabama

This is a work of fiction. All of the characters, organizations, and events portrayed in this novel are either products of the author's imagination or are used fictitiously.

SPACE CITY

ISBN-13: 978-1-7326412-7-3

Published by Up Past Dawn. Find us at https://jareddanielaustin.com

Dedication

For Dana,
who helps me reach for all my dreams

Acknowledgments

While writing a book can be a lonely endeavor, revising and publishing it is not. And there are many people who have played a role in getting this book published that I most heartily give my thanks!

There are many friends and fellow writers who read this story or listened to me read it over numerous writers group meetings and offered advice, edits, and most important, encouragement to keep going. Those people include Dana Austin, Karisa Austin, Mel Howard, Kay Glover, Amy Herring, Darren Gannuch, Heather Montgomery, Nellie Maulsby, Lin Cochran, Shirley Garrett, and many others at both my Teach to Write and the North Alabama Science Fiction and Cake Appreciation Society (NASFCAS) writing groups.

I'd also like to thank Amy Herring and Bryan Jones for consultation and support in my cover revisions.

And of course, thank you, my readers, who are giving *Space City* a chance! It has been a long journey from my first imagining the story, to writing, and finally sharing it with you. I promise more to come soon!

Chapter 1

Neil's Recruitment

Neil clutched his grandfather's silver coin in one fist and a fake ID in the other as he worked up the courage to enter the Air Force recruiting office. Enlisting now was a long shot, but he had to try. His mother's dying wish was for him to seek help here when he turned sixteen; bizarre advice, considering the Air Force didn't accept recruits until seventeen. He just wished he had something better to wear than a tattered grey shirt and holey jean-shorts to make a good first impression.

The recruiting office was next door to Army, Navy and Marine recruiting offices in a long, beige shopping center. In the corner was a cheap buffet serving seafood and sushi. He had eaten there a few times with his mother as a child. That buffet was one of the reasons why Neil couldn't remain in Huntsville, Alabama any longer. Once a dear home, it was now haunted by the memory of his mother. He knew the cost of living chained to the past, like his uncle.

Standing tall like a young bear, feigning fearlessness, Neil squeezed his grandfather's coin, a gift from Winston Churchill. Roughly the diameter of a silver dollar, but thicker, one side of the coin had the American Bald eagle with the American flag hanging from its talons, representing freedom. On the other side was a lion beneath the British flag, a symbol of bravery. His grandfather had told him the two were paired together because freedom could not truly exist without bravery. Churchill had commissioned a limited number of the coins as personal thanks for American soldiers who heroically aided Great Britain during World War II. The coin was also the last thing Neil's grandfather had ever given him.

His grandfather had only accomplished those feats after first enlisting, and that knowledge compelled Neil into the Air Force recruiting office.

A recruiter wearing a light blue shirt adorned with a silver nameplate on his left breast, ribbons on his right, and the U.S. insignia and occupational badge—sat behind a desk and talked to an old man. The wall calendar, flipped to August, displayed a picture of an F-16 Fighting Falcon aircraft with the slogan "Aim High" above it.

The recruiter eyed Neil as he entered, but didn't rise. "Can I help you, son?" His voice revealed a slight southern drawl.

Neil's suddenly leaden tongue, like an anchor tied to legs in the ocean, refused to work. What's so hard about talking to the man who can decide your future for years to come?

Straightening in a valiant attempt to add height to his 5'8" frame, Neil attempted to channel his grandfather's confidence. "I'd like to enlist, join the Air Force."

The recruiter rose from this chair. A head taller, and a good fifty pounds larger, the recruiter stared down at Neil. The recruiter asked. "How old are you?"

"Just turned sevenTEEN, sir!" Neil's voice cracked for the first time in quite a while. Was his whole body turning traitor today?

Despite suddenly burning cheeks, Neil stepped forward and offered the fake ID. He had memorized the license number, date of birth, address, and even the expiration date. The photo had come out pretty well—he had always liked his unruly red hair. He could live with the name Rick Sanders. Better that than begging his dad's brother to let him return to his rat-infested hole.

The recruiter accepted the card. Without glancing at the ID, he dropped it on top of a neat stack of papers on the desk. His thin eyebrows slanted in a frown. "Impersonation is a crime. How old are you, honestly?"

Neil wished for a drink of water, if only to delay a response. He hated lying, but surely his desire to enlist made up for it. The recruiter's hard eyes said he wasn't interested in good intentions, though. Stick to the facts.

Neil weakly answered. "Sixteen, sir." His palms started to sweat.

"What's your name?" the recruiter asked, retrieving a steaming mug of coffee from beside the keyboard.

How could anyone drink coffee in the summer? Neil wondered. August in Alabama was way too hot and humid, and this year was no exception.

Mistaking the delay in Neil's response, the recruiter's eyes narrowed. "Don't you dare lie."

"Neil Ericson." Mercifully, Neil's voice held steady this time. Even so, he felt ashamed at the pleading tone underlying his words.

"Why do you want to enlist?"

The question caught Neil off guard. Had he misjudged the recruiter? Perhaps he would understand.

Neil explained. "I need to get away from my uncle."

"Why?"

Neil closed his mouth and stared at the ID. He was reluctant to elaborate about his uncle. He had gone down that road before, and it never ended well.

The recruiter chuckled and gave a knowing glance to the old man. "Your uncle refuses to let you waste all day watching TV? Won't buy the latest video games?"

Neil hated when adults scoffed at his problems, as if his concerns were trivial. "All his money is spent on alcohol, and the tightwad doesn't share."

The recruiter grimaced. "Sorry, son. But joining the Air Force isn't an option at your age, even if I'd sometimes wish otherwise."

Neil had expected that answer; yet, it was still a punch to the gut.

"Come back on your next birthday," the recruiter suggested. "A year isn't that long. I'm sure your uncle will sign off on your enlistment. You'll have to shave that red mop on your head."

Neil shook his head, refusing to accept no as an answer. "Isn't there something you can do? An exception to the rule for special circumstances? I could clean. My uncle already thinks I'm the maid."

The recruiter smiled slightly, but crossed his arms. "Can't join until you're seventeen. But the day you are, I'll help you."

Neil considered confessing everything. If he failed now, he would be forced to return to his uncle's home after promising himself that morning that he'd never go back. His uncle was a ghost, clinging to the past. A once promising baseball prospect playing in the minor leagues, he'd shattered his ankle in a collision at home plate. Now all he did was drink and watch ballgame after ballgame on TV, while raving about his glory days. If he got too depressed or angry about the lost fame that was his due, he would take it out on Neil.

Having observed his uncle for years, Neil understood the danger of living solely in the past. The longing for what once was made a person bitter. Neil had no intention of forgetting his mother. But he was afraid that if he remained here too long, even one more year, his own growing bitterness might drown him.

"I could pass for seventeen," Neil insisted.

The recruiter shook his head. "Come back after your birthday. I'll keep the ID so you don't get any more clever ideas."

Shoulders slumping, Neil turned and departed the recruiter's office. He briefly considered the other three recruitment offices in the shopping plaza before turning to face University Drive. The lunch time traffic bustled along, people hurrying back to their offices to finish up their work-day so they could go home to their families. After all, Huntsville was a family-friendly city. But without his family, Neil felt like an outsider.

What now?

"What's the real reason you want to join the Air Force?" a voice called from behind.

The old man from the recruiter's office had followed him out. He was dressed in a silver, button-down shirt with the sleeves rolled up and black slacks. Only a few wisps of white hair remained on his head. He had a large round nose paired with a toothy smile that made him seem kind and harmless. But his rigid, near-march gait marked him as a military man as well.

Neil started to repeat what he had told the recruiter.

"No, no," the old man waved dismissively. "I heard your story. There are a lot easier ways to escape an unpleasant home life. Why the Air Force?"

If the recruiter couldn't help, how would this old man?

The old man would probably just tell him how when he was Neil's age, he had worked one job before the sun came up, another two after school, and had only slept during the walks in between.

Still. What could it hurt to explain?

"My grandfather. Before my mom died she told me stories about him. He was a fighter pilot in World War II. She knew tons of stories about his heroics. Ever since, I've wanted to fly jets."

"What was your grandfather's name, son?" the old man asked.

"Rurik Ericson."

The old man grinned, as if confirming something to himself. He gestured forward, and they resumed walking.

"Did you know him?" Neil asked.

"I've met him." The old man offered his hand. "My name is Harold Chapman."

Neil shook Mr. Chapman's hand while a ton of questions scrambled through his head.

"I may know a way you can start training now," Mr. Chapman said before Neil could ask. "I used to work for a prestigious academy, and sixteen is the age to join."

"Is it an Air Force academy?" Neil asked. He was pretty sure the Air Force Academy in Colorado Springs wouldn't accept him yet. Could the old man be serious?

"Better." Mr. Chapman's green eyes shone and his smile broadened. "You'll not find a better academy in the universe."

Neil stopped in his tracks, doubtful. "The academy would accept me?"

"You marched into that recruiting office with a lion's determination," Mr. Chapman replied. "And if you're anything like your grandfather, the academy needs people like you."

Neil was desperate for something good to happen to him. Was this his chance to escape his uncle and start a new life? The academy wasn't the Air Force. He had always dreamed of the day he would wear an Air Force uniform, like his grandfather.

"Any siblings?" Mr. Chapman asked.

Neil shook his head, unsure why that mattered. "I always wanted some."

"This is an opportunity you can't pass up," Mr. Chapman said.

Neil's desires and Mr. Chapman's assurances were hard to ignore. If he changed course now, was he betraying his mom and grandfather, solely to escape his uncle?

Neil opened the hand clutching his grandfather's silver coin, the side with the eagle holding the flag facing up.

Freedom.

He yearned for freedom from his uncle. Yet, he had always hoped to earn some type of coin of his own in the Air Force one day. But who was to say this academy couldn't be his path to the Air Force? He showed Mr. Chapman the coin. "My grandfather gave me this coin before he disappeared. I was six. He told me life sometimes offered impossible choices. Whenever he came across a tough decision, he flipped this coin and let fate decide."

"You can't know what the future holds," Mr. Chapman said. A cab pulled up to the curb beside him and he opened the door, but stood waiting.

Neil held out the coin, the eagle and American flag facing Mr. Chapman. "Heads, I wait until next summer and return to that recruiter's office. Tails, I go with you and join this academy."

Neil flipped the coin. On its fall, Mr. Chapman reached out and caught the coin and climbed inside the cab, leaving the door open.

Chapter 2

Neil Beyond the Sky

Neil scrambled into the taxi after Mr. Chapman to retrieve his grandfather's coin. The cab driver was a middle-aged man with a well-groomed salt and pepper beard. Jazz played on the radio.

"The Arsenal, please," Mr. Chapman said to the driver. He held out the coin, bravery side out, toward Neil. "This isn't an opportunity you dismiss. Your grandfather would've agreed."

Neil snatched the coin and slipped it into his pocket. What did the old man know about what his grandfather would have agreed with? Adults always thought they knew what was best, even when they didn't know you at all. But Mr. Chapman's words had implied that he knew Neil's grandfather, not just met him. The old man had surely served. Behind his big smile, he possessed a firm quality, like a seasoned military officer. Maybe he and Neil's grandfather had served together.

Mr. Chapman surprised him. "Tell me about your grandfather."

"But you've met him, right?"

"Yes, but you're his grandson."

Before his mother's death, Neil had spent countless evenings playing with model airplanes or drawing fighter jets by the fire as she recounted stories of his grandfather's military feats. He had flown for the British to defend London during the Blitz. Later, during the war, his grandfather had barely bailed from his plane before it collided with a Nazi jet near Paris. As he talked, he heard his mother reciting the stories to him as clearly as if she sat in the cab with them. He wished she were here telling the stories to Mr. Chapman.

The cab stopped at the back of a line of cars approaching the Redstone Arsenal gates, breaking Neil's reverie. He hadn't traveled onto the arsenal in years, since his grandfather last brought him. His pulse quickened at the prospect.

The six lane gate resembled the starting gate of a horse race, the cars entering like stallions loading up before shooting forward to start the race. The guard standing beside the booth they had pulled up to smiled and spoke to Mr. Chapman as if they were old friends. Mr. Chapman handed a badge to the guard, and the cab driver forked over his driver's license. The guard eyed Neil a moment, but didn't ask him for identification.

Fortunately, he didn't have the fake ID on him anymore. Prison was not the step up from his uncle's house that he hoped for. Then again…the food was probably better.

The guard examined the badge and driver's license for a moment, before he handed the IDs back and wished them a good day. Was he accustomed to Mr. Chapman bringing new academy students with him?

For the next half mile, open fields on either side of the road were filled with amarums—a knee high, thin plant with small, yellow flowers at the tips. The fields gave way to tall, southern pines intermixed with eastern red cedars. The trees, crowding the roads on all sides, created a buffer zone around the Arsenal.

They continued on past a ten-story, gray NASA building with the U.S. flag flying from the top. In front of the building, three rocket engines were on display. He knew them well, having studied most air- and spacecraft thanks to the books his grandfather had left him. The shortest engine, the J-2, was nearly twice the size of a full-grown man. On the top portions of each engine was a typical engine block with turbopumps, ducts, valves, and manifolds tightly wound together. The engine blocks rested on a large metallic thrust chamber, which resembled the bottom half of a ballroom gown, as if the engines were prepared for a dance.

To Neil's surprise, the cab carried them past many new and aging office complexes and out to a remote area overgrown with crab grass, amarums and kudzu. The driver parked beside a single, large white building, a little smaller than the NASA office they had passed earlier.

Neil doubted anyone had used the building in the last twenty years. Surely this place wasn't the campus.

Mr. Chapman paid the driver and exited the cab. Frowning, Neil climbed out after him. People love to say "don't judge a book by its cover" in moments like these. But come on. This was not what he pictured for a prestigious academy.

The old man, grinning now like a child headed to an amusement park, marched across the cracked and uneven parking lot straight for the entrance. "We've got a decent flight ahead of us. Are you ready?"

Neil stumbled, taken aback. "Flight? What are we flying in?" He stared at the wall of the building as if he might suddenly see through it to what awaited them inside. Was the building actually a hangar? Where was the academy?

Mr. Chapman held his badge to a black card reader beside the door. The card reader beeped and he pulled the door wide. Sunlight flooded onto a spacious concrete floor. In the middle of the room, a futuristic silver ship rested on top of an enormous, tank-like vehicle with a flat top. The vehicle resembled the crawler transporter that NASA had used to carry the space shuttle to the launchpad.

Neil's jaw dropped.

The ship faced bay doors at the rear of the facility. A logo with a blue planet and a single green continent, with the letters SC in the middle, adorned the ship's vertical stabilizer. The musty air was laced with gas fumes. Cranes that nearly touched the ceiling, a fuel pump, and other equipment and tools lined the perimeter, but the majority of the floor around the ship was spotless. Overhead lights beamed off the ship which rested on two vertical engines that capped short wings on either side.

This ship was the coolest thing that Neil had ever seen, but a thought occurred to him which made him fear this was all for naught. "How much does this academy cost?" His uncle, who had little money as it was, would never agree to pay tuition when public schools were free.

"You'll have a chance to apply for scholarships." Mr. Chapman hit a button that opened the bay doors. "Hang here for a minute."

He marched over to a door in the gray crawler. As he approached, a set of stairs extended to the ground, allowing him to climb to a raised platform and enter the crawler. Its engine fired up, and he slowly drove the crawler and the ship out through the bay doors.

Neil followed the crawler outside, the hair on his arms standing up. Were they seriously going to fly in that ship? Despite Mr. Chapman's earnest appearance, Neil considered the possibility that this was all a prank of some sort. Perhaps the recruiter and the old man liked to play jokes. That seemed implausible, but so did the idea of an academy recruiting random kids using state-of-the-art aircraft, even if the recruiter knew his grandfather had been a war hero.

Mr. Chapman emerged onto the stairwell. "Come on. Our flight's not getting any shorter." He turned and climbed a second set of stairs toward the platform on which the ship rested.

Not waiting for a second invitation, Neil ran to the crawler. He paused right before the stairs and glanced up at the two-story vehicle, unable to believe his luck. He pinched an arm just to assure himself that he was not asleep. When the crawler didn't vanish, Neil reverently climbed the steps. He gripped the rail the entire way, not to support himself, but simply to confirm this was real. This was happening.

On the first level, a pair of wide doors led into the crawler. Neil wanted to check it out, but was afraid of holding the old man up, since he had not offered a tour. Neil lingered a moment longer before climbing the second flight of stairs to the crawler platform.

Once more he slowed to a stop, taking in the sight of the beautiful silver ship shaped a little like a stingray, but not as thin in proportion. Who had built this ship? He had never seen anything like it.

Neil slowly approached the open door just before the wing and entered a cabin. Mr. Chapman stood next to an open cabinet, donning a gray one-piece suit. A smaller version of the logo Neil had seen on the tail of the ship adorned his left breast.

Mr. Chapman pulled a matching suit from the cabinet and tossed it to Neil. "Put that on."

Neil hesitated, wanting to put it on, but a little overwhelmed. "Are you sure?"

Mr. Chapman zipped his own suit. "This academy offers a one-of-a-kind opportunity. I can't go into too much detail yet, for security reasons, but no other school will offer you a better future." He spoke to Neil man-to-man, easing the doubts. Plus, Neil couldn't pass up the chance to fly on that ship, not even if his uncle beat him every day for a year.

Neil pulled the flight suit on over his clothes before following Mr. Chapman toward the cockpit. "Let's fly!"

Wait until Brent hears about this when I get back to school.

Except if he joined the academy, high school was a thing of the past. The academy must be way cooler than public school.

In the cockpit, Mr. Chapman grabbed two flight helmets and handed one to Neil. The helmet slid on snugly. The old man pressed a button on the side of his helmet and a glass shield lowered from the top of it to his suit. "In case of emergencies," he said.

Neil found the button on the side of his helmet and pressed it. A second shield lowered over his face, sealing him in. The suit and helmet made him feel a little claustrophobic, causing him to tense up.

"Take a seat." Mr. Chapman tapped the button to raise his face shield back up and gestured to the rear of two seats in the cockpit.

As Neil took a seat, he tapped the button to raise his face shield, but Mr. Chapman motioned for him to close it again. He grabbed a device that was hooked to the back of Neil's chair. The old man plugged the other end into the back of Neil's helmet.

"For oxygen," Mr. Chapman explained.

He took the front seat facing numerous screens, hooked himself into the emergency oxygen system and closed his face shield, and started pressing the screens with gloved hands. The engines fired and the deafening blast prevented Neil from asking any further questions. He sat back and tried to relax and enjoy the takeoff, but it felt like the moment right before bungee-jumping off a bridge, multiplied by a hundred.

The ship rose straight up in the air, lifting off from the crawler. Neil gripped the chair arms, his stomach plummeting as the ship launched.

Was this a good idea?

The ship's nose angled upward and they accelerated. His nervousness quickly gave way to excitement.

Where was this academy located? He couldn't imagine how he had never heard of this ship, so he guessed they must maintain a high level of secrecy, maybe in some isolated mountain range or on a remote island.

The ship shook from heavy turbulence as they rose through the clouds. Neil shouted his excitement. The launch had confirmed his desire to fly. Joining this academy was the right choice if they trained him to fly a ship like this. Only his mother being around to send him off would have made this flight better.

To his surprise, the ship didn't level out after a short ascent. Before long the ship shook violently and the roar grew. Neil tried to get the old man's attention.

"What altitude are we at?"

The engine's roar, combined with turbulence, swallowed his words.

As they soared upward, his excitement drained. Why hadn't they leveled out? Had Mr. Chapman passed out, leaving the ship racing upward until they burned up in the atmosphere or lost control and crashed?

Neil grabbed at his seat buckle, trying to free himself. His heart raced. He yelled again, but couldn't hear his own words. Unbuckling himself became the most important task in his life—

The ship calmed.

Neil glanced out the windows and forgot about trying to free himself. Stars filled his view, myriad diamonds bespeckling the blackness of space.

They had left Earth's atmosphere. Surprisingly, the moon hadn't changed. It remained the same as it looked from Earth during a full moon, except not nearly as bright.

The ship changed angles, revealing the Earth out the window. The ocean was like a clear blue sky. He spotted North America, which gave him chills. An entire continent that at the moment seemed like a miniature replica. He had never imagined the opportunity of seeing the planet from space.

"Wet yourself?" Mr. Chapman asked, glancing back over his shoulder. He hadn't passed out, as Neil had feared. He had flown them here intentionally.

Unable to tear his eyes off this unexpected unveiling, Neil asked, "Is the academy on the moon?"

The old man chuckled. "Close, but I'll let you discover for yourself."

Neil grabbed at his seat belt again, this time effortlessly unbuckling himself. His entire body rose, drifting toward the ceiling, but the sudden weightlessness made him uneasy. He grabbed the chair arms and pulled himself back down. He re-buckled.

When he had gone to bed last night, his thoughts had revolved around his desperate hope of Air Force enlistment. People dreamed about the last things on their mind before sleep, right? Maybe his subconscious was embellishing his desires to fly into this impossible dream.

"I'm sure you have questions," Mr. Chapman said. "We have a long flight, so I'll answer as many as I can. Let me start by saying the academy is located on Space City."

A logo, the same from the ship's tail, appeared on the right window, which doubled as a screen.

"Space City is home to a secret alliance that explores the universe and makes contact with the inhabitants of distant planets."

"Aliens exist?" The words tumbled from Neil's lips. The stunning revelations kept coming, and he didn't know how to process them all. Part of him wanted to tell the old man he was crazy, yet here they were flying above the Earth.

"Azzaro, Kali, Macab, and many more," Mr. Chapman confirmed.

A blue-skinned humanoid with two short horns on its head and jaws that looked like the skin was missing, leaving bluish muscles on the surface, replaced the logo on-screen. Images from every movie or show Neil had ever seen involving aliens flashed through his mind. A cynical voice in his head noted that the man could easily be wearing body paint.

"Where do I even start?" Neil heard the incredulity in his voice.

The old man chuckled again.

"What's with the logo?"

"That's your first question?" Mr. Chapman asked. "I tell you that aliens exist and you're going to live on a ship in space, and you ask about a logo?"

"The picture of the Earth with just a single continent struck me as odd is all."

"Hmmm," Mr. Chapman mused. "Well, when the alliance first formed, the founders wanted it to represent the entire Earth, not just one country or continent. Unity is needed to successfully explore space, because it is so vast and dangerous. The single continent is Pangaea, the name of the Earth's continents when they were all one. It symbolizes unity. The humans living on Space City come from nearly every country on Earth."

An alliance comprised of people from all over the Earth, and most people had no idea that it existed. How was that possible?

"Space City was founded shortly after Neil Armstrong took his first step on the moon," Mr. Chapman said. "On a second, follow-up mission, we had our first encounter with another race, the Azzaro. Those involved in that first contact decided Earth wasn't ready to meet the universe. The Cold War raged on as the Vietnam War ground to a halt. So many countries divided. Space City's founders chose to act as a shield until the Earth laid aside its violent differences."

"How do you keep this a secret?" Neil asked, studying the Earth. "Surely people saw us take off?"

"We're cloaked. And people in Huntsville are used to all sorts of strange booms and blasts coming from the arsenal. You'd be surprised how much people ignore what doesn't immediately affect them."

Neil smacked his hand against the side of his helmet. He should have guessed the answer. He had seen Star Trek and Stargate. "When will I get to learn to fly this thing?"

"Not right away, I'm afraid. You'll have to complete quite a few training classes first."

Neil groaned. "I just want to fly."

"You can't get anywhere you want in life without a good education," Mr. Chapman chided. "Space City is no different. But you'll find the classes at the academy much more interesting than what you're accustomed to back home. Much more hands-on."

Neil doubted that. Adults always insisted an education was important. True or not, school was dull. He did enjoy some classes, but too many teachers lectured all day. He found it hard to focus by just listening to a teacher drone on.

Would he have to learn new languages to speak with aliens?

The closest he had come to speaking in a foreign language was burping the alphabet after downing a soda. Pretty awesome, sure, but unless the Azzaros spoke burp, he doubted that skill would help.

A young man in a gray uniform similar to the ones they wore popped on-screen. "Mr. Chapman, it's good you're returning. We've intercepted a Dahakan transmission discussing plans for an infiltration."

"I've got a new recruit onboard," the old man said. Neil recognized the disapproval in his tone.

"Excuse me. I... I didn't realize," the young man said, face panicked.

"That's why we have protocol in place for all communications," Mr. Chapman said.

The young man flushed. "Yes, sir. Won't happen again. Your orders are to report to Council headquarters when you arrive."

"I'm retired. I don't have orders."

The young man opened his mouth. Mr. Chapman just turned off the communication.

"Who are the Dahaka?" Neil asked. He imagined some horde of angry monsters invading the Earth. Were they in trouble? Was that the job of the alliance, to thwart alien invasions?

"Nothing for you to worry about," Mr. Chapman assured him.

"But the man said—"

Mr. Chapman cut him off. "For now there's nothing to do. We need to sleep and reorient ourselves to Space City time."

"I'm not even remotely tired," Neil said, angered. What was the old man withholding from him? If he was going to be in danger by joining this academy, surely he deserved to know about it.

"Don't worry, you will be in a moment."

What did that mean? He suddenly smelled lemons—not quite like the actual fruit, more like cleaning solution—inside his helmet. Where had that come—

His mind went blank.

Chapter 3

Neil's Lunar Flyby

Neil woke to drool running down his chin. He tried to wipe it away, his mind a little foggy and disoriented, but his hand struck the transparent shield covering his face.

"Drooling on yourself? Don't tell me my newest recruit needs a padded cell." Mr. Chapman looked over his shoulder from the cockpit's front seat. His face shield was raised.

Neil hastily pressed the button to raise the shield and wiped away the drool. As he did so, he remembered why he had been asleep. "What did you do to me?"

"Macab sleeping agent," Mr. Chapman said. "Delivered through the air filtration system. We're coasting behind the moon to conserve energy. Once we're back in direct sunlight, we'll speed up."

"What's sunlight matter?" Neil snapped.

"You'll appreciate the sleeping agent later. For now, I need to focus."

Still angry at being drugged, but unsure what to do about it—after all, he couldn't climb out of the ship and hail a cab home—Neil glanced out the left window and spotted the moon. It was larger than he imagined—a planet itself. The gray, crater-pocked surface loomed like the Death Star. Would the force be with him?

"How long did I sleep?" Neil asked, wondering how the moon had gotten so big so fast.

"A little over eight hours. We're not far now."

A bright light drew Neil's focus ahead where he expected that the sun was emerging from behind the moon.

His jaw dropped.

The sun *was* present. Behind a city—hovering in space.

Towering structures shone with a legion of multicolored lights. Enormous, gear-shaped edifices were randomly spaced on vertical poles. The constructions were intermixed with other giant, hive-like buildings. And also sporadic, transparent, flower-shaped sky scrapers—a celestial flying city. Like a mighty beacon, it beckoned, drawing them in from the cold and darkness.

"Welcome to your new home," Mr. Chapman said, amusement and a little awe in his voice.

"How? How is this possible?" Neil asked, staring in wonder.

"I remember my first time," the old man said. "I was much older than you, already an adult. Thought I'd died. Asked my recruiter if he'd transported me to the afterlife."

"She's just hanging there," Neil said.

The city stood on a broad surface like the ground when seen from a plane, but below that was a dark metallic surface. Despite his grandfather's many adventures as a fighter pilot, Neil felt positive he also would have stared in wonder.

"Seeing her from space never gets old. I miss her when I'm away too long."

The ship couldn't land fast enough. Was this what immigrants felt when arriving in America and seeing the Statue of Liberty for the first time? Did the sight fill them with hope that today's promises for the future dwarfed the frustrations and disappointments of the past?

The ship approached the city and hit turbulence, similar to when they left Earth, as if they passed through an atmosphere. This time the tumult hardly concerned him and seconds later their flight smoothed back out.

The sky brightened as they descended toward a spaceport filled with numerous ships of varying sizes far from the city's outskirts. The spaceport was surrounded by high walls. The lone exit from the spaceport passed through a sizable garden that led to a campus with four large buildings, maybe five stories tall each, on the four sides of a courtyard filled with people. Numerous other buildings surrounded the main cluster. A couple of miles of open fields separated the campus from the city that Neil had seen from space.

Between the campus and the now blue skies overhead, they could have been landing back on Earth rather than onboard a floating city.

Had everything he'd seen moments before been simply an illusion? He put his hand on the window as if to touch the sky and make sense of everything.

"Space City is an artificial, flying planet. Her atmosphere's designed to mimic Earth's own," Mr. Chapman said. "The founders built it to mirror life back home. The Earth protects life in so many ways, and the ship replicates that. Plus, people feel most comfortable in an Earth-like environment."

Neil's first day in a new world. The morning hadn't held such excitement since his mother had been alive. He wished she could share it with him.

"Based on Space City time, it's ten in the morning. The ship rotates during the day so that the sun seems to cross the sky. At night, shields darken the skies. You'll feel like you're back on Earth, except for the moon in panorama."

In the sky, the giant moon out-sized the sun at least ten to one. Space City was like a satellite in the moon's orbit.

Mr. Chapman landed the ship in the spaceport. Neil removed his helmet, unbuckled his seat, and after sitting the entire flight, his legs shook when he stood. He used the walls to steady himself as he made his way back to the exit.

The spaceport possessed various spacecraft, landers, and rovers. Neil counted a dozen ships like the one they'd flown in, plus behemoths the size of giant aircraft carriers.

The day was hot but pleasant. A breeze ruffled his hair, as it had on good days when he'd helped his mother in her rose garden. It was amazing to know that he stood on a ship in space and felt like he stood outdoors on Earth.

A man with two long, dark brown braids draped over his shoulders rounded their ship. Possessing a wiry build, he marched toward them. He wore a uniform consisting of a light-blue, buttoned-down shirt and navy-blue pants. An insignia denoting his rank marked both shoulders, and a Space City logo was pinned on his left breast below a small nameplate.

"Neil, I'd like to introduce you to Senior Master Sergeant Shilah Nez," Mr. Chapman said. "He's an instructor. He'll take you to the academy and orientation."

Instructor Nez nodded and spoke formally. "Welcome to Space City. If you'll remove that flight suit, I'll get you to registration."

"Yes, sir." As Neil stripped off his flight suit, he asked, "Your title is Senior Master Sergeant?"

"It is," Nez replied.

"This is a military academy?"

Mr. Chapman shook his head as he took Neil's flight suit. "The Space City Preparatory Academy is a private academy for promising students aboard Space City. It has a Junior ROTC program you can join if you wish." He carried the flight suits back inside the ship.

"So why are you a Senior Master Sergeant?"

"I'm retired." Nez motioned for Neil to follow him and set off at a brisk pace. "Let's get you to registration."

Neil took a step after him, then paused. Mr. Chapman remained inside the ship. "Aren't you joining us?"

Mr. Chapman emerged and waved. "I'm needed at headquarters. Not sure how long, but I'll try to check in on you later."

Neil wanted to say more, but Nez marched on without pause. Neil hurried after him.

"The academy demands hard work, but you're cut out for it," Mr. Chapman yelled.

*****

Nez led Neil from the spaceport into the lavish garden. A series of oval flowerbeds, each with a different type and color of flower, alternated with dwarf fruit trees. A thick wall of vines surrounded the garden so that the only path from the spaceport led directly through the entire garden. Neil spotted apples, pears, peaches, oranges, and several nut varieties among the trees in the garden. Throughout the orchard, human-shaped yellow robots picked fruits and nuts, pruned branches, and watered the flowers. Neil considered asking one of the androids for a peach. Would it talk or understand him?

Neil had only ever eaten fruit when a neighbor, Mrs. Stevenson, had shared with him. His uncle's idea of a meal was fast food. Around the holidays, Mrs. Stevenson had prepared homemade pies, and usually baked a mini one just for him. He would miss her sweet and juicy peach pies with flaky crusts.

Nez checked the flowerbeds as they passed each one, but said nothing.

"Any chance I won't get in?" Neil asked, still worried this might end when they discovered his C+ student average. Mr. Chapman had invited Neil to join the academy after learning who his grandfather had been. Had the old man's knowledge of Neil's grandfather gotten him here?

"The flowers approve of you," Nez said.

The flowers? Neil stared at the series of flowerbeds as they passed. Roses, lilies, lilacs, and several other varieties he couldn't name. Nothing strange about any of them that he could tell. What did the flowers have to do with his acceptance into the academy? And what did Nez mean by *they* approved?

Nez didn't elaborate on the flowers. "If you fail, there are always opportunities within the city. Everyone on Space City can play a role."

Neil exhaled. They weren't sending him back. Even if he never flew, he was free of his uncle's ghostly existence.

"In a few rare instances, particularly undesirable students are launched into outer space, though," Nez added.

Neil stopped, eyes darting to the instructor's face, but he kept walking. Surely he joked.

They exited the garden and headed toward the campus in the direction of the five-story glass buildings. Their tinted windows reflected the garden. As they headed toward the closest building, Neil studied the immense open courtyard in the campus' center. In each corner stood enormous oak trees. People milled about the square, many in uniform. Would he receive a uniform?

He suddenly felt self-conscious wearing his worn-out clothes. He'd had only one real friend to speak of back home; everyone turned up their noses at his holey clothes, which weren't the good kind. Someone had even started a rumor that he was homeless.

Nez ignored the square and proceeded to an entrance in the building's rear corner, which led into a large room filled with other prospective students. The students came from a variety of cultural backgrounds and spoke several different languages that Neil didn't understand.

Had the potential students come on ships from all over Earth?

Even with shields hiding the ships, Space City must expend a lot of effort recruiting new students while maintaining secrecy on Earth.

Congregated in approximately five lines, the students proceeded toward counters along the back wall where assistants helped them.

"You'll wait in line to sign up." Nez pointed to the end of the nearest line. "The assistants help with everything you need, from schedule to room assignments. Good luck."

Without waiting for questions, Nez strode off. Neil wanted to ask for a little more guidance from the instructor. Instead, he shuffled toward the nearest line and stopped behind a boy and girl, both with blonde hair. Neil had an inch or two on them. A trident tattoo marked the back of the boy's left hand.

"What ya staring at?" the boy demanded with a thick Irish accent, catching Neil glancing at the tattoo.

"I just noticed your tattoo." Neil hunched down unconsciously. "Thought it was cool is all."

The blonde girl offered Neil an apologetic glance. She had striking emerald eyes and a petite nose. "Don't mind my brother. Riagan never learned manners." Her Irish accent was less pronounced than her brother's, but still there.

"I'm suspicious of unwanted attention." Riagan looked him up and down. Apparently deciding Neil was ok, he offered a handshake. "However, he appears to have good taste."

Neil shook the boy's hand followed by the girls. She had extremely soft hands.

"I'm Rois," she added, smile warm and contagious.

"Neil," he replied, but his own smile felt awkward. To divert her attention, he gestured at Riagan's tattoo. "Did it hurt much?"

The boy grinned. "It didn't. I have a connection back home. He did it for me as payment. Do ya know what it symbolizes?"

Neil shrugged, wondering what he meant by payment. "Poseidon carried a trident."

"The wielder of a trident holds great power." Riagan traced the outline.

Rois rolled her eyes. "Ya so full of yourself. Seriously. What power?"

"Nothing like a sister to shoot ya down," Riagan complained, giving Neil a *see-what-I-have-to-deal-with* look.

"Just a reality check," Rois said, eyes twinkling in amusement.

Eyeing the line ahead, Neil asked. "Been waiting long?"

Riagan raised his voice as he glanced toward the counters. "Waiting too long without a snack or something to drink."

Rois punched her brother's arm. "Behave. We're after landing."

Soft and pretty, but with a cunning strength, like a Margay, she was exactly the type of sister Neil would've wanted.

"And at the rate we're moving it'll be lunch time before we get through," Riagan said. "Already missed breakfast."

Neil's own stomach growled, reminding him that he hadn't eaten since yesterday morning. Or this morning. What time was it on Earth?

"I say we find a mess hall and come back later," Riagan suggested. "Maybe the lines will have shortened."

Five people entered, each bearing trays with pastries and cups of water. A boy, several years older than Neil, approached him and held out a tray. "Would you like a snack?"

Neil grabbed a few raspberry pastries and water. Riagan and Rois also grabbed some food.

"Happy now?" Rois asked around a bite of a blueberry muffin.

"I'd prefer food." Riagan held up both hands as if holding something weighty, but then stuffed a pastry in his mouth.

"Forgive my brother. He's downright beastly sometimes."

"Ham or bacon and eggs wouldn't hurt," Neil said as the server continued along the line. He should've grabbed another pastry or two.

"Right," Riagan agreed, clapping Neil on the shoulder. "This man understands. Pastries don't fill ya up."

"Boys! Ye all alike," Rois said, but her exasperated smile belied her words. Even the shake of her head seemed to say *they're family, what am I going to do?*

The person at the head of their line departed through double doors beside the front counters. Everyone else shuffled forward six inches and reality set in. Summer had come to an end.

School was back in session.

Chapter 4

Riagan Runs Afoul

Riagan had enjoyed the sweet ride from Earth, and the sudden appearance of a city in space was like a video game coming to life. Once they'd landed, his excitement had hit a snag. Adults ordered him around and forced him into school at summer's end when he had so many better things to do. It seemed to be one of their favorite pastimes.

He had waited over an hour just for an ID. Only with an ID could he obtain a wrist-comp for class, receive meals in the mess hall, and pretty much do anything else at the academy. Did he need the ID to go to the bathroom, too?

Attendants had ushered Riagan, Neil, and Rois through double doors into an auditorium. Tables along the walls bore tuna or chicken salad sandwiches, various fruits, including some strange purple melon, and water or tea, but no crisps. Who ate sandwiches without crisps? Nevertheless, he piled his plate with tuna sandwiches and a banana, before choosing a seat on the last row.

Students quieted as Instructor Shilah Nez, at the front of the room, introduced himself. "Welcome to the Space City Preparatory Academy. This'll be your home for the next four years. Period."

Riagan stuffed down a tuna sandwich. Their recruiter, Mr. Collins, had already informed them that if Rois and he joined the academy, it would be years before they returned to Earth, if ever. That was fine with Riagan. He had left nothing behind.

Shock was registered on quite a few faces in the room.

"Most of you have some or all of your family here on Space City," Nez continued. "For those who left loved ones behind, you will occasionally be allowed carefully-monitored virtual communication.

This is for the protection of you and your loved ones. Our secrecy is of the utmost importance."

Riagan snorted. Adults always insisted their rules and restrictions were for everyone's safety. It was their default answer to questions. That or *because I said so*.

"Now, it's important for all of you to understand the two tenets upon which the academy is founded—scientific achievement and social evolution." Nez paused to let his words sink in.

"Science is an examination of the processes that create the universe. If you want to know why we exist or how everything came to be, science is the gateway to understanding." Nez stood tall and rigid, hands clasped behind his back as he strode back and forth in front of the recruits. He immediately struck Riagan as someone who was tough and enforced the rules to the extreme.

"All of human progress has resulted from examining our world and asking how and why things work, and determining how we can build upon that. From the invention of the wheel to populating the Earth, pushing out into space, the creation of this city and everything on it, all of this has come from scientific pursuits and technological achievements."

Riagan peeled his banana, wondering when they would be let loose. Nez looked ready to drone on for hours. Rois was leaning forward, listening intently. They had recruited her precisely for her scientific brilliance, and she would believe in the promises that Space City offered. Riagan didn't consider himself a cynic, he just had a harder time accepting that their lives would suddenly change into something amazing. But he would try for her.

"Through our scientific pursuits, we've learned the importance of evolution. Just as an expanding gene pool makes life stronger and more complex, so does the exchange of knowledge and ideas advance us as a species. The more inclusive we can be of others with different backgrounds and viewpoints—social evolution—the faster we learn and grow. This idea isn't confined to humans, but to every alien species. As we explore and meet new species with their own understanding of the universe and our shared knowledge bases grow, the scientific feats of which we are capable will increase exponentially."

Rois applauded, along with a handful of others. Riagan considered calling her a suck up, but his mouth was full.

The ideas were good, but putting them into real practice was a different story. Equality was fashionable on Earth. While most people agreed with the idea, they usually drew a line somewhere. Often the line appeared in regard to people who practiced different religions or followed a different political party. They would promote equality in some ways, but reject it in many others. Was it even possible to believe in absolute equality, regardless of how it was measured?

"Now that you know the importance of why you are here, here's a short movie with more details about Space City and the academy," Nez said.

The lights dimmed in the auditorium, and a video started to play on the wall behind Nez.

Folding his empty plastic plate, Riagan pointed it past Rois to the exit doors. "Let's leave the kids to their nap time and check out the sites."

"They wouldn't have this orientation if it wasn't important," Rois whispered.

She always followed the rules despite his best efforts, so Riagan appealed to Neil. "We haven't had a moment of freedom since our arrival. Ya saw the city during landing. We've got to explore this place. The details can wait."

Neil bit his lip and seemed to be weighing whether to go. He needed a nudge.

"C'mon, there's got to be some amazing things in the city," Riagan said. "Ya don't want to be afraid to live, do ya?"

That seemed to make up Neil's mind. "Lead the way."

"Are ye attention spans that short?" Rois asked before finishing her last bite of a sandwich. She had forgotten it during the speech.

"They only wanted ya anyway." Riagan rose, but not to full height where he'd draw attention. He hurried behind the last row of chairs toward the exit. Several students eyed them as they passed, but none said anything.

*****

The exit doors led out to an empty hallway. Neil and Rois in tow, Riagan crossed to glass doors and pushed his way outside. Riagan knew Rois had only come to keep him out of trouble.

The paved courtyard at the center of campus was peppered with grassy areas and lilac trees, in addition to the four large oaks on the corners. Students and instructors hurried about their business, talked to friends, read wrist-comps on benches, or relaxed on the grassy areas. Most wore uniforms with light-blue, button-down shirts and dark slacks, but a few wore t-shirts and jeans.

Two flagpoles stood on the left side of the courtyard. Hanging from one pole like a banner was the Space City flag—gray background with the blue Earth, green Pangaea, and white SC. The second flag showed a griffin, wings spread wide, holding twin lightning bolts in its talons.

"Right, how do we get to the city?" Riagan asked.

"We can't leave the academy grounds without permission," Rois warned, arms crossed. "We need passes from an instructor, and they only hand them out on the weekend."

"How do ya know?"

Rois smiled. "A magician never reveals her secrets."

"Ya researched all this on the ship's computer during our flight here, didn't ya?" Riagan guessed.

Rois pursed her lips and eyes flashed annoyance. "One of us has to learn the rules to keep ya out of trouble."

"Great. Ya can fill me in later," Riagan replied.

On the far side of the courtyard, lizard-like humanoids with olive scales leaned against the north building. Everyone walking by gave them a wide berth.

"C'mere Neil, we found our first target." Riagan strutted straight for the lizards, eager to meet his first alien species. He passed guys raving about some championship match over the weekend.

"Wait for me," Rois said.

But Riagan was too excited and he pressed on ahead.

Seconds later Rois squealed in shock. Riagan spun around to find a wall of red fire that had suddenly appeared out of nowhere. Rois quailed before the fire, holding her hands up protectively.

Where had the fire come from so suddenly?

Riagan rushed to Rois' side to pull her away from it. As he neared, he realized that the wall was actually five distinct fires. The flames seemed to be encompassed by invisible barriers. Near the top of each fire, two small blue flames slid back and forth. Riagan had a strange feeling those were eyes, moving from him to Rois and back. Were these fires alive?

The five fires all moved slightly toward Rois, the flames changing shape beneath invisible skin. Rois stepped back, eyes wide. Other students backed away all around them. Riagan moved in front of Rois to shield her, but made no move to touch the fires. A thin white flame appeared on one below its blue eyes. With the emergence of the white flame, cracks and pops like wood in a fire arose, but in rapid succession. Was it speaking?

Riagan just stared, at a loss as to how to react.

"Fresh off the Earth," someone in the crowd behind them taunted.

The crackling and pops rose in volume as the other fires joined in, and a blast of heat washed over Riagan, forcing him back a step. Others around them cried out in shock and surprise, and everyone fell back.

At that moment Neil stepped to Riagan's side, creating a wall with him between the fires and Rois. Riagan was glad for the support.

"We're not here for trouble, just looking out for our friend," Neil said.

A tall woman with blonde hair tied in a bun behind her head and wearing a uniform rushed over, speaking in the same crackling language as the fire aliens. The blue eyes from the middle fire shifted toward the woman and it kept speaking.

"They nearly trampled my sister," Riagan said, wanting to make sure the woman had the whole story.

She waved him off and spoke more with the red creature. What were they discussing?

Riagan wanted to say more, but Rois grabbed his arm to prevent him.

"I'm fine," she whispered.

After the woman exchanged a few more words with the fires, they moved on past. Riagan stared after them a moment, wondering what kept them from burning everything around them. Would he get burned if he touched them? They certainly possessed the heat of a fire, though it fluctuated, as if they could control how much they gave off.

With the trouble diffused, everyone in the courtyard turned their attention back to other things. Having calmed the fire aliens, the woman rounded on Riagan, Neil, and Rois. The nameplate on her right breast read Tereshkova. "I assume you new students? Anyone here a week would know better than to start ruckus like that, especially with Traga. They extremely short-tempered."

"We thought they were threatening Rois," Neil protested. "That they might burn her."

"He's fire marshal," Instructor Tereshkova said, stone-faced. "And instructor."

"Fire Marshal? Does he start them first to keep himself employed?" Riagan was relieved that the standoff was over.

"With reckless teens aboard, he has no worry about job security. And you will address me as Instructor Tereshkova, or Instructor."

"Yes, Instructor," Rois answered politely. She elbowed Riagan in the ribs when he said nothing and he grunted.

Tereshkova pointed back at the main office. "They teach you how to avoid stupid mistakes like that in orientation."

"We received orientation from our recruiter on the *long* flight here," Riagan said. When she glared at him again, he added, "Instructor."

Why hadn't their recruiter mentioned the fire aliens first? Or Nez could've started off the orientation warning them.

"Truth is, between the flight and the morning's registration, we needed a break," Riagan said. "We actually intended to introduce ourselves to the lizards." He pointed to the three scaly creatures still idling across the courtyard.

Tereshkova glanced at the lizards. She smiled as if she had a secret. "How did you propose to speak to them? Shout like you did at Traga?"

Riagan shrugged. He hadn't thought about it. "Don't they speak English, Instructor?"

She laughed again. "At orientation, you receive tradutors." She pulled out three black earphones, handing one to each of them. "Tradutors are language translators. When someone speaks to you in a foreign tongue, earphones translate."

"Cheers!" Riagan slipped the earphone into place. Never need to take a foreign language class again. If he'd had these back home, he would have sold one to every student in school.

"We can talk to the lizards with these?" Neil asked, disbelief in his voice.

"You won't speak with anyone anytime soon if you don't address me properly," Tereshkova said.

Riagan bit back the response rising to his lips. No point in ticking off an instructor needlessly.

"Since you intent on meeting Malsain, you fetch something from Instructor Tanith for me," Tereshkova said. "She has book she promised to bring back. Get from her and I'll let you return to orientation without further punishment."

"A book?" Riagan asked, making a perplexed face. "All this technology aboard a flying city and you still read books."

"Some of us still enjoy physical books," she said drily. "Now do you want to fetch or shall I reconsider my offer of leniency?"

"One book coming right up," Riagan said, voice dripping with mock kindness. He'd planned to visit the Malsain anyway. If fetching a book kept them out of trouble, that was fine with him. Especially after their encounter with the fire aliens. What had she called them? The Traga. If they got out of all this without getting burned, they were doing all right.

When Riagan closed within a few feet of the Malsain, Neil and Rois at his heels, he realized why everyone avoided them, and why Tereshkova had sent him rather than retrieving the book herself. The Malsain reeked. If you combined sewage with rotten eggs and let skunks spray it, the Malsain stunk worse.

Riagan regretted his haste, but refused to balk now. Eyes tearing a little from the stench, Riagan marched right up to the Malsain. The lizard creatures resembled upright walking komodo dragons, which made him a little uneasy. They studied him, their faces twisted into bizarre grins. Forked tongues sampled the air.

"Instructor Tanith?" Riagan asked, eyeing each in turn.

"Yessss?" the sulfurous yellow one said. Her voice sounded like a mix between a hiss and a raw-throated growl. The translation from the tradutor was clear over the growl, though.

A fresh wave of the Malsain's foul breath turned Riagan's stomach. He gulped to avoid losing his lunch. "My name is Riagan." He was no longer certain how long he could maintain this conversation, but had to try long enough to avoid looking like a dog returning to its master with its tail between its legs.

"Ask for the book." Rois covered her mouth with a hand.

Riagan gritted his teeth, refusing to let a little stink drive him back too quickly. Correction, the worst stink he had ever come across. Visiting the Malsain's home planet had to be considered cruel and unusual punishment.

"We're new students at the academy. I heard you're an instructor?" Riagan asked, doing his best to smile.

The Malsain croaked rapidly like frogs, which, combined with leering grins, he took for laughing.

"Our odor makes you gag?" Tanith asked in amusement, tongue flickering toward Rois.

Riagan ignored the question. "Where ye from?"

Neil stood steadfast at his side, but Riagan noticed his face had paled and his mouth twisted like he tasted something awful. You knew something reeked when you could taste the foulness you smelled.

Riagan breathed through his mouth, wanting to hold his nose, but that was almost as bad as running.

"Are you going to get sick?" Tanith asked Rois, tongue tasting the air again. The constant flicking of the tongue from the Malsain was unsettling.

Rois held a hand to her mouth, gulping. "Please, Instructor Tereshkova asked us to retrieve a book from ya."

"Is our breath too much for you, darling?" Tanith asked her again slowly, stench pouring out with each word.

"No, ya wonderful," Rois lied. "I amn't having a good day, thanks to my brother."

Riagan didn't protest. She had a point. He could've come alone.

The three Malsain studied Rois for a moment before burping a yellowish vapor from their mouths. The putrid spray hit them in the face. Bile rose into Riagan's throat, but he forced it down. Rois was not so lucky. She turned and emptied her lunch on a grassy mound.

"What space cadets!" shouted a boy, pointing at Rois as she bent over the grass, gagging.

Riagan groaned inwardly, knowing he would pay for her embarrassment later.

While Neil checked on Rois, Riagan decided to speed things up. "Mind if I get the book ya borrowed from Instructor Tereshkova?"

Tanith studied him for a moment, and Riagan feared she might spray him again. He steeled himself, doubting he could handle another round, but instead she pulled the book from a cloth bag and handed it to him. He sighed in relief as the Malsain huddled together, dismissing him.

The book was well-used. *Astrobiology for Ourania, the 5th edition.*

Grim-faced, Riagan turned to Rois. She had a hand covering her stomach and her face was pale, but she appeared fine.

"Right, are ya done torturing me?" she asked.

Riagan nodded grimly and they returned to Tereshkova. He took measured paces, head held high, and handed her the book.

She accepted it, her nose wrinkled. Her corresponding smirk indicated she had gotten what she wanted. "Most people would choose detention for a month rather than endure Malsain up close."

"Guess we're tougher than most." Riagan gloated, glad he could show her he was not afraid and could handle himself.

"Foolish, actually," she replied. "Never lie to Malsain. They have zero tolerance for lies. They know how bad we think they stink."

"Right, good to know I could've avoided this if I was after keeping my stupid mouth shut," Rois said.

"I take back." Tereshkova pinched her nose, which only made Riagan feel more triumphant. "Returning you to orientation would be cruel punishment to other students. Get to showers."

She pointed them toward the dormitories across the way. Riagan walked, head held high and shoulders back as the other students in the courtyard cleared out of their way. Several snickered while others pinched their noses and jeered, but he did not care. He held his head high all the way to the showers.

Chapter 5

Neil Plays Substitute

"The funk is fading," Neil said in the shower. "Or my nose broke."

At first the shower had intensified the stench from the Malsain, and Neil had lost his lunch in the adjacent stalls. After that he had breathed through his mouth while bathing. Thirty minutes spent scrubbing, rinsing, and repeating. The greasy film from the Malsain came off quite easily, but the odor lingered. Neil had washed several times before feeling clean.

"I'm sure my nostrils are deserters right now," Riagan replied, toweling off. "Kept my lunch down, though, unlike you *girls*."

"Pretty sure Rois will hold you responsible for that." Neil had a feeling that being on Rois' bad side wasn't fun.

Riagan grimaced. "She can hold a grudge."

They returned to the changing room benches, but the uniforms that they received on their way in had been replaced by silk costumes. Neil had been thrilled at receiving the uniforms. Nicest thing he'd had since the suit his mother had made him wear to church as a child. Now he hadn't kept the new uniform for a whole hour.

"Ya kidding," Riagan said, holding up a red and yellow costume.

The outfits reminded Neil of harlequin costumes. His own had a lavender right arm and left leg, green left arm and right leg, and a lavender-and-green checkered torso.

"I amn't wearing this." Riagan held his in clenched fists. "Who stole our clothes?"

On cue a group of boys, all wearing academy uniforms, stepped into the doorway, howling with laughter.

"Just fulfilling our responsibilities," one said, easily the shortest in the group. The boy possessed jet-black hair, menacing brown eyes, and a nose that pointed upward sharply, as if he was physically stuck up. "I'm Patrick Duffy." He offered a handshake. When Riagan didn't accept, he shrugged.

"This is my second, Caleb Thorton."

Patrick gestured to a taller boy with large ears that stuck out wide from the sides of his head. His short-buzzed hair only served to spotlight his elephantine ears. Caleb offered them a fake smile, his cold blue eyes giving it away. He didn't offer a handshake.

Behind the boys was a small fire, which Neil quickly realized was another Traga. Maybe a student? Neil eyed it warily, and it shrank back slightly.

Riagan crossed the room and shook the costume in the boy's face. "Where are my clothes?"

Neil hurried after him in case of a scuffle, though they really needed to avoid making any more waves today. They had already incurred Tereshkova's displeasure, and he didn't want to generate a reputation among the instructors on his first day. Nor did he wish to make Mr. Chapman regret recruiting him.

Patrick sneered. "We're toughening up the Earthlings."

Caleb and the other boys laughed derisively.

"Earthlings?" Neil asked.

"You're fresh off Earth," Patrick said, eyes dancing in confident pleasure. "You're ignorant of what it takes to survive here. Some aliens will kill you over an untimely glance. The universe is much tougher than Earth. Baby boys won't survive."

"What are ya going to teach us, Napoleon?" Riagan dropped the costume and balled his fists.

Patrick hopped back into the hall—not afraid, more like he was baiting them.

Neil arm-barred Riagan to keep him from pursuing Patrick. But Neil felt like he was a passenger on a runaway train. A collision awaited and he was powerless to divert it.

Patrick sneered at them. "You must complete a test to earn your uniforms. All baby boys do before they can grow up." He pointed at the costume on the floor. "Probably want to put those on before you come out." Laughing, he strolled back outside, his gang at his heels.

"I'll stuff ya into these costumes," Riagan shouted after them.

The gang laughed louder. Neil clenched his fists in an effort to calm himself. If they were to avoid the train wreck, he had to remain level-headed.

"Hey, where are my clothes?"

Neil spun around to find another boy limping out from the showers, his left leg moving stiffly. The boy had bleach blonde hair that reached his jaws. He reminded Neil of a surfer.

"I guess Patrick took your clothes with ours," Neil said. He felt bad for the boy. He was in the wrong place at the wrong time.

"Not again," the boy complained in an Australian accent. His shoulders slumped. "Can I help it his father lost money betting against Aidan in a race?"

"Maybe he just mixed yours with ours," Riagan replied. "I'm Riagan Byrne."

"Cade Martin. Is there a third costume?"

Neil glanced around the room, but found only the two. "We could try to get yours back with ours."

Cade smiled at Neil's offer, but shook his head. "You won't get them back on your own. I better come with you."

The costumes zipped up in back, which forced the boys to help each other. Neil felt like they were girls in dresses, and Riagan's face glowed beet-red. It was a toss-up between them and Cade, wearing only a towel, as to who had it worse at the moment.

Fully clothed, they stormed out into the hallway with Cade hobbling behind them. Neil matched his pace to Cade's own; he didn't wish to add to Cade's embarrassment.

They found Rois waiting for them at the entrance to the boys' dorm, her hair wet. She had changed into the Academy uniform after showering. At sight of them in their brightly-colored costumes, she fought to keep a straight face, but lost that battle. "Is it Halloween so soon?"

Neil and Riagan swept past her without comment. Neil felt her eyes on his back and wondered if his face had turned as red as Riagan's again.

They were greeted in the courtyard by an eruption of laughter and jeers from a gathered crowd of thirty or more students. The Malsain croaked as well.

"Adorable Earthlings." Patrick pointed up two flagpoles. They had seen the flagpoles on their way in, which at that time had held two flags. Those now lay draped across a nearby bench. The aluminum flagpoles were a little more than two stories high, and stood on a grassy hill about waist-high. Their clothes were tied to the top of the poles, right under mini white rockets that pointed skyward.

"Let's test how well you climb," Patrick said. "On some planets it's a vital survival skill."

"When in danger, just climb a flagpole?" Neil scoffed. He had no desire whatsoever to climb the poles. Could they request new uniforms instead?

Caleb knelt on the grassy hill surrounding the flagpoles and hit a button. A red light started flashing.

"The flagpoles double as launch towers," Patrick said. "Caleb set the countdown for five minutes. After the launch, good luck retrieving your uniforms. It's cold in space."

Neil stared upward in disbelief at his clothes. Both cheers and jeers issued from the crowd of students. Others whistled. The crowd had expanded in all directions, pulsating excitedly. Had the entire student body gathered to witness their humiliation?

Neil and Riagan had two choices. Climb the poles or endure taunts forever.

"Where are my clothes?" Cade asked.

"Caleb?" Patrick asked. "Didn't we do something extra special with his?"

"Of course!" Caleb moved over to the bench where the flags rested and retrieved a uniform from underneath the bench. The uniform was covered in a slimy muck. Caleb tossed the uniform at Cade's feet.

Cade stared at the uniform, nonplussed. "I wasn't wearing a uniform. I had my own clothes."

Patrick grimaced. "Guess yours are up the pole. Better get to climbing."

"Climb the… You know I can't climb with this leg," Cade replied, face reddening with humiliation.

Patrick shrugged. "Not my problem."

"But—" Cade just looked at his clothes, flying atop the pole, completely at a loss.

Neil felt ashamed that anyone would act so callously. It was one thing to pull a prank on Riagan and himself, especially with their academy-supplied uniforms. Doing this to Cade was just cruel. Neil studied Cade for a moment, came to a decision, and approached the pole with Cade's clothes at the top. He eyed Riagan. "We do it together?"

Riagan nodded, teeth gritted.

Neil jumped and grabbed the pole, the aluminum cool to the touch. He tried supporting his weight with his legs and feet. Thanks to the costume's silk fabric, his feet slid down the pole. More snickers from the crowd caused his ears to burn. Dropping to a sitting position, he tried tearing at the fabric around his feet. Riagan joined him. The fabric stretched, but Neil couldn't rip it. He kept at it, trying to tear even a meager hole. How much time remained?

"Give up. You'll never make it," Patrick taunted.

Maybe I should deck Patrick, Neil thought. *No one would call me a coward for that.*

"Got to be more resourceful," yelled a voice from the crowd.

"Four minutes left," Caleb shouted with too much pleasure in his voice.

Rois came up to Neil and pulled scissors from her purse. "These should help."

"Thanks."

Neil cut the fabric off at his calves, baring his feet and ankles. He tossed the scissors to Riagan.

Riagan quickly cut his feet free. "Cheers, sis."

"Ready?" Neil asked, rising to his feet and grasping one pole again.

Riagan nodded and they started up again. Calves and feet bared, Neil gripped the pole with his legs, freeing his arms to help pull himself higher. He quickly climbed the first story with Rois and Cade shouting encouragement. Each time he reached up with a hand, his arms grew more tired.

"My hands are starting to sweat," Riagan said, a few paces below. He grunted. "I'm having a hard time hanging on."

"Ready to give up?" Patrick shouted to the crowd like a circus ringmaster. "Two and a half minutes left."

"Riagan, we can't let him win," Neil said. He refused to be beaten like this. He forced himself to keep reaching up one hand at a time. The higher he climbed though, the more he felt the pull of gravity, a yoke trying to pull him down. If he paused for even a second he would lose his momentum and slide all the way down. And he wasn't sure he could get himself going again.

When they neared the second-floor windows of the adjacent dorms, others in the courtyard started cheering, competing with the jeers. Neil gasped for air, arms and legs screaming now for a rest, but the countdown had to be close to zero. Gritting his teeth, he fought his way to the top. Applause filled the courtyard as he reached and grasped pant legs—jeans.

"You with me?" he asked Riagan. With trembling hands, he picked at the knotted clothes, which were tied around the rockets— more like rocket boosters, but no more than a foot long and maybe six inches in diameter.

"Almost there."

"Ten. Nine. Eight," the crowd chanted.

It was difficult to support himself while untying the shirt and jeans, especially with hands shaking from exhaustion.

"I'm after climbing," Riagan shouted as he reached the top and set to work on freeing his clothes.

"Six. Five. Four."

After getting the first knot loose, the second came free much easier. Neil yanked Cade's clothes free. He dropped them to Rois. Riagan's knots weren't as tight, and he freed his own.

"Two. One. Zero," the crowd shouted.

Not sure what to expect from the launch, Neil loosened his grip and started sliding down the pole. A fuse fired out from the end of the rocket, startling him and he let go and fell to the grassy little hill, landing on his back. He gasped, the wind knocked out of him. Riagan landed beside him, curling into a ball from the impact.

The crowd whistled and applauded. The mini-rockets shot out sparks, but didn't launch.

"Surprise attack," Patrick announced.

Neil barely noticed that Patrick and his friends had paint ball guns before they started to fire at him. The first couple spattered the hill around him with orange paint. He instinctively covered his head with his arms. Paint balls slammed into his arms, legs, and back. Neil's muscles tensed and he gasped from the shock and pain of so many strikes at once.

"Enough," a familiar female voice ordered.

The shots ceased and Neil slumped in relief, unable to do more than lay there and take comfort that it was over. Instructor Tereshkova emerged out of the crowd, glaring at Patrick and his gang, before eyeing Neil and Riagan in their paint-covered costumes. Seeing they didn't appear seriously harmed, she rounded on Patrick.

Patrick's gang held the guns loosely at their sides, heads lowered slightly. They knew they had been caught.

"Why am I not surprised that you are involved?" Her eyes blazed.

Patrick shrugged, but kept his eyes on her feet. "Just teaching them the ropes, Instructor."

Several students in the crowd booed at this response. Everyone remained packed around, enjoying the show.

"They stole *my* clothes, too, Instructor," Cade said. "Fortunately, Neil helped."

Neil finally caught his breath, but remained unable to speak. He was grateful that Cade was speaking up for them. Neil really wanted to rip the guns away and beat Patrick with them. No one but his uncle had ever attacked him like this; the embarrassment of enduring such a beating in front of an enormous crowd only made it worse.

Cade defending them helped, though.

"Apparently, you forgot my warning that it's instructors' jobs to prepare students, not yours to prey on your peers," Tereshkova told Patrick. "You only a first year yourself."

"Didn't you hear the cheers, Instructor?" Caleb protested. "We put them in a position to earn our admiration." The gang echoed his words.

More boos from Cade, Rois, and the crowd disagreed.

"I guess I should reward your charity, Caleb Thorton," Tereshkova said. "All of you drop and give me one hundred. And since you like to help out, for next three days you all help me clean hare dogs' cages."

Patrick's gang whined. The crowd cheered.

"No one got hurt," Patrick complained.

"One hundred, now!" Tereshkova said. "I expect all of you ready to clean in fifteen minutes."

Patrick shot Neil a glare, as if this were his fault, before dropping to the ground. His gang joined him.

Neil sat up. He exchanged satisfied grins with Riagan. He quickly hid it when Tereshkova turned to them. They hadn't done anything wrong, but she might not see it that way.

Studying their paint-covered clothes and faces, she shook her head. "Back to showers. Your intrepid natures have certainly gotten you noticed." She started to turn away, but paused and gestured to the flags. "Put flags back up."

Neil started to argue, "It was Patrick's gang that took them down—"

Her warning glare stopped him.

"Yes, Instructor," he said sheepishly. At least she wasn't giving them detention, too. Still, he couldn't help feeling they were losing esteem in her eyes. But this was no fault of theirs!

The train hadn't reached the station unscathed.

Neil stood and grabbed Cade's clothes. A few splotches of paint streaked the green shirt and jeans, which Neil handed to Cade. Hopefully the paint would wash out.

"Thanks," Cade said, quickly pulling on the green shirt despite the paint. He and Rois had managed to avoid getting hit.

After Tereshkova departed, students crowded in and congratulated them. A short kid with close-cropped sable hair shook Neil's hand. "About time someone showed Patrick up. You're a space ace. I'm Jiro Takeda." He eyed Patrick's gang with distaste.

"Anand Singh," a chubby boy said. He possessed a bald head and prominent cheekbones. "You're lucky Colonel Terror didn't punish you further."

Neil arched an eyebrow. "Colonel Terror?"

A slender girl standing next to Anand spoke up. "Instructor Tereshkova. She's a retired Space City officer. But don't ever call her Colonel Terror to her face, obviously."

"Are all the instructors former officers?" Neil asked. "I met Senior Master Sergeant Nez this morning."

"Some are." The girl closely resembled Anand in the face, but she had long dark hair that started to curl just below her jaw. She gave

Neil a petite smile. "And I'm Anand's twin sister, Devika Singh. We'll get the flags and run them up for you."

"Thanks. I'm Neil."

He still wanted to pay Patrick back, but after the congratulations from others, he felt somewhat avenged. Whatever they might have lost in Tereshkova's eyes, they had gained from their classmates, which more than made up for it to Neil.

Once the flags were flying again, he and Riagan trekked to the showers for the second time that morning. Neil hoped this wasn't the start of a trend.

Chapter 6

Neil Meets a Volcano Diamond

Neil headed toward the lounge for the academy's school year kickoff party. It served as an introduction for new recruits to current students and other important figures in the Space City community. He wore the academy uniform—navy pants, white button-down shirt, and a navy jacket with gold buttons in the front and at the wrists, and yellow epaulets on the shoulders. He felt a little ridiculous dressed up like this, but having new clothes confirmed that he was living a better life, free of his uncle.

The thick, white stone rails lining the steps to the lounge doubled as flowerbeds. Small red roses grew in the beds. Ahead of Neil, a boy walked up the steps and the roses suddenly transformed to white. Neil paused, staring at the roses. What had caused them to change color?

A stout man in uniform at the lounge entrance moved to block the boy. "Empty your pockets," the guard ordered.

"What for?" the boy asked, fidgeting with the pocket flaps on his jacket.

"Always someone thinks they can sneak alcohol past the roses," the guard answered.

Sneak alcohol past the roses? He must have heard that wrong. Except he had just seen the roses change colors before his eyes as the boy passed them.

The boy's shoulders slumped and he removed a small flask from the right jacket pocket. The man took the flask and let the boy enter.

"How does that work?" Neil asked, eyeing the roses, which turned back to red as he climbed the steps.

The man eyed him levelly, and Neil realized that he possessed a fake left eye. Neil did his best not to stare, but it was difficult not to focus on it now that he had noticed it.

"You must be a new recruit," the guard said.

Neil nodded.

"The roses are genetically modified to detect alcohol. Similar to bomb-sniffing dogs, but significantly more sensitive. Every year a few of you think you're smart enough to sneak something past the roses. Never works."

"At least that you know of," Neil said, focusing on the roses to avoid staring at the eye. The roses didn't look different from any he might find back on Earth.

The guard laughed haughtily. "You're welcome to try."

Neil stared from the man to the roses and back. "I'm fine without." He stepped past the guard and entered the lounge.

White couches lined a good bit of the place. Small wooden tables with murals of stars, planets, and other space visuals carved into their sides were placed between the couches. In a corner of the room was a large bar beside a line of tables bearing trays heaped with food.

"Neil." Mr. Chapman, a champagne glass in hand, waived him over. He relaxed on a white couch. He was dressed in uniform with a Lieutenant General insignia—three stars on either shoulder.

Neil moved over to join him, sitting on the opposite end of the couch. "It's good to see you."

"How are you enjoying your first day? You've had an interesting introduction, no?" Mr. Chapman smiled broadly.

"You heard?" Neil asked.

Mr. Chapman gestured around the room. "Everyone is talking about it. You've left a lasting impression."

More than a few people in the lounge cast amused glances in Neil's direction, making him want to sink through the couch.

"Since my return to campus a couple of hours ago, this is my first reprieve from questions about my newest recruit." Mr. Chapman's smile didn't waiver. He seemed to be enjoying this. "There's rampant speculation over how you'll fare at the academy."

Neil shifted uncomfortably. He had backed Riagan with the Traga and Malsain because that's what friends do for each other. As for the flagpoles, he'd learned long ago that bullies tend to focus on the weak.

They shy away from anyone who seriously challenges them. Climbing the flagpole was a warning to Patrick and others like him to focus elsewhere. Besides, Patrick's prank on Caleb had been too cruel to turn a blind eye.

"What about you?" Neil asked, trying to change the conversation. "How did your meeting go? What's with the Dahaka infiltration?"

Mr. Chapman's lips tightened and he glanced uncomfortably around him, as if checking to see if anyone had overheard. "I told you earlier it's nothing for you to worry about. I'd appreciate it if you'd drop the matter." The old man gave Neil a warning look, but there was also a hint of unease in his eyes. Whatever he'd learned at the Council headquarters hadn't been good. Probably dangerous.

Neil wanted to ask more questions. Who were the Dahaka? Was he in danger here? But Riagan and Rois entered the lounge just then, spotted him, and made their way over.

"Cheers. What's the story?" Riagan asked as they approached.

Neil forced himself to smile, dropping the questions for now. He would talk to Mr. Chapman alone again later.

Riagan wore the same academy uniform. Rois wore a long, sea-green dress that accentuated her eyes. A silver necklace with a circular pendant that reminded Neil of a maze hung around her neck. The two sat on an adjacent couch, Rois' necklace reflecting the light.

"That is an unusual necklace," Neil said.

Rois fingered the pendant. "It's a shou. It symbolizes long life. A gift from my parents on my eighth birthday, right before their deaths."

Neil considered kicking himself. "I'm sorry. My mother died when I was eight, too. Never knew my father. I lived with his brother."

"Foster parents," Rois replied flatly.

"Well, the pendant has kept you safe," Neil said, hoping the positive statement avoided any more foot-in-mouth moments. "I guess it works."

Riagan snorted. "I've kept her safe."

"My parents gave me the necklace and Riagan to watch out for me," Rois said. She smiled, but pain crept into her eyes. Neil wished he had not asked about the necklace at all, but it had seemed like the easiest thing to start a conversation.

"You'll face many challenges during your time at the academy," Mr. Chapman said, changing the subject. "Coming from similar backgrounds, you can understand what each other is going through. You'll need to support each other to succeed."

Neil started to agree when a girl entered the lounge who made him forget the words rising to his lips. She wore a flowing, rose-red dress, yet where the skirt billowed around her calves, it changed to deep orange. A scarlet pimpernel graced her long chestnut hair above her left ear. She wore a silver necklace with a reddish-orange pendant and matching earrings that adorned petite ears. Bracelets covered with miniature crimson flowers ornamented her slender, slightly pale arms.

As she advanced, the dress transformed from rose into a bright orange and back. With each step the dress flowed back and forth between rose and orange, as if two painters battled over her ethereal form.

Everyone else in the room became indistinct shadows.

She glided toward the center of the lounge, and in her wake Patrick glared at him. Neil evenly returned his gaze, before realizing Mr. Chapman was talking to him.

"-ughter of Dr. Trevena, the lead scientist here," Mr. Chapman said. "If memory serves, she's also a first year."

"What's her name?" Neil asked, wanting to hear everything Mr. Chapman knew about her.

"Maellyn Trevena," Mr. Chapman said. "Brilliant, like her father."

Upbeat music filled the room, and Maellyn broke into a dance, putting on her own show. She swayed, twirled, and jived to the beat. A female voice broke into song with the melody, but in an alien language. Neil sat transfixed by Maellyn as she spun, dress whirling rose and orange around her. After a moment, others in the crowd joined in, their movements synchronized with hers. But she was the leader.

"Why did they choose music we can't understand?" Riagan complained.

Neil frowned at the disturbance.

"Did you receive your tradutors?" Mr. Chapman asked.

Neil had left his in his room, but didn't care. He only wanted to watch Maellyn. Everything else was a distraction.

More people joined in the dance, but Neil's focus remained on Maellyn. He had never before considered dancing; it seemed unmanly. But as she danced, he found himself wanting to join her. He had never seen a girl like her in his life. She was confident and in complete control of the moment.

The music abruptly ended and people around the room applauded, Neil among them, rising to his feet. The dancers dispersed and everyone went back to talking amongst themselves. Maellyn, in her shimmering rose and orange dress, moved toward the back of the lounge. Neil longed to go introduce himself, but what would he say? He liked her dancing. What else?

"Anything to drink? Ginger ale? Purple melon?" A female-shaped creature with silver scales that flashed with rainbow colors, depending on how the scales caught the light, stood over them. She held a tray with drinks.

What sort of alien was she? Neil refrained from asking to avoid saying something else stupid.

"What's purple melon?" Rois eyed a long-stemmed glass with a violet drink on the tray.

"You'll like it," Mr. Chapman said. "The fruit comes from the Macab. It's like a cross between a watermelon, a grape, and a kiwi. The juice is traditionally prepared as a ceremonial punch for events like these."

"I'll take one," Rois said. The server handed her a glass.

"I'll try one, too," Neil added, intrigued. He accepted the glass from the girl and took a cautious sip. He agreed with Mr. Chapman's assessment of the punch, except it possessed a subtle tartness. "This is excellent! These melons grow out by the spaceport, right? I saw them this morning."

Mr. Chapman nodded. "A gift from Instructor Fintan. The purple melons grow on his home planet Niveum. The melon trees can reach over a hundred feet tall. We've developed a dwarf version here."

Rois eyed her glass, lips curved with pleasure. "Cheers. This punch is fantastic. I have to try the fruit."

A short time later, they made their way back to the food tables. Neil chose roast with new potatoes covered in beef gravy, green deviled eggs like in the Dr. Seuss story, and a couple of purple melon slices. As an afterthought, he added a golden, syrupy fruit called *pyrns*.

The roast was tender and he chewed slowly to savor it. The deviled eggs tasted like they were crossed with grass. Neil swallowed the first bite. The rest he left untouched. Must be an acquired taste. He finished off two more glasses of the purple melon punch with the meal. How long since he'd eaten like this?

Feeling stuffed and needing some air after the meal, Neil excused himself and headed for the balcony at the lounge's rear.

Outside, white spheres the size of oranges floated in the air overhead, lighting up the balcony. Off to the side, a couple sat huddled together on a bench, the girl in a light blue dress that matched the boy's uniform. She had a glass of punch in her hand. The boy, his blue shirt stretched tightly over a heavily muscled torso, whispered to her and she giggled.

Beyond the balcony walls was a substantial lawn with a pathway through the middle that led to a stadium.

The cool night air ruffled his hair.

The technology that Space City used to simulate life on Earth amazed him. Artificial wind, an atmosphere, and even temperature fluctuations as the day progressed. If not for the gibbous moon filling nearly the entire night sky, he might have believed he stood on a balcony on Earth rather than a ship in outer space. Well, the moon and the total lack of any animal sounds. No crickets singing in the night, or bugs dive-bombing the overhead lights or him.

Strangely, all of it made him feel closer to his mother than he had in a long time. He had spent countless nights studying the stars, searching out the constellations and imagining finding her one day among them. Suddenly he had found her, or a part of her.

Approaching steps from behind interrupted his reverie. He turned to find Maellyn. Her dress appeared mostly rose now, but glimmers of orange sprouted where it caught the light. She made her way over to the balcony wall, several feet away from him, and stared out into the night.

Up close, Neil realized that the silver necklace and earrings she wore each had a reddish-orange flower that grew in a little pot—the tiniest flowers he had ever seen. The dress and flowers accented her rosy complexion.

"I've never seen a dress change colors quite like that." Neil hoped his voice didn't crack as it had at the recruiter's office. "You made quite an entrance."

Her eyes measured him for a moment. With a smile, she said, "Not like the entrance you made."

Neil frowned and checked his clothes, expecting something out of place on his uniform. Everything looked straight. Did he have a zit on his face? His body had been a traitor lately.

"The dress is made from *valm*, a fabric similar to silk," Maellyn said. "Its color is heavily influenced by light. The Alfar made it for me."

Neil adjusted the jacket slightly, and wished to check his face in the bathroom. What had she meant by the entrance he'd made? "Who're the Alfar? It's my first day, so I don't know many aliens."

"I'm aware of how much you don't know, considering your exploits this afternoon," Maellyn said.

Neil's cheeks burned as he realized what she'd meant. At least it wasn't a zit. "You heard, too? Has everyone?"

"Saw it myself," she said. "I want to thank you for helping out my cousin, Cade. The nerve of Patrick Duffy, running Cade's clothes up the flagpole." Her nostrils flared a little at that.

"You're welcome," Neil mumbled, still embarrassed, but pleased that by sticking up for Cade he had also earned her admiration.

"To answer your earlier question, the Alfar are more commonly known as elves," she said.

"I love the Alfar," interrupted a female voice. The girl in the blue dress. She rose and dragged her boyfriend over. "Have you heard that if someone is invited to undergo the immortality process on Ourania, their true love can join them? Isn't it romantic?" She wore a dreamy expression.

"Elves? Really?" Neil asked.

"They're a very scientifically advanced species," Maellyn said. "Visited Earth in the past, which is why they exist in our myths and legends."

"And they're immortal, like in the stories?" Neil asked, finding that hard to believe. But he *was* standing on a ship beyond the moon.

"As long as they never leave Ourania," the girl answered sadly. A lock of her chestnut hair fell across her face, and she brushed it back behind her ear. "Those that leave age as we do, their immortality lost forever. Few leave Ourania now. They are devoted to studying the universe and how it works, so they've developed advanced technologies which they send out to explore and deliver data back to them for analysis."

That would be disappointing, Neil thought. Like staying home all the time and watching TV to see the world.

"Let's go, Fran," her boyfriend said, bear-paw-sized hands on her shoulders, pulling gently. "Not everyone wants to hear your Alfar praises. Besides, your glass is empty."

Fran let her date draw her away, leaving Neil alone with Maellyn on the balcony.

"Elves exist and are immortal," Neil said, happy to be alone with her again. "They can grant immortality to others. And they design dresses that change color as you move. Anything else I should know?"

Maellyn smiled. "You have to do a great service to the Alfar to receive the gift of immortality from them, but there's a catch."

"Always is with promises of immortality," Neil said, shaking his head and mock-sighing. "Usually something that ruins everything and the person promised immortality ends up dead."

Maellyn laughed. "If you receive immortality, you can never leave Ourania again, just like the Alfar. Otherwise, you lose your immortality and age rapidly."

"Fine print gets you every time."

"It is romantic, though."

"Gaining immortality, then being stuck on one planet or you die?"

Her laughter was melodic and sweet. He wanted to keep her laughing.

"Spending eternity with your true love," she answered. "We humans promise to love each other forever, but mean 'til we die. Or 'til it's inconvenient. They truly choose for eternity."

"How will you know who your true love is?" Neil asked. "What if you choose wrong?"

Maellyn held up her left wrist and touched the bracelet. Immediately, a large diamond hologram floated in the air above her wrist. "Shortly after my fifth birthday, I came across a volcano diamond for sale in the city."

The diamond was filled with lava. Neil was tempted to reach up and touch it, despite knowing it was nothing more than an image.

"It was the most beautiful thing I'd ever seen," Maellyn said. "The merchant selling the diamond said it came from a mysterious planet few have heard of, and even fewer have seen. Supposedly, the planet is a dark wasteland where the ground is cracked and continually spews hot lava over the surface, which runs in rivers. The creatures that survive in those conditions are deadly and prey on anyone foolish enough to step foot on the planet's surface."

"Sounds like a great vacation," Neil deadpanned. He certainly didn't want to volunteer to visit the place. "Is the planet rare because no one can find it… or no one *wants* to find it?"

She grinned. "His story horrified me, but as I stared at the volcano diamond, I thought it all the more wonderful. Amid such an awful place, something beautiful had formed.

"The volcano diamond is several times harder than any diamond found on Earth. After that I daydreamed that one day I'd know my true love when he gave me a volcano diamond; proof that love really is stronger than anything else." She snorted. "Silly little girl's dreams, huh?"

"What's silly about a dream?" Neil thought he'd journey straight into a volcano if he could find the diamond for her. Maybe he would volunteer to visit that planet.

"My name's Maellyn, by the way."

"Neil," he answered, happy for the chance to talk with her. Back home a girl who looked like her wouldn't have bothered with him. Maybe it was the uniform.

"I caught your name this afternoon," she said, still studying the sky.

Neil flushed at the reference, but she smiled and he didn't feel quite as bad.

"Maellyn, it's time for the countdown," A voice said. They turned back from the balcony rail. A tall man in a suit stood in the doorway. His short, dark hair had grayed on the sides.

"Yes, father." She turned back to Neil and inclined her head. "Goodnight."

Inside, Maellyn's father led her off into the crowd. As she left, Riagan approached, offering Neil another glass of purple melon punch.

"Cheers. I underestimated ya, lad," Riagan said. "She's the hottest girl I've seen since we arrived."

"Got lucky. She wandered out after I did," Neil replied, excited by the little bit of time spent with her, but not sure it meant much.

"Wish I was so lucky. I'd climb another flagpole to get your luck ... with the second-hottest girl, that is."

Neil hoped to see her again soon. Maybe they'd share a class or two.

"Ten. Nine. Eight." Everyone in the room started to count down. To what? At zero, everyone shouted "To Mars!" and drained their drinks.

"To Mars?" Neil asked, unsure if he'd heard that right.

Riagan nodded. "Apparently, the first night of each new school year the ship sets off for Mars. We arrive at the end of the school year. Final exam takes place on the red planet."

They were headed for a new planet. For the second time, Neil feared this might all be nothing more than a fanciful dream. Setting foot on Mars, or any new planet, seemed too good to be true.

How different would it be from walking on Earth? He wanted to find out now, rather than wait until the end of the year.

"According to Mr. Chapman, the ship replenishes resources from the asteroid belt during the stop," Riagan said.

Neil waited for the ship to move. Nothing happened. "Is there a malfunction?"

Everyone around the room celebrated as if everything was normal. Maybe it was. The ship simulated life back home and no one felt the Earth revolving around the sun.

Neil spotted Rois by the dessert table. She scooped up a few cupcakes and joined them. "Cheers. Have a cupcake." She handed them both a rocket-shaped cupcake—chocolate with green frosting.

Biting into his, Neil found to his delight that it had a fudge center. Riagan's cupcake was a yellow cake with Italian cream in the center.

"I'm going to need at least six more," Riagan said. Neil agreed.

Chapter 7

Riagan Duels a Dragonfly

Their first class took place that Monday after a weekend to adjust to the academy. Fifteen students met in an enormous white warehouse filled with rows of ten-foot-tall metallic cylinders. The facility resembled a sterilized lab. Most of the students surrounded an Azzaro and the Traga from Patrick's group.

Riagan ignored them and studied the cylinders. They had doors and rested on movable mechanical platforms, but he could not find controllers to operate them.

The class was titled, "Introduction to New Worlds," but what did these cylinders have to do with that? Perhaps the cylinders, when turned on, displayed a holographic planet, like a large, digital globe on which to examine the continents and oceans that comprised different worlds.

Riagan wore a Velcro case, strapped around his left arm, which held his paperback-book-sized wrist-comp. It contained some information about the academy. He considered searching it for details about the facility or cylinders.

Instructor Shilah Nez strode into the classroom pulling a rack of gray suits, one of which he wore. He was followed by a short albino monkey with four arms. The monkey had a squash-shaped face, rounded out by thick fur on the sides and top of its head, and pale yellow eyes. Roughly four feet tall, the monkey walked more fluidly on two legs than any monkey Riagan had ever seen.

"Attention," the monkey said. A couple of students straightened and saluted.

Riagan's jaw dropped, and several other students murmured excitedly. He had thought maybe Nez had brought the monkey with him as a trained assistant, but it could speak.

"Welcome to Introduction to New Worlds. I'm Instructor Fintan," the monkey said with a deep voice for his size. "Instructor Nez and I work together."

The monkey was an instructor. How many people could he offend on Earth with that?

"Since many of you are new to Space City, I'll give you a little background on myself." The ape pointed at his chest with both left arms. "I am a Macab. My home planet is Niveum, which we will explore today."

A girl with long, curly, strawberry hair raised her hand.

Instructor Fintan pointed his lower right arm at her. "Yes, Aileen McKensie."

"We're traveling to Niveum now?" A huge smile spread across her face, and she looked ready to burst with excitement.

Fintan shook his head. "Actually, you won't visit any new planets your first year."

Most of the students grumbled.

Riagan hadn't even considered the possibility of leaving the ship, but the sudden discussion was upsetting. Setting foot on a new planet had never been a life goal before, but now that it was a possibility, he couldn't imagine anything he wanted to do more.

Fintan held up all four hands to silence the protests. "New worlds are dangerous for those uneducated," he said. "The academy believes providing students a solid foundation from the safety of the ship best prepares them for future exploration."

Riagan rolled his eyes at Neil. Adults always underestimated their abilities, setting unreasonably small boundaries and claiming it was for their well-being. Neil frowned and nodded back.

"Despite this limitation," Mr. Fintan said, "I assure you our exploration will satisfy your curiosity and reckless natures."

"Let me correct one thing," Nez said. "You will remain on the ship at all times during the year, until the final exam on Mars' surface."

Several students murmured excitedly.

"At the start of every year, I like to offer a deal to my students." Nez wore a challenging smile. "If anyone can correctly answer the following question, you pass the class whether or not you attend another session this semester.”

Several students shouted an endorsement of the challenge. Riagan hoped that he knew the answer, no matter how unlikely. An extra free hour three times a week!

“An eighteenth-century astronomer, Thomas Wright, once speculated that there are nearly four million stars within the Milky Way Galaxy, and how many planetary worlds like ours?” Nez asked.

“Ten million,” shouted Aileen.

“Twenty million,” Anand and Devika Singh shouted simultaneously.

“A billion,” Riagan said, intentionally guessing high. *Has to be some ridiculous number.*

“Wright estimated sixty million planets,” Nez answered. Several students groaned in disappointment, Riagan included. Goodbye free hour.

“We now know those estimates take up just a fraction of our night sky,” Nez said.

Maybe he was close after all? Riagan held his breath in anticipation.

“At present, scientists estimate there are trillions upon trillions of stars in the universe, and even more planets around them. If we spit out a number, say in the septillions, it’s just a word with no real meaning. An amount that dwarfs anything we know.”

Riagan gaped. He’d only thought he had shot unrealistically high. The actual number was mindboggling.

“To put that in a little context, the Earth’s population is around seven billion,” Nez said. “If every single human controlled one thousand planets, we’d still have countless more left unexplored.”

“A thousand planets for me.” Anand gestured to Devika. “And a thousand planets for you only.”

“Only a thousand, Anand?” Devika asked in mock sorrow, her eyebrows drooping. “I need at least ten thousand, or claustrophobia is coming.”

“How long would it take you to explore a thousand worlds?” Nez asked.

Riagan didn’t know, but he wanted the opportunity. Travel to a planet, explore it for a few months. When he tired of it, move on to the next. Never visit the same place twice. His life could be an endless adventure—a Tom Crean of the universe.

"This is what Space City is preparing you for," Nez said, glancing at each of them in turn, as if to instill in them the significance of his words. "We may never discover the limits of the universe, but we want to prepare you to try. Now, each of you grab a suit from the rack and we'll get started on your first thousand."

Nez' words stirred Riagan, and he hurried for a gray suit with standard-issue black boots, and started to dress. Two red stripes ran down the suit's length, and a golden Space City insignia marked the left breast. The one-piece uniform resembled a wetsuit, but possessed a little thickness, like a jumper. Nevertheless, it felt light as a cloud and included gloves. Riagan completed the uniform by slipping on the two pieces of the tradutor, one in his ear and the other under his tongue. The tradutor was required in all classes.

Nez pushed the rack over to a wall out of the way. "The suits are standard issue in the field. You are required to wear one at all times in class."

Riagan checked himself out. He nodded approvingly. The uniform fit comfortably, if not quite his size, and made him feel like a professional explorer. For the first time since his recruitment with Rois, Riagan felt like there might be something in this for him. He didn't have to be here only because they needed her.

"The suits are specially designed for protection," Fintan said. "They're fire-resistant and withstand temperatures up to three hundred degrees or negative one hundred."

Neil leaned over to Riagan and whispered. "So our bodies will survive without our heads."

Riagan grinned, stifling a laugh. "Ya could pull off the headless horseman."

"Or a chicken," Rois teased as she joined them.

"Choose a cylinder," Nez said. "Doesn't matter which, but only one student per cylinder."

Still curious what they were for, Riagan climbed into one. He searched it for anything that might explain how they would explore planets from here. No screens that he could see.

Once everyone stood inside a cylinder, including the instructors, Nez said, "activating the simulation," and they suddenly stood on a grassy plain next to a river about a mile wide. The facility and cylinders had vanished, replaced by a landscape covered with strange creatures. Riagan spun around, trying to take it all in. Had the instructors lied and taken them to another planet after all?

Alarmed, Riagan sought out Rois, finding her a few feet away, eyes bulging.

"Relax, this is simulation of Niveum," Fintan said in a calming voice.

"A simulation?" Rois' asked, voice filled with disbelief.

Riagan shared her incredulity. This was too real to be a simulation. Thin, zebra-striped cattle-like creatures grazed on calf-high brown grass. Riagan caught a whiff of cow dung and crinkled his nose. Mini kangaroos, no taller than his knees, hopped along and used armadillo-like snouts to scavenge insects. Some trees dotted the landscape, their branches growing straight up and ending in hundreds of green shoots that reached toward the sky like a dense candelabra. And the sky. It was a teal color, rather than the deep blue of Earth.

The heat from the sun warmed his face. Could all of this be fake? He found it hard to believe that he still stood in a cylinder in the facility, but the teal sky assured him they weren't outside aboard Space City. Or back on Earth either.

"We are still in cylinders," Fintan assured them, "but you see complex computer simulation. Provides controlled environment to explore Niveum without facing danger."

This is going to be better than any class I've ever taken, Riagan thought. Real or not, it felt like traveling to an exotic planet. He had talked to Rois for years about traveling the world when they turned eighteen. Leave child services and everything else behind, and live their life on a permanent holiday. Now he didn't have to wait. Could these cylinders show any place on Earth? Or any other planet in the universe?

Mr. Fintan led them to the river's edge where dwarf elephants, their short trunks barely longer than their mouths and tusks, floated in the current. Based on the river's depth, the elephants stood about as high as his waist. He guessed they weighed double the largest hog he had ever seen. Maybe three times. Still, they paled in comparison to those on Earth.

"These are meerphants," Mr. Fintan said. "They spend majority of time in water. Meerphants typically remain in shallows unless food is scarce or to avoid land predators."

"They're cute," one girl remarked. She was very short with tiny feet and curly cinnamon hair. Her cheeks were peppered like a freckled orchid. "Can we pet them?"

Mr. Fintan gave her a severe look. "Christel Manikas, examine those tusks. If a meerphant gores you, expect an extended infirmary visit, if you survive at all."

Riagan leaned over to Neil and said conspiratorially, "Let's jump on a couple and ride them."

"It's just a sim. We probably can't ride them," Neil replied. "They can't actually gore us."

Riagan grimaced at having already forgotten. The meerphants appeared solid enough. If he tried to ride one, would it disappear like a mirage? "That takes the craic out of exploration."

Neil frowned. "Craic?"

"Means fun or excitement," Rois explained.

"It is correct that no real physical harm occurs within these sims," Nez said. "But this is an extremely advanced sim. If you touch the meerphants, you will feel their rough hide. Put a piece of grass in your mouth, and you'll taste the bitterness.

"The sim also monitors everything that happens. If you're attacked in a manner that normally leads to a serious or fatal injury, you're dropped from the sim and receive a failing grade for the day."

"What if it's an accident?" Christel asked, brow furrowed. "What if we can't avoid it?"

"No do-overs in life. If you get attacked, you suffer injury," Nez answered, his face stern as if they should feel ashamed if they allowed themselves to be harmed. "After your first year, if you sustain a fatal injury in the sim, you fail the class, not just the day. If you do as you're told, you'll get through this year without difficulty.

"Now, please take out your wrist-comps, point them like a camera at a meerphant and press the scan button. Your wrist-comp will create a link for you to the appropriate class reading material and videos. I expect you to scan every animal, plant, tree, or anything else I point out during class explorations. Tests will cover the materials you scan."

Riagan removed his wrist-comp from its case. Pointing it at a meerphant, he pressed the scan button near the screen's bottom. A status bar moved from zero to one hundred percent. *Saved* appeared momentarily on the screen. He hoped the reading was short. Why couldn't they have videos instead?

"Meerphants are extremely skittish creatures that stay close to their herd all their lives," Fintan said. "Some herds are domesticated. They're strong creatures, so we use them as transport across rivers."

Behind the group, the twins, Anand and Devika, withdrew a pair of white mice from their suits, mischievous grins on their faces.

"We must domesticate entire herd, however, and only separate them for short stretches," Fintan said, unaware of the prank in motion. "If separated from herd, a meerphant endures extreme depression and dies in short time period."

Anand stepped forward and launched his mouse like a hand grenade over the class and into the shallow water near the meerphants. But Devika moved behind him and dumped her mouse down the back of his suit. The herd of meerphants broke out in squeals of terror, sounding more like pigs than elephants. At the same time, Anand shouted in surprise and clawed at his suit, dancing around.

"Get it off. Get it off," he shouted.

Devika doubled over with laughter.

Riagan loved the double-cross. She had done it perfectly, as if she was the sister of Loki.

Mr. Fintan, not knowing what was wrong with Anand, effortlessly grabbed him with his four arms and tossed him into the water.

Riagan's jaw dropped. This was amazing!

The frightened meerphants splashed water everywhere in their panic to escape and doused the students who were close to the water's edge. Aileen and Christel screamed as well, sounding like the meerphants, in Riagan's opinion. Meanwhile, Anand lurched out of the water, gasping, face shocked. He resumed wriggling to free the mouse from his suit, while the meerphants stampeded downstream.

Riagan laughed so hard that he had trouble breathing. He doubled over and nearly lost his balance.

"What was that for?" Anand bellowed after he'd freed the mouse and scrambled back out of the river.

Mr. Fintan hurried to Anand's side, face concerned despite having thrown him into the river himself. "Are you ok? I feared a shrub snake had slithered up your leg and the easiest way to deal with them is drowning." Fintan's sincerity only made Riagan laugh harder, and this time he did lose his balance and plop to the ground.

"I'll expect you in detention after your classes are through today," Nez said to Anand. The Instructor cast an annoyed look at Riagan as well.

"Oh, come on. I got the worst of it only," Anand complained, pointing at his drenched suit. A few of the other students were pretty wet too from the meerphant stampede.

The mouse Anand had first thrown into the water dragged itself on shore and Devika quickly scooped it up before the instructors noticed. Anand shot her a reproachful glare. Her face was expressionless, but her eyes danced merrily.

Nez didn't show any sympathy for Anand. "Report to Instructor Tereshkova at sixteen hundred hours and give her the mice."

"Yes, Instructor," Anand mumbled, not meeting the instructor's eyes.

Apparently Nez hadn't noticed Devika's hand in things. She was sly, pulling that off. Riagan was impressed. He'd have to keep an eye on her.

Fintan led them away from the water toward thicker, waist-high grass. Beyond that towered palm trees. He motioned for everyone to keep quiet. The tall grass seemed like the kind of place that might hold a lion or some other predator. Riagan had no wish to fail a day of class, nor was he sure what having a lion leap out at him would be like, even if it wasn't real. But despite hushing them, Fintan offered no warnings as they waded through the grass.

They quickly came across a dog-sized horse munching on the grass. The miniature horse's russet coloring resembled that of a deer. Riagan took another step forward to scan the animal, but a rotted log he hadn't seen crumpled underfoot, startling the little horse. It bolted away.

The log revealed a bug's nest. Gray bugs fled the sudden exposure. Some crawled over Riagan's boots and he shook his leg in disgust, trying to dislodge them. *Some luck I've got*, he thought sourly.

Several female classmates gave him dark looks for scaring off the horse, but it wasn't like he had done it on purpose.

"Propal," Mr. Fintan said. "Unlike horses on Earth, Propals are hunted as food among the Macab. Difficult to domesticate, they provide little other viable use."

"My Little Pony is a delicacy," Patrick deadpanned. Caleb snickered. The Traga made a noise like a crackling fire, presumably laughter as well.

"An excellent meal," Mr. Fintan agreed with Patrick, missing the joke.

Rois paled at the Macab's words.

Riagan suppressed a grin.

The high grass near the river soon gave way to more low-lying vegetation inland, as well as the enormous palm trees. The trees possessed scaly bark. Riagan scanned the tree, curious, before his attention was drawn by exclamations as another rodent-like creature, about two feet tall, bounced past. The animal shared the same russet coloring as the Propal, along with white spots on its back, like a fawn.

"The lepteer is a carnivore that eats insects and small lizards." Mr. Fintan pointed at the rodent. "Lepteers are great trackers due to their superb sense of smell, and often used by hunters to pursue game."

At that moment, the lepteer jumped and snatched a moth from the air and munched greedily. Riagan had a hard time seeing the lepteer as a formidable creature, especially one that would be useful in a hunt. The lepteers, like all the creatures he'd seen so far, were strange but appeared harmless. Where were the predators?

"Lads, I'm after seeing the petting zoo animals," Riagan said. "Let's check out the ones we need to guard against. Otherwise, why are we in a sim instead of the real deal?"

Mr. Fintan blinked. "How will you defend yourself against more dangerous animals?"

Riagan shrugged. "Isn't that why we're here, for ya to teach us?"

"We're introducing you to new environments," Mr. Fintan said, lips compressed in a thin line. "We don't introduce dangers you're unprepared to handle."

Riagan rolled his eyes. Apparently that standard position wasn't restricted to human adults. "Are all the creatures on Niveum miniatures like ya?"

"You jape with the ape?" Mr. Fintan asked, catching laughs from several students. "Do cubs think they can hunt because they can growl?"

Riagan opened his mouth to reply, but Rois kicked his shin hard, sending a bolt of pain through his leg.

"You're irascible," she hissed. "Ya give out too much."

"Let's keep going," Nez said. He typed something into a little black device in his hand.

Riagan limped after them. Rois had no reason to kick him. So he had complained a little. He wanted something a little more exciting. What's the harm in telling the instructors? But she always made sure that he knew when she thought he was out of line, most often to the detriment of his legs.

Seconds later a loud buzzing sound drifted out from beyond the palm trees. Riagan frowned. An insect, albeit a loud one. Or a swarm? Were they about to face killer locusts? Students searched the trees for the source of the buzzing. From the trees flew an eagle-sized dragonfly. Flying swiftly, it dove at Christel Manikas. She screamed as it darted around her head.

"Those are poisonous!" someone shouted.

Instinctively, Riagan grabbed a fallen branch and leapt at the dragonfly to protect Christel. Neil joined him and they tried to drive it away. This only seemed to anger the dragonfly as it buzzed louder and darted faster, turning its attack on them. Riagan swung cautiously, trying to avoid getting stung if it was indeed poisonous. The insect zipped out of reach, too fast for him. After another miss, the dragonfly plunged forward and clamped to his face, its legs digging painfully into his temples. He froze in shock and terror before it promptly disappeared. He gasped and searched wildly for it, tensing for another attack. He felt his face, trying to see if it had gotten him anywhere.

Patrick, Caleb, and a third boy with sallow skin doubled over in laughter.

"You three are nebbish," the third boy, with a French accent teased. "Like most newbies."

"Like ye could do better," Riagan said. Not finding any bites on his face, he pointed the branch at the trio.

"Enough," Nez ordered to silence them. "Adrien Laroque, do I need to visit with your father?"

Adrien quieted and shifted back a couple of steps.

"That was a Megaera," Nez said, ill-tempered. He glared from Riagan to Neil. "It *is* poisonous. Once it clamps onto your face, you're dead. One bite is fatal within ten minutes. Two might kill you before we got the creature off."

Riagan tried to hide his embarrassment at failing to drive away an insect, albeit a large, vicious, poisonous one. He appreciated that Neil had had his back without asking. He had someone else besides Rois to count on, something he had not experienced in a long time.

Eyes blazing, Nez continued. "There's an antidote for a Megaera's poison, which none of you know. Every planet has dangerous creatures. Our job is to introduce you to the environment and cautiously add in dangers so you can learn. Megaera are territorial. You don't know how to spot their nesting areas to avoid them, which is preferable considering their speed. They're difficult to hit with any weapon, much less a branch."

Patrick and Adrien snickered. Riagan clenched his fists, chagrined. He had overreacted to a sim. When it had attacked Christel, he'd forgotten that it posed no danger and had simply acted. But he'd rather look foolish, than stand by and let a girl get hurt. This sim was supposed to prepare them for real encounters after all.

"I'm giving you one break, Riagan, since it's your first day," Nez said. "After this, you fail the day as I warned you."

Patrick and Adrien still smirked, enjoying Riagan's humiliation. He wanted to snap at them, but his shin still stung from where Rois had kicked him and he did not relish the idea of getting another. Nor did he want the instructors focused on him any more than they already were at present.

Nez pressed a button on the black device and the Megaera reappeared. Riagan tensed. To his pleasure several other students, including Patrick, flinched in surprise.

The giant dragonfly flew in place, no longer menacing.

"No brandishing sticks?" Patrick asked Neil and Riagan in feigned surprise. "I guess the newbies can learn." But his words had little effect after he'd flinched, too.

"You're getting a second chance to scan the Megaera," Nez said.

Riagan quickly complied, as did the rest of the class. How much reading went along with these scans? Maybe Rois would give him the highlights.

"On another note, you'll work in teams for your final exam," Nez said. "In a couple weeks we'll group you into two teams for the semester. You'll learn to function in those teams. Every instructor will evaluate your performance in your classes to determine your roles. Some will be chosen as team captain for the final exam, a role you'll carry into your second year if you successfully pass."

"No pressure for you, though," Patrick said to Riagan and Neil. "Newbies are rarely chosen team captains. Too green."

"A challenge then?" Neil asked.

Patrick chortled. "Try if you like. You haven't a chance."

"Good yoke it's not up to ya," Riagan snapped.

Already, plans were forming in his mind for training with Neil to best Patrick and become a team captain. Riagan was not going to be shown up by Patrick. Of course, to prove to the instructors that he should be a team captain, he could not give out about how boring or easy class appeared. The instructors would expect him to stay in line and follow orders.

The academy had really only wanted Rois. He had something to prove to all of them.

Chapter 8

Neil's Printed Lunch

Food machines, bearing a resemblance to an arcade machine without controls, supplied meals in the academy mess hall. You selected foods from a touch screen and received the meal in a slot below.

Standing in line waiting to choose their lunch, Neil showed Riagan and Rois his class schedule on his wrist-comp. "Pre-calculus and the Science behind Space City sound terrible," Neil complained. And no flying lessons. "Besides Introduction to New Worlds, only Battle Tactics 101 sounds interesting."

He had sought out Mr. Chapman, hoping to follow up about the Dahaka infiltration, only to find out his recruiter had already been sent off ship. Nor would anyone tell Neil where Mr. Chapman had gone. Only that he was on a mission. It must have something to do with the Dahaka infiltration. Did Mr. Chapman's being sent elsewhere mean the threat was elsewhere, too?

"Astrobiology!" Riagan stared at his own class schedule, eyes widening in alarm. "That's why Rois was recruited. Why do I have it?"

Neil glanced at Riagan's schedule. They shared four classes. At least they could commiserate in Astrobiology and Space City History 101 together.

"I'll help you through it," Rois promised Riagan. She showed them her schedule. She shared one class with Neil and Riagan, and one with each of them separately.

The best news Neil had heard so far was that their classes wouldn't start until nine a.m. each morning. Apparently, their circadian rhythms—an individual's internal clock—begins to shift at age thirteen and peaked at nineteen. This shift made it natural for teens to stay up later at night and wake later in the morning. Scientific studies showed that for classes that started at 8:35 or later, students had higher Math, English, and Science scores than those who started earlier. In addition, classes starting later had higher attendance rates, lower depression rates, and reduced car crashes among teens. Whatever. Neil was just happy he wouldn't have to wake up before eight to get ready for class.

When Neil reached the ruby-colored food machine, it prompted him for his student ID number, which he entered. *Welcome Neil Ericson* appeared on-screen. Below his name the screen listed his height, weight, and other health statistics he did not understand. After searching through a few different food categories and ignoring the *Recommended* button, he settled on spaghetti, garlic toast, and green beans. He did not really want the beans, but the computer prompted him to choose a vegetable. No steamed spinach for him. Brownie for dessert? Yes, sir.

The machine hummed while the screen told him to *Please Wait*. "Think it's microwaving a frozen dinner?" he asked Riagan and Rois.

"Can't be worse than mess hall lunches back home," Rois said, not looking particularly hopeful.

A lid in the machine rose, revealing a steaming plate of spaghetti and meatballs, green beans, and toast. The smell made Neil's stomach grumble and mouth water. Hope this tastes as good as it smells.

The screen read *Your Food has been Printed*. Below that the screen listed the calories and nutrients in his meal and his requirements for the day.

"Printed?" Neil picked up the plate, suspicious despite the food looking freshly made. "What are they feeding us?"

"I'm too hungry to care." Riagan pushed past Neil to the machine, choosing pizza, roasted peppers, banana pudding, and peach cobbler.

Neil ogled when the machine delivered two desserts. "You can get more than one?" Why hadn't he thought to try for two?

"The dessert genie grants my every desire." Riagan snatched the tray as if afraid the machine might change its mind and pull the plate back.

"Rois, will you get me an extra?" Neil asked hopefully.

"Or two?" Riagan suggested.

"Ye going to make yourselves sick," Rois said. Nevertheless, she chose an apple pie for Neil along with chicken Alfredo and broccoli, corn, and carrot cake for herself. Once her food printed, they searched for seats in the mostly full mess hall.

"C'mere, let's sit with Jaya." Rois pointed at the blue-skinned humanoid. The Azzaro from their first class was sitting alone. Jaya was bald with a shallow nose and a ring in his left ear. His cheeks curved inward and resembled uncovered muscles. And his irises were a pale blue with tiny black pupils.

When they reached his table, Rois asked, "How's the craic, Jaya? May we join ya?"

Jaya nodded. As they sat, he eyed the extra desserts. "You have a weekly limit."

"What?" Riagan frowned.

"The machines track meals to ensure you get a balanced diet. The beginning of each week you're allotted two free meals. For the rest, the computer limits your choices so you're eating fruits, vegetables, carbs, and limiting sweets. If you eat whatever you want up front, your options are restricted the rest of the week. Desserts are allotted one per day."

"Guess I'm the exception." Riagan scooped up a mouthful of banana pudding.

"You get two free meals a week," Jaya repeated. His own plate had salmon with spicy rice, creamed corn, and chocolate ice cream for dessert. "You choose more than one dessert during your two free meals, you'll go without on a different day."

"Would've been nice for someone to explain that," Riagan said.

"They did… in orientation," Jaya replied drily.

Rois punched Riagan in the arm. "I told you."

Neil cast Rois an apologetic grimace. "Sorry. I owe you a dessert later." That's what he got for being greedy.

He took a bite of his spaghetti and found to his delight that it tasted incredible. Back home, spaghetti consisted of overcooked Ramen noodles, canned tomato sauce, and either hot dogs or spam. This spaghetti had a little spicy kick that made him want to stuff his face. The 'printing,' whatever that meant, caused no ill effects to the flavor.

"I'd suggest using the *recommended* button for most meals, and choosing from there," Jaya said. "I typically save my free meals for the weekend."

Neil sampled the green beans and was amazed when he liked even them. The food compared favorably to Mrs. Stevenson's best, his neighbor back home. She had always invited him to dinner whenever she saw him, but she was retired and on a fixed income. He hadn't wanted to mooch off her, so he had limited his visits.

"Surely there's a way around the system," Riagan said.

"You could try to convince other students to give up their desserts," Jaya said.

Neil snorted.

"Who would do that?" Riagan looked at Jaya as if he were mad.

Jaya grinned. "Didn't say it was a good option, but you won't get around the machines monitoring your intake."

Neil found himself smiling, too. He liked Jaya already. "Any other way to get candy or other desserts?"

Jaya leaned forward and answered in a hushed tone, "Nico Colombo runs the candy black market. His dad owns a store in the city and keeps Nico supplied. That's your best bet."

Unfortunately, Neil didn't have any money. There had to be ways to earn some, though.

Rois speared some broccoli with her fork. "The food machine said our food was printed. How?"

"The food is 3D printed," Jaya replied.

"You can 3D print food?" Neil paused, his fork with food held halfway to his mouth, and stared at it. How did they print food that tasted this good?

"3D printing is used to make most objects here," Jaya replied. "It's vital to living in space because it reduces the amount of supplies stored on the ship, which drastically reduces mass. Basic materials are stored. The printers combine them to create almost anything."

"That's amazing, but food?" Riagan asked in disbelief.

Jaya nodded. "Foods are made of simple compounds."

Neil shook his head. What would the food look like as the printer added layer upon layer until you had a steaming plate of spaghetti?

"We've met some Malsain and Traga since arriving, but not many are students," Rois said. "Are we in the wrong classes?"

Jaya picked at his spaghetti. "Most prefer their own forms of education, which is different than humans. My parentals are engineers here for about five years. Before coming here, I attended an Azzaro Lore Center on Sundara."

"Ya home planet?" Rois asked, all her focus on Jaya.

He nodded.

"What's it like?" She picked absently at her corn.

"Sundara has two suns, but it only orbits one," Jaya said. "It's strange though, because the visually smaller sun is actually the larger of the two. It's further away. Due to the two suns, we have much shorter nights than you are accustomed to. In the winter, the longest night has six hours of darkness. During the summer, our nights are twilight."

"That would actually depend on ya latitude on Sundara at night," Rois corrected.

"Cheers, oh brilliant one," Riagan deadpanned to Rois. She flushed, and he turned back to Jaya.

Neil hid a smile.

"Must need heavy curtains in the summer," Riagan added.

Neil nodded his agreement. One of the few good things about living in his uncle's basement was its minimal windows. During the summers, he'd covered them with heavy blankets and slept 'til noon.

"During the twilight nights, there is a peak outside the city you can climb," Jaya said. "From that vantage point the amethyst sky casts everything in a reddish purple hue." He focused on Rois. "There is a belief that if a woman takes a man to the peak during twilight, she'll know if he's her true love because a Glory will appear around his head."

"Ya lived on the ship for five years?" Riagan asked. Through slightly narrowed eyes he watched Jaya and Rois' studying each other. "So, ya know a lot of the other students?"

Neil hid a smile at the not-so-subtle diversion.

Riagan caught the scowl Rois shot him, so he diverted all his attention to Jaya.

What was it like to look after a younger sister? Neil thought. Not for the first time, he wished his parents had given him a brother or sister.

"I've met a few new recruits such as yourselves. Most of the other first years I've met at earlier schools." Jaya kept his focus on Riagan, but cast Rois furtive glances whenever Riagan glanced down at his food.

"How did you get recruited?" Jaya asked, directing the question to Riagan. Neil would bet Jaya was more interested in how Rois got recruited.

Riagan grimaced. "They didn't recruit me, actually. Rois wrote a paper on colonizing Mars for school, and her teacher helped her get it published."

"Published? Wow!" Neil said. "Must've been an impressive paper."

Rois blushed. "It was just published in our town newspaper in West Ireland."

"Published is published," Jaya said. "And if it got you recruited, it had to be a good one."

"Agreed," Neil added. He had never met anyone who had gotten a paper published. His esteem for her grew.

"They were knocking on our foster parents' door a week later," Riagan said. "They wanted to bring her here that day. Me, not so much."

"I told them I'd never go without ya," Rois said, leaning toward Riagan with a cajoling smile.

What would it feel like to have something published? Had to be pretty great.

Neil finished off the last bite of spaghetti. He stared mournfully at his plate. What were the rules on getting seconds? Having already eaten an extra dessert, he didn't want to cost himself even more. He would just have to wait until dinner.

"Have you guys gone to the city?" Jaya asked, covering his plate with his napkin.

"Not yet," Rois replied, brightening. "But we'd love to see it."

"I can show you around during our pass weekend," he offered. "Our first pass weekend will come around end of September."

"We'd love to," Rois blurted.

Riagan gave Rois a suspicious glance, but Neil piped in. "We're game."

Chapter 9

Neil Learns of the Invasion

After lunch, Neil and Riagan split off for Space City History 101, while Rois and Jaya shared a Physics class. Riagan glowered after Rois and Jaya as they walked across the courtyard to their class.

The bell rang.

To distract Riagan, Neil said, "Bet you lunch in the city I beat you to class."

In answer, Riagan broke into a run. The cheater. Neil had longer legs, though, and in the open courtyard he outpaced Riagan. Once Neil yanked open the door and darted into their building, however, students filled the hallway and meandered toward classrooms. He weaved through the crowd, anxious to keep Riagan from catching up. But when he neared their classroom, Riagan stiff-armed him into a short, plump female instructor who was closing her classroom door.

"Oh," she squawked.

Neil righted himself with the door, his face burning. "I'm sorry."

"You should be more careful," she said, nodding disapprovingly.

"I will. I'm sorry."

He hurried after Riagan into their history class.

"You cheat," Neil said as they slid into seats at the back of a bowl-shaped classroom with stadium seating. On his other side sat an athletic girl he recognized from class that morning. She offered a smile and brushed her short blonde hair out of her face. He smiled back.

Down in the room's center, the instructor introduced himself as Louis Aldrin; a medium-sized man with short, curly red hair.

Riagan tapped Neil on the shoulder and pointed to Instructor Aldrin's right. The Malsain they had met on their first day, Instructor Tanith, sat alone in the front row and Aldrin introduced her as the co-instructor for the class. Her yellowish scales rippled as she rose to her feet. Her forked tongue tasting the air, Tanith smirked up at Neil and Riagan. Neil's stomach churned as he remembered her noxious breath. He forced himself to smile back, trying to hide his discomfort. What were the academy's rules on transferring classes?

"I like to begin the first class each year asking what everyone would like to learn most," Instructor Aldrin began. "That way I know where your interests lie and also get a feel for what you know. Any suggestions?"

One person requested the Kali rebellion. Another the Nereus crash. Fran, the elf-fanatic from the kickoff party, requested the Alfar alliance. The Dahaka invasion was the overwhelming favorite, however.

"The Dahaka invasion is nothing new," Aldrin chided. "Everyone knows about Commander Vairya's ploy to build the greatest empire in the universe."

This revelation alarmed Neil. Mr. Chapman had assured him not to worry about the message concerning an infiltration, but if it had happened once? Neil wanted to ask, but was afraid that he was the only one who didn't know. He didn't want to embarrass himself by revealing his ignorance.

The blonde next to him raised her hand.

"Yes, Eris," Aldrin said.

"You actually fought in the Dahaka invasion, correct?"

"I did," Aldrin confirmed.

"So you can tell us firsthand," another boy suggested, a birthmark coloring the left side of his neck. He was short, and his accent sounded Italian.

"The new recruits from Earth know nothing of the conflict," Eris added. "Plus, you have an Eidetic memory. You can give us details others can't."

Neil frowned. Was an Eidetic memory like a photographic memory?

Aldrin grimaced. "All right, I'll give you today. I'll answer any questions you ask, but no more for the rest of the year."

Neil was thankful that Eris had spoken up.

"What about the Alfar Alliance?" Fran asked.

"Fran, you know enough about the Alfar to teach a class by yourself," Aldrin said as if he'd received this request from her a thousand times. "Probably do a better job than anyone else here at the academy. We're here to learn new subjects."

Aldrin pressed a few buttons on the nearby desk and a large, 3D image popped up in the air showing a pale-skinned man, large as a WWE wrestler, wearing obsidian armor. He was bald and a pair of long white tusks decorated the armor covering both forearms. The man possessed crimson eyes with black pupils. A chill rippled through Neil as he stared at those otherworldly eyes.

"The Azi Dahaka hail from Siavash, in the star cluster Hyades," Aldrin said. "Siavash is a planet teeming with dinosaur-like creatures similar to what existed on Earth during the Permian period two hundred and fifty million years ago."

The image in the air changed to a video of a battlefield where an Azzaro Army fought Dahaka invaders among city rubble. The Dahaka, at nine, maybe ten feet tall, towered over the Azzaro. The Dahaka also moved with incredible speed despite their size. In addition to their onyx armor, they wore black helmets that left only their necks exposed.

"Commander Kathra Vairya led the Dahaka attack on Sundara." Aldrin pointed to a Dahaka warrior impaling an Azzaro with the tusk on his right arm. The Dahaka pumped his fists in the air, the slain soldier hanging like a carcass on a meat hook. "The Dahaka use savage displays of brutality to cow enemies into surrender."

The dead warrior resembled Jaya, and Neil was glad the Azzaro wasn't present. Had Jaya lived through this invasion? If so, Neil could only imagine the horrors he must've seen.

The Dahaka on-screen caught another Azzaro between powerful arms. It squeezed like a snake, choking the life from its prey. Once the Azzaro went limp, the Dahaka threw the body against a crumbled wall. The savagery mesmerized Neil. He couldn't turn away. Would they have to face the Dahaka?

"You'll notice that the Dahaka Army lacks modern weapons. Their ships in the background are outfitted with primitive missiles."

A vague outline of ships covered the horizon.

"They prefer their own natural abilities, relying on superb armor to protect them."

The Azzaro forces fought from rooftops, firing laser weapons at the Dahaka. Their bursts reflected harmlessly off the armor. How was the Dahaka armor able to withstand laser weaponry?

Only direct shots to the neck, between their masks and armor, wounded or killed the Dahaka. Thanks to their speed, few shots hit the mark. The Azzaros who braved the ground, attempting to get closer, more accurate shots, soon fell before the giant invaders. Some managed to wound or kill a Dahaka before being overwhelmed by others.

Neil wished that the Azzaro would flee, despite knowing that this battle had ended long ago. He would not wish this on anyone, even Patrick. Neil wanted Instructor Aldrin to turn off the footage and yet he couldn't look away.

"How were the Dahaka able to overrun an Azzaro city like this?" the boy with the birthmark asked. "Everyone knows the Azzaro have the second-best defensive technology, next to the Alfar, while the Dahaka are well behind."

"During the Dahaka invasion on Sundara, the Azzaro technology wasn't what it is now, Nico Colombo," Aldrin replied. "We gained the technology to build this ship through an alliance with the Azzaros. They could explore space. But we both received our superior defensive systems through an alliance with the Alfar. Since they are confined to Ourania, they have focused on defensive technologies to make their home planet an impregnable fortress. An attack on Ourania by any other race in the galaxy is laughable.

"But at the time not only were the Azzaros not as strong, the Dahaka had developed a cloaking technology that allowed them to attack Sundara without warning. The Dahaka ships laid waste to the city before sending forces on the ground to finish off the attack. Fortunately, we had recently formed our Alliance with the Azzaros."

On the video screen, silver ships similar to the one Neil had flown in from Earth, joined the battle and fired on the Dahaka army. After the Azzaro troops had withdrawn from the field, other ships dropped bombs that decimated the Dahaka forces.

"Between our combined forces, the Azzaro and Space City drove the Dahaka from Sundara and destroyed their fleet, ending the Dahaka

Invasion. Not long after, we reached a treaty with the Alfar, and with their help our defensive technologies have improved to the point that any Dahaka incursions are quickly repelled."

Another scene flashed back to the Dahaka setting fire to any buildings that still stood in the decimated city. "Another reason the Dahaka were beaten is that they destroyed everything in their path, rather than acquire enemy resources. That short-sighted approach keeps them technologically inferior."

"Did you face the Dahaka up close?" Neil asked with a mixture of dread and fascination.

Aldrin nodded. "I did. I was part of special units sent in to assist the Azzaro, to finish off the remaining Dahaka. We had hoped to capture some and study their armor to learn what makes it so strong. We were never able to capture one, however, and they never leave their dead behind."

Would Aldrin train them in combat? Surely he was as qualified as any on the ship.

Aldrin's face became haunted. "That day we reached the remains of the city at 8:24 a.m. The smell of burnt copper intermixed with sulfur overwhelmed the senses. I remember the grotesque carnage that caked the city's ruins. I could tell you everything I saw, smelled, and touched during every second of those eleven days as we drove out those remaining Dahaka.

"I promise you, an up-close battle with a Dahaka is horrifying. As fast as they appear in that video, they're faster. As vicious as you've seen, they become barbaric when cornered. I witnessed a Dahaka tear five men apart as they attempted to take him down. It took ten more to kill him.

"Like the ancient Spartans, the Dahaka spend their lives training for battle. Warriors and hunters all, they thrive on a world where dinosaurs still roam. They are forced to become ruthless to survive. Our resistance, along with a great many other races, depends on technological superiority. Without that, we don't stand a chance in a war against them."

The video ended with a Dahaka bearing down on an Azzaro. The Azzaro barely realized the danger before the Dahaka swung his arm and impaled him with a tusk and slammed him into a wall.

Neil imagined himself in the Azzaro's place. He almost felt the tusk piercing his chest. He shivered and felt sick to his stomach, this time not from Tanith's foul breath.

"We could take one together," Riagan whispered, clapping Neil on the arm, a confident smile on his face.

Neil did not want to find out. Enduring a gassy Malsain or climbing flagpoles was one thing. Fighting a heavily armored giant that charged like a bull sounded insane. He wasn't sure he would ever be ready to face one, regardless of the training he received here on Space City. Had his grandfather ever fought battles on the ground? All of his mother's stories had involved his grandfather in a plane. Neil couldn't imagine his grandfather backing down though, even to the Dahaka. Could he ever be that brave?

Chapter 10

Riagan's Skunk Sack Surprise

Riagan walked into his Astrobiology class and immediately wondered if he could change to another. Behind the twin teachers' desks sat Instructor Tereshkova talking with a Traga. Likely one of the Traga that Riagan had argued with in the courtyard last weekend.

Neil started to laugh.

"Don't say it," Riagan warned.

Behind the instructors, a 3D video showed a harpist playing a soothing melody, but it did little to lighten his mood. He grabbed a seat at the back and slouched, hoping the Traga would not notice him. Luck was not in his favor. The Traga's blue-fire eyes narrowed when he spotted Riagan. After a moment's regard, the Traga diverted its attention back to Tereshkova.

"Guess I can skip this class," Riagan said. "We're not even through the first week and I've already failed if the Traga has any say on grades."

"Keep your current pace and you'll wind up a trash collector before you know it," Neil teased.

A white sheet covered the left wall from floor to ceiling. In front of the sheet were tables upon which rested pots in which one- and two-foot, amber, egg-shaped pods grew.

Nico Colombo sat in a chair in front of them. He had his wrist-comp out and played a game on it. Riagan leaned forward over Nico's shoulder. The game was a first-person shooter hunting Dahaka in a jungle.

"How did ya get that?" Riagan asked, thumping Nico on the shoulder. "I checked mine for games and didn't find any."

"Have to get around the school's encryption and download them," Nico replied without taking his eyes off the screen.

"Show me?" Riagan asked, pulling his wrist-comp out.

"Bring it by my room later tonight. I'll set you up."

"Do you sell candy?" Neil asked.

Riagan remembered the conversation with Jaya in the lunchroom. "Yeah."

Nico eyed the instructors. They hadn't heard, so Nico turned back to them and gestured for quiet. He whispered, "Tonight. My room."

Riagan started to press Nico, but the bell rang and Tereshkova rose to address the class. All the students stood and saluted. After a short hesitation, Riagan set his wrist-comp on his desk and joined them. He was already on thin ice with Instructor Tereshkova and the Traga. He needed to at least skate by in the class if he wanted to be a team captain.

"Welcome to Astrobiology," Tereshkova said in greeting. She introduced herself and turned to the Traga, who stood on his chair in order to see over the table. It was unsettling that the Traga stood so close to the wooden desk. Riagan half expected it to catch on fire.

"This is my co-instructor, Aodh." Tereshkova said.

"A sun-filled day to you," Aodh said. His coloring changed from a dull red to cherry for a moment, then lightened again.

Now Riagan understood why the tradutors were required for every class. They had an alien co-instructor in each. What other alien instructors awaited them?

"Before we start, take out your wrist-comps," Tereshkova said.

Many already lay on desktops, but a few students fished theirs from backpacks. Riagan left his on his desk and waited for Tereshkova's instructions.

"Now scan yourselves," she said.

"We have to read pages about ourselves for homework, Instructor?" Nico asked. Riagan chuckled.

Tereshkova ignored the question. "Scan measures your heart rate, blood pressure, and other health factors and transmits them to infirmary. Everyone is required to scan each morning. Doctors use to monitor your health."

"Seems like an invasion of privacy, Instructor," Riagan said. He did not want to remember to scan every day. That would be a hassle.

"Scans help doctors catch sickness early, before you notice or spread to your classmates," Tereshkova said. "Information is stored in AI neural network. If you get seriously injured, network alerts doctors about your drug allergies or other complications that might prevent certain treatments or procedures. Daily scan is for your own well-being."

"They just like giving orders," Riagan whispered.

"I barely remember to dress in the morning," Neil replied drily.

"What did you say?" Tereshkova asked, eyebrow arched.

"Um, nothing, Instructor Tereshkova," Neil stammered.

Riagan kept his face blank so she wouldn't turn on him next.

"Speak up," Tereshkova said. "If you have something to say, say for whole class."

Neil grimaced. Loud enough for the class, he said, "I just said it'll be difficult to remember first thing in the morning, Instructor. I'm usually in a rush so I'm not late for class."

Tereshkova snorted at the last part. "What if you get hurt and knocked unconscious in your battle tactics class? If doctors treat you for wrong injury or illness, you might die from efforts to save you."

"Yes, Instructor," Neil said, already preparing to scan himself. "I'll remember."

Riagan was relieved she wasn't focused on him.

"That's better," Tereshkova replied coolly.

For the next thirty seconds, everyone fumbled with their wrist-comps, trying to scan themselves. Riagan knew he'd have to set a daily reminder. If he wanted to become a team captain, he probably couldn't afford to miss too many times.

After everyone had complied, Instructor Aodh continued, surveying the class. "How many of you have seen a Hyaenodon up close?"

No one raised their hands. Tereshkova stepped over to the sheet-covered wall and pulled a cord, which raised the sheet up to the ceiling, revealing a ten by twenty-foot cage with iron bars. Inside the cage was a hyena-like beast the size of a rhinoceros. The Hyaenodon growled at the class, flashing razor sharp tusks. Several of the students closest to the cage jumped to their feet in alarm, a few gasping. Riagan rose to his feet as well to get a better view. From the shoulders up, the

Hyaenodon had chocolate brown fur. Back from the shoulders, the beast was black-and-white striped like a zebra.

"Hyaenodon are swift predators with bone crushing jaws," Aodh said. "Anyone know the best way to deal with one?"

"Shoot it from a distance, Instructor," Nico said. Riagan agreed. If that failed… run.

"Hyaenodon possess superb smell sense and strong eyesight," Aodh said. "They'll discover you first, set an attack, and close in too fast to avoid."

"You might get off lucky shot to kill one," Tereshkova added, "—but Hyaenodon hunt in packs. Usually at night. Good luck shooting them all."

Riagan wanted to move over to the cage for a closer view.

"Any other guesses?" Aodh asked. The Traga focused on Riagan, as if challenging him.

Riagan shook his head. He didn't like it, but he didn't have an answer.

"You'd survive fewer than a week on Anthea," Aodh said.

Was Instructor Aodh dismayed or unsurprised at what they didn't know? It seemed unfair to judge them at this point. Riagan had not known that any of this existed last week.

"Over course of year," Tereshkova said, "we'll teach physiologies of many animals and plants you'll come across once you explore off-ship. Many pose great dangers, while others heal or protect."

"For today, we're examining skunk sacks, which ward off Hyaenodon." Aodh gestured toward potted plants along the wall. "Take one to your desk."

Several of the students moved cautiously toward the table holding the pots. But Riagan hurried to the table and peered over at the Hyaenodon. The beast tensed and crouched, glaring at him. An icy shiver ran across Riagan's back between his shoulder blades, and his body tensed to run, but he forced himself to ignore his fear and meet the beast's angry gaze. They remained locked that way for a few seconds until Tereshkova interrupted.

"Riagan, please grab skunk sack and return to your desk."

Her words startled Riagan. He had momentarily forgotten anyone else in the room. Now he sheepishly grabbed one of the pots and carried it back to his desk. But he kept casting glances over at the

Hyaenodon, wishing they were doing more with it instead of examining these skunk sacks that grew on lily-pads on the soil.

"How do these pods protect us from that?" Riagan asked, pointing at the Hyaenodon. The beast, apparently deciding no one posed a threat, had lain down at the back of the cage, but kept its eyes on them.

"Maybe they'll eat the pods and we can escape," Neil suggested.

Riagan shrugged. Seemed unlikely that a beast like that would ignore fresh meat for some stupid pod. He wouldn't.

"Skunk sacks are the infant form of Timbrosias, the vastest trees on Anthea," Aodh said. "Similar to Giant Redwoods on Earth, Timbrosias grow and mature inside protective skunk sacks until achieving about five feet in height, before consuming the sacks."

"Five-foot eggs? That's one heck of an omelet," Riagan whispered to Neil.

At the front of the classroom Aileen McKensie turned her back on her pod and covered her mouth, face pale. Her chest heaved as if she was about to vomit. Taking another breath, Riagan discovered why. He searched the floors for a skunk, or a Malsain.

"Somebody punctured a pod," Aodh said, an amused grin on his face.

Everyone had covered their noses and mouths with a hand or their shirt and stepped back from the pods. The Hyaenodon sat up and whined. It paced the back of the cage. Riagan knew how it felt. He wished he could run away right now, too.

"Skunk sacks are the protection Timbrosias developed," Aodh said. "During infancy stage, the shoots are soft and tender. Many animals find infant Timbrosias immensely tasty, so the sacks protect the shoots until the trunks harden. They're filled with juices similar to skunk excretions. If an animal wants the shoots, it must break the sack and endure the odorous juices. If you crack a skunk sack wide open, the stench is tenfold worse. Your nostrils are stung by only a whiff right now."

"So our best defense against a Hyaenodon is to imitate a skunk?" Eris asked, voice nasally from covering her nose.

Juice squirted into the air from in front of Riagan, spraying across his skunk sack, desk, and shirt. He jumped back in disgust, nose wrinkled. Then he glared at Patrick.

"What're you going to do?" Patrick asked, smiling smugly while Caleb and Adrien chortled on either side of him. "Tattle to Colonel Terror?"

Riagan actually debated cutting open his own sack to return fire.

"Patrick Duffy, that is Kitsch," Tereshkova scolded.

Patrick turned back to her. "An accident, I promise, Instructor." He slapped Adrien on the back. "Adrien didn't expect the juice to shoot out like that."

"My apologies, Riagan," Adrien said flatly.

Patrick turned back toward Riagan, shielding the glee in his eyes from the instructors while he mouthed "newbie" at him.

Riagan pressed a knife against his skunk sack. Neil grabbed his wrist and shook his head. Riagan gritted his teeth, but didn't fight him off. There was nothing he could do right now without coming off as the bad guy. It was always the one who retaliated who got in trouble.

"Wash up," Tereshkova told Riagan, pointing to the sink. "Adrien Laroque, be more careful next time."

Lips pressed together as he fought to control his anger, Riagan marched over to the sink. He grabbed a wash rag and soap and started to clean the stain on his azure shirt as Tereshkova resumed the discussion.

"Never underestimate any method for warding off danger. Skunk sacks can disguise you from an enemy on a mission."

"The stench would ward them away," Eris said. Others voiced their agreements amid chuckling.

"The juices in the skunk sacks aren't the lone value." Aodh held up a lily-pad. "When the leaves are crushed up, they secrete a salve to treat flesh wounds to prohibit infection. If you're clawed by a Hyaenodon and escape, you'll want skunk sack leaves to clean the wound."

Riagan finished washing his shirt the best he could, but the stink remained as he returned to his seat. Now he'd have to do laundry tonight. Stupid Patrick.

Aodh showed them the best way to procure the foul juices from the skunk sacks without harming the pods. They stored the liquid in vials.

When class ended, the students quickly filed out. Patrick and his gang passed by and he gave Riagan a conspiratorial grin. "If you wear some skunk juice in Instructor Tanith's class, you might become teacher's pet." Caleb and Adrien snickered as they left.

Frustrated at Patrick's cockiness and repeated attacks, Riagan noticed a petite skunk sack on another classmate's table. Tereshkova and Aodh had their backs to him. Slinking over to the sack, Riagan grabbed it. The sack broke off from the lily-pads pretty easily. If the teachers caught him with this, he would be in serious trouble, but he had to repay Patrick. Cradling the sack to his side with one arm, Riagan hurried from the room.

When he got into the hallway, Neil glanced at the egg and asked suspiciously, "What is that?"

"C'mere." Riagan rushed ahead.

"Is that a skunk sack?" Neil persisted.

"C'mere."

Riagan chose a circuitous route to their dormitories to avoid the courtyard. They snuck into Patrick and Caleb Thorton's room. Twin beds lined opposite sides of the room with a desk and chair in between. A dresser stood at the foot of each bed. Like all the rooms in the boys' dormitories, it was immaculate. Inspections occurred every morning.

Riagan glanced from one bed to the other, unsure which bed belonged to Patrick. He chose the right one.

Pulling back the sheets, he stripped the pillowcase off and tossed the pillow aside. In its place he set the skunk sack.

"Riagan, that's a little much," Neil said, but making no effort to stop him.

Riagan glared at Neil. Retrieving the Swiss army knife from his pocket, he moved to cut the pod. Neil grabbed his arm, but he shook him off.

"He's earned this," Riagan said. "Ya know he has."

Neil didn't argue, so Riagan sliced the sack in half. The pod split, juices spilling over the sides and pooling on the sheets. In the middle of the pod grew a sapling. Riagan slipped the pillowcase over his right hand and pulled the sapling out and set it aside. Breathing through his mouth, he spread the juice all over the sheets using the pillowcase. The empty pod he threw underneath the bed.

He replaced the pillow, set the shoot and pillowcase on top, and remade the bed, taking care that no visual clue gave away the mess. The room reeked, though.

Neil held an arm over his nose and mouth.

"Did you see that loser's face when he got sprayed with skunk sack juice?" Patrick asked from down the hall.

Neil flashed a panicked grin. They had nowhere to hide. Riagan searched for an escape, happy he'd gotten his revenge. He ran for the window and raised it. Neil climbed on the desk and leapt out into an alley. Riagan scrambled after him. A twist of the door handle caused him to panic and fall from the window to the alley below. He landed on his arm, the wind knocked from him. At least the dorm room was on ground level.

From the room behind, Caleb asked in disgust, "What is that smell?"

Chapter 11

Neil's Dahaka Countdown

"Who did this?" Patrick demanded from the dorm room above.

"Man, that's my bed," Caleb complained, voice muffled.

Crouched in the alley beneath the dorm window, Neil grimaced. They hadn't gotten Patrick after all. Caleb deserved it, too, but that wasn't as satisfying. Even less satisfying if they were discovered.

Neil moved in a low crouch away from the window. At the first right, he and Riagan entered a maze of research facilities and classrooms that filled the campus, providing ample hiding places.

From around the corner behind them, Patrick said, "They can't have gotten far. Find them."

The chorus of several feet pounding on the ground toward them sent Neil and Riagan racing ahead and ducking left down an intersection.

"This way. I hear them," Caleb shouted, not too far off. How had Patrick and Caleb summoned help so quickly?

Neil ran through a couple of more intersections. Nearby, a busted grate partially covered a window well. He pointed at the opening. "Let's hide down there."

He reached the grate and dropped to his knees, scrambling through the hole and dropping down into a basement filled with dusty lab equipment.

Riagan landed beside him. "Let's get away from the window."

There was a single door on their right. Neil shuffled toward it and eased it open to see if they could hide anywhere. Inside the room, Neil spotted a Dahaka in obsidian armor. Neil's eyes widened and he froze.

What was a Dahaka doing on the ship?

Fear flooded like a swift icy river through Neil as he ducked back out the door.

"That's a Dahaka," Riagan whispered as he joined Neil.

Thanks Captain Obvious, Neil thought. He listened in terror for a sign that the Dahaka had seen him, but instead it continued speaking unperturbed with someone else around the corner.

"My master is displeased with the CME progress," the Dahaka said. Fortunately, Neil had not removed his tradutor after leaving class.

The other man in the room replied calmly. "We're on schedule. Delivery will occur as agreed."

Neil didn't recognize the voice, and since they appeared unaware of the intrusion, he found himself peeking around the corner.

"We require the CME before next summer." The Dahaka flickered out of existence, then reappeared.

Neil frowned. How had the Dahaka done that?

"What was that?" Riagan asked.

Neil punched Riagan and held a finger to his lips.

"Next summer is impossible," the man scoffed. "We agreed on one year. Building the CME and getting it off ship unnoticed in less time is unthinkable."

"Delivery in six months," the Dahaka insisted. "We'll pay double."

"Ormazd, you're being unreasonable," the man complained. Tendrils of smoke drifted through the room. "What good is payment if I get caught?"

The Dahaka disappeared momentarily again, and Neil realized why. He leaned close to Riagan and whispered. "It's a sim. Like class."

Riagan's shoulders relaxed, but he kept his voice hushed. "Is it a movie? Training sim?"

Neil shook his head, not quite sure what to make of this. The Dahaka was real, whether it was onboard the ship or not. Its conversation with whomever was in that room was real, too, and that made Neil uneasy. Why was someone on their ship meeting with a Dahaka? This had to be tied to the infiltration that Mr. Chapman was investigating.

"Six months," the Dahaka repeated. It disappeared again, this time for good.

The man around the corner swore.

Neil eased the door back shut. He wanted out of here. They hurried back to the window and peeked outside. No signs of Patrick and his gang. The street was empty. Neil gave Riagan a boost out the window. Once Riagan was up on the street, he turned back and Neil took his hand to climb out of the window.

Back on the street, Neil felt a sting on his neck. He smacked the spot, expecting to find a mosquito. His head suddenly turned foggy, his vision swimming. Overwhelming dread slammed into him. He placed his hand against the wall to steady himself. What had gotten him? He blinked to clear his vision, terrified at what was happening.

Riagan was doubled over as well. There was nothing else in the alley that could explain the sting Neil had felt, or the disorientation. Riagan gasped and lurched upright. He broke into a run back the way they had come. Not wanting to be left here alone, Neil gave chase. He took deep breaths as he ran, which cleared his vision. But the sudden, indescribable fear drove him onward.

They raced through the campus maze until reaching the road that led toward the spaceport. They took refuge in the garden. On the opposite end of the garden, closest to the spaceport, an old man tended to a flower bed while robots pruned trees or picked fruit. The man had thin strips of white hair that hung halfway down his back, and a cane rested against the stones surrounding the bed. He turned to them, smiling, and waved. Chest heaving, Neil breathed deeply to calm himself and waved back. The gardener turned back to his work.

Neil watched and listened for pursuit, still unsure what had gotten them. He hadn't seen bugs on the ship before, and the sting had subsided. Had it been nothing?

"I think something stung me," he said, feeling his neck again for the spot.

Riagan doubled back over, as if still fighting off the dizziness and fear.

"Are you ok?"

"I don't know," Riagan admitted.

"Maybe we should visit the doctor," Neil suggested.

Riagan forced himself upright once more and shook his head vehemently. "No!"

The tulips in a flower bed behind Riagan started to turn white.

Neil frowned. "Riagan, do you have alcohol on you?"

Riagan shook his head. "I don't. Why?"

Neil studied the tulips a moment longer. Why had they changed color? The flowers weren't their most pressing concern, though.

"Is a CME a weapon?" Neil asked.

"It doesn't matter. We never heard about it."

Neil gaped. "What do you mean? The Dahaka—"

Riagan cut him off as he pointed back the way they had come. "Do ya know who the Dahaka spoke to?"

Neil shook his head.

"Exactly," Riagan said. "We don't know who is involved, and we want to avoid the attention of anyone with the power to secretly deal with the Dahaka. What do ya think he'd do to preserve his secret?"

Neil's skin crawled at the thought.

Riagan's eyes flashed. "Men like that will crush us to protect their interests. Sticking our necks out will only get us killed."

"This is tied to an infiltration I heard about," Neil said, sure of the connection. "A Space City officer informed Mr. Chapman about it, and he was sent to investigate."

"The Council knows, then. Let them handle it."

"If the Dahaka want a CME, it's not good for us," Neil argued, not liking the idea of doing nothing. That seemed cowardly.

"We need to find out more first," Riagan argued. "They discussed a spring deal. We can ask questions. Maybe tip off the right people anonymously."

Riagan set off for campus, leaving Neil behind to mull over his words. Neil didn't believe his grandfather would've done nothing, but Riagan had a point. Someone helping the Dahaka likely had no qualms with killing them, and they didn't even know the traitor's identity. What if they spoke to the wrong person? Mr. Chapman was gone.

The uncertainty made Neil feel powerless, unsure what to do.

Thinking about Mr. Chapman brought his grandfather and his silver coin to mind. Neil fished out the coin. Neither choice was a good one so let a toss of the coin decide. Heads, he spoke with the next instructor he found. Tails, he searched for more information and kept quiet, for now.

Neil flipped the coin.

"Students are not allowed off the road," a mechanical voice said behind him.

He spun about so fast that he nearly toppled over. A few feet away, a silver robot with a generally human-shaped body held a bundle of pruned branches.

"Students must remain on the road," the robot said.

Neil looked for his coin, anxious to depart.

The robot stepped closer. "Students are not allowed off the road."

Not seeing the coin, Neil panicked and spun in a circle, desperate to find it. He could not lose his grandfather's coin. Lifting his right foot, he realized he had stepped on it. He let out a breath of relief. Snatching the coin from the ground, Neil hurried back toward campus. Only later did he realize that he'd forgotten to check on which side the coin had landed.

Chapter 12

Neil's Request

Neil agonized over what to do about the traitor as he did his health scan the next morning. An uncomfortable silence hung over the room. Riagan was acting like they hadn't seen the Dahaka. Any time Neil started to bring up the subject, Riagan hissed him quiet. Finally, if only to get away from the tension between them, Neil left to get breakfast in the mess hall.

As he exited the boy's dorm, Neil spotted Maellyn across the courtyard. She read her wrist-comp on a bench. Unfortunately, they did not share any classes, making it difficult for him to run into her. He decided to go talk to her, but as soon as he started across the courtyard he wondered what to say to her. He could ask what she was reading, but what if she thought he was just being nosey.

Absorbed with reading, Maellyn did not notice Neil's approach. With nothing coming to mind, he almost panicked and turned around, but managed to keep himself going until he stood in front of her. Wanting to avoid standing like a mute idiot in front of her, he said the first thing that came to mind.

"The moon is steadily shrinking."

He groaned inwardly, feeling stupid for stating the obvious. Riagan probably never had difficulty talking to girls.

Maellyn jumped, startled. Her surprise flustered him further, but she relaxed once she realized it was him and returned a welcome smile.

"Before long you won't even see it anymore," she said. "That's the one thing I wish Space City would fix. Put a fake moon in the night sky." She wore a pair of tiny lavender flower earrings, not much larger than her bottom lobes, which matched her top. The little flowers lent a natural quality to her beauty that was rare.

He realized she waited for his response. What were they talking about?

His face started to burn as his mind scrambled. "I like your earrings. Do you own many flower earrings?"

What a silly question, he chided himself. Why couldn't he come up with something clever to talk about?

But she smiled. "Four. These are columbine flowers. Lavender is my favorite color. I have the scarlet pimpernels I wore at the party, a pair of yellow daisies for spring, and also white lotus blossoms."

"I've never seen flowers that small." He still felt awkward, but as long as she continued to smile that had to be good. Right?

"These earrings were made using 3D printers. The flowers were engineered to this size."

"That's cool," he said. Unsure what else to say about the earrings, he pointed at her wrist-comp. "Homework?"

She glanced at it and nodded. "Plenty of assigned reading. Scanned a lot yesterday. I'm in a third year engineering class thanks to my father." She added this last bit with a sigh.

He felt as if he had just driven onto the highway during his first learner's lesson. She was obviously really smart. He hoped she didn't ask him what classes he had.

"Your dad's a lead scientist, right?" he asked, wanting to kick himself. All of his questions sounded lame the moment he said them.

She just nodded. "For twelve years."

"How long have you lived here?"

"Nearly my whole life," she replied. Her wrist-comp started to beep and she glanced at it. She rose to her feet. "Will you walk me to my class?"

"Sure," he said, hoping he didn't sound too eager. Inside he wanted to jump for joy.

She retrieved a light green bag from underneath the bench and dropped her wrist-comp inside. She slipped the bag over her shoulder as they walked. "I was born in New York. We lived there off and on until I turned five while my dad supervised a secret project."

"What project?" he asked. They reached the math and science building and he grabbed the door for her.

"I don't know. He shows me some of his work, but most projects are classified."

Would her father know about CMEs? As a lead scientist, he must know. Maybe he'd told her about them.

Neil was hesitant to involve her and put her in danger, yet if he could discover something about a CME, about the danger they posed—

"What is it?" she asked as they passed through the crowd of students milling about on their way to class.

"What?" He was startled from thought.

"You want to ask me something," she said matter-of-factly. "What is it?"

"Oh, nothing," he said, downplaying the question. "Have you heard of a CME?"

She frowned. "I'm not familiar with it. What is it?"

"Just something I heard someone mention."

She placed a hand on his shoulder, stopping him. He turned and her eyes had narrowed, but she had a hint of a smile on her lips. "You're afraid you're the only one who doesn't know because you're new?"

Before he responded, the bell rang. He was also a long way from class. "Just curious."

"I can check with my dad."

He started to protest. The last thing he wanted to do was include her father. That might lead to too many questions. He shouldn't have said anything. "Don't worry about it. It's nothing."

She pushed him playfully. "I'm sure he'll know, and now I'm curious." Before he could respond, she pointed at a classroom door. "I better get inside."

He grinned nervously. "Yeah, I better get to class, too."

"Maybe we can have lunch?" she asked.

"Great. I'd love to." He wanted to pump his fists in triumph, but that would look stupid.

Aileen McKensie and Christel Manikas emerged out of the crowd of students and surrounded Maellyn. Whispering, they rushed her into class.

Neil wished he could skip his morning classes and go straight to lunch. He doubted he would be able to concentrate during class now.

The halls were quickly emptying, so he hurried off toward Battle Tactics, hoping to avoid an instructor stopping him for being late. The last thing he wanted to do was miss lunch with Maellyn because he was in detention.

Chapter 13

Riagan Corners a Bull's Eye

Riagan narrowed his eyes and braced himself for bad news as Neil, red-faced and wearing a foolish grin, arrived on the Battle Tactics field, located in a large, outdoor stadium. Despite Riagan's best efforts to convince Neil to be careful about revealing what they had seen, he had left early this morning claiming he was headed for breakfast. Riagan had gone to the mess hall a few minutes after Neil, only to find he wasn't around. Now Neil showed up, pleased as a cat who had brought its master a dead bird, leaving Riagan to wonder what trouble he had gotten into after leaving their dorm. He clearly wasn't going to let the Dahaka sighting go.

"Where did ya go?" Riagan asked.

Neil gasped, breathing heavily. "Just making lunch plans."

That sounded better than Riagan had expected. Maybe Neil had listened after all. Riagan waited for him to elaborate, but his friend just stood there grinning like an idiot. Riagan decided to let it go for now.

The field for Battle Tactics was odd. A white line split the field into halves. On the left side loomed a towering oak forest. On the right half, a rapidly inclining stone hill was split by several pathways. The back of the rocks, near the far end of the field, stood nearly as high as the top of the forest. Stands surrounded it all.

"What do you think is played here?" Eris Zeigler asked, joining them.

"Gladiatorial games?" Riagan ventured. "Fans cheer on fights to the death?"

"Does Space City have twelve districts to pick fighters from?" Neil asked, grinning foolishly.

Eris laughed, a little too hard for that joke if you asked him.

"What if that's the reason they brought us from Earth?" Riagan loved the idea of testing himself against aliens. Maybe not battles to the death, but it would give him a chance to show Patrick and everyone at the academy to not take him lightly.

Those thoughts were forgotten as the instructors arrived. Behind them, a pair of older students pushed a rack with gray suits like the ones from the New Worlds class. One of the instructors was a mountain of a man. Easily a head taller than anyone else, he possessed a mammoth-sized torso with thickly muscled arms and legs. He wore a gray suit with a green target on the chest. Next to him stood a dense, coal-colored cloud in the silhouette of a man. The smoky figure lacked specific features; he just generally looked like an adult man.

"I am Instructor Glenn," the large man bellowed. He gestured to the smoky figure next to him. "Stribog is my co-instructor."

"General Stribog," Eris whispered, eyes wide.

The general bowed, his billowing smoke body constantly shifting. More substantial than a ghost, he still possessed a supernatural quality.

The chance to learn battle tactics directly from a general excited Riagan. This was going to be his favorite class, he was sure of it. How would the general fight? Maybe choke people. Could he wield a weapon? Being made of smoke had to offer great advantages as an assassin. Pass through bars. Flow under doors. Was he bound by gravity? Riagan imagined flying to a high tower to bypass security and take out a target. The general must have great stories.

Instructor Glenn was no slouch either. Not too many people would be able to endure a single blow from a man that size. In fact, he looked like he could probably break off the larger branches of the nearby oaks with his immense arms if he wanted; perhaps even uproot one.

"General Stribog is renowned for the fighting prowess he displayed during the Dahaka Invasion," Eris said reverently.

Riagan chuckled to himself, imagining the Dahaka trying to spear the general with the tusks on their armor. Nothing to pierce. Their speed and strength would avail them nothing against such a fighter.

"He led his people, the Kali nation, to support the Azzaros, which was strange considering the Kali traditionally ally with the Dahaka," Eris added.

That only increased Riagan's esteem of the general.

Eris leaned in close and whispered conspiratorially. "Some think he helped the Dahaka invade Sundara in the first place, then switched sides to weaken both."

A frown creased Neil's forehead. "If he's untrustworthy, why is he here?"

Eris shrugged. "That's just what some say."

That last bit had to be false. People loved rumors. More often than not they had little basis in truth. The facts were that the general had led the Kali against the Dahaka, and probably possessed more battle knowledge than anyone they had met, except for perhaps Instructor Aldrin.

"Today we begin field training," Instructor Glenn said. "Suit up and we'll begin."

Several students cast General Stribog uncertain glances as they retrieved suits and pulled them on over their uniforms. But Riagan felt a compulsion to stick his hand into the black smoke to find out what would happen. Was any part of the general tangible? Not quite brave enough to do it, Riagan marched over to the rack.

After everyone had donned suits, some with green targets on their chest and others with yellow, Glenn pointed his gloved right hand at a nearby oak. A metallic target hung on its trunk with a bullseye, two space rings surrounding it, over a larger square panel. For a brief second Instructor Glenn's fingertips glowed red, then the entire bullseye on the target lit up, flashing orange. A direct hit.

Several girls murmured to each other.

Riagan searched the instructor's hands for a weapon, but found them empty. Why had his fingertips glowed?

Glenn grinned at them. "Bet none of you guessed the suits have built-in laser weaponry."

Riagan excitedly examined his gloves. Tiny red holes on his fingertips connected to lines running along the back of his hand. The lines converged at the wrist, ran along his arm, and disappeared into the suit at the shoulder.

"How do they work?" Neil asked.

Riagan searched for a firing mechanism, anxious to test out the suit's weaponry.

"They fire by thought." Glenn pointed at a second target, this one up in the branches, and fired again. This time the top half of the targets outer two rings flashed orange, but bottom half and the bullseye at the center stayed dark.

Grinning with anticipation, Riagan pointed at another target. Now that he was looking, he spotted a number of targets on trunks or up in branches. In his mind, he ordered his suit to fire. Nothing happened. Several other students pointed at targets, but also failed to shoot. Riagan tried again, but was once more unsuccessful. "What's the command word?"

An asthmatic chuckle and booming laughter reverberated around the stadiums from the two instructors.

"Firing your weapon is a thought *process*," General Stribog said. His words sounded breathed as opposed to spoken. "Imagine the laser firing from the igniter at your back, traveling along your arm and out through your fingertips."

Determined to be the first one to successfully shoot, Riagan focused on a tree. He imagined lasers flowing from his back and along his forearm before diverging at his wrist into five separate lines that ran to his fingers and shot forth. The target panel to Riagan's right flashed orange once a half second before Riagan's own target panel did the same. The target's rings, where he'd aimed, remained dark.

Still, Riagan was thrilled at his own success. He turned to brag to Neil before realizing that he was the one who had fired first, and was already aiming again. Grunting with annoyance, Riagan revised his goal to becoming a better marksman than Neil. He had always been competitive.

A couple more students succeeded in hitting the target panel, but none lit up the rings or struck the bullseye.

Glenn nodded approvingly. "The process gets simpler the more you practice until it becomes automatic."

Riagan aimed again and fired. This time the bottom right corner of the outer ring lit up, flashing. It continued for about ten seconds before resetting. For a few minutes he watched others shoot, seeing many miss their targets altogether, and a thought occurred to him.

"Right, our shots aren't real?" he asked.

Glenn's face grew serious. "Can't have you hurting yourselves or others because you're untrained. Training suits fire light beams that pose no real threat."

In that case.

Riagan pointed his gloved hand at Neil's chest and thought about shooting him. His gloves glowed briefly and lit up the yellow target on Neil's chest.

"Et tu, Brute?" Neil asked in mock protest.

"I don't like coming in second," Riagan replied before smiling broadly.

They lined up and practiced while the instructors moved along the line giving individual instructions on how to improve their aim. After Riagan managed to light up both rings several times, Glenn stopped behind him for a moment. Riagan took aim at the bullseye, unnerved at being watched, and hit the target panel a couple of times.

"Aim slightly above your target," Glenn said. "Lasers are line-of-sight. They aren't affected by gravity, but it looks like what you think you're aiming for is a little off of reality. I think a slight adjustment high will help."

Riagan flushed but did as directed and his next shot lit up the bottom right corner of the bullseye. Finally!

The instructors let everyone practice for twenty minutes, then gathered them around. Pointing at one of the two older students who had wheeled in the rack of suits, Glenn said, "All students with a yellow target follow Team Captain James Hardin."

Hardin was tall and muscular, like a quarterback on a high school football team.

"Those with green targets will follow Team Captain Spencer Gilbright."

Gilbright stepped forward. The older boy reminded Riagan of an outdoors type who liked to camp, hunt, fish, and hike. Gilbright led Riagan and the students with green targets toward the stone uprising side of the field, while Hardin led Neil and the yellows into the forest.

Riagan searched casually about as they climbed the rocks. Barriers, ledges, nooks, and crannies abounded everywhere. Gilbright didn't say a word as he led the way. What were they doing? Marching just for the sake of it?

Halfway up the rocks, a light blow to Riagan's chest, as if someone had punched him, was accompanied by his target lighting up. He flinched, not expecting the physical impact. Annoyed by the unexpected attack, or maybe at himself for flinching, he searched for the shooter. Several other students stumbled back, targets flashing, startling everyone, before an older student emerged from behind a boulder twenty yards up.

"Lots of places to lay ambushes in these rocks," Gilbright said. "You must always be vigilant when exploring."

"We didn't even know we were training," Aileen McKensie squealed.

Riagan bit his tongue, but he had to agree that a little warning would've been nice.

"We're always training," Gilbright said, face stern. "The second the year started your training began. This is a lesson. When you explore new planets, enemies won't alert you about their plans. You must always be prepared for attack." Gilbright turned to the boy who had ambushed them. "Thanks Dirk!"

"No problem." Dirk disappeared back into the rocks.

Riagan hated being shot first. It made him feel weak. Gilbright should have given them some warning. An enemy would not share its plans, but a commander's job was to prepare his men. Instead, Gilbright had thrown them like mice into a snake's pen.

Using some small device in his hand, Gilbright deactivated their flashing chest targets and led them onward. This time Riagan followed a few paces back, his arms held loosely out from his sides, ready to shoot at any threat. He carefully studied their surroundings, searching for another ambush. He was not a blind mouse.

The rocky high-rise ended at twenty foot cliffs that partly surrounded an open bowl roughly thirty yards wide. Half a dozen pathways split through the high-rise and several drop points from the cliff walls allowed entrance to the bowl. What was the bowl's purpose? The field was obviously meant for some game, but Riagan had no idea what. He still liked his gladiator idea.

"We're under attack," several students shouted at once.

Riagan spun around. Chest targets flashed everywhere in the group. Ducking behind a nearby rock, he searched for attackers. The rest of the group huddled together like sheep as more chest targets lit up.

Eris ducked in beside him.

"Quick thinking, Riagan," Glenn said over the tradutor, which also served as a long range communication device.

"Cheers," Riagan replied while searching for the shooters. He spotted a face peeking out from a small cave about a foot off the ground a good twenty yards away. He took aim and fired at the face, but missed. Eris fired beside him, also missing.

"All right, that's enough," Gilbright ordered, stepping in between them and the ambushers. "Cease fire."

Riagan waited, not about to rise first. Three aggressors appeared—one hidden in a small cave, a second underneath a ledge, and the third rose from the rocks in plain sight. Riagan frowned, unable to figure out what had shielded the third from view.

Gilbright marched back and forth in front of the class like a displeased military trainer in front of incompetent recruits. "Only two of you heeded my warning."

Everyone's chest targets flashed except for Riagan and Eris. Riagan stood straighter, head high and shoulders back, proud that he and Eris had passed this test.

Gilbright's voice grew heated. "Those two were prepared and took cover. The rest of you bunched together in the open, making yourselves easy targets. In a real attack, you'd all be dead, leaving Riagan and Eris outnumbered in enemy territory."

Most of the class wore surly expressions. Gilbright had thrown them to the wolves, then berated them for failing. They didn't like it.

Riagan gloated. In his mind, Gilbright had already given them a warning. If they failed to heed, shame on them. He whispered to Eris. "We've already got a leg up."

"Space Aces," she said, grinning.

This had been the first class where the instructors hadn't treated them like children unable to do anything. Gilbright had tossed them out to sink or swim. They would learn rapidly this way. Riagan liked the challenge.

Gilbright led them back toward midfield. Most of the chatter quieted now. Everyone examined their surroundings for further attacks. When they reached the open center field, Gilbright gathered them back in close.

"I'm going to separate you into smaller groups to search the forest," Gilbright said. "Riagan, Eris, and Jiro, you're on one team."

Riagan hadn't seen Jiro Takeda since their meeting on the first day after climbing the flagpoles, but he had seemed reasonable. Riagan liked having him and Eris on his team. Once Gilbright had them all broken up into groups, he sent them on ahead.

The woods were thick with trees, some of the oaks growing so closely together that they formed natural barriers. Good locations for traps.

How many students had the instructors hidden in the forest to test them? Riagan had no intention of getting ambushed again.

A second later a pebble bounced off Riagan's back. He froze, gritting his teeth. Had someone snuck up behind them after all? They were barely into the forest.

He turned back to find Eris and Jiro crouched behind two oaks. Eris pointed a warning finger past Riagan. He dropped behind another tree. Peeking out, he saw only an empty forest. He turned back to her, holding both hands up in question. She pointed again, but this time up into the canopy ahead. A single student, wearing camouflaged clothes, hid in a tree ten or fifteen yards to the northwest. No wonder he had missed the boy at first.

The boy hadn't noticed them yet. Riagan searched for others, but found none.

What should they do about the one? He was a little too far away to shoot.

Before Riagan could develop a plan, Jiro charged past, surprisingly quiet. He was fast and used the trees as shields. When Jiro neared the student's position, still unseen, he scooted into a fallen log. The space from the log to the oak was clear. If Jiro exited the log he would make an easy target.

To Riagan's surprise, the boy's chest target lit up. The startled student cursed and searched for his attacker. Jiro remained hidden in the log. After several seconds the ambusher dropped from the tree and ran off.

Impressed, Riagan ran beside Eris to catch up with Jiro as he emerged from the log.

"Excellent shot," Riagan congratulated.

Jiro half smiled. "I trained all summer."

If team captains got to choose their team for the final exam, Riagan wanted Jiro.

They started to explore further, but Glenn ordered everyone back to midfield using the tradutors. Riagan wiped his forehead with a sleeve and tasted warm saltiness as sweat slid from his upper lip into his mouth. A good class.

When they reached midfield, everyone gathering around the instructors, he found Neil, purple-faced and sweating.

"What did ya do? Ya as red-faced as a Traga," Riagan teased.

"Ha." Neil gasped for air. "Hardin ran us the whole time."

It was a good yoke he had ended up with Gilbright, Riagan thought.

"Science of Interplanetary War is assigned reading," General Stribog said, his form shifting as if a breeze struck him from all sides. "Everyone needs to learn stratagem. We uploaded the book to your wrist-comps."

"Too much assigned reading for the first week," Riagan muttered, but he was already formulating a plan to convince Rois to give him the highlights. If he offered her a couple of his weekly desserts, or maybe candy from Nico, she'd probably go for it.

"Quiz on chapter one next class," Glenn said, receiving moans.

Riagan shook his head in disgust. Teachers should not give quizzes during the first week.

As they removed their suits, Gilbright approached Riagan. "You pick things up fast," Gilbright said. "I have an opening on my Taurus team for the Academy Games. You should try out."

"Academy games?" Riagan asked as he hung the suit back on the rack. He was glad Gilbright had noticed him. Hopefully the instructors had, too.

Gilbright nodded. "You'll like it. Come try out."

"Sounds great," Riagan agreed.

Hardin pulled Neil aside and invited him to join another team. Riagan would have to convince Neil to team up later. For now, Riagan was happy with his success.

Chapter 14

Neil Becomes Monkey Food

Neil forced himself to nonchalantly pull on his gray suit when Maellyn entered the Introduction to New Worlds facility midway through their second week of classes. What was she doing here? Only half-listening to Riagan rave about his first practice with Taurus, Neil did his best to act casual, but couldn't stop himself from glancing in her direction. When she caught him spying, he quickly diverted his eyes to Riagan. He hoped she didn't notice his embarrassment, but the heat in his cheeks tattled.

"Next practice is Sunday afternoon," Riagan said. "Bring Maellyn to watch. It'll impress her. I'm sure Gilbright will let ya join."

Neil's cheeks burned hotter. Riagan had noticed him watching Maellyn, too.

"I already have practice with Ursa," Neil replied.

Riagan had tried several times to convince him to join Taurus. Neil liked the idea of teaming with Riagan, but he wanted to play for Hardin and Ursa. He couldn't explain why, but he felt that Hardin offered him the best chance to become a team captain, too.

With Fintan in tow, Instructor Nez arrived. "Class, today we will explore a Niveum jungle. Before we start, do a quick body scan with your wrist-comps."

Neil frowned, having already scanned himself before leaving his room. Several students said they had as well.

"Body scans are mandatory from this point forward to start and end each class," Nez said. "The scans help doctors monitor how you handle different environments and stresses."

Neil had scanned only fifteen minutes ago, recent enough for doctors to collect any data they needed, surely. But Nez crossed his arms, unwilling to hear arguments. Everyone complied before climbing into the round cages, which allowed them to move through the sim without running into each other.

Nez activated the sim for the Niveum jungle.

Thick vines grew everywhere in the steamy jungle, including up trees that resembled giant umbrellas. The gluttony of foliage limited their view. Mosquitoes buzzed everywhere which, combined with the vines, created a claustrophobic atmosphere.

Nez divided them into two groups and handed each student a machete for cutting their way through the jungle. "No dueling," he ordered.

Neil pressed his finger against the sharp edge of a machete. It felt real enough to cut his finger open. His skin tingled in uneasy anticipation. Could it actually cause real bodily harm?

At that moment, Riagan ran his own thumb over the blade. No cut. "That takes all the craic of out these yokes," Riagan complained.

Neil agreed. It would be cooler to use real blades. He started toward Maellyn, trying to come up with a good joke about the machetes, but Patrick beat him to her. Neil paused and waited awkwardly a few steps away.

"I'm hosting a party Friday night. You can make it?" Patrick asked confidently, expecting her agreement.

She gave him a regretful smile. "I need to study. Homework is crazy already." She turned to Neil.

"The party will be fantastic." Patrick smiled slyly at Neil. "I might invite Neil and Riagan to reprise their roles climbing flagpoles for entertainment."

Before Neil could retort, Maellyn spoke up. "Mr. Fintan, may Neil and I hike to the waterfall? I'd like to check on our Apidium experiment."

"I don't think that's a good idea during center of class," Fintan said. "We need to remain together."

Neil didn't know what the Apidium experiment was, but he was all for going off with Maellyn alone. Too bad Fintan hadn't agreed.

Maellyn walked over to the Macab and put a hand on his lower left arm. "I'd really like to check on our insect traps. I promise to regale him with our summer lessons."

Fintan relented, much to Neil's surprise. Eris eyed Maellyn coldly from behind, appearing upset with her for the request, though Neil didn't understand why.

Patrick smoldered, too. But that made Neil's day. As he followed after Maellyn, Neil smirked at Patrick, who glared back and punched his other palm.

Once Neil and Maellyn were on their own, he said, "I'm surprised you're here."

They hacked at foliage blocking their path. The vines were as thick as his fingers in some places, but the machetes cut cleanly through them. It still amazed him that the machete and vines were nothing more than computer simulations. Everything felt, looked, and smelled real. How could a sim fool all the senses?

"Transferred in," Maellyn said as she lifted one vine over her head with the machete. "Scheduling conflict."

"I'm glad we'll have this class together," he said. Now he would see her at least twice a week!

"Me, too."

Neil smiled, but didn't know what else to say.

The steamy jungle smelled musty, and sweat beaded on his forehead. Mosquitoes zipped around their heads, and he instinctively swatted at them. *Stop that, they're not real,* he chided himself.

"Dad told me a CME is a Coronal Mass Ejector," Maellyn said, revealing her reason for taking him with her. "He didn't elaborate on what exactly a CME is, but was alarmed about how I heard about it." Concern was clear in her voice.

A gray snake with scarlet stripes slithered along a branch right by his head. Neil jumped backward, inhaling sharply. He hated snakes, especially unfamiliar ones that might be poisonous.

"What is it?" Maellyn asked, before spotting the snake.

It tasted the air with its tongue.

"That's a firebrand," she said softly, as if to avoid disturbing the snake. "It possesses a toxin that will make you think you've badly burned your entire body. It's temporary and they only attack if threatened."

Nevertheless, he sidestepped away from the snake, and eyed it uneasily until they were several feet past it. He remained braced for an attack until they had left the snake well behind.

"So how did you hear about the CME?" she asked.

He answered by telling her about Riagan swiping the skunk sacks from Tereshkova's class. Maellyn laughed hard, easing the tension as he described Riagan splitting the sack and dumping its contents all over Caleb's bed. Everyone on campus had heard about the incident. Rampant speculation had varied wildly over who had accomplished the deed. But the consensus among the first years was that Caleb had deserved it.

Neil recounted their escape out the window, making their getaway, followed by overhearing two men discussing a CME. He did not elaborate on who he had overheard or what they had said about the CME. Her father's concern only reinforced Neil's unease about discussing it with her. He would have to avoid coming to her for any more information.

Maellyn accepted his story without question, to his relief.

When they reached the waterfall, she turned her attention to a pack of mini monkeys climbing through the trees. The thin monkeys were no more than a foot tall with tan fur except for a white ring that circled their face.

"These are Apidium monkeys," she said as she led him toward one tree that had several monkeys lurking in its branches. "A similar species once existed on Earth, an ancestor of our modern monkeys."

"They're cute," he said. "Instructor Fintan studies them?"

He suppressed a laugh as he pictured a monkey studying other monkeys.

"My father and Fintan are close friends. I've known him all my life," she said. "Every summer since I was little he's given me lessons using the sim. He conducts experiments here because the sim provides accurate results of what we'll find in the real world. The Apidium are endangered so we are running an experiment to protect them."

Maellyn held out her right hand toward a young Apidium eating berries in the tree. The monkey hopped onto her arm and offered her some purple berries.

"No thank you, Harisha."

The monkey held out the berries a moment longer, questioning her. When she didn't take them, Harisha resumed eating.

Maellyn stroked the fur behind his head. "From the first time we came across the Apidium and Harisha here in the sim, I loved them. I asked Fintan about bringing a real one on the ship, but their numbers are dwindling so fast. That broke my heart. We've designed a means of protecting them and are testing it out."

"Why are they dying off?" Neil wanted to help since she liked them so much. Plus, that might give him another excuse to hang out with her.

"The Apidium love to eat fruit and insects. They favor two kinds of insects—a harmless fly and a black mosquito. The mosquitoes carry a virus with a high fatality rate for Apidium."

"Have you tried using pesticides on the mosquitoes?"

She shook her head vehemently. "The Macab never wipe out any creature. They believe every creature forms a necessary part of their world, and eradicating one upsets the balance. We had to devise a method that saves the Apidium without risking the well-being of the mosquitoes."

She showed him some small, clear spheres hanging from branches in the trees like ornaments. Tiny gray flies fluttered around pink flowers inside the sphere. "Earlier this summer we developed an insect catcher designed to attract and trap the flies while repelling the mosquitoes."

Holes in the top of the spheres allowed the flies to enter. Neil was not sure what stopped them from escaping the same way.

Harisha finished eating his berries. Maellyn placed him back on a branch as she said, "We've spent the summer teaching them to reach into the spheres through an opening in the bottom to get the flies. We're hoping as the Apidium realize how easy it is to grab flies from the spheres, they'll spend less time trying to catch flies on their own, reducing the likelihood they'll eat the mosquitoes."

"Does it work?"

As if in response, an Apidium crept over to a sphere. The monkey reached through a rubber flap in the bottom and pulled out a couple of flies. When it withdrew its hand, the flaps sealed off the bottom, preventing the flies from escaping.

"It took three months to teach them the spheres held food. Now they increasingly head for the spheres when they're hungry. Harisha here has learned to move the spheres to other branches where he knows the flies congregate, don't you?" She cooed to the little monkey.

Harisha pulled back his lips, flashing a bizarre smile.

Neil reached up to pet the monkey, and Harisha bit a finger. Neil yanked back his hand. The bite had felt like a soft pressure on his finger, as if Harisha lacked teeth, but it had still startled him.

"Harisha!" Maellyn scolded.

Harisha cringed and disappeared further up into the tree.

"Sorry about that," she apologized.

"It's fine," Neil said. "Maybe I taste better than the flies."

She smiled. "I bet you do."

"So are you putting these spheres on Niveum?" Neil asked, impressed that she had developed a method for saving an endangered species. What had he accomplished like that? That thought stung as he considered what little he had done about the traitor.

"We need more tests on the effects the spheres will have on the Apidium before the Macab will approve it."

"What about the gray flies?" Neil asked. "Isn't catching them endangering them?"

She shook her head. "The Apidium don't consume enough flies to threaten the population, and their natural predators will keep their numbers in check if we succeed."

She seemed to have considered everything.

"You really are brilliant," he congratulated.

She blushed. "I want to become a scientist and save other endangered species. Fintan has shared his work with me for as long as I remember. I loved the animals he introduced me to, and once I learned that some might one day go extinct, all I've wanted to do is protect them. Science has given me the tools to do so."

Without warning, a rain shower started to pour down on them. All the Apidium scurried for cover.

"This way." Maellyn ran under a massive tree nearby where a tarp was tied between two branches overhead, providing shelter. They were already soaked by the time they reached cover, though.

"I guess we wait for the instructors to turn off the sim?" Neil wondered how long they were stuck here.

"I've got my own sim controller." She took a seat against the trunk. "The instructors can end the sim while we remain until we're ready. The sim can run indefinitely, which is why we can conduct these experiments."

He sat beside her, enjoying their time alone, even soaked. Small price to pay. "How can we explore other places if this sim is always running?"

"Each cage is capable of running its own sim. Or any combination of cages can run the same sim together."

Sitting there watching the rain, Neil wracked his brain for something else to say.

"I have a confession," she said. Her expression was guarded.

"What?" he asked, worried at her sudden reservation.

"During the new year kickoff, your red hair reminded me of the volcano diamond, especially after you stood up to Patrick for my cousin. I thought you were brave. That's partly why I told you about the diamond."

Thrilled, he wanted to tell her that he planned to find one, so that he could give it to her. But the words stuck to his tongue, immobilized by the war between his wishes and fears.

For a few seconds they sat in silence, staring at the rainfall, until she added, "Do you mind if we stay a bit longer?"

"Not at all." He would spend all day here if she wished.

Chapter 15

Neil's Caramella Experience

Everyone finally received passes to visit the city on the last weekend of September, and Neil, Riagan, Rois, and Jaya hiked over from campus. Lily-stem-shaped skyscrapers soared overhead, connected to hive-like buildings and gear-shaped structures by a vast web of hundreds of bridges at varying heights. Tinted glass walls with unlimited design variations strengthened that web.

The tallest skyscrapers, which towered hundreds of feet overhead, seemed even larger here in the city than they had from the academy grounds. As Neil stared skyward, several of the bridges spanning between the buildings shifted so that one end of the bridge connected with a new building or other bridges. People traversed those bridges in new directions. Neil felt a chill run up his spine at the thought of crossing one.

"How is that safe?" Neil asked, drawing Jaya's attention to the bridges.

Jaya glanced at them, unconcerned. "The buildings are 4D printed."

Neil stopped in his tracks and someone behind him bumped into him. Startled, Neil glanced at the man.

"Sorry," the stranger mumbled, and continued on his way.

"My fault," Neil called after him before turning back to Jaya. "What does 4D printed mean?"

"All of the buildings on Space City were 4D printed from a substance that can modify its shape over time," Jaya explained. "The bridges are designed to change direction based upon the flow of people around the city. Computers monitor how many people are moving in different directions. The computers send directions to the bridges to move in a way that improves the flow of people."

"That sounds aggravating," Rois said with a frown. "If ya used to taking a path somewhere and suddenly the bridges change direction on ya."

"It's just something everyone is accustomed to," Jaya replied. He rolled the sleeves of his olive wool jacket up to his elbows and lowered the zipper halfway down, revealing a gray shirt underneath.

No cars filled the streets. Neil had hoped to find private planes like those the Jetsons flew; not that room existed for either on the ship. Instead, moving walkways carried people through the city, allowing them to stand or walk, where they found room, until exiting at their stop. For faster transportation, a vast monorail system twenty feet above the street was filled with bustling people. Most people traveled by monorail from the residential areas into the heart of the city. From there they used the moving walkways for shorter trips. Both transportation modes were overloaded with far more people than Neil had ever expected to see on Space City.

On their way to meet Maellyn, who had gone home for the weekend, they stopped at a coffee shop. Rois wanted a café mocha. Despite her gray jacket, she shivered in the cool morning air. It was cool enough that Neil wished he had worn something more than a jade-colored t-shirt and jeans.

At the coffee shop, Riagan bought a potato, mushroom, and onion piroshky. He tore off a piece and a bit fell on his sable shirt. He tossed the bite in his mouth then brushed the food from the image of Poseidon holding a trident on the front of his shirt. The smell of the piroshky reminded Neil of hashbrowns, and he quickly regretted eating breakfast in the mess hall before coming.

They wasted no further time getting to the railway stop to meet Maellyn.

"Morning," Neil greeted when he saw her. "Ride in ok?"

She nodded, adjusting her pink blouse on her shoulders. "Great. Enjoyed sleeping in my own bed."

"I miss mine," Rois said glumly.

"Want to stay with me tonight?" Maellyn asked her. "I've got a spare. Girls Saturday night?"

"Cheers. I'd love it," Rois said before sipping her coffee.

Probably the one thing Neil missed about life on Earth was the mattress set his neighbor had given him after she upgraded a few years back. The cheap twin mattresses on the beds in the dorms were hard slabs by comparison.

"Where are we headed?" Maellyn asked.

"Street fair on 8th and Park. Thought they might enjoy the lavish, colorful food and universal gifts," Jaya replied, eyeing Rois in particular.

"Perfect," Maellyn agreed. "Great introduction to the city."

With Jaya leading, they crossed a bridge over the street and stepped onto the northbound walkway. They barely squeezed onboard. Jaya wrapped an arm around Rois to keep her from getting knocked around in the tightly packed crowd. Riagan's jaw tightened, but he said nothing. Neil was amazed that Riagan controlled himself about that when he so easily popped off at anything else he didn't like. If Neil had to wager, Riagan held his tongue because of what Rois would do to him if he didn't.

Following Jaya's example, Neil offered an arm to Maellyn and was thrilled when she accepted. She smelled lightly of peaches. Shampoo or perfume?

A grand banner, showing a team in mustard and brown-colored uniforms, hung from a skyscraper they passed. The banner proclaimed the Thorny Devils as Space City Cup champions. A cartoonish depiction of a mini rhinoceros covered in spikes served as the team mascot. Another banner a block away promoted the Quasars, who had dark red uniforms tinged with black and a logo of a dense cloud circling a black hole.

"What sport are the teams in?" Neil asked, pointing at the Quasars' banner.

"Space City Games," Jaya said over Rois' head. "A professional version of the Academy Games."

"Can we go to a game?" Riagan asked, interest brightening his face.

Jaya shook his head. "The league plays in the summer. The Thorny Devils won the Cup about three days before you arrived."

"Shame," Neil said, doubting he could afford a ticket anyway. He had earned a little money from washing the bad nut beetles' cages and feeding them for Tereshkova, but most of it went to Nico for candy.

"Can't wait for our first game," Riagan said.

"Professional games are different," Jaya said. "Way more involved."

Riagan peppered Jaya with questions about the Academy Games as they rode the moving walkway. Maellyn and Rois discussed their prospects for shopping at the street fair, so Neil contented himself with examining the city around him.

Sizable 3D commercials and images played in the air above building entrances. Ads for toothbrushes that cleaned your teeth for you while you dressed, 3D-printed perfect pets created in an afternoon while you shopped, and Space City Games memorabilia competed with a thousand other products to lure customers into stores. Neil wanted to check out the pet store, curious what a printed dog looked like. He had always wanted a dog, but his uncle had refused his requests, free or otherwise. Just as well. His uncle would've viewed a dog as another source to vent his frustrations on.

One colossal skyscraper, as wide as a city block, housed a History of the Universe Museum. How long would a tour of that take?

When they reached the street fair, Neil marveled at the four skyscrapers which ringed an open square filled with carts where vendors sold food, clothing, jewelry, and other exotic items. The fair wasn't confined to street level either. The skyscraper balconies surrounding the square housed additional market stalls from the ground to the high rises. In order to attract customers to their floors, the merchants all had large, square hologram advertisements displayed in front of their stores at the edge of the balconies, so that each of the four buildings resembled patchwork quilts.

"I'm going to go broke fast," Rois said as she stared in awe at the myriad of items for sale.

Neil wished he had asked Tereshkova if she had any other tasks that she'd pay him to do before today.

They passed a stand with pots from which flames burned. The flames changed colors depending on the powder poured onto the fire. Rose for romance. Gold for wealth. Pink for a young girl's birthday party.

For a snack they purchased Butternells, a warm bread with a creamy center that tasted a little like butterscotch. The Macab selling the pastries assured them that she made them fresh every morning. She kept them warm in a small oven.

Since the girls still shivered a little from the cold, Jaya bought them hot spiced teas. Rois thanked Jaya, her face beaming. Jaya eagerly returned her smile. Neil felt a stab of annoyance that Jaya had bought one for Maellyn, too, preventing him from offering to buy her one. Jaya was just being nice, though.

Neil and Riagan both purchased purple melon punch. They carried their snacks toward benches surrounded by small grassy squares, but found only two seats for the girls. Tired from walking, Neil started to sit on the grass, but Jaya and Maellyn protested.

"That's not grass, it's an internet mesh network," Jaya said.

"A what?" Neil asked.

"The grass is here to imitate life on Earth, but actually serves as the network providing internet service for Space City," Maellyn explained. "If you sit or stand on them, you risk damaging the network."

"How about a little warning sign saying keep off the grass," Neil muttered.

Maellyn pointed to Neil's left. He turned to see a sign with bright red lettering.

Please Keep Off the Grass to Avoid Damaging Internet Service

His cheeks rose in a guilty smile and his face burned.

"Pretty much everything on the ship serves a dual purpose," Jaya said. "The glass skyscrapers accumulate solar energy. The entire ship is solar powered."

"The tinting on the windows also serves as electronic skins that monitor the buildings wear over time, ensuring their safety," Maellyn added.

"So if I walk on the grass, I might knock out the internet?" Riagan held one foot over the grassy median, his expression challenging.

"Riagan!" Rois exclaimed.

"Relax." Riagan pulled his foot back. "I amn't harming anything. Just curious how stable this is?"

No one else in the area appeared alarmed at Riagan's antics.

"You'd probably cause no more than a minor disruption," Jaya explained. "Still, no reason to deliberately cause problems. Any trouble we get in is reported to the academy. They are always threatening to eliminate city visits."

"Right, get off my back," Riagan said, glowering and backing away from the grassy squares.

"It'd be nice if we knew how to tell the difference," Neil said.

An edge creeping into her voice, Maellyn replied. "All the grass in the city is part of the mesh network."

Not sure what was upsetting her, Neil gulped the last of his purple melon punch. He searched for a trash can, but found only recycling containers. "What goes in recycling here?"

"Everything," Jaya answered. "Everything on Space City gets recycled, or at the very least burned to create more energy."

"Cheers. We're the prime example of going green," Riagan said facetiously, tossing his own empty cup in the recycling container.

Neil found it laudable that everyone worked so hard to avoid waste. Everything was treated as a precious resource that was consumed and refashioned for another purpose. But there should be an introduction to the city for new recruits, so no one made mistakes like sitting on grass.

"Neil! Riagan!" a familiar voice shouted from overhead.

Nico Colombo waved at them from a second-floor balcony, urging them to come visit his father's candy shop.

They rode an elevator to the 2nd floor walkway, which led to Colombo Caramella.

"Great you came!" Nico said. "Dad, these are friends from school."

A portly fellow who reminded Neil of an Italian chef strode over, a wide smile on his face. "Welcome. Nico's friends are always VIP guests." He tossed toffees to them, which they happily popped in their mouths.

"Rumor has it Neil and Riagan got Patrick Duffy with a skunk sack," Nico told his father mock-secretively.

Neil turned to Maellyn, but she returned an innocent look. He just shook his head.

"Put away your money, Signorina," Mr. Colombo said to Rois as she fished money out of a coin purse. "Your money is no good here. Anything you want, it's on the house."

"Cheers!" Rois smile brightened the room. "Ya wonderful."

Mr. Colombo waved dismissively. "Patrick has pulled pranks on Nico for years, but my boy, he's too generous to confront anyone."

"Dad," Nico cried, shoulders slumping slightly as he stared at the ground.

Nico always displayed confidence in class, except when someone asked too loud about buying candy in front of the instructors. His sudden discomfort was strange.

Neil joined Riagan and Jaya in ogling all the candy varieties. Fudges in every color. Caramel toffees. Rainbow beans. Purple melon gummies. Chocolate ships, stars, and planets. Gate crashers. Pumpkin canes. Licorice in seven different colors and flavors. Lemon slices. Chocolate covered cherries, strawberries, oranges, and cranberries. White chocolate blueberries and raspberries. Coconut cakes. Sour gums.

For the first time in his life, Neil understood the expression *like a kid in a candy store*. So many choices and Nico's father had offered them whatever they liked.

Neil felt a little greedy as he stuffed his pockets. "Are you sure we can't pay you for some?"

"Nonsense," Mr. Colombo said. "I'm fat enough to be good-looking. I can afford to treat Nico's friends. Have some fudge." He handed Neil a raspberry fudge slab.

"This place is amazing," Riagan said. "When did ya open it?"

"Actually, I took over the shop when the previous owner died about five years ago," Mr. Colombo answered. "Before that, we lived in Torcello, a small island near Venice."

Nico's mouth soured, apparently unhappy with his father for this revelation. What bothered him about them knowing that?

"Ya grew up in Italy?" Rois asked, longing on her face.

"Until his tenth birthday," Mr. Colombo confirmed. "He knows Venice by heart, don't you, Nico?"

Nico just grimaced.

"One day you'll have to show us around," Rois begged.

"Jaya can pretend to be one of the Blue Man Group," Riagan said slyly.

Jaya frowned. "Blue Man Group?"

Neil guffawed, but quickly hid it as Rois rounded on her brother, glaring. "Don't mind him."

After getting their fill of candy, they left the shop to continue exploring the market. They meandered along the walkway and stuffed their mouths with candy. Past a sushi restaurant Rois and Maellyn took a detour into a camera shop. But Neil spotted Anand and Devika, so he hurried over to talk to the siblings, Riagan and Jaya in tow.

"Where'd you get the candy?" Anand asked, practically salivating as he eyed Neil's fudge bar.

"Nico's dad's shop." Neil pointed back the way they'd come. He wrapped the rest of his fudge bar and slipped it in his back pocket. "Anything worth visiting?"

"Rory's Weird and Unexplainable," Devika suggested.

"Oh, we're definitely going there," Jaya agreed.

Devika's eyes gleamed. "Symphonic stones that perform any song played once in their presence only. Salamanders that turn invisible when bright lights shine on them."

"Wish we had those for campus," Anand said wistfully.

Devika grinned mischievously. "We do, no?"

"Oh, right," Anand said, feigning sudden remembrance as he held up a cloth sack.

He opened the drawstring sack and held it out for them to peek inside. Four opaque salamanders scrambled around. Devika removed a small flashlight from a blue purse and focused it on the salamanders. Miraculously they disappeared. Only the shifting cloth gave any sign that the salamanders remained in the bag. Anand pulled the drawstring back tight.

"Could put those in the girl's dormitories after curfew," Riagan mused.

"Put what in our dormitories?" Rois asked. She and Maellyn each carried a bag.

Neil muttered to himself. Riagan was going to get them in trouble. Hoping to divert the girls' attention, he asked, "What have you got there?"

"Picture frames." Not to be distracted, Rois put her free hand on her hip. "Put what in the girl's dormitories, Riagan?"

"They thought loosing salamanders in the girl's dorm would be a good idea," Devika said. Her expression was pitying.

Neil gave the girls a blank stare and took a step away from Riagan. What was Riagan thinking making such a suggestion in front of a girl, even one as mischievous as Devika?

"Got to run," Devika said. As she passed by the girls, she cast a smirk back at Riagan and Neil.

Neil wanted to yell at her for tattling.

"Colombo's Caramella here we come," Anand added before scurrying off after his sister.

Rois arched an eyebrow and looked ready to flay Riagan. "If ya set foot in the girl's dormitories with salamanders or any other creature, I'll get another skunk sack from Instructor Tereshkova and pour it all over ya bed… while you're still in it. Then smear it all over your room so that ya can't ever remove the smell."

"I'll help her," Maellyn added, lips thinning as she glared at Neil, clearly believing he was involved, too.

Neil grinned uneasily and considered chasing after the twins.

Riagan held up his hands defensively. "We're only joking."

Jaya stepped closer to Rois. "So you got picture frames?"

Rois stared at Riagan reproachfully a second longer before her face transformed to eagerness as she pulled a lilac disc the size of her palm from the bag. The disc had a sticker of a white cat on its side.

How did girls do that? Change moods like flipping a coin. Neil didn't get it, but at least they appeared soothed. Why they were so uptight about it in the first place, he didn't know. Salamanders never hurt anyone. Releasing them in the dorms was nothing more than a harmless prank.

"My first 3D frame." Rois pressed a button near the bottom of the frame and a small 3D image of her and Maellyn popped into the air over the disc. The picture quality was stunning, like miniature clones.

"The guy in the store took our picture. A couple actually," Maellyn said. She pulled out her own picture disc and showed them an image where the girls posed, nearly cheek to cheek.

Neil had to admit the pictures were good. Not as useful as invisible salamanders or as satisfying as candy, but his pockets were full. He doubted he could hold another truffle.

"Thought we'd hit Rory's Weird and Unexplainable next," Jaya said, trying to steer them onward. "And if everyone's up for it, I've got extra tickets to tonight's races."

"Races?" Neil asked. "What kind of races?"

"Let's get a group picture first." Rois stopped a passerby to request they take a photo. She pulled Riagan, Jaya and Maellyn close.

Maellyn struck a pose, then called to Neil. "C'mon Neil, get in here. There's room here with me."

For the first time in his life, Neil hurried to get his picture taken.

Chapter 16

Riagan Scrapes the Wall

Standing in a line along the perimeter of a weaving track, Riagan gaped as he studied the state-of-the-art arena. Smooth, metallic walls lined the course over clear floors that revealed an immense pool below. What did that have to do with racing?

Riagan turned to mention the pool to Neil, but he was focused completely on Maellyn. Jaya and Rois were also huddled close. Why was Cupid running rampant with his stupid arrows?

"Apparently love is in the air at the races," Riagan complained to Jaya's father Jarl.

Taller than Jaya, his father was dressed in a suit as if ready for a business convention instead of a race. Unlike Jaya, his head was completely bald, not even eyebrows, and his blue skin gleamed from the lights. Jarl chuckled. "That's why I left my wife at home. Only way to enjoy a race."

"Little hope for these four," Riagan said.

Jarl laughed more heartily this time. "No hope for any of us. We're at their mercy ninety-five percent of the time. You learn to live for the five percent when you can do what you want."

"Doesn't seem worth it."

Jarl gave him a knowing smile. "One day you'll find yourself just as hopeless, and unwilling to imagine yourself otherwise."

Before Riagan could disagree, Jarl pointed to a guy in a leather jacket with shoulder-length blonde hair signing autographs.

"That one's a rising star on the circuit," Jarl said. "Aidan Martin. He and his partner, Sophie, had a rough rookie season, but they're turning heads this year. Already won a few races."

"He's my cousin," Maellyn said, emerging from her couple bubble to point out the connection. "Cade's older brother."

Aidan looked calm and confident as he signed autographs and joked with fans. His demeanor contrasted greatly with Cade's solemn fade-into-the-crowd attitude. In fact, Riagan had hardly seen Cade since Patrick had run their clothes up the flagpole during their first day aboard. Riagan wondered if Cade's limp was the sole reason for the difference in Cade and Aidan's dispositions.

A man at the front of the line unhooked a rope, allowing the crowd to surge forward toward a row of ATVs at the starting line. Riagan pressed forward, too. He couldn't wait to drive. Fans got a chance to race for fun early before the pros came out for the real competition.

Neil and Maellyn headed straight for a silver ATV. Neil climbed into the driver's seat, while Maellyn slid into the one behind him.

Rois and Jaya headed straight for a yellow quad with brown ends, but he gestured for her to drive, insisting he'd driven plenty of times. Riagan bit his lip. He didn't like how close she and Jaya were getting. Riagan hadn't decided if Jaya was trustworthy. He and Rois had been burned countless times trusting others, and if he didn't look out for Rois, who would?

Left on his own, Riagan chose a red ATV with orange flames, while Jarl headed up into the stands. The ATV bucket seats had a waist strap, and two more for the shoulders to buckle them in securely. Riagan wondered if they could ram each other like bumper cars. Attendants made their way through the line of ATVs, checking everyone's seat belts to make sure they were secure, then hitting a button on the side of the vehicles and a blue sphere lowered from the top of the ATVs to form a dome around the vehicle which turned invisible. Riagan reached out to the side, his palm touching the clear barrier. He started to ask the attendant what it was, but the man had already moved on to another ATV.

The others had started up their engines, so Riagan turned his attention back to driving, turning the key. The ATV hummed quietly. Once the attendants had cleared the track, stoplights on either side of the starting line changed from red to yellow to green.

Out of the gate, they had three steep hills to drive over. The drivers in front took off. Riagan accelerated up and over the first hill, taking it slowly at first. He started to speed up as he reached the second hill, but at the top a large ram slammed into his left side, striking the invisible barrier which flared blue momentarily. He was knocked sideways into another ATV. Riagan tensed, gripping the steering wheel.

What the—

The ram retracted back into the wall lining the course. As soon as the way was clear, the ATVs behind Riagan continued along the course, heedless of the wreck as if it was completely normal.

For a few seconds Riagan sat there in shock. The ram hadn't hurt. It had just surprised him. The invisible dome covering the ATV had shielded him. No one had warned him that they could be attacked. Nevertheless, the other guy which Riagan had hit maneuvered his ATV clear.

Riagan, now at the back of the pack, pressed the accelerator and the ATV jerked forward. He steered back toward the middle of the course, and the quad veered sharply left, forcing him to break hard before he collided with the far wall.

The rest of the racers were leaving him behind. A little annoyed that he was the only one who had been rammed, Riagan gave chase after the rest. They entered a series of sharply winding curves and Riagan kept running into walls or other ATVs as he tried to get comfortable steering. Everyone seemed to have trouble controlling the quads, only making it more difficult as they careened through. With great satisfaction, Riagan passed Neil and Maellyn, who were stuck in a corner, a couple of other ATVs wedged up against them. Riagan waved.

He rounded another turn and the track opened up, allowing several drivers to split wide and pick up speed. His path clear for the first time, Riagan accelerated, wanting to see how fast the ATV would go. A rocket fired from a cannon straight into an ATV ahead and to the right. The ATV swerved, but not fast enough. The rocket slammed into the ATV's left panel, knocking it on its back. Riagan slammed on his brakes and reached to unbuckle himself so he could check on the driver. Other ATVs raced on, heedless of the flipped one. Before Riagan could even get himself unbuckled, two metallic arms extended from the rear of the downed ATV. The arms planted in the ground and the ATV righted itself, and the arms disappeared back into the vehicle. Apparently unharmed, the driver accelerated and re-joined the race.

Riagan couldn't believe it. What other hazards were in store for them? He immediately floored the ATV, anxious to find out.

Around the next two curves, several rockets were fired at the ATVs, and Neil ran directly into another ram. Riagan skated through the traffic, but up ahead, a wall blocked the way forward. A single door in the wall alternated sliding open and closed. He accelerated toward the opening, but at the last second he realized it had started to close again. It was too late to brake. He kept his foot slammed on the accelerator and gritted his teeth as scraping metal shrieked in his ears. Sparks flew as the ATV scraped the wall on its left, but he made it through. He exhaled in relief.

Looping around, he crossed a bridge and floored the ATV down the back stretch across the finish line. He wasn't first, but had managed to beat Neil and Maellyn. After he had pulled off to the side, parked, and started to reluctantly climb out of the ATV, he spotted Rois racing Neil down the backstretch. They were racing tight, but at the last second Neil's quad fish-tailed a little and Rois pulled past him and across the finish line.

Rois pulled to the side and parked. She threw her arms straight up in the air as she turned to Neil. "Cheers! I beat you!"

"Ahem." Riagan tapped his chest as he strode over to them. "I believe I finished ahead of all of you." He decided not to point out that others had finished ahead of him.

Rois hopped out of the ATV. "That was awesome! Do we have time to go again?"

"We'll never get through the line for a second round before the actual race starts," Jaya said. "Might as well get some refreshments, then join my dad in our seats."

"Are you sure?" Neil asked, wistfully studying the line of the next round of people waiting to drive.

Riagan was tempted to join the line again and press his luck, but instead they all headed for concessions where he grabbed a warm butternell and purple melon punch.

Once the professional race started it turned out to be a relay. Four ATV drivers raced through the obstacle course, and at the completion of a lap, four partner submarines raced through a second course in the pool below for a lap. They watched the subs race on screens in front of their seats.

In the pool, the subs had to watch out for torpedoes and mines. Unfortunately, fans couldn't drive the racing subs. Riagan would've jumped at that opportunity. There was a second set of stands below for people to watch the subs race up close. He had to get a ticket to sit down there next race.

"Thank you so much for the tickets!" Neil told Jarl on their way out of the arena.

Jarl nodded. "Any time. Let Jaya know if you want to come again. I'll get tickets."

"Definitely can't wait," Riagan said. He would look up the schedule when he got back to campus.

"There goes Cade." Jaya pointed him out. "Too bad he's got that bad leg. Won't ever race like Aidan."

"Let's go talk to him," Maellyn said. But despite his limp, Cade quickly slipped away into the crowd. Riagan thought he didn't look in the mood to talk.

They headed for the monorails to drop off Maellyn and Rois.

"Before we split up, I want a memento." Rois pulled out her lilac disc and set it on the ground. She linked arms with Riagan and Jaya. "Everyone together."

The disc floated to eye level.

"Smile," Rois said.

Riagan barely had time to fake a smile before a bright light from the disc nearly blinded him.

Rois squealed happily. She darted forward to retrieve the disc. She brought up a 3D image of them squeezed together. "Cheers. That's a good one."

"Text me after you make it?" Riagan asked Rois as she returned with the disc.

She hugged him. "I'll text ya."

Riagan knew she had never had many girlfriends back home. In foster care, they usually wound up with strict families that viewed them as slave labor. Here, it seemed like they were finally getting a chance to be normal, which felt great.

After the girls departed on the monorail, Riagan and the guys started back toward campus. To their surprise, Jarl headed with them.

"I got a new lab on campus," Jarl said when questioned. "I didn't tell you before now because I wasn't sure if the deal was going to happen."

Jaya and Neil questioned Jarl about the lab, but Riagan let his mind wander. He glanced at the star-filled sky and wondered how many of those planets he would one day explore. He had been excited for Rois when the academy recruited her, but thought that when he got here he would find nothing for himself. Instead, he had found a whole new world opened to him. Or rather, a multitude of worlds. He no longer felt trapped by the realities that imprisoned him back on Earth, where most decisions were made for him.

Here, in a city among the stars, he felt he could make his own decisions. He could decide his fate. So, what did he want?

Chapter 17

Neil Tongue-Tied

Neil felt like an acolyte entering an exotic temple as he and Riagan entered the girls' dormitory to pick up Rois and Maellyn. The dorm wasn't strictly off limits to guys, except after dark, but few ever entered. Normally, Rois and Maellyn met them in the mess hall.

"Thought this would be cooler," Riagan said, eyeing each room they passed as if he might find something glamorous inside.

"Yeah," Neil agreed. He had expected perfumes effusing the entire dorm, pillows everywhere, girls powdering their faces, scented candles, and if they were lucky, maybe a girl or two still dressing.

Instead, girls departed their rooms for breakfast and class, most already in uniform. Through open bedroom doors Neil spotted perfectly made beds and well-organized rooms, not much different from his own. Daily inspections by the instructors forced everyone to adhere to a high standard, unless you wanted to land on the latrine cleaning crew. Even the floors here had the familiar lemon cleaner scent.

A girl in pink pajamas shuffled out of her room, rubbing sleep from her eyes. She disappeared into the latrine. Finally, a little bit of the allure they had hoped for.

Neil stared after her and tapped Riagan on the arm. "Do you see—"

"Yes."

"She's in—"

"She is..."

"They're pajamas," Rois said from a few doors away on their right, startling both boys. "Everyone wears them." She rolled her eyes and darted back into her room.

Neil and Riagan both flushed at getting caught. They hurried after her. Neil half hoped to catch Maellyn in pajamas as well. Instead, he found her fully dressed and staring in a mirror while putting on the white lotus flower earrings. Her reflection smiled at him.

Neil hid his disappointment. He imagined her in a pink, silk nightie that revealed too much of her thighs. The thought forced him to stare at a bed as his cheeks colored again. He hoped she didn't notice.

A cinnamon aroma filled the room, which made his stomach growl. On the window ledge, Rois' 3D picture frame cycled through pictures of them outside the arena before and after the race last weekend. The white cat sticker on the lilac disc faced outward. Sunlight, shining in through the window, made the pictures gleam like something out of a fairy tale. The current image showed Rois hugging Riagan, her smile ecstatic while he grimaced.

"I love how the sunlight highlights your tattoo," Neil teased Riagan.

Noticing the image, Riagan's expression became pained. "Ah, c'mon, sis. Do ya have to display that?"

"I do," Rois said, brushing her hair. "The frame is solar powered. Maellyn suggested I put it in the window to recharge."

"Ya don't have to show the photos, though."

"I like them."

Neil covered a smile with his hand, enjoying Riagan's discomfort. *Better Riagan than me*, he thought.

Maellyn slipped on a white lotus flower necklace that matched her earrings. "A one-day charge ought to last a month. Dad and I put our frames in the windowsills during the day. We return them to their spots in the evening."

"I'm starving." Riagan checked his wrist-comp. "Twenty minutes 'til class." Not giving them any more time, Riagan herded the girls out to the courtyard.

As they approached the mess hall, Neil thought a cinnamon roll sounded appetizing. His stomach rumbled. Maybe he'd get two.

"Neil Ericson?" A plump boy with tiny eyes and a bulbous nose asked, interrupting Neil's contemplation.

"Yes?" Neil didn't recognize the boy from any of his classes.

"You're to report to General Dardanos." The boy fidgeted. He glanced at the girls, back at Neil, then the ground.

"What for?" Neil asked.

The boy shrugged. His message delivered, he hurried past them into the mess hall.

Neil's heart beat faster and a chill swept through him. What did the academy's headmaster want with him? He hadn't done anything wrong. No detentions.

"What do you think he wants?" Maellyn asked, concern tingeing her voice.

Neil shook his head. "Not sure. I guess I'll see you later."

The girls entered the mess hall, but Neil tugged at Riagan's shirt to slow him.

"Think this is about the Dahaka?" Neil asked. They hadn't spoken about it since that day.

Riagan's lips tightened and he checked their surroundings. No one was close enough to overhear them. "Did ya tell anyone?"

"No," Neil said, thankful his nose wouldn't grow from a lie. He hadn't really told Maellyn anything.

"How would he know then?" Riagan hurried after the girls.

Neil followed him inside. "What if someone spotted us?"

"He'd have summoned us both, and a lot sooner," Riagan replied through gritted teeth, refusing to return Neil's gaze. He started searching through the food options.

"Maybe I should tell him about the CME." Surely he could trust the headmaster, if anyone.

"Ya do, leave me out," Riagan growled.

As soon as the cover lifted, revealing a tray with his breakfast, Riagan snatched it and practically ran to the table where Rois and Maellyn sat, already eating.

Neil's hunger had gone. It was unfair. Why was this all on him to figure out? Riagan had seen the Dahaka, too. Yet Riagan's refusal to even discuss the situation left Neil trapped, unsure where to turn to for help. If he told someone else, he might be putting them in harm's way. How had his grandfather ever made his heroic decisions when any move might be the wrong one?

He hurried to the academy headquarters and pushed the button for the elevator. While he waited, he considered Riagan's argument, but doing nothing, trusting no one, eliminated hope, which made him feel too much like his uncle. His uncle had given up hope, the first step in his downward spiral.

The elevator ran too smoothly, carrying Neil to the fifth floor. The doors opened unceremoniously onto a waiting room with an administrative assistant's desk guarding General Dardanos' office. The blonde assistant hadn't noticed him and he found himself rooted in place, unable to move forward or back. He longed to press a button while escape remained possible. But he guessed someone other than the timid boy would be sent next to retrieve him, so he stepped off the elevator.

Perhaps ten years older than Neil, the assistant's pink lips faintly smiled as she typed on her wrist-comp. Neil couldn't bring himself to disturb her. When she noticed him, he sucked in a deep breath, momentarily more nervous in her presence than at the prospect of visiting the Academy head.

"Neil Ericson, I presume?" The girl had blue eyes like a summer sky.

He tried to reply, but his lips didn't budge. He managed only a slight nod.

"General Dardanos is expecting you."

Neil tried to smile, but the movement felt strange. He feared that he made some bizarre grimace, which increased his desire to flee. Still, he had to proceed to Dardanos' office, so he focused on the glass doors as he walked toward them, too self-conscious to glance in the assistant's direction again.

Dardanos' office paid homage to the military. Books on military strategy, real life stories of soldiers in the field, and commanders' memoirs filled the shelves on the left. Next to the bookshelf, a glass case displayed a gray Space City suit with quite a few badges. Additional glass displays lining the opposite wall showcased two samurai swords, an automatic rifle, and several other weapons Neil didn't recognize. Were those weapons from other planets? On the wooden desk in the room's center rested a couple of Space City spacecraft models.

Dardanos sat behind the desk, measuring him. A grizzled veteran, he possessed a flat-top haircut, decorated uniform, and a confident grimace that left no mistake that he had the upper hand.

"I need to know what you witnessed with the Dahaka." Dardanos' tone indicated this wasn't a request. He placed his fists on the desk.

Neil gaped. Despite guessing the reason for the academy head's summons, he wasn't prepared for this matter-of-fact questioning.

"Preferably before lunch," Dardanos added. The command in his voice compelled Neil to answer.

"I was fleeing Patrick and his gang. I passed an open window, so I dropped through it down into the basement. I was looking for another way out when I spotted the Dahaka talking with someone." The story flooded from his lips. He didn't mention Riagan's involvement, at least managing to keep that secret.

Confiding in the General did offer some relief. He surely knew how to thwart the Dahaka's efforts to steal the CME. All Neil had managed to do was agonize over it.

"You're sure it was a hologram?" Dardanos asked.

Neil shifted from one foot to the other. "Yes, sir."

"Do you know whom the Dahaka spoke with?" Dardanos' eyes seemed to boar into Neil's, as if to confirm the truth of Neil's words on their own.

Neil shook his head. "No, sir. Blocked from view. Only saw the Dahaka's back."

"What about the man's voice? Could you recognize him speaking again?"

Neil considered for a minute, trying to recall the scene. Shock at seeing the Dahaka had overwhelmed him. He struggled to recall what the man had said in the hope that if he remembered that, it would trigger the memory more clearly. To his chagrin, he remembered only the Dahaka's deadly tone followed by the dizziness and unexplainable fear before they fled. Should he mention that part?

"I don't know…maybe…" Neil remembered one word and seized on it. "Ormazd. The Dahaka's name was Ormazd."

"Ormazd."

Neil nodded. Hoping to help further, he added, "The CME has something to do with a coronal mass ejection."

Dardanos blinked in surprise. "You seem to have discovered quite a bit."

Neil rushed on before Dardanos asked how. "Don't know what a CME is exactly, but if the Dahaka want one, I'm guessing it's not a good thing."

Dardanos looked troubled. "Why didn't you come forward with this?"

Neil's stomach turned. "As I said, I didn't know the man. He could've been anyone. I didn't know who I could tell."

Dardanos' countenance was grim, but he seemed to accept this. "In the future, I'd prefer such information come to me directly. I'm in the best position to address such issues, rather than a scientist."

"Yes, sir."

Maellyn's father had informed Dardanos about his questions, it seemed. That didn't explain how Dardanos knew he had seen the Dahaka, though.

"How did you know I'd seen the Dahaka?" Neil asked.

"We have security cameras covering the entire outdoor campus."

Neil felt a surge of hope. "You must know who was in there."

"Unfortunately, no," Dardanos said. "According to our footage, no one had entered that building for a good six months before your encounter."

"How did you know about the Dahaka?"

"That's evidence you don't need to know. You or Riagan."

Neil colored. He knew about Riagan, too. Why hadn't he been summoned, too?

"I'm personally investigating." Dardanos wheeled himself around the desk. "I'd prefer you kept this quiet. We don't need to tip off the traitor. Or cause a panic."

"Of course, I won't talk to anyone," Neil said, staring at the wheelchair. It didn't make Dardanos any less fierce.

"By the way, why were you running from Patrick and his lackeys?" Dardanos' eyes seemed to bore into Neil, as if warning him against lying.

Riagan was going to be so pissed.

"Riagan and I put a skunk sack in Caleb's bed," Neil confessed.

Dardanos nodded, as if that was what he expected to hear. "Report to Instructor Tereshkova for detention. Riagan, too. You're dismissed."

Relieved to have that off his chest, Neil hurried from the room, more than willing to accept that punishment. A small price to pay now that he didn't have to worry about the Dahaka or the traitor.

His eyes instinctively turned to the assistant's desk. She was gone. Relief and disappointment mingled through him. Rather than wait for her to return and risk Dardanos summoning him back, Neil hurried for the elevator and chose the bottom floor.

Thrilled to have this off his shoulders, Neil jumped excitedly as the elevator stopped at the bottom and the doors opened. The assistant stood there waiting on it. Neil immediately colored. She had seen him jump for no apparent reason. She smiled, stifling a laugh.

This was awful!

He shot her a distressed smile. Thankfully, she said nothing as he exited and slipped past.

Chapter 18

Neil Slows Riagan

Neil was so hungry that his belly button had started gnawing on his backbone. Having woken up late that morning, he had only managed to grab a purple melon and peanut butter crackers before rushing off to Battle Tactics. Once Pre-Calculus ended, he had darted out of class and had to restrain himself from shoving everyone out of his way as he charged for the mess hall. Hunger could do strange things to people's normally polite behavior.

"C'mere. Wait up," Riagan called as he tried to push through the crowd of students flooding out of classrooms.

Neil didn't slow. He wanted to get to the mess hall before the lines got too long. Riagan would catch up. Neil pushed through the doors outside to the courtyard.

Jaya and Rois lounged on a bench not far away, her back pressed against his chest and his arms enfolding her. She read to him. Over the last month, since the race, they had spent an increasing amount of time together, despite Riagan's frustration and snide remarks.

Riagan had told Neil a little about life in the system since their parent's death. Riagan had scared off a few foster parents looking for a boy, because they didn't want two kids. Rois had had no one but him to rely on, and he wouldn't abandon her for any reason. She had later done the same when good foster parents came looking for a girl, despite his insistence that she leave him behind. They had been placed in a couple of homes together, but soon learned that most foster parents were either in it for a government check, or didn't want kids as much as they thought. Riagan had known if he didn't look after Rois, no one would.

Now Rois was infatuated with love, which took up a lot of her time.

At that moment Patrick and his gang, including a few girls, passed in front of Rois and Jaya.

"Lamia," someone in the group spat.

"Little green woman," another yelled. Several others in Patrick's gang repeated the insults, sounding like an angry mob.

Neil clenched his fists, ready to confront Patrick, but when the group passed, Rois' face was a mask of horror. Her gaze chilled him. What had they done?

Her eyes were riveted on a six-inch hologram emerging from a lilac disc with a white cat sticker on the ground. Neil recognized it at once. Her 3D picture frame. The image depicted Jaya with red horns, a pointed tail, and holding an onyx trident while standing next to a green-skinned woman in a wedding dress.

Tears welled up in Rois' eyes as she stared at the image.

Neil moved around in front of the hologram, and his breath caught in his throat. His gut hurt as if a horse had kicked him. The woman depicted was Rois, but not only was her skin colored green, but she possessed a full, crimson-stained pregnant belly.

Riagan caught up and when he saw the hologram his whole body shook with fury. He charged after Patrick. Neil followed, feeling like an active volcano about to erupt. Rois always had a kind word for everyone. She tutored girls in her dorm simply to help. How could Patrick stoop this low?

"Patrick!" Riagan roared. He was a bull who had seen the red flag. But before Riagan reached Patrick, Instructor Nez rushed in and blocked his path.

"Hold up," Nez ordered.

Riagan tried to sidestep him, but Nez shoved him back into Neil.

Neil paused, fury giving way to wariness.

"What is this about?" Nez asked.

Riagan tried to rush past again.

Nez blocked him. "Stop now or you're suspended."

Knowing the threat meant little right now, Neil threw his arms around Riagan to hold him back. Riagan struggled violently. Neil longed to let Riagan loose on Patrick, who deserved whatever he got. Instead, Neil held on tightly. He would not let Riagan be the one punished here.

"They attacked Rois," Jaya said, marching past them and furiously waving the now profane device. He shoved it into Nez's face, causing the image to undulate. Nez gaped at the hologram. His expression quickly darkened and he spun to face the gang. Patrick Duffy stood defiant at the head, but the others shuffled uneasily, ready to abandon ship.

"Who demeans this girl?" Nez seized the device and shook it at them. Several girls paled as they got a closer view, as if seeing it for the first time. "Who dares to belittle her so?"

Patrick leaned away from the image as if disgusted, but replied calmly. "I don't know where that came from. We didn't make that."

"Liar!" Riagan struggled to free himself. Neil tightened his grip. Nez was an electric fence between them, and Riagan was too angry to recognize the danger.

"You're all innocent?" Nez tone was thick with disbelief.

"Just passing through," Patrick said, pulling out a pass from his pocket. "I've got permission to practice in the stadium. I got a group together and we were headed there now."

Neil gritted his teeth. *Conniving coward*, he thought. He wanted to force Patrick to admit what they'd done.

"They hurled insults at us first," Jaya said coldly. "Called Rois a demon and a green woman."

"Did you see them place the device?" Nez asked.

Neil didn't like the question. Was Nez going to let Patrick get away with this?

"How could they when we didn't do it?" Patrick's upper lip curled in a sneer.

"Rois and I sat on that bench for the last half hour." Jaya pointed back where Aileen McKensie and Fran Snelling now huddled around Rois, trying to soothe her.

"They passed by, insulted us, and the hologram lay on the ground in their wake."

"You will all be summoned by the Academy Council on this," Nez said. He clicked a button on the disc, turning off the image. "I'll take this as evidence."

"You're letting them go?" Neil asked. Nez couldn't really *believe* Patrick's lies. It was too clear what had happened.

Riagan slipped Neil's grasp and tried to charge Patrick again.

Nez rounded on them. "Hold!"

Riagan halted midstride. The anger on Nez's face now blew away their own.

"No one is off the hook," Nez shouted, face flushed. "The council will get to the bottom of this." Turning back to Patrick's gang, he waved the abhorrent disc in their faces. They shied back. "When we discover who is responsible, they will be punished." Turning his glare back on Riagan and Neil, he added, "The instructors enforce the rules, not students."

Rois passed by Neil and stepped in front of Riagan, tear stains streaking her face. "Let's go… now."

Riagan glared over her head at Patrick, who stood smugly in front of his gang.

Rois grabbed his arm, pulling him away. "C'mere. I want to go now."

Nez ordered them all to be on their way. Riagan let her guide him, Jaya reluctantly following.

Patrick grinned at Neil, clearly believing he had just won. Neil clenched his fists, but with Nez present, he just turned and followed after Riagan and Rois.

"Should've chosen better friends than an alien's lover, her fool brother, and the Smurf," Patrick shouted after him.

Neil ground his teeth, but kept on walking.

"You now have detention after your classes today," Nez told Patrick, but to Neil that did little to make things right.

Up ahead it was Rois trying to soothe Riagan. She held her head high despite what had happened. This gave Neil a pang of guilt. Somehow he owed her more. He had always wanted a sister and he guessed his feelings for her matched that desire. Should he wait and see if the council punished Patrick and the others? Was that enough?

Something inside him said that more was expected from a brother. He knew Riagan could not be satisfied with the academy dealing with this. Neil longed for his grandfather's advice. He slipped his hand in his pocket, fingering his grandfather's coin.

Maellyn arrived and Jaya filled her in. She gasped at the insults, then paled about the hologram.

"Blimey. How can these prejudices persist?" she asked. "With our education and advancements, and all that we witness and the good people we meet across the universe, some—a tiny minority, I assure you—still exchange one prejudice for another."

Tears brimmed in Rois' eyes, but she quickly brushed them away. "Do you…" She hesitated, eyes on the ground now. "Do you think it's weird we're dating?" Her eyes rose back up to Maellyn.

Maellyn immediately pulled her into a hug. "Of course not. You two are wonderful together. There is nothing wrong with that."

Neil felt his throat tighten. He'd never considered that Rois might worry that they wouldn't approve of her dating Jaya. But when Rois turned to look at Riagan, he realized that all of her brother's snide remarks had affected her. She had worried that he didn't approve.

Riagan coughed, shifting nervously before speaking. "If ya want to date Jaya, I have no problem with that."

"Are you sure?" she asked, studying him closely. "Ya always make little comments."

"Because ya spend all your time with him now," Riagan replied, voice quiet. "It used to be just us."

Rois flushed, her eyes pained for a different reason. "I'm sorry. I didn't think."

"It's fine," Riagan mumbled.

"I'm cool with you two, as well," Neil said. He felt like it was important that he let Rois and Jaya hear that from him, too. That he not remain silent.

Rois nodded at him, then reached out and grabbed Jaya's hand. Her tear streaks remained, but they were drying. "I like ya and I won't let anyone ruin this."

"Me either," he replied, squeezing her hand.

Neil's stomach growled, reminding him that he still hadn't eaten and he reddened with shame when everyone turned to look at him. He felt like he had just minimized the situation. "Sorry," he mumbled.

"How about sneaking off campus for lunch in the city?" Maellyn suggested. "We all need some time away."

Rois nodded and led the way, linking an arm through Jaya's.

Chapter 19

Furry Riagan

The Academy Council conducted its affairs on the fifth floor opposite General Dardanos' office. Following the administrative assistant into the council chambers, Riagan was ready to demand justice for Patrick's gross mistreatment of Rois. Almost a week had passed—too long in Riagan's opinion—but the council had chosen to conduct the hearing on a holiday to avoid their missing class. Riagan thought the offense was worth missing a few hours or a day of class.

Rois, rubbing her arms nervously, followed Jaya. Neil and Maellyn brought up the rear. For some reason, Neil blushed and carefully avoided looking at the assistant.

"If you'll have a seat, the council will arrive soon." The assistant directed them to chairs behind a wooden rail on the left side of the room. Rois chose the middle seat in the front row between Riagan and Jaya. Neil and Maellyn took the back row.

At the front of the room was a massive wooden desk on a raised dais which resembled a federal courtroom. The Space City and academy flags adorned the back wall. The formalness of the setting assured Riagan of the seriousness with which the council would handle the situation, but he wasn't sure if that boded well for them or not. Formality and seriousness did not assure justice.

A few minutes later, the blonde assistant showed Patrick and his gang, all dressed properly in their uniforms, into the room. Patrick strode for the chairs behind a wooden rail on the room's right side. Riagan tried to catch his eye, but Patrick focused straight ahead as if they weren't there. Adrien Laroque brought up the rear, looking paler than usual and wringing his hands.

Alongside them marched a man in a suit with a briefcase.

A lawyer?

What was he doing here? Riagan wondered. If they thought a lawyer would get them out of trouble…

Riagan imagined the whole group spontaneously combusting, flailing about as balls of fire. Contrary to his wish, they proceeded to their seats unburned.

The man in the suit sat in the front row next to Patrick. He possessed the same jet-black hair as Patrick, and the same sharp, pointed nose. Older brother? Cousin?

Rois, for her part, gave Patrick and his followers a single glance, her lips pressing together in a thin line as she fingered the shou pendant on her necklace. Riagan reached over and placed a hand on her left arm for reassurance at the same moment Jaya grabbed her right hand. She smiled at Jaya before turning it to Riagan.

Optimism remained in her eyes. That continual buoyancy often surprised him considering the many homes and terrible guardians they had suffered through. She had always managed to let that sorrow slide off her the way mud washed away in a shower, leaving her untarnished. That didn't mean they hadn't hurt her. Patrick's attack had hurt her a great deal. Yet pain and sorrow never weighed on her for long. Riagan dreaded the day when she failed to shake off such ill-treatment. He loved the perpetual starlight in her eyes, and felt a burden to protect it.

General Dardanos and Instructors Nez and Tereshkova entered the room. Jaya immediately stood and saluted. Riagan and the others followed suit, as did Patrick and his lot. The headmaster moved to the middle of the desk, and the instructors took seats on either side of him.

"At ease," Dardanos said. Everyone sat and he studied the older man by Patrick for a moment. "We are here to investigate student misconduct. Nez, will you take the lead?"

"I will." Nez moved to the floor in the center of the room.

He proceeded to relate events as he had witnessed them, pulling out Rois' lilac disc and activating the image as evidence. Maellyn gasped, seeing the image for the first time. The General's eyes had a fire in them, which pleased Riagan.

Nez pointed to the horns and tail. "As you can see, Jaya is depicted as a devil, a highly offensive image."

Rois kept her chin up, but she avoided the image and a tear slid down her cheek. Riagan wished she could leave for this part.

"That alone is bad enough," Nez said. "Such bigotry threatens our relationship with both the Azzaros and other alien races, undermining everything Space City and this academy represents."

Tereshkova looked ill as she studied the hologram.

Nez continued. "Rois Byrne is depicted pregnant, and presumably the victim of a violent, horrific attack. We might easily infer from this that the devil attacked her."

Rois' face had colored, eyes dropping to her hands clasped in her lap. Riagan bit his lip, suppressing the urge to demand Nez turn off the contorted memento. The council needed to see it. They needed to understand the full extent of Patrick's viciousness. But it was cruel that in order to obtain justice, victims had to relive their suffering. One time wasn't enough?

Nez returned to his seat and invited Rois and Jaya to provide their accounts to the Council, followed by Neil. The others had a clearer memory. Riagan mostly remembered his rage.

Finally, Riagan corroborated what the others had already shared as best he could. He felt his anger burning on his face, and every time his voice rose, as he started to lose control at the memory, Rois placed a calming hand on his back. And once he started he could not look in Patrick's direction for fear that he would find a sneer and that would make him lose all control, which would not help them.

Riagan finished and returned to his seat. Rois squeezed his hand encouragingly. He hoped it was enough.

Throughout their recounting, the council listened, stone-faced. Their only show of emotion had occurred when seeing the hologram. Occasionally Tereshkova asked a question, but that was it. Why didn't they show more outrage at what Patrick had done? Riagan expected open condemnation of the act.

Nez invited Patrick to address the council. Riagan steeled himself for lies, but Patrick didn't rise. Instead, the man in the suit stood and took the floor.

"My name is Dougal Duffy," the man introduced himself. "I will speak on behalf of Patrick and his friends."

"We are here for student testimony only," Dardanos replied, clearly displeased at Dougal's presumption. "It is highly irregular for legal counsel involvement in a student disciplinary hearing."

Dougal held up his hands in apology, but a lawyerly smile covered his face. "Normally their parents would attend disciplinary hearings, but they have all requested that I stand in for them in these matters."

"Very well," Dardanos said through clenched teeth.

"I'd first like to thank Instructor Nez for giving his account of events." Dougal reminded Riagan of lawyers who got their clients released due to a technicality. Everyone knew the defendants were guilty, but the lawyer found a sleazy way to get them off the hook anyway. "The passionate recounting makes me wonder about his neutrality in this matter, though."

"Are you challenging this council's integrity?" Dardanos' face reddened. "I have the power to excuse you, regardless of the parents' wishes."

Dougal held up his hands once more to placate the academy head. "I'm merely trying to protect these students, as I know you are doing. Please forgive any missteps on my part."

Riagan wished Dardanos would toss Dougal out. The longer Dougal spoke, the more Riagan expected him to find a technicality.

"Have you had the device inspected?" Dougal asked, pointing to the disc sitting on the oak desk before Nez.

Nez nodded. "Yes, we analyzed the device."

"And were you able to discern anything that might confirm who loaded the image onto it?"

Nez grimaced, clearly unhappy. "The driver was damaged."

Dougal smiled like a rat who has found cheese.

Jaya buried his head in his hands.

Growing nervous, Riagan leaned toward Jaya. "What does that mean?"

Jaya didn't answer.

"The device programming is irretrievable?" Dougal asked.

"Not without great difficulty," Nez admitted.

"What does the programming matter?" Riagan asked, still confused.

Jaya leaned over and whispered to Rois and Riagan, "If the driver is damaged, only an expert can discover who created the image.

Paying an expert to trace where the programming came from is expensive, more than the academy is likely willing to pay to determine a student's guilt."

"They're off the hook?" Riagan asked, louder than he intended.

Dardanos gave him a warning glare. Riagan clamped his mouth shut, but he didn't shrink back under the General's disapproval.

"Fortunately, I happen to have connection," Tereshkova said. "We can have results in three days. I'd suggest culprit and anyone involved admit so now. Our judgment will be harsher if they continue to hide what they've done."

"I did it. I created the image," Adrien Laroque said, jumping to his feet. "I claim complete responsibility for the device. No one else had any knowledge of what I did."

Riagan's jaw dropped. Adrien was part of Patrick's group, but Riagan had never considered him brave enough to try something like this on his own. And as Riagan thought about it, he didn't remember Adrien among Patrick's gang that day in the courtyard.

"I am solely to blame for the image," Adrien said, eyes wide with fear. "It was meant as a simple prank."

Riagan jumped to his feet, stabbing a finger at Adrien. "He's taking the fall. They were all in on it. Don't believe them."

"Enough!" Dardanos' nostrils flared. He glared at Riagan as if ready to strangle him.

Rois pulled Riagan back down on his seat. *Surely Dardanos would see through this*, Riagan thought. Patrick had somehow convinced Adrien to take the fall, probably by threatening him with something worse.

"In light of this confession," Dardanos began, "Adrien, you are suspended for one week. You will vacate the campus by curfew tonight."

Riagan jumped back to his feet. "Ye can't let them get away with it! It's a lie!"

Dardanos pounded his fist on the desk. "I will not accept this recalcitrant behavior. Control yourself."

Neil and Jaya seized Riagan's arms, pulling him back from the rail.

"Let me go," Riagan demanded. "They can't let Patrick off."

Neil and Jaya held on tight, though. He struggled, but they hauled him from the room and toward the elevator. Despite his protests, they didn't release him until the elevator doors had closed and they were descending.

"What're ye doing?" Riagan asked, glaring at them. "He's guilty. Ye both know it."

"We have no proof," Neil said, but he lowered his eyes, as if recognizing that explanation meant little. "We can't prove they lied."

Not wanting to hear their traitorous excuses, Riagan bolted the moment the elevator doors dinged open. If the council refused to hold Patrick responsible for his actions, it was up to him. He alone cared about Rois.

*****

Riagan stormed straight for Instructor Tereshkova's classroom, ignoring Neil's and Jaya's pleas to stop and think. He refused to accept this. They needed to choose whose side they were on, because if they did nothing, they were saying what Patrick had done was ok.

Shoving open Tereshkova's classroom door, Riagan headed for the bad nut beetles. Their slime was perfect. Retrieving gloves from the hook beside their cage and pulling them on, he turned and grabbed a leather pouch to carry the little brown beetles. They were easily mistaken for pecans if you weren't paying close attention.

As he moved to open the cage, Neil cut him off.

"Get out of my way." Riagan shoved him back into the cage, furious that after everything Neil would actually try to stop him.

"You can't do this," Neil said, having seen Riagan's burns from the beetles. "That's going too far."

"You'll only get in trouble," Jaya added, joining Neil to create a wall.

Riagan balled his fists, furious at their inability or refusal to understand. "Too far? Ye think it right that Patrick get away with this?"

Neil grimaced. "No way, but revenge won't help."

"It will," Riagan hissed, pointing a finger in the general direction of the academy council building. "He's not afraid of the instructors. He knows he can escape punishment."

Neil crossed his arms. "Who is this revenge for?"

Riagan stared at him. Had Neil gone mad? "This is for Rois. If ye care as much as ye claim, help."

"Rois doesn't need this." Neil stepped closer and put his finger on Riagan's chest. "You do."

Riagan snarled at Neil, batting his hand away. "Ya know nothing of family."

Neil recoiled at the rebuke. Jaya clenched his fists, but said nothing. He just stood beside Neil.

"Ye think standing with us when it's not hard is enough?" Riagan asked.

"What's going on?" Tereshkova stood in the doorway, eyes narrowed as she studied the three of them.

Riagan flinched. *Great*, he thought sourly. They just killed this with their whiny protests.

Tereshkova crossed the room at a measured pace, noticing the gloves Riagan wore and the pouch for beetles.

After spilling a couple of beetles on his wrist earlier in the week, Riagan's skin had burned badly the rest of that day. Nothing had soothed the burn either. Ice and medicine hadn't helped. He had endured the pain until it dissipated. He had slept that night only after exhaustion had finally overwhelmed him. Even then, every time his wrist had touched something he had bolted awake, gasping in pain. Fortunately, the effects wore off after a day.

Tereshkova snatched the pouch from Riagan. "Apparently you never heard me say attacking classmates is not acceptable."

Jaya and Neil started to protest, but Riagan shouted over them, not bothering to hide what was plain to them all. "The council did nothing."

"Nothing?" Tereshkova arched an eyebrow. "Adrien received suspension for maximum time a student may miss in year. If he misses one more day for any reason, he'll have to repeat year. That is not trifle punishment."

"Adrien wasn't involved, Instructor." Riagan doubted that she cared, though. "He wasn't even there."

She turned on her heels. "Come with me."

Neil and Jaya followed without argument. Riagan contemplated ignoring her, grabbing the beetles, and making a break for it. But he'd never get near Patrick with them now. He'd only increase whatever punishment Tereshkova had in store for them. Grunting in anger, Riagan yanked the gloves off his hands and threw them and the pouch against the cage, but didn't even get a satisfying thud from that.

Tereshkova led them out to kennels beside a broad, penned-in area behind her classroom. Rat-faced, beagle-sized dogs filled the kennels. She placed a hand on a kennel. "Hare dogs' kennels need cleaning. Consider this your detention for your paltry behavior. Student retaliation isn't taken lightly."

"Yes, Colonel Terror," Riagan said, knowing the words were a bad idea, but not caring.

Tereshkova's eyes smoldered as her lips drew into a thin line. "For that, you'll bathe hare dogs as well. Anything else to say?"

Neil and Jaya groaned.

Riagan glowered, but didn't argue further. Adults never cared about fairness. They handed out punishments when they wanted to whether it was deserved or not.

Tereshkova reached over and opened a cage. "We need to put hare dogs in pen."

A hare dog emerged from the open cage and Tereshkova grabbed it by the collar and led it toward the pen. The dog tugged her forward, ears pointed straight up. Tereshkova opened the pen gate and released the hare dog inside where it raced around, happy for the freedom.

Unable to believe that he had woken up that morning believing that Patrick would be punished for his crime, and instead it was himself in detention, Riagan opened a cage and reached inside for another hare dogs' collar. The dog snapped at his fingers, and he jumped back in surprise.

"Nearly bit me," he complained, wanting to slam the door shut in its face.

"Let come out first," Tereshkova instructed. "They extremely territorial, allowing only mate or young into dens."

Riagan backed away from the kennel door. The hare dog eyed him warily for a moment before it gingerly stepped outside. Riagan eased his hand toward the dog's collar. This time, the hare dog took no notice of his hand. He gently grabbed the collar and the dog pulled him toward the pen. Inside the pen it darted after the first. The two started playing and Riagan, despite his frustration, couldn't help but grin at their excitement.

After moving the dozen hare dogs to the pen, the three boys stood facing the kennels, which reeked. Molted fur, mud, leaves, and twigs covered the floors and walls of the cages.

"My sister gets attacked and we get punished," Riagan complained, trying to come up with an excuse to get out of cleaning the cages. She really was Sergeant Terror.

For response, Tereshkova handed them rakes. "Don't pretend you blameless. We all know why you were in my classroom."

Riagan didn't argue, but it shouldn't matter. Patrick deserved a little payback for what he had done to Rois. How could Tereshkova not understand that?

As if reading his thoughts, she said, "If their involvement is proven, council will punish. You must acquiesce to rules if you going to succeed."

Riagan shoved the rake in the kennel and pulled matted fur from it.

"Put fur in fire pit." Tereshkova pointed to a small round hole in the ground.

Riagan carried his rake over to the hole and shook the matted fur into it, before returning to the cage. Neil and Jaya had already started raking out other cages.

"I was under impression you three wanted to become team captains," Tereshkova said. "You giving me serious doubts about abilities to lead."

Riagan slammed the rake against the back of the kennel, scraping at a dirt clod. How could she question his ability to be a team captain over this? He was attempting to protect Rois from an aggressor. Wasn't that what leaders did?

Once they'd cleared most of the debris from the kennels, Tereshkova gave them hoses to soak the cages, followed by soap and scrub brushes to thoroughly clean them. Riagan bit his tongue, but he wouldn't be so gracious to Neil when they returned to the dorms.

"Alyona, do you have the latest class health scan results?" Instructor Aodh asked as he drifted back from the classroom. He paused when he noticed them, then chuckled with recognition. "I'm sorry, Alyona. I didn't realize you were occupied. Not your most sciential students."

"I find a little manual labor does wonders for student behavior and focus," Tereshkova said. "Scans on my desk."

Aodh grinned and departed.

Tereshkova turned back to them. "Speaking of health scans, you three keeping up with daily's?"

"Daily and before half our classes, Instructor," Riagan griped, scrubbing the bars. He almost called her Sergeant Terror without thinking. He had to watch that. He didn't relish adding to his workload.

"Those scans go into neural network," Tereshkova said. "With each new health issue recorded, network learns from experiences and mistakes. More data leads to improved recommendations to doctors."

Riagan wanted to shout that he didn't care about a neural network or how well doctors did. He just wanted to finish the cages and return to his dorm to be alone.

In order to completely clean a kennel, they had to move them— weighing forty or fifty pounds each—in order to clean the outside. By the time they had finished with all twelve, as well as the two spare, evening had set in.

Muck covered Riagan's clothes. He itched all over, and sweat poured down his forehead and cheeks. He was too exhausted to even hold onto his anger any longer.

Tereshkova examined the newly cleaned kennels with approval. "I should hire you three to clean regularly." She then turned her attention to the hare dogs, who lay inside their pen panting from their play. "Now to bathe."

That was another ordeal. The hare dogs didn't like getting wet and would fight to get away. To get the hare dogs clean, two of them had to hold one of the dogs, while the other hosed and cleaned them down. But at least it was cooler than crawling around inside the cages.

When they'd finally finished, the sun was setting. Riagan clenched his jaws and waited for Tereshkova to dismiss them. He was exhausted and wanted nothing more than a shower and bed.

She walked over and stood before him. He met her gaze squarely.

"All of this because you think you need to protect Rois," Tereshkova had compassion in her eyes.

Riagan snorted.

"Rois doesn't need protection. She only needs support."

Chapter 20

Neil's First Match

The stadium stands reverberated as people searched for their seats and argued over who would win the opening Academy Games match between Ursa and Chamaeleon. They would all watch and judge every single move Neil made during the game. That unnerved him a little, but he did his best to tune out the crowd noise.

Maellyn and Rois waved from the stands with Jaya and Riagan. The girls had donned Ursa sweaters which matched Neil's reddish-brown, grizzly bear-colored jersey. "Ursa" and a depiction of the constellation Ursa Major were emblazoned on the front.

Riagan played a game on his wrist-comp. He had likely only come because Rois had made him. He had hardly spoken to Neil or Jaya over the past month no matter how much either apologized. Rois had even argued with him on their behalf, but in his mind, apologies didn't erase betrayal.

Neil had thought that if he could prove Patrick's involvement in the attack on Rois, that might soothe Riagan. Neil and Jaya had hatched several ideas, but they had all led to dead-ends. Patrick had a talent for covering his tracks.

With less than five minutes until match start, Team Captain Hardin called the offense together for a final word. Neil, Eris, Dirk Fischer, and Trini Flores joined him while their three defensemen filtered into the forest to take up positions. Anand and Devika guarded home base.

"All right, we get giant armadillos," Hardin said.

Neil had heard mention of animal defenders in the games. The animals identified one team as co-habitants and the opponent as invading predators. Giant armadillos sounded underwhelming, regardless of their size.

"Serpent hawks guard the Chamaeleon's eggs," Hardin added. "They're large, fast, and territorial."

Sounded a lot cooler than giant armadillos. Advantage Chamaeleons.

Neil searched the empty sky for the hawks. They were probably released after match start. How dangerous were they?

"Stay focused at all times," Hardin said. "Stay disciplined. Follow orders. Do that and we'll win."

Neil nodded absently as he studied the Chamaeleon players spread out on the opposite half of the field with the rocky uprising. They wore camouflage uniforms with their name and the constellation on the front.

Standing among the Chamaeleon players, Patrick spotted him and yelled. "Neil, you know what they say about children born with red hair, right?"

Neil averted his eyes, but unfortunately couldn't close his ears. Well, not without looking childish.

"A pig slept under your mother's bed."

The squeal of laughter from one of Patrick's teammates sounded like a pig. If the opportunity came, Neil would shoot Patrick three times to knock him out of the match. Maybe that would earn him a little forgiveness from Riagan.

"Fall back once the match begins," Hardin said over their tradutors to make sure they were all on the right frequency, separate from the Chamaeleons.

Three successive horn blasts signaled the start of the match and the crowd roared in delight. Neil retreated behind the closest oak tree as ordered. Light beams, fired by Chamaeleon players, bounced off the trunk. Eris, Dirk, and Trini joined him behind other trees, all in defensive positions.

Across the midfield line, one Chamaeleon was already headed for the medical area, Hardin having shot the target on his chest. Medical was simply a sideline area where each player that had been shot had to get their target reset before resuming play.

Neil aimed at Bennett Stanton who was charging across the midfield line, headed left away from them. Bennett had an odd twist to his nose as if it had been previously broken. Neil's fingertips lit up, but the shot struck Bennett's left shoulder. Neil bit his lip in annoyance. Luckily, Eris' shot lit Bennett's chest target.

"That's one for me!" Eris gloated.

Bennett halted, shook his head in disgust, and headed for medical. His left arm hung limply at his side. It was a feature of the suit that the academy used for training purposes. To mimic real conditions, if you were shot anywhere, the suit around the spot locked up to simulate a wound. Bennett would only be able to unlock it by visiting medical. However, a player could only be shot in the chest or back target three times before they were out for the rest of the match.

With two Chamaeleon players headed for medical, and Patrick and the other offensive players charging into the forest, the middle of the field was clear.

"Offense to me," Hardin ordered.

Dirk and Trini, the fastest Ursa players, reached Hardin first and took the lead as advanced scouts. A former track runner, Dirk was tall and thin, but athletic. He was also always cracking jokes. Trini was short, quick, and feisty. In practice, she had often screamed like a banshee when charging a defender, flustering them so that they didn't get a good shot on her. She would then take them out in close range. She was a poor shot beyond ten feet, unlike Eris, who nearly matched Hardin.

Dirk and Trini scampered up the rocky outcropping in Chamaeleon territory, keeping a wary eye out for enemy defenders, while Hardin led Eris and Neil down a sinuous path through it. Every practice, Hardin had started them off running along all the paths through the rocks and over them, grouped in threes, to memorize the layout. He had insisted they know every nook. Then he had set ambushes to keep them guarded.

Their training kicked in. Neil immediately sought out potential hiding spots for traps. But the rocks angled upward quickly and fifteen yards in they were already well above his head.

Hardin reached a side path and rushed through while Neil checked the right path and Eris the left. Clear both ways.

On the other side, Hardin paused. "Dirk, Trini, have you crossed the side path?"

"I cross," Dirk replied over the tradutor.

After a five second pause, Trini whispered, "C4 above your line."

Hardin had assigned each Chamaeleon player an identifying number. C4 meant Nico. Besides being the school's sweets supplier, Nico was an excellent shot. If he discovered them, they'd present easy targets in this narrow confine; fish in a barrel.

"Can you take him out?"

Another five seconds passed. "Yes, but I'll need time."

"Negative. Head right on your own," Hardin ordered. "Engage only if forced."

"Understood."

"Dirk, layout?"

"Clear."

They retreated to the left side path and found purchase to climb the ten feet onto the rock ledge. At the top, Neil immediately started scanning for defenders. The crowd roared behind them, and Neil instinctively swiveled back.

"Twins under attack. Moving to assist," Jack Johnson said over the tradutors.

Pressure skimmed over the back of Neil's hand and he leapt backward, searching for a shooter. From practice, he recognized the pressure as someone's laser shot grazing his hand.

Hardin raced across the rocks and fired into a cleft. Neil chased after, embarrassed that he was nearly shot due to distraction. By the time he caught up, C7 had emerged with his chest target flashing. He scowled and headed for medical.

The ambush thwarted, Hardin glared at Neil. "Without discipline, success is beyond control."

"Yes, sir," Neil replied. He hadn't anticipated the distraction from the crowd, but refused to make excuses. He wouldn't get caught unaware again.

They caught up with Dirk at the cliffs surrounding the bowl that was the Chamaeleon base. Neil's excitement turned to disbelief and trepidation as he laid eyes on six serpent hawks strutting in the bowl. Around ten feet tall, the hawks resembled a giant, lean ostrich with a parrot's beak. But they possessed long, sharp talons on the ends of their feet and moved with measured steps as if hunting, every bit like predators. The serpent hawks guarded two lines of five bronze boxes in the bowl's center. The first line of boxes held bronze eggs the size of an apple. The goal of the game was to capture all five bronze eggs and return them to their base. The second line of boxes were for the eggs the Chamaeleons stole from Ursa.

"If the roosters wildly fight and strut, take note, you'll soon observe a change in the weather," Dirk said, grinning.

Neil frowned in confusion.

On the far side of the bowl Trini appeared and exchanged fire with C9, who guarded the base. A serpent hawk strutted in Trini's direction, shielding C9 from her. The hawk screamed in fury, spreading its wings wide, the charcoal comb on its head raised indignantly. What affect did their laser shots have on the serpent hawks? Neil doubted they would obediently head for medical if shot.

"Eris." Hardin gestured at C9, wanting her to take him out.

Eris ranged right, seeking a clear shot. She fired and hit C9's back target before giving them a thumbs up.

Behind her, Nico Colombo stepped into view.

Neil shouted a warning and fired at Nico. His shot barely missed. Eris dove, spinning as she fell and shot Nico in the chest. Nico's own shot struck her right leg. Eris tried to rise, but she was unable to bend her leg.

"My suit is locked around my leg," she said.

"Provide cover until we get an egg," Hardin ordered, "then head to medical."

Neil started to volunteer to back her up to medical, but her determined look caused him to keep quiet. She never tolerated appearing weak.

With C9 now gone, the bowl was empty. Trini raced in for the first egg. Neil's breath caught in his throat as she engaged the serpent hawks. She ran straight at one. A few feet before she reached it, she fired into its eyes. The hawk reared back, angry, but there was no apparent harm. Must be something about the lasers that affected the creatures even though it didn't hurt them, Neil reasoned. Trini took advantage of it and sped past.

Hardin studied the bronze boxes with his glasses. "Trini, the far right box is unlocked."

She dropped to the box, and pulled it open. She yanked out the first bronze egg. As she clambered to her feet, all six serpent hawks ringed her. Neil knew the bronze eggs were fakes, but the Serpent hawks seemed to think otherwise.

"Dirk, grab an egg," Hardin said. "C9 alerted his teammates after getting shot."

Another rule Hardin had taken great pains to instill in them. A flashing target equaled dead. They could not participate in the match or use radio communication before visiting medical. Any infraction resulted in the forfeiture of an egg. Each team could capture one egg at a time from the lone unlocked box. The other boxes were locked until the stolen egg made it to their home base, preventing one player from trying to carry all five back at once and ending the match. But if the other team cheated, a second box unlocked, allowing them to steal two eggs at once.

Dirk immediately climbed down into the bowl to get a second egg.

"Shoot the hawk blocking the center path," Hardin told Neil. "Aim for the head."

Neil took a deep breath to calm himself. Dirk and Trini depended on him. Focusing on the eyes of a hawk, Neil fired. It's beak jerked to the right and it screamed in rage. The shot wouldn't hurt the hawk, but did seem to infuriate it. Eris shot a second hawk, briefly immobilizing it as well and opening an escape route. A third hawk darted at Dirk, swiping with its talons, but Hardin shot it in the face to blind it. They kept shooting, trying to hold the serpent hawks back until Trini escaped the bowl. The hawks broke off pursuit at the bowl's edge, as if penned in by some invisible barrier. They turned all their focus to Dirk, but he managed to retrieve an egg before escaping down a second path from the bowl.

Neil and Hardin raced down the rocks to rendezvous with Trini and Dirk while Eris headed for medical. At midfield a couple of Chamaeleon defenseman emerged. Trini and Dirk shifted away from the defenders as Hardin and Neil moved to shield them. One of the defenders aimed past them and shot Trini in the back. Hardin took him out. The other defenseman, all alone, darted for cover.

"Neil, grab the egg," Hardin said, firing after the remaining defender.

Neil fell back. Trini had dropped her egg on the ground and was already racing to medical. He retrieved the egg and followed Dirk back through the forest. As they closed in on their own base, they found the giant armadillos.

Large as SUVs, the armadillos had cow-like heads and unexpectedly short snouts. A Chamaeleon player shot at one armadillo, which seemed pointless to Neil. The laser would bounce harmlessly off the thick carapace covering its body. But it still angered the armadillo, which swung a massive spiked tail that narrowly missed the player and splintered a tree trunk.

Neil skidded to a halt, suddenly revising his opinion of the armadillos as a defender. Despite assurances that their animal defenders wouldn't hurt them, an icy chill ran down his spine. But Dirk didn't hesitate as he charged past the armadillos and into their base. The armadillos paid him no mind. Neil took a deep breath and chased after Dirk. The armadillos let him pass unchallenged, and he let go of a breath he hadn't realized he had been holding.

Their base was hidden inside a large ring of tall holly bushes. Two wide pits surrounded the bushes all the way to the stadium walls, preventing anyone from sneaking into the base from behind. One path between the pits, front and center, allowed entrance into the base. Between the pits and the bushes was a ledge that held bundled piles of hefty oak branches. During practice, those ledges had been clear, allowing someone to attempt to circle around and enter the base from the side, but not now. The bundles of branches would be too difficult to climb over.

Neil ran down the center path and entered the base where Anand and Devika were standing guard over silver eggs in silver boxes. Neil noticed two other exits from the base back by the stadium walls on either side, but with the pits blocking access to them, he wasn't sure what good they would do.

"Those are awesome, no?" Anand pointed out at the armadillos.

Devika's eyes flashed excitedly. "Imagine one free on the quad."

Neil fervently hoped the twins didn't find a way to make that happen as he and Dirk put the bronze eggs in two empty bronze boxes.

During their second raid, Trini and Eris were both shot again, while a serpent hawk slashed open Hardin's left cheek, forcing him to medical for actual treatment. After an hour and a half, they'd captured four bronze eggs, and still held two of their silver ones. They had sustained heavy losses, though, with three defensemen and Trini sidelined, forcing Hardin to move Eris back into defense. By Neil's count, the Chamaeleons outnumbered them eight players to six. And if he was shot in the chest or back again, he was out.

Readying for a final charge, Hardin and Dirk headed up the rocks, while Neil headed for the far left path. The plan was for Hardin and Dirk to draw the defenders away, leaving the serpent hawks for Neil to get past.

Neil reached the bowl unchallenged as planned, but C9 remained, guarding the final egg with the help of the serpent hawks. Neil wouldn't get close without taking C9 out. He lined up a shot, but Dirk fired first from the cliff top. C9 scuttled for cover, returning fire as he ran, but Dirk's next shot took him out.

Seeing his chance, Neil rushed for the last bronze egg. Almost immediately, the serpent hawks turned on him, screaming their hatred. The more eggs that had disappeared, the more frenzied the serpent hawks had become at protecting them.

Two hawks leapt into his path. Neil fired into one's eyes. The bird barely flinched, then snapped at him. Neil dove left, narrowly avoiding it. He wasn't so lucky dodging the second bird. Claws scraped his neck below his right ear. Pain wrenched a gasp from his lips.

He rolled as he hit the ground and popped up a few feet away. Blood ran down his neck and stained his suit. The berserk hawks screamed and stomped around him, forcing him to dodge quickly.

With the hawks focused on him, Dirk had a clear path to the last egg. While Neil fired at the hawks to distract them, Dirk descended into the bowl and raced to retrieve the last egg. The moment he had it in hand, C7 rushed into the bowl and fired at Dirk. His first shot hit Dirk's left shoulder. On instinct, Dirk hurled the bronze egg at Neil before C7's next shot lit up his chest target, eliminating him.

The bronze egg landed a couple of feet from Neil. He ducked out of reach of a second gouging from a hawk, then lunged for the egg. *Please don't let the hawks get me*, he thought.

Grabbing the egg, he sprinted toward the closest path from the bowl. His back tingled as he braced for claws or shots from C7. He pushed himself to run harder and overextended himself. Losing his balance, he tumbled forward. He threw out his arms to break his fall, hit the ground and rolled over.

Panicked, he lunged to his feet, expecting the hawks to pile on him, but no attack came. Cries of rage from mere feet away echoed around the bowl, so that it seemed like he had thwarted an army of serpent hawks instead of six. He turned to find the hawks stomping at the bowl's edge, mere feet away. He had tumbled just beyond their reach.

A surge of exhilaration and relief washed through him. A light beam from C7 shot past Neil's head and he got going. He raced back along the path toward midfield. Over his tradutor, Eris and Devika shouted that they were under heavy attack. He had to get back fast. Where was Hardin?

Neil ran as hard as he could ever remember in his life, reaching midfield and passing through the forest unchallenged. Closing in on their home base, Neil found chaos. Six Chamaeleons were attempting to get past the armadillos and into the base. Two of the giant armadillos blocked the lone path through the pits. The armadillos furiously swung their tails at any Chamaeleon that got too close, and in the process they had splintered the trunks of several nearby trees, knocking one completely over.

Neil couldn't navigate through the Chamaeleon attackers and he wasn't sure he wanted to test the giant armadillos blocking the path at this point. They might mistake him for a Chamaeleon in all the pandemonium. He needed an alternate route.

He surveyed the base and pits, and an idea came to him. He hollered excitedly into his tradutor, "Eris, come out your left exit."

He would get one attempt. Jogging around to the far right side of the base, Neil charged for the pit, feeling a bit of nervous exhilaration. He reached the edge of the pit and leapt. The gap was too wide for him to clear, but he hit the far wall at chest level and scrambled to grab a hold of the branches on the ledge. The oak bundle budged a little, but held.

Neil grunted in relief.

The delighted crowd roared.

Eris raced out from the base to the ledge. She stepped onto a bundle of branches and reached to pull him up.

"No, the egg," he gasped.

By now the Chamaeleons had noticed and were shooting wildly at them. Eris returned fire, then grabbed the egg and raced back into the base.

Neil held on and was shot for his troubles. His suit locked and he dropped into the pit, landing on his back. He was out. The wind was knocked out of him. He gasped for a few seconds, desperate for air. Finally, air surged back into his lungs as the trumpet signaled match end.

They had won!

The crowd cheered wildly as Anand and Jack Johnson arrived to help him out of the pit. The game over, Neil's suit unlocked and he climbed to his feet. Jack brushed his dreds out of his eyes with a hand almost as dark as his hair, before reaching down with long, gangly arms, and with Anand's help, hoisted Neil out as the rest of the team arrived.

"That leap across the pit was space ace level," Trini said, face beaming. She must've run here from the sidelines the moment the game ended.

"That's the risk I like to see." Hardin clapped Neil on the back, before noticing the cut on Neil's neck. "You should get that checked out."

Now that his adrenaline was slowing, the cut started to throb. Neil gritted his teeth, hoping it wasn't as bad as it felt. Eris recounted different parts of the match as she'd seen it as they walked back to medical to get his cut checked out. They found Maellyn, Rois, Jaya, and Riagan waiting to congratulate them.

When Maellyn realized Neil was injured, she worriedly eyed his neck. "Is it bad?"

"Its fine," he said as a nurse came over and began cleaning the cut. "Doesn't hurt much." He lied about that last part.

"Sit." The nurse pushed him down onto a bench.

"I'll be great by tomorrow," Neil added, because Maellyn still looked concerned.

The nurse snorted.

Riagan played on his wrist-comp and ignored them. Behind him, the black smoke that was General Stribog talked with Chamaeleon players.

Neil pointed at the general. "Riagan, what do you get if you shoot off General Stribog's arms and legs?"

Riagan scowled and kept playing his game.

"It's just a flesh wound," Neil said, imitating a British accent for emphasis. "I'll bite your leg off."

The joke might as well have fallen on deaf ears. Riagan paid no heed to any of them and finally Rois huffed loudly. When he still didn't respond she punched him in the side. He merely glared and went back to his game. Nothing seemed to get through to him, and quite frankly, Neil was tired of trying.

The nurse rubbed a thick gel on Neil's neck and he inhaled sharply as his muscles tensed. The cold gel briefly increased the sting before it started to soothe. The nurse grabbed a syringe with a long needle.

"What's that for?" Neil eyed the needle uneasily.

"Nanoshot," the nurse said. "Injects nanobots to help stitch your wound. You won't feel them."

Neil tensed as she stuck the needle in his neck. The sharp pain from the needle wasn't bad, but he still hated it. Didn't everyone hate shots?

He also didn't know what to make of nanobots being injected into him. But Maellyn and Jaya accepted this as routine, so he didn't protest. Besides, he didn't feel as bad as a Chamaeleon player looked as he limped by, arm in a sling and the right side of his face purple with bruises.

"What happened to him?" Neil asked.

"You didn't see?" Jaya's eyes threatened to pop out of their sockets. "Giant armadillo caught him with its tail. Sent him flying into the bushes."

Neil's jaw dropped. "That's crazy!"

"Boys." Maellyn rolled her eyes at Rois. "He could've been seriously hurt and they are excited."

"Too bad it wasn't Neil," Riagan muttered.

Rois punched him again. A kick followed for good measure. This time Riagan scowled and stalked off.

Neil wondered if he had lost his best friend for good. Was there anything he could do to fix it? Did he even want to try? He supposed planning a revenge move against Patrick would help, but he refused to go that far. Rois had asked them all to let it go and Neil didn't want to jeopardize his place at the academy just to soothe Riagan. Was that wrong?

"The suits offer great protection," Jaya said to steer the conversation back to the Chamaeleon boy. "The armadillo spikes didn't pierce anything. The holly bushes caused most of the damage to that guy's face."

Neil grinned. "Bet the replay was sweet."

"You've no idea. I must've replayed it on my screen ten times."

"Despite our protests to stop," Rois said, grimacing.

The nurse placed a bandage on Neil's neck. "Time for visitors to head home."

They said their goodbyes and departed. Eris stayed with him since she was on the team, but that earned tight-lipped scrutiny from Maellyn. Neil couldn't guess why.

"Need anything?" Eris asked.

Neil shook his head. "I'm good. Thanks."

"Want me to scan you?" She gestured to his wrist-comp. They had to scan themselves before and after games, too. The academy really over did it on all the health scans.

"I can manage," he said.

"Are you sure? I'd happily scan you," she said, grinning mischievously.

Retrieving his wrist-comp, he scanned himself and sent it to the medical department. He felt only dull pain from the cut on his neck now. How quickly would the nanobots heal the wound in his neck? The thought of them moving around inside his neck made his skin crawl.

"There, done." He put the wrist-comp away.

"Great, now we can head over to Anand's room," Eris said. "The twins are throwing a team celebration for our first win."

Neil shook his head. "I promised Maellyn we'd grab a bite after the match."

"Oh. Well, if you change your mind." Eris left, a disappointed smile twisting her lips.

Neil was too excited about dinner with Maellyn to consider why.

Chapter 21

Neil's Thanksgiving with Maellyn

Neil stepped off the monorail into the residential neighborhoods, though little distinguished it from downtown. People lived in condominium skyscrapers. The lower floors included private balconies, and restaurants or convenience stores filled most ground floors. Large oak trees lined the moving walkways through the neighborhoods, their leaves gold and red, imbuing everything with a sense of fall. Strangely, no leaves littered the ground. Neil expected the chilly fall breeze to whisk leaves everywhere, but maybe they were artificial and served dual purposes like the internet grass.

He pressed through the crowd and stepped onto the moving sidewalks. Maellyn had told him not to worry about bringing anything, that her father always prepared too much food for Thanksgiving. But if Neil had ever dared bring a friend over to the house empty handed, his uncle would've complained incessantly about one more mouth to feed.

On his way, he had stopped by Colombo Caramella to restock on sea sours and pumpkin canes, and a small gift for Maellyn. Mr. Colombo had talked so much that Neil had despaired he might end up late for the meal. He wanted to avoid making a bad first impression with Dr. Trevena. Only Nico's reminder that they were running late for their own dinner plans had finally freed Neil.

Riagan and Rois had spent every holiday on their own in Ireland and decided to keep up that tradition here on Space City, but Neil suspected it was at Riagan's insistence. Neil had just shrugged when Rois told them. He was done trying to appease Riagan.

Jaya also had his own traditions with his dad, which included a trip to the race that afternoon. Neil was a little jealous that he'd miss it, but he couldn't say no to an actual Thanksgiving dinner invitation. Especially one from Maellyn.

The scent of fresh baked bread in the bakery on the bottom floor drew Neil into Maellyn's complex. He purchased one sourdough loaf and then pompe de noel bread because the baker insisted it was a necessity for any Thanksgiving meal. Neil's stomach grumbled as he carried the loaves to the elevator, but it probably wasn't kosher to bring partially eaten food to a party.

Exiting the elevator on the thirteenth floor, he shuffled nervously down the narrow hallway to 13C and knocked on the white door. To his relief, Maellyn answered. Flour dotted her left cheek and covered her hands, elbows, and harvest wheat-colored shirt.

"Just in time." She held the door wide for him to enter. "Dad's making a mess of the apple pie."

Unsure how to respond to that, he offered her the loaves. "I brought bread."

She grabbed the loaves, eyes devouring, and held them to her nose and inhaled. "I love pompe de noel."

Neil was grateful for the baker's suggestion.

"Also got some cherry blossoms from Nico for you." He handed the small red gift bag with the chocolates to her, too.

"Thanks." Her eyes twinkled before she turned on her heels.

Neil followed Maellyn through a short hallway past two small rooms and a bathroom, through a spotless living room, and into the disaster site that comprised their kitchen.

"Dad, Neil brought bread," Maellyn said. "We don't have to eat your burned cornbread after all."

Neil cringed at her words, hoping her father wouldn't be annoyed.

Dr. Trevena simply greeted him with a "Happy Thanksgiving" as he scooped up apple filling from the island countertop around an overfilled pie pan.

Spilled flour, sugar, cornmeal, and other baking ingredients covered the island. Dirty dishes filled the sink and overflowed onto the surrounding counters. Bits of food clung to cabinets and the fridge, as if someone had lost control while mixing batter.

"Happy Thanksgiving," Neil said, gaping at the wreckage.

"Cooking is a contact sport," Maellyn explained in amusement. She removed a plate from a cabinet and placed the loaves on it.

Dr. Trevena spread dough strips across the pie and tossed it into the oven. "The quality of the meal is directly proportional to your mess in the kitchen."

Bread plate in hand, Maellyn grabbed a tea pitcher from the fridge and ushered Neil to the feast on the table. Mashed potatoes, dressing, sweet potato pie, cranberry sauce, ham, green bean casserole, deviled eggs, winter squash, gravy, carrots, burnt cornbread, pumpkin pie, pecan pie, and a twenty-pound turkey. Enough food to feed a dozen people.

Maellyn found spots for the bread and tea while her father started cutting the turkey. He carved off a dozen or so slices, placing them on a serving plate.

"Thank you for inviting me," Neil said, overwhelmed by the feast. His recent Thanksgiving meals had consisted of fast food before football started on TV; he always slipped out no later than the third quarter when his uncle started drinking heavily.

Maellyn gestured for Neil to take a seat at the table. She took one herself and added green bean casserole, mashed and sweet potatoes, and dressing to her plate. She offered each dish to Neil in turn.

After carving off several slices of turkey, Dr. Trevena seated himself. "My daughter tells me you're new to Space City and don't have family here."

Neil scooped a helping of cranberry sauce onto his plate. "None back on Earth, either."

"Tell me about yourself." Dr. Trevena started to slice the loaves of bread.

"Last name is Ericson." Neil poured gravy over his mashed potatoes and turkey.

Dr. Trevena's eyes widened slightly, but he focused on slicing the bread.

"Heard the name before?" Neil asked, curious at his expression.

"I have. Your grandfather?" Dr. Trevena asked.

"Yes, sir," Neil said, surprised to have met a second person who had heard of his grandfather. Dr. Trevena must have military connections as well.

"Neil plays for Ursa," Maellyn told her father. "He won their first match with a daring move."

"Which animal guardians did they use?" Dr. Trevena asked.

"Serpent hawks and giant armadillos," Neil said, taking a bite of the sourdough bread, which was warm and fluffy.

Dr. Trevena nodded. "Good introductory defenders. Capable but not overly aggressive."

Neil choked on a bite, coughing twice. If the serpent hawks weren't overly aggressive, what animals did Dr. Trevena think were?

"What other creatures are used?" Neil asked, cutting a piece of turkey smothered in gravy and placing the bite in his mouth. The turkey was moist and hot. Neil chewed slowly to savor the taste.

"Seashell lizards, club tails, and other, more aggressive species," Maellyn said around a mouthful of squash. "Nothing too dangerous for academy teams. The professional teams are a whole different story. Double-horned rhinos and boardons are common there."

Seashell lizards didn't sound dangerous. Double-horned rhino, though…

"Why are animal defenders used in the games?" Neil asked. "We're learning to shoot and work in teams against an enemy, but why add in the guardians?"

"To prepare you for exploring new worlds," Dr. Trevena answered. "You're going to encounter such creatures that pose serious threats to yourself and your team. The academy is familiarizing students with the dangers they may eventually face, but in a controlled setting."

If the academy wanted to challenge them, though, why were meerphants the biggest danger they had faced in Introduction to New Worlds?

"What about the Dahaka?" Neil asked. "Shouldn't our training prepare us to defend against an attack? The Dahaka pose the greatest threat, don't they?"

"Dahaka soldiers are well beyond a first year's abilities." Dr. Trevena's countenance turned serious. "You'll train for years before encountering them. I've seen a ten-year veteran ripped to shreds in seconds by one."

"What if they obtain a CME? What if they attack?"

Dr. Trevena shook his head sadly, as if misunderstood. "The CME isn't intended for use as a weapon. Never was. Plus, there's little chance the Dahaka will acquire it. CMEs are hard to move, and there are many security measures to go through before one is transferred."

"So the threat of a Dahaka attack is low?"

Dr. Trevena paused, carefully considering his response. "Angra Mainyu is a clever leader. He uses subterfuge masterfully to convert enemies to allies, which is one reason we're wary of him."

Neil hadn't heard of Mainyu, but Dr. Trevena's words certainly didn't reassure him.

Dr. Trevena's face was grave. "Mainyu seized power from Commander Vairya after the failed Dahaka invasion of Sundara. He is significantly more dangerous. Commander Vairya was a brute conqueror. He used strength to lead the Dahaka. Mainyu is cunning. He served as Commander Vairya's advisor, and most people suspect his planning allowed Commander Vairya to attack Sundara without warning. Do you know the Dahaka hail from Siavash, a dinosaur planet?"

Neil nodded. "Learned that in class."

"In order to survive, the Dahaka developed a very hard mentality. Weakness means death. After the failed invasion, many Dahaka soldiers reasoned that Commander Vairya's weakness led to their failure. Seeing an opportunity for advancement, Mainyu invited Vairya and other Dahaka leaders to a feast. Once they were sluggish with food and drink, Mainyu ordered his private guard to enter and slaughter them all. Without rivals, he rose to power unchallenged."

For the next few minutes they picked at their food in silence. Neil regretted starting the conversation until the oven timer for the apple pie went off. Dr. Trevena brightened and rose from the table.

"My masterpiece." Dr. Trevena pulled on gloves, scooped the pie from the oven, and set it on the island to cool. "The crowning achievement."

"You'll love it," Maellyn said.

Just like that the mood turned cheerful again. Dr. Trevena and Maellyn made jokes as they finished eating. Afterward, Neil helped clear the table for dessert. While Maellyn poured mulled cider into mugs, Dr. Trevena cut three slices of the warm apple pie and served them.

The apples in the pie were soft and cinnamony and the crust light and flaky; Neil ate with gusto. After finishing the last bite, he pushed the plate away, unable to remember the last time he had eaten so much. Dr. Trevena groaned and excused himself to the couch for a nap while Neil helped Maellyn put away the leftovers.

"How are you feeling about midterms?" Maellyn asked as she dumped potatoes into a storage container.

"Not even close to ready. I've heard Instructor Tereshkova's exams are long and difficult with tons of animals to remember."

"I know what you mean. I've already set a study schedule with several girls in my dorm."

"Are we washing the dishes?" he asked, wearily observing the mess in the kitchen sink.

For answer, Maellyn marched over to the pantry and opened the door. Inside stood an amber, human-shaped robot dressed in a butler's uniform. Maellyn activated it.

"Good afternoon, Miss Trevena," the robot greeted formally, its voice deep and human-sounding, as it stepped out of the pantry and headed for the sink.

"Charlie will clean the kitchen," Maellyn said.

The robot started clearing out the sink, setting dishes on the surrounding countertop.

"You have a robot to clean your house?" Neil asked, wishing he had one to clean his dorm. He was impressed at the robot's efficiency as it quickly stacked the dishes to clear the sink. Could Charlie make beds and hang clothes?

"He can cook, too, but we prefer to do that ourselves," Maellyn said. "Come on. I'll show you my pet, Iris."

They passed into the living room where Dr. Trevena rested on the couch. A slate device on a stand in the corner showed a hologram of the race.

"Who's winning?" Neil asked.

"Diantha and Petra at the moment," Dr. Trevena said.

Numerous 3D photographs of Maellyn, her father, and presumably her mother hung on the walls. Where was her mom? Maellyn never spoke about her. Rather than ask about her, Neil focused back on the hologram of the race, which looked so life-like.

"The technology and wealth I've seen since coming to Space City is incredible," Neil said as Dr. Trevena rewound and zoomed in on a barbed wire Oliver Dunn fired at Diantha's ATV, just missing her left rear tire.

"We have many more resources from other planets and asteroids than what is found on Earth," Dr. Trevena said. "With an entire universe filled with resources, we have more than we'll ever need and we also maximize our use of everything."

"I know. Dual purposes for everything," Neil said.

Dr. Trevena nodded. "That's part of it, but we maintain a technology sharing system. Companies can provide basic details on their latest breakthroughs for others to review. Often those ideas lead to spinoff technologies, which reduce costs and can lead to whole new avenues for making money."

"Don't they worry about competitors stealing?"

"Companies release basic details on the tech sharing system. If another company has an idea for the tech, the two arrange a mutually beneficial agreement. The idea came from NASA, which develops complex technologies for use in space, then provides that research to independent U.S. companies to create spinoff technologies. The United States has benefited a great deal from the technologies created by NASA."

Maellyn grabbed Neil's arm, pulling him back toward the hall. "I'm taking Neil back to visit Iris."

"Ok, Lyn," her father said, turning back to the race. "Leave the door open."

Back in her room, Maellyn opened her closet, which was filled with a cage. A small, flying reptile rested on the branch of a fake tree inside the cage. The creature chirped and spread leathery bronze wings, which spanned two feet in length from tip to tip. A baby, no larger than Neil's forefinger, slept in a nest on the floor.

"This is Iris." Maellyn opened the cage. She stuck her hand inside and the mother hopped onto her arm and croaked happily. "She's five years old."

Neil gazed in wonder at the little dinosaur. A real one, not a replica. "This is amazing." He wanted to touch the creature, but hesitated.

Maellyn raised her arm. The little mother leapt into the air and flew around the room before darting out into the hall. "She loves to wing about the place. Sometimes I'll take her to the garden by the spaceport and let her exercise, give her more space."

"Who is the baby?" he asked, eyeing the sleeping creature.

"Haven't named him. He's about eight weeks old. I've given away his siblings, but am still looking for a home for this little guy."

"What do you feed them? Do you train them?"

She carefully picked up the little guy. "Iris eats insects and fruits. Sometimes our houseplants if I don't have time to pick up more food. She doesn't require a lot and keeps some for the little guy."

The baby fit easily in the center of Maellyn's palm. He looked so fragile. "I taught Iris a few tricks. She can fetch some light things for me. Do you want him?"

Neil did. He'd love to. He'd never had a pet. "Can I keep him on campus?"

"No. You'd have to leave him here for now, but it would give me an excuse to keep him."

He was crestfallen, but not really surprised.

The little dinosaur woke up, noticed his mother had gone, and started to cry. Maellyn placed him in Neil's hand, much to his pleasure, and moved to retrieve a small bag from her dresser.

Neil cupped his hands together protectively. The baby had smooth, snake-like skin. "What species are they?"

"Teinyosaurus," Maellyn replied. "They come from the Dahaka homeworld, Siavash."

"Really?" Neil asked in surprise.

The little dinosaur studied him. It croaked plaintively.

"Missing his mother?" Neil asked.

"Probably hungry. Usually is when he wakes."

Iris returned and landed on Maellyn's arm. The little mother eyed Neil warily as she nibbled at Maellyn's white lotus flower earrings. Maellyn brushed her away, then pulled dried fruit from the bag and offered them to Iris, who took them in her mouth, but didn't swallow.

"Put him on the bed," Maellyn directed.

Neil set the baby down and Iris hopped from Maellyn's arm to the bed. She moved over and dropped the bits of fruit in front of the baby, who ate greedily.

"Any ideas for names?" Maellyn asked.

"Petey," Neil answered, thinking about his favorite childhood dinosaur movie.

"What do you think Iris?" Maellyn asked, scrubbing the back of Iris' head. "Is Petey a good name for your baby?"

Iris focused her full attention on feeding Petey, though. Once he'd eaten, she set about cleaning him.

"I'm glad you invited me," Neil said as Maellyn put Iris and Petey back in their cage. "And thanks for Petey! Too bad I can't keep him in the dorms."

"I'm glad you came," Maellyn said shyly. "I like hanging out with you."

"It's nice just the two of us." He was nervous now that Iris and Petey weren't the focus.

Maellyn waited patiently for something else, but what?

"Your home is nice," he said.

She sat on the edge of her bed. He searched for a place to sit, but not finding a chair, he cautiously sat next to her, thrilled to be so close, yet unsure what to do. Maybe he should suggest they watch the race, though he wasn't all that interested anymore.

"Jaya asked Rois to be his girlfriend," she said.

"They like each other a lot."

"I'd ship them," she said.

He felt the urge to touch her cheek.

"Rois says Jaya's a great kisser." She blushed at that statement.

He felt a stab of jealousy, not from a desire to kiss Rois, but because he hadn't dared try with Maellyn. Jaya was lucky.

Maellyn brushed back her hair. She met his eyes, saying nothing. Just waiting. She liked him. At least he thought she did. When they rode the walkways to the street fair, she often slipped an arm around his, huddling close. He loved that contact. Loved the peach shampoo that scented her hair.

She tilted her head slightly upward, still saying nothing, just waiting. He wanted to kiss her, yet doubt warred with his desire. What if he misjudged her feelings? He didn't want to ruin their time.

She smiled, eyes asking a question he didn't recognize. He felt the urge to reach for his grandfather's coin, but that would only force his hand. And the explanation would sound foolish.

She closed her eyes, her chin rising a little higher.

That had to be a sign, right? Slowly, he leaned forward.

"Maellyn!" her father called.

Her eyes shot open and they both jumped up from the bed, quickly turning toward the door.

"About ready to go for our walk?" Dr. Trevena asked from the living room.

Neil felt his cheeks burning. He was relieved that Dr. Trevena hadn't seen them. Dr. Trevena wouldn't likely be enthused if he found Neil trying to kiss his daughter.

Maellyn blushed as well and moved over to the clock on her nightstand, so that her back was to him. "We take a walk every Thanksgiving after the meal. It's tradition. Maybe you could come with us?"

She turned back to him, her expression a little nervous.

"I wouldn't want to intrude." He wanted to spend more time with her, but he felt awkward now.

"I'm sure he'll be fine with you coming," she said, taking his hand in hers. "You'll love it."

Chapter 22

Riagan Solves the Midterm

The sun hung low on the western horizon. The resulting twilight on the planet was darker than Riagan expected. Must be some weird aspect of the sim.

Thin, four-foot-tall, asparagus-like black plants topped with black buds dotted the desert landscape. The black plants grew in clusters of five or six and bowed slightly from the wind. A shallow river, ten or fifteen feet wide, snaked toward the sun. A soft insect hum filling his ears, Riagan searched the landscape for predators, but came up empty. He had run a search of the planet, Hawking-30c, on his wrist-comp, only to find that all research was presently restricted. They had to go in blind, as if they were the planet's first explorers.

He didn't like it.

"For your midterm exam, you'll split into two groups, each with your own tasks to complete," Instructor Nez said. "Team assignments and the first task are loaded on your wrist-comps."

Riagan activated his wrist-comp and searched for the Introduction to New Worlds midterm exam folder.

"Each of you grab a pack." Nez gestured to backpacks lined up next to Instructor Fintan. "You'll find a 3D printer, along with containers holding the supplies you'll need to complete your tasks."

The 3D printers were eight-inch obsidian rods about as wide as two fingers, which connected wirelessly with the wrist-comps. The printers were introduced in class after Thanksgiving, and they'd had only two weeks to practice with them.

Riagan, Neil, Rois, Maellyn, Eris, Nico, Anand, and Devika comprised team #2. Jiro and Jaya were teamed with Patrick, Caleb, Christel Manikas, Aileen McKensie, and Adrien Laroque.

Classes had been tense since Adrien had returned from suspension, but the instructors had all kept close eyes on them, preventing encounters between Riagan and Patrick and Adrien, except for occasional verbal barbs. Even then, the instructors had stepped in before things escalated. Worse, Neil had remained silent every time. He just didn't get what it meant to stick up for family. But how could he? He was an only child.

"Hawking-30c doesn't rotate as Earth does," Nez said, gesturing toward the planet's sun. "It's tidally locked. The west side endures perpetual daylight and average temperatures are around sixty-four degrees Celsius."

Several students whistled.

"What temperature is that?" Riagan whispered to Rois.

"A hundred forty-seven degrees Fahrenheit."

"Wow." Now Riagan knew why they had helmets with face shields that could be lowered to seal into their suits. Small oxygen tanks attached to the backs of their suits right above their packs. But for now they kept the face shields up.

"The east side experiences constant night," Nez continued. "Temperatures routinely fall to minus forty-seven degrees Celsius."

Several students muttered their displeasure with taking an exam on a planet with such temperature extremes.

They're all soft, Riagan thought. How many nights had he and Rois slept outdoors during a cold winter's night after running away from a bad foster home with nothing more than a blanket to warm them? Here they had suits that regulated body temperature. *And* this was only a sim.

"Team one, I'll take you to your starting point." Nez gestured with his hands for team one to follow him. "Team two will accompany Instructor Fintan."

Nez used the sim controller to transport team one somewhere completely out of view. How far away had he taken them? Or had they been taken to an alternate version of this sim?

Fintan led them to the river's edge. "Your first task is listed on your wrist-comp. Upon completion, you'll receive instructions for next task. Nez and I monitor progress remotely. Safe luck." He then disappeared from the sim.

Almost immediately, a strong wind picked up, whistling around them. Riagan clicked on the task list file. Inside, he found: *Task 1 – Retrieve the cylinder from the water trap.*

"Anyone spot a trap?" Nico asked, peering out over the shallow river.

Despite using tradutors for comm, it was still hard to hear over the wind.

"Spread out," Riagan said. Without the instructors, they needed a team captain. Might as well be him.

Algae grew along the river's edge, but not densely enough to conceal a cylinder. Riagan waded a few steps into the river, nearly losing his balance from the wind whipping around them. Shadows rippled along the bed, an illusion from the flowing water. It was cold, chilling his feet for a few seconds until the boots adjusted temperature. Rocks, all smaller than his fist, lined the riverbed. They seemed unlikely to cover the cylinder, so Riagan pushed upriver into the darkness while also wading in deeper. The center of the river rose just above his calves.

A few feet away he spotted a gleaming round object, about the size of a baseball. He moved closer to examine it, but it darted away in crab-like fashion. So there was more life on this planet than just insects, which meant predators were likely.

After searching for ten minutes, Nico shouted over the tradutor. "I've found something. Down river."

Anand and Devika stalked along the shore further upstream, poking at something along the river's edge. Neither gave any indication that they had found anything important, so Riagan hurried ashore to join Rois and they headed toward Nico.

"Right, what do ya think he's after finding?" Rois asked.

Riagan shook his head.

As they moved downriver toward the sun, the wind kicked up dust clouds, counterbalancing the increased sunlight. They found Nico huddled up with Neil, Maellyn, and Eris halfway into the river around a black hole. Dark creatures swam around inside it.

"What are they?" Maellyn asked, revulsion on her face.

Riagan held his wrist-comp over the hole, activating the flashlight to illuminate the creatures. Black snakes, maybe? He scanned them with his wrist-comp.

Oil eels popped up on-screen. The name came from a toxin they excreted, which paralyzed their prey. The eels fed primarily on fish. Individually, they presented little danger, but could be deadly in a group. Riagan estimated at least six in the hole.

He sent the file to everyone's wrist-comps, though for a moment he considered not including Neil. Then he waded back to shore where the twins had finally caught up.

"Says here they're repelled by rank weed." Eris showed them a picture of the plant on her wrist-comp, the same ones Riagan had noticed earlier.

Nico scrunched his nose. "Rank weed repels me, too."

"You avoid your mother?" Anand asked in feigned shock.

Riagan stifled a grin, but Nico's mouth tightened, as if the suggestion really did bother him.

Neil approached a patch of the black plants, broke off a stem and sniffed the black bud. "Doesn't stink. Are you sure this is it?"

The others joined him.

Riagan compared it with the picture on his wrist-comp. "That's obviously it. Ya blind?"

Neil scowled, but said nothing.

They each broke off a stem and returned to the river. Anand tossed his into the water first. Almost instantly, a sulfurous stench filled the air.

"Ugh," Devika groaned as everyone covered their noses.

Riagan gasped for breath. The smell was nearly bad enough to rival the Malsain. He would've expected a plant that stunk like that to grow on their home planet, Gleeson. Too bad he couldn't take some of the weed with him from the sim. It might earn him some bonus points with Instructor Tanith. He could use all the help he could get in history.

"Stinks like Nico's mom, right?" Anand said through his hand.

Nico grumbled under his breath, but Devika dipped the black bud of her weed in the water. She turned and rubbed it all over Anand's face.

"Gross!" Anand shoved the bud away and retreated.

Devika followed, waving the bud at him.

"Why do I put up with you?" Anand complained.

"Cause you're stuck with me, right?" Devika replied, swatting him once more with the bud, before tossing it away.

Riagan fingered his own stem and wondered how close they needed to be in order for the weed to drive off the oil eels. Would he have to worry about the residual toxin from the fleeing eels?

"Riagan and I can get rid of the eels," Neil offered.

Riagan bristled. He'd prefer to go by himself, but Neil was already wading out toward the hole. Riagan hurried after him, grinding his teeth as he followed. Who did Neil think he was?

"Let's drop both our stems in the same spot to amplify the effect." Neil held his stem over the hole.

He was clearly attempting to usurp the position as lead for the exam.

Riagan knew he needed to respond. But how? He hit upon an idea. He took a couple of steps upstream. "We need to drop them before the hole. If ya drop them on the hole, the stream will carry the buds away before the stench can disturb the eels much."

"Good idea." Neil joined him. "On three. One."

Riagan gripped his stem tightly. Neil thought he could just assume leadership. He had repeatedly tried to do the same after they had discovered the traitor. He had tried to force Riagan's help.

"Two."

Neil was arrogant. Riagan considered not dropping his stem and hoping Neil failed on his own, but that wouldn't help his cause.

"Three."

They dropped their stems on the river. The overwhelming stench immediately filled the air.

This time even covering their mouths and noses did little to help block the stench. The two moved closer to the hole to check if it was working. The eels thrashed about as the stems floated past. Riagan wondered if the stink was worse to the eels. After all, farts stunk worse in the shower. Regardless, the oil eels didn't flee. He searched for the cylinder, but couldn't make out anything through the flailing black mass. Maybe while the eels were disturbed he could try to snatch it?

But his inability to spot the cylinder to verify that it was actually there, combined with the danger of the paralyzing eel toxin, held him back. The smell dissipated after ten seconds or so and the eels calmed.

Part of Riagan cheered that this attempt had failed. Now he had the chance to devise his own solution. But what else could they do to get rid of the eels?

"What happened?" Rois asked from shore.

"Nothing," Riagan shouted back. They needed something bigger than the stems to lower into the hole to at least confirm the cylinder's presence.

Rois consulted with the others, then answered, "C'mere. Maellyn has an idea."

Pushing to shore, Riagan found Maellyn drawing a pair of long metal tongs on her wrist-comp.

"That could help," Riagan said. "Or a pair of long-handled pliers."

Nico fished out his 3D printer from his pack. Rois had pulled out a container of liquid CO2, along with a few other materials. She had quickly mastered the ratio of different materials for printing various objects. Whatever she printed was routinely stronger and more durable than what anyone else in class created.

Rois poured the CO2 mixture into the printer materials slot and spread a printer cloth out on the ground. Instructor Nez had informed them that Space City had equipment that captured CO2 given off by people breathing and from other sources. The CO2 was used in the 3D printers to create plastic parts. Sometimes it seemed that those onboard Space City had thought of everything.

Maellyn typed a command in her wrist-comp and the printer rose into the air, hovering about a foot off the ground. A white laser from the printer moved back and forth over the cloth, building the tongs layer by layer using the CO2. After a few minutes, they had a newly printed pair.

The moment the printer laser stopped, Riagan snatched the tongs, intent on being the one to try for the cylinder.

Maellyn held her rank weed stem out to him. "You should be able to hold several stems with these and stuff them into the hole. Neil, maybe you should go with him so that if it works, you can quickly grab the cylinder."

So *that* was their intention for the tongs. Riagan had to admit that if it drove off the oil eels, it would be the easiest way to find the cylinder. He wanted to be the one to actually retrieve it, though.

"Why do I get all the dirty work?" Neil asked.

"Rois and I made the tool." Maellyn's tone indicated they'd done their part.

Riagan offered the tongs to Neil. "Want to trade?"

Neil accepted, much to Riagan's satisfaction. Now *he* would get the cylinder.

"I'll help," Nico offered, taking the stems from Maellyn and Rois.

Anand snorted with laughter. "He's used to his mom's stench only."

Devika put hands on her hips and stared at Anand. "That's getting old, no?"

"It's ok," Nico said flatly. "Apparently he never learned not to bite the hand that feeds him. A candy shortage may be in his future."

"See," Devika said, smacking Anand's arm.

"I'm joking only," Anand said, a pained expression on his face as he pulled away from Devika. "I'm sure his mom's a great lady."

Riagan retrieved Maellyn and Rois' rank weeds and traipsed back out to the hole with Neil and Nico.

Neil held open the tongs. "Give me the bunch."

Riagan handed his pair to Nico who offered the combined bundle to Neil.

"Ready?" Neil clutched the rank weed with the tongs just above the water.

Riagan took a deep breath and held it. Nico just nodded.

Neil plunged the tongs into the hole. Once again the eels thrashed about, but this time after a couple of seconds they retreated into underwater tunnels, exposing a slender silver cylinder. Unsure exactly how far the eels had fled, Riagan snatched the cylinder. He thrust it overhead triumphantly a moment, before they fled the river to escape the vile odor and the possible return of the eels.

Back on shore, Riagan examined the cylinder. There was a seam in the middle. He gave it a twist and the cylinder split apart, revealing a thumb drive. He plugged the drive into his wrist-comp and their second objective popped up on the exam list.

A timer next to the task began ticking down from one hour. A map showed a path running south across the river.

Riagan grinned. Playing soccer was one thing he and Rois had both enjoyed when they had a chance to play. Even when they hadn't been able to play on teams through school, they had played together on their own. Seven miles was easy.

Riagan showed the instruction and timer to the others. "We better get running."

Anand groaned.

Without time to waste, Riagan crossed the river and set off at a jog, Rois at his side. Neil, Nico, and Maellyn all kept pace, but Anand and Devika quickly fell behind. Riagan suspected Devika simply kept pace with her brother so as not to embarrass him.

Low-lying hills created numerous nooks and crevices from which yellow eyes studied them. Riagan never caught more than the eyes, though, leaving him unsettled. Were those predators he needed to guard against or could he dismiss them?

Making matters worse, the clouds moving in were storm clouds. Already, lightning lit the air in the distance, still a good distance away.

When they reached the halfway point, they had to cross two consecutive rivers, the second forcing them to wade through water nearly up to their waists, slowing them down considerably. Riagan gritted his teeth, his legs tiring from the strain of pushing through the water.

"Thirty-two minutes left," Maellyn announced as they emerged on the far shore.

Riagan smiled wide. Plenty of time. Now that they were running on land again, he got his second wind. He felt good. If they didn't have to cross too many more rivers, they would reach the end well before the time ran out. At least some of them would. Hopefully they weren't all needed at the finish line.

"I don't like that we're being watched." Rois pointed out a pair of eyes.

"We've got weapons if they threaten," Neil said to soothe her.

An attack from the creatures wouldn't actually cause physical harm. The creatures were nothing more than sims after all. But if they failed to ward off an attack, they would fail the exam. Riagan had learned that this particular midterm weighed heavily in the determination of team captains for the final exam. Failing would eliminate him from consideration. Losing teammates might hurt his chances as well.

He decided to preemptively strike. He fired at the next pair of eyes that peeked out from the shadows. He wasn't a great shot on the run, scoring the ground short of the eyes. But it worked as intended. The eyes instantly winked out. A few others disappeared as well.

"Up ahead." Nico's face lighted up and he pointed toward two square stone altars about a mile ahead.

Riagan pushed himself, quickly covering the last mile. One of the two stone altars had an opening in the top. Out of that opening protruded a plastic stem holding another silver cylinder. The stem was lowering down into the hole. He reached the altar and grasped the cylinder before the stem had completely sunk into the altar. The second altar held nothing.

Rois, Neil, and Maellyn crowded around Riagan as he examined the second cylinder. Eris and Nico joined them a few seconds later as Riagan tried to twist it open, but it was locked. A series of small keys with strange symbols marked the side of the cylinder.

"Is that a lock of some sort?" Maellyn asked, echoing Riagan's thoughts.

He shrugged and handed her the cylinder. She examined it, Neil looking over her shoulder, but didn't touch any of the keys.

"Hold on." Rois bent down in front of the altar. She ran her fingers over several indentations in the stone.

Riagan realized the indentations matched the symbols on the cylinder, but in a different order.

"It's the password," Riagan said.

Maellyn checked the symbols on the altar and started to press the corresponding ones on the cylinder. After entering the password, she tried to open the cylinder. It wouldn't budge.

"Still locked," she said.

The twins finally caught up, Anand wheezing from the run. "Seven miles isn't good for my health," he complained.

"Let me try," Riagan said.

Maellyn handed him the cylinder and he carefully entered the code a second time, tried to open it, but it remained secure. He frowned.

"Maybe it's backward," Nico suggested.

Riagan tried the code in reverse with similar results.

"I think I've got it." Rois remained bent down examining the altar. She raised a hand toward Riagan and he gave her the cylinder. She typed in a shorter code, twisted, and the cylinder opened, revealing a thumb drive.

"Fantastic, sis," Riagan congratulated, clapping her on the shoulder as she stood. "How did ya figure it out?"

"Every other symbol has a faint diagonal line through it," she replied. "I only entered the unmarked symbols."

Riagan bent down before the altar to get a closer look, and sure enough, the even numbered symbols had a thin line chiseled through them.

Rois handed the thumb drive to Nico, who already had his wrist-comp in hand. He plugged the drive in.

"It's a weather app," he said.

What does a weather app have to do with the exam? Riagan wondered. They could already see the storm building.

"Anything on that second altar?" Eris asked.

Riagan shook his head.

The altars were identical, so it stood to reason they both had held something. Had this been an intersecting point for the two teams? If so, that meant Patrick's team had already been here and was in the lead. The instructors hadn't indicated that the two teams were competing. Yet Riagan recognized that if he wanted to become a team captain, everything became a competition. And Patrick had his group out front.

Successive lightning bolts split the sky. Riagan jumped. Eris inched closer to Neil, a decidedly uneasy expression on her face.

"I don't see a new task." Neil reviewed his wrist-comp. "Have we missed something?"

"We didn't find anything else," Rois said. "The timer hadn't expired, but maybe we were still late?"

Riagan didn't think so. Both teams were pursuing the same final task, he was sure of it. Knowing Patrick, he had probably swiped both teams' clues to keep them from completing their final objective. If that was true, though, why hadn't Patrick taken the second cylinder? Maybe he had been prevented from doing so?

The weather app finished downloading, and Nico activated it. On the screen was a massive storm system, much bigger than they'd realized, approaching from the west. The app indicated dangerously strong winds in addition to heavy lightning. This wide-open location wouldn't remain safe for much longer.

"Final task or not, we need to move," Riagan said.

"More running?" Anand asked, hands on knees as he gasped for air.

"Which way?" Neil asked.

"East," Riagan replied. "We came down from the north. I think the other team came up from the south, and we can't travel into the storm."

East was deeper into the cold and darkness. Something moved a couple of miles ahead, among foothills. Patrick and his team? The instructors hadn't said how wide the center band was where the temperatures remained reasonable, but not every planet would have pleasant weather.

"We have no tasks sending us east!" Eris protested.

Before Riagan could respond, a bolt of lightning struck the ground, blinding them. Everyone hunched down like frightened animals. The corresponding thunder hurt Riagan's ears so much that he clapped his hands over his ears. Everyone else did the same, Nico dropping his wrist-comp on the ground.

The thunder quieted and Riagan retrieved Nico's wrist-comp, flashing it at the team. The radar on the screen showed numerous lightning strikes in red. "We can't stay here. There's no shelter. I say we go east."

He was sure that's where they needed to go and that they were already behind. He didn't like losing period. Losing to Patrick would be unbearable.

"I'm with Riagan," Neil said. He stared hard into the darkness as if he had also seen Patrick's group and come to the same conclusion.

Once Neil agreed, everyone else relented. Riagan wasn't sure if that was due to his logic or because Neil concurred. Either way, Riagan had what he wanted.

The temperature dropped rapidly as they headed east, about ten degrees in half an hour. After a couple of hours of hiking through lifeless, low-lying hills, the temperature had dropped from seventy-five degrees to thirty-two.

From time to time Riagan observed movement ahead, but in the darkness he could never determine exactly who or what. They no longer saw golden eyes watching them, so Riagan felt confident they pursued Patrick's team.

The lightning storm followed at their heels. They started passing patches of black ice and before long the temperature dropped close to zero, forcing them to lower their face shields and activate the oxygen tanks. The suits maintained a comfortable body temperature, even when it dropped to minus ten out, but Riagan wondered what their limits were.

"What is that?" Neil sprinted forward.

Riagan thought he spotted a faint light from the ground ahead. A single ray like a grounded spotlight.

Everyone charged after Neil. He reached it—a metal hatch in the ground. He tried to open the door, but it wouldn't budge.

"Let me try." Riagan pushed Neil aside. He knelt and threw his weight into lifting the hatch but it was stuck tight. Neil scooted beside him and they heaved to no avail.

Riagan pounded a fist on the hatch. "They locked us out." He should've known Patrick would cheat, barring their way so he could finish the last task without competition.

Nico stepped behind the hatch, examining its sides. "I might be able to get us in."

"How?" Riagan asked, anxious for any solution to get inside.

Nico worked on his wrist-comp. "There's a keypad here. Will you give me the weather app thumb drive?"

Riagan retrieved it from his pack and handed it over. Nico connected the drive to his wrist-comp and rapidly typed away.

"Are ya searching for the lock code?" Rois shivered. They would all appreciate getting inside.

Nico didn't answer. He finished typing, removed the drive and dropped to one knee. He pulled out a short screwdriver from his pack, removed the keypad cover, attached the thumb drive, and resumed typing. "This might not work, but it's a shot."

If Nico got the hatch open, they might still have time to beat Patrick. And with the instructors absent, Riagan thought he might have an opportunity to teach Patrick a lesson, too.

A couple seconds later the hatch clicked and Nico yelled triumphantly. The hatch door was heavy and Neil and Riagan strained to lift it, but they finally hauled the lid open. A ladder extended down to a bunker below.

Riagan scrambled onto the ladder and started down.

"Right behind you," Neil said.

From the depths of the bunker, out of sight, came the familiar voices of the other team.

"Someone's coming," Christel Manikas said from below.

"Positions," Patrick ordered.

Positions? Had they almost completed the task?

Riagan hopped off the ladder, desperate to get to Patrick before he completed the final task. A doorway, perpendicular to the ladder, led into the bunker. Neil was nearly down, but Riagan was not waiting. They might already be too late. He ran straight into the bunker and barely had time to notice Caleb and Adrien aiming for him before they shot his chest target, which started flashing.

"What is this?" Riagan demanded.

Patrick stood behind them, grinning malevolently.

Before Riagan could call out a warning, Neil darted into the bunker, shooting straight at Patrick. One shot struck Patrick's left shoulder, a second his arm. Caleb and Adrien shot Neil.

Riagan felt a moment's satisfaction—Neil had had his back, even if he had failed to take Patrick out—before outrage at getting shot took over.

"Ya dirty cheater." Riagan clenched his fists and started toward Patrick.

Jiro Takeda hurried from behind Patrick and held out both hands for Riagan to stop. "This won't help. I know it isn't fair, but the instructors are watching."

Riagan paused, but glared past Jiro at Patrick. He was tired of Patrick getting away with his crimes.

"If it helps, I'll assist your team with the final task," Jiro offered. He was a standup guy and a good Academy Games player.

Riagan shook his head. If Jiro switched sides, Patrick would take him out, too. Still, it felt nice that Jiro had offered.

Anand and Devika stuck their heads in the room. Caleb and Adrien fired at them, forcing the twins to duck back out of sight.

"None of you can come in," Patrick said. When Riagan glared at him, Patrick shrugged. "Just ensuring we win. With you guys out, I only need to figure out how to get the final cylinder."

Since he couldn't attack Patrick, Riagan punched the wall to release his anger. The pain that shot through his hand made his eyes water.

Neil, a little calmer, marched past Caleb and Adrien. "What have you got?"

"I won't let you have it." Patrick moved to block him.

Neil pointed at the still flashing target on his chest, brow furrowed in anger. "You already made sure we wouldn't win. Won't hurt you if we look."

Patrick eyed him a moment, before stepping aside. Riagan followed, staring down Patrick as he passed. Patrick returned his glare, unfazed. It took every ounce of restraint that Riagan had to walk past him without lashing out.

Jiro led them back to where Caleb Thornton and Christel Manikas studied a pair of roughly fifty-gallon fish tanks. One tank hung on the wall above the second. Inside the top fish tank was a third silver cylinder, identical to the two they had obtained already.

"What happened to Jaya and Aileen?" Neil asked.

Surprised at the question, Riagan checked the room. He hadn't realized the two were missing.

"Jaya was attacked by saber-toothed panthers," Jiro said as he glared at Patrick, who shrugged disinterestedly. "Patrick somehow missed a clear shot on the panther from ten feet. Some team captain. Instructor Nez took Jaya away. Said we had to finish without him."

"What about Aileen?" Riagan asked.

"Oil eels."

"Toxin?"

"Yeah. Her whole body seized up. We dragged her to shore. Instructor Nez took her, too." Jiro was clearly frustrated that they'd lost two members of their team.

Riagan felt buoyed that their team had all made it here, but his enthusiasm was dampened when he remembered he and Neil had been taken out by Patrick.

Neil pointed at the tank. "What's the problem?"

Caleb held up a metal bar. He swung and hit the tank. Riagan jumped backward, expecting the glass to shatter and the water to rush out at them. But the bar rebounded off the glass with a dull thud.

"Unbreakable glass," Caleb said.

Christel tapped the bottom tank. "We think we need to empty the top tank into the bottom, but haven't figured out how."

Riagan studied the aquariums. There were three scant holes in the bottom bracket holding the top tank, but otherwise there were no obvious means of opening it. "Can I bring in my team or will ye shoot them, too?"

"Only you," Patrick said. "They can still beat us, so I'm blocking them out."

Riagan grimaced and took a picture of the tank.

"Hey, what're you doing?" Patrick reached for Riagan's wrist-comp.

Riagan pushed him back. "Don't touch me!"

Patrick gritted his teeth and raised his arm to shoot, but noticed the flashing target on Riagan's suit.

"That's right. Already shot me."

Riagan pushed past Patrick and returned with Neil to the entryway where the rest waited. Eris, Anand, and Devika had taken aim, but they relaxed.

"What do they have?" Maellyn asked, stepping forward.

Riagan showed them his wrist-comp. "Fish tank with the cylinder. Unbreakable glass. Three holes here in the side." He sent the picture to their devices, so they could all examine it.

"If you and Neil have been shot, isn't this cheating for you to take a pic to show us?" Rois asked. "Does this disqualify us?"

Riagan grimaced, not having considered that. Either way it was too late, he'd already shared the pic. "I don't know. Guess we'll find out."

They studied the pic in silence for a few minutes. Riagan wracked his brain, trying to think of what might be used to unlock the top tank.

"How about a trident?" Rois suggested.

Riagan stared at the picture, puzzled by that leap. "What's a trident have to do with this?"

"Ya tattoo," Rois said. "Maybe the instructor's remembered it when they devised this task. Stick the trident in the three holes."

"Isn't Aileen's father an oceanographer?" Eris asked.

"She got knocked out earlier," Riagan answered, but he got the connection. The holes appeared to be properly spaced apart for a normal trident.

"It's worth a shot," Rois said. "We can print one."

"Already working on the design." Maellyn drew on her wrist-comp. "Ready to print in thirty seconds."

"Right, but are we going to hand this over?" Riagan asked as Nico pulled out his printer. "Patrick won't let ye in without a fight."

"I'm up for a shootout," Eris replied.

"Annihilate 'em," Anand added. He was always ready for a fight.

Neil tapped Riagan's chest. "They could use you and me as human shields."

Riagan grinned at that idea. "That would work!"

"We can't," Rois said. She was mixing the liquids for the trident. "If ye were dead, we wouldn't be able to lift ye."

"Speak for yourself," Anand replied.

Maellyn pointed toward the door into the bunker. "Taking them out aren't our goals. We need to remember what we really want. We only need to solve the problem. We should get points even if we don't get to implement the solution."

Riagan didn't like it, but the girls made sense. Yet how could he just hand the solution over to Patrick?

When the trident finished printing, Neil picked it up. "The girls are right. We should still get points for solving the task."

Riagan grimaced, desperate for another solution. "Not Patrick."

"Jiro, then?" Neil asked.

Riagan sighed, but nodded. "We're coming in."

Neil held out the trident as they re-entered the bunker. Patrick and his team were all targeting the two of them. All except for Jiro, who hung back, shamefaced.

"Don't shoot." Every part of Riagan wanted to fight, but he forced himself to speak civilly. "We think we found the solution."

"And you're going to hand it over?" Patrick asked suspiciously when the rest emerged with their hands raised high.

"Better to get partial credit than none," Neil said.

Riagan ground his teeth.

Patrick strode forward, gloating, and reached for the trident. "Told you they'd fold. Don't have the guts."

Neil pulled back the trident from Patrick's grasp. Patrick opened his mouth to demand they hand it over, but Neil pointed the trident at Jiro. "We'll only give it to him."

Patrick's lip curled in a snarl, but Jiro hurried past him and retrieved the trident. For a moment Riagan thought Patrick might shoot Jiro in the back, but he stepped aside, apparently deciding that all that mattered was that his team won.

Jiro carried the trident back and inserted it into the holes in the upper fish tank. The bed opened and the water and cylinder poured into the open bottom tank. Patrick seized it triumphantly.

Riagan snarled and without thought lifted his arm to shoot Patrick. He couldn't stand it that they'd let Patrick win.

The sim instantly disappeared and they stood in the cages of the empty facility. Riagan blinked in surprise, dropping his hand to his side. That was it. The exam was over.

"We won!" Patrick shouted as he emerged from a cage. He pumped the cylinder in his fists. Riagan hated it, but there was nothing he could do.

"The exam is complete," Nez said. "You're all dismissed. Please leave your cylinders on the table on your way out."

"How did we do, sir?" Maellyn asked.

"You'll receive exam grades in a couple of weeks," Nez replied.

Patrick, Caleb, and Adrien celebrated as they dropped their cylinders on the table and removed their suits.

Riagan couldn't believe it. They had lost. The instructors hadn't reprimanded Patrick. He had cheated, and the instructors had allowed it.

Neil approached him. "We'll be fine." They walked to the table and dropped their two cylinders on it. "It's just one exam. You know we'll make up ground in the Battle Tactics midterm. Plus, we can legally shoot him there."

That did little to lighten Riagan's mood. He hated the condescending way Patrick competed. Patrick seemed to believe that he had already earned a team captain. Maybe he had. The instructors certainly weren't chastising him for his actions.

Was that what it took to make team captain? Win at all cost?

No excuses.

No apologies.

Just win.

Chapter 23

Neil Screws Up?

Neil eyed the spaceport, unable to believe five months had passed since he first arrived. He had since learned a great deal about the different types of Space City ships. The Gigantes freighters carried supplies. The Chimera capsules carried a four-person crew or could be split in two with each half holding a pair. Eagle IVs, one of which he had traveled on from Earth, were the fastest ships in the fleet; he had his sights set on flying one someday.

Exams were finished and grades were due out this week. After the Introduction to New Worlds exam—how had they been graded by the instructors considering Patrick's scheming?—he thought he had done well in Space City History, Battle Tactics, and Selected Literature from the Known Galaxies. Tereshkova's Astrobiology exam had been ridiculously hard, but studying with Maellyn and Rois the night before the midterm had helped him enough to pass, he was sure.

Now he just wanted to enjoy his first winter holiday here.

"I'm cold." Maellyn rubbed the dark green sleeves of her sweater as they circled around toward the back of the spaceport to watch the meteor shower that was set to commence shortly after sunset. Rois had been anxious to see it and Jaya had assured them that the spaceport provided the best view.

Neil removed his new Ursa jacket and slipped it over Maellyn's shoulders. "You should've grabbed a hot chocolate on campus."

"Already had one on my way in from the city." Maellyn squeezed the coat tightly around herself.

Iris and Petey circled overhead. Petey had nearly doubled in size since Thanksgiving and was enjoying his first trip out of the house, darting everywhere while Iris nervously hovered near him.

"What are those?" Riagan pointed toward a dozen gray, one-story cannons at the back of the spaceport.

Students typed on wrist-comps in front of half the cannons. Every few seconds, a canon fired a laser into the sky; a few led to explosions in space. A new competition, perhaps?

"Meteor showers bring out the best shooters," Jaya explained. "The cannons are part of the SCADSat system. Space City Asteroid Detection satellites. The satellites orbit the ship, monitoring asteroids and meteors to determine if they're on a trajectory to hit us. Any meteors too large to burn up in the atmosphere are automatically shot by those cannons and destroyed before they get too close."

"We can shoot meteors?" Riagan's eyes flashed greed like a miner who has struck gold. "Cheers."

Neil listened intently, too.

"Shouldn't professionals man the cannons?" Rois asked. "What if someone misses?"

"The four cannons on the right are automated," Jaya said. "Only the other eight can be used for target practice. People love to test their skill, attempting to hit the smallest meteors before they burn up in the atmosphere. Particularly skilled shooters aim for the largest meteors before they come within the automatic cannons' range. Maybe three people on Space City can outshoot the auto cannons, though."

Riagan jogged to the last empty cannon, wrist-comp in hand. Neil wished he had brought his, too, but settled for observing over Riagan's shoulder.

An app had to download to Riagan's wrist-comp in order to control the cannon. The app created a sensor screen with the green outlines of a dozen small meteors moving across it. Riagan placed one finger on the crosshairs onscreen and dragged it to a meteor. He pressed the *Fire* button in the bottom right corner of the screen. A burst of energy shot from the muzzle of the cannon. They studied the sky, waiting. No explosion.

Neil bit his lip in disappointment.

On the sensor, the meteor advanced past the crosshairs. Riagan dragged the targeting reticle to the meteor once more and fired a second time. The shot missed again as the meteor drifted past the crosshairs.

Neil was tempted to ask for the wrist-comp, sure he could do better, but held his tongue.

"How am I missing?" Riagan asked, jabbing the screen. "The meteor is in the crosshairs when I shoot."

"The timing is hard," Jaya said, still arm in arm with Rois, his thick gray cloak matching her sweater. "Put the crosshairs a little in front of the meteor. Shoot where it's going, not at it."

Rois frowned. "Lasers move at the speed of light. Why would he need to lead the target?"

"But meteors move at an average of 11 kilometers per second," Jaya explained. "How long do you think it takes from lining up the crosshairs on your sensor before you hit the fire button? Half a second?"

Riagan sighed and dragged the crosshairs slightly ahead of the meteor. The cannon fired.

Third miss.

The meteor reached the atmosphere and for a few seconds flared orange across the evening sky before burning up completely.

"Plus, there's a small delay in transmission of your order from your wrist-comp to the cannon," Jaya added. "At the speed the meteor is traveling, the small delay can mean a lot."

Neil couldn't hold back any longer. "Let me try."

Riagan grumpily tossed him the wrist-comp. Neil picked a new target and guessed where to set the reticle, then fired. He missed, too, much to his chagrin.

"Not so easy, is it?" Riagan asked.

Ignoring the jibe, Neil lined up a second shot, but watched as the meteor reached and passed through the crosshairs. The meteor tailed slightly downward. Adjusting the reticle accordingly, he fired again. This time the meteor exploded in a bright orange ball followed by a firework-like crack-boom. Cheers rose from the gathered crowd.

Neil turned to Maellyn. "Did you see that?"

"Nice shot," she replied coolly, arms crossed as if unimpressed. Did she think she could shoot better?

Two more explosions lit the sky, garnering cheers from the onlookers.

"I was hoping for a bigger shower," Rois said, disappointment etched across her face.

"A little later we'll see a lot more," Jaya promised. "We're catching the leading edge right now. More in the welkin than can be shot."

"I thought we came to play with Iris and Petey?" Maellyn's tone was sulky.

Neil frowned, taken aback. Behind her, Petey was having a great time flying dizzying circles around Iris.

Riagan grabbed his wrist-comp back. "Ya play with the pets and I'll shoot meteors."

"Yeah, ok," Neil said. He half wanted to retrieve his wrist-comp from the dorm. Take him ten minutes to get there and back. Maybe if they played with Iris and Petey for a bit, Maellyn would warm back up, and then he could fetch his.

Neil whistled to Petey as Maellyn had taught him, attempting to lure the two flying lizards over, but they refused to approach the crowd. Giving up, Neil attempted to slip his arm through Maellyn's but she squeezed them to her sides and pulled away.

What was she upset about? He had come out here specifically for her.

He had spent most of his free time since semester's end visiting the Apidium monkeys with her to monitor their progress with the fly feeders. The experiment was working beyond expectations. Unfortunately, Maellyn and Fintan wouldn't gain approval to use the feeders on Niveum until this coming summer. In the meantime, Maellyn was worried about the losses to the Apidium population. But Neil didn't think she was upset about that in particular at the moment. Still, he didn't want to ask in front of the group.

Since Iris and Petey would not come, Neil decided to go fetch them. Maellyn kept pace; her arms remained crossed and her expression cold. Rois and Jaya followed.

As they neared the two lizards, Maellyn pulled a bag containing diced pyrns from her jacket pocket. She removed a few pieces and whistled to Iris, who dropped to her arm and gobbled the proffered fruit. Petey followed, landing on Neil's shoulder. The little guy's head swiveled around as he searched for his share.

"May I have some?" Neil asked.

Tightlipped, Maellyn handed him a couple pieces.

"Thank you."

Maellyn kept her focus solely on Iris.

What had he done wrong?

Neil offered the pyrns to Petey, who greedily snatched them up, the fruit puffing out his throat as he swallowed.

"He is *so* cute," Rois said, reaching out to scratch Petey's back with a finger. The little guy arched into her finger, but started to cry when Neil ran out of pyrns. Maellyn handed him extra.

"May I?" Rois asked.

"Of course." Neil handed the fruit to her. Petey leaned forward, anxiously watching Neil's hand, before transferring all his attention to Rois.

She held out one piece of the fruit to Petey, which he devoured.

"I'm jealous," she gushed. "Wish I had one."

Maellyn stuffed the fruit bag back in her pocket. "We'll let Iris have another litter in the spring. I'll keep one for you."

"Ya would?" Rois asked, eyes beaming as she gave Petey the next bite. She scratched the back of his neck again and the little lizard made a noise that Neil would describe as purring.

Maellyn smiled. "Sure. Dad won't love three around the house, but he can't say no when I tell him it's for you."

"Ya wonderful." Rois hugged her.

Neil hoped Maellyn's smile meant she wasn't angry anymore.

Their snacks finished, Petey and Iris set off flying again. Petey zoomed around wildly, nearly crashing into his mother on a couple of occasions, much to Neil's amusement. Each time, Iris chirped admonishingly at her son.

Ten minutes later the meteor shower commenced in earnest, and they sat on the ground to watch. Riagan continued to shoot at the incoming meteors and appeared to hit a couple. Was he getting better or had the increased numbers improved his odds? Neil longed to rejoin Riagan at the turret, but a few minutes into the meteor shower, Maellyn scooted over and leaned against his shoulder. He still wasn't sure what had upset her, but now that she appeared happy again, he wasn't about to mess it up if he could help it.

*****

Few girls remained awake in their dorm, and those that were frowned in disapproval. Boys were forbidden after twenty-three hundred hours. They had only been allowed in after Neil had promised Instructor Tanith that they were only here to drop the girls off. Tanith had agreed to give them five minutes to walk the girls to their room and return, or she would come hunting. She had promised them a worse encounter than their first meeting if she had to come find them. He had no intention of testing her.

Rois opened her bedroom door, flipped on the light, and froze. Standing beside her and holding Iris and Petey in their cage, Maellyn gasped. Neil stood on his toes, trying to peek over the girls' heads. Something green marked Rois' bed.

"What is it?" Riagan asked.

Neil took a step forward between the girls. It was a message written in green goo.

Watch your back green woman.

The message chilled Neil's gut.

Rois started trembling, and Maellyn set aside the pet travel cage and pulled her into a comforting embrace. Alarmed, Riagan and Jaya pushed past them into the room. When Jaya spotted the message, he rushed to the bed and grabbed the blanket, which he dumped in a heap on the floor to hide the words.

"He's going to pay," Riagan said, balling up his fists.

Neil didn't wait for Riagan. He turned and ran back to the girl's dorm entrance, shoving the doors open and hurrying outside. A voice in the back of his head screamed that they should go find Instructor Tereshkova. Yet what had she or anyone else done to stop these attacks? They had accepted Patrick's excuses and lies. And now he had struck in Rois' bedroom, a place she should feel safe in. She didn't deserve to keep suffering because Patrick had a talent for squirming his way out of trouble.

Neil yanked open the door to the boy's dorm and nearly collided with General Dardanos. Surprised, Neil backed straight into Riagan, the thud knocking a gasp out of him. He ignored the pain in his back and straightened up.

"Where are you two headed in such a hurry?" Dardanos asked in irritation as he rolled his wheelchair out the door.

Neil gaped, his mind going blank. He did not want to end up on the headmaster's bad side. Riagan's hands remained curled into fists, but he clenched his jaws and said nothing, nostrils flaring.

"Out with it!" Dardanos' eyebrows dipped into a frown.

Trying to keep emotions in check, Neil said, "Patrick grafittied Rois' bed."

"And you thought you'd pay him back?" Dardanos asked in a dangerous tone.

Neil's brain scrambled for a plausible excuse. "We were headed to Instructor Nez." He *was* the hall monitor in their dorm.

"Liar!" Dardanos' eyes flashed.

"It's true," Riagan insisted. He hadn't unclenched his fists and the heat in his eyes matched the academy head's own.

Dardanos studied them for another moment, as if searching for hints that they were lying. "If I find out either of you were doing otherwise…" He let the threat linger.

At that point, Tereshkova came striding across the courtyard, headed for the girls' dorm. She noticed them and changed course.

"You heard?" Dardanos asked.

Tereshkova nodded. "Tanith called. I'm headed to investigate."

"We'll show ya." Riagan took a step toward the girl's dorm.

Neil nodded, hoping Dardanos would let them go without further discussion.

The headmaster jerked his thumb over his shoulder. "You two return to your room. If Instructor Nez sees either of you out again tonight for any reason, you'll serve detentions for the rest of winter break."

Riagan reached for the door, but Dardanos blocked him. "We'll handle this. Do you understand?"

"Right, like ya handled it last time?" Riagan's jaw jutted forward. This time he didn't meet Dardanos' eyes.

Dardanos reddened until Neil thought he might blow steam out his ears like an old cartoon character. "Don't cross me boy. We'll get to the bottom of this. I don't permit student attacks on one another."

Without answering, Riagan shoved his way into the dorm. Neil started to follow.

"Neil, a word," Dardanos said as Tereshkova departed.

Neil paused reluctantly. It was difficult to keep calm considering he wasn't sure how far he trusted them to protect Rois.

"Have you remembered anything further about the Dahaka?" Dardanos asked.

Neil blinked. He had not expected this question. He shook his head. "Told you everything I remember."

Dardanos pursed his lips and nodded.

"You haven't found anything then?" Neil asked, suddenly alarmed. He had believed things would get resolved once it was in Dardanos' hands. If the Council wasn't making any progress, how much danger were they in?

Dardanos straightened in his wheelchair. "The investigation's progressing. Just wanted to make sure you didn't leave anything out."

Neil wanted to make a snarky comment about the academy council's inability to solve problems lately, but he didn't relish another round of Dardanos' wrath.

The headmaster started away, but then stopped and regarded Neil seriously. "One more thing. You and Riagan might consider speaking with Rois and Jaya about continuing to be open about their relationship. For all the advancements and improved education here, some prejudices remain."

Neil gaped, shocked to hear that from the academy head.

"I meant what I said about protecting all students from ill-treatment, but when you leave the grounds I can't ward against those who harbor such prejudices. You could protect yourselves by not being a target."

"Yes, sir."

Dardanos continued toward the girl's dorm.

Neil couldn't believe it. What about social evolution being a tenant upon which the academy was founded? Hiding punished the victim and appeased prejudice, allowing it to flourish. It was anti-evolution. Neil couldn't believe Instructor Tereshkova would share those sentiments. Nez either.

Rois had taken the high road, refusing to seek revenge and certainly not letting others dictate how she lived her life. She liked Jaya and refused to let anyone take that away from her. No, bowing to Patrick or anyone else was not something Neil could do. Or in good conscience suggest to Rois and Jaya. Regardless of Dardanos' claims, he was apparently not in their corner.

Chapter 24

Neil Uncovers a Traitor

Neil lay in bed and wrestled over what to do for the day. Maellyn had taken Rois for a girl's day alone in the city. Riagan left early for the stadium to blow off steam with shooting drills before practice. Neil could check with Jaya to find out his plans, but Dardanos' revelation that they had discovered nothing further about the traitor aiding the Dahaka troubled him.

Instructor Tereshkova had mentioned that the science labs next door on the Space City U campus possessed a research room that stored all of Space City's scientific knowledge, only a portion of which was accessible from his wrist-comp. Could he find answers there?

Thirty minutes later, after grabbing a quick breakfast, he entered the science building. The facility was comprised of one central corridor that intersected two longer side ones. All three corridors housed smaller labs where scientists studied life and other phenomena across the known universe, and developed new technologies to aid in exploration.

In the first lab that Neil passed, scientists examined Petri dishes. He felt pretty sure that wasn't what he wanted. A few labs down on the right, a scientist and a Traga sat facing each other in metallic chairs that hovered several feet off the ground. They studied each other as if in a staring contest.

At least a hundred scientists walked along the first side corridor. No one paid him any mind. According to Tereshkova, the research room was located at the end of this main hallway, so he pressed on past an expanded lab where a team worked on two new rover designs.

He had been shocked to learn from Instructor Nez that Space City had over two thousand rovers currently conducting missions on uninhabited planets and moons of interest.

After pressing through an also-busy second side corridor, Neil spotted the research room on the left. Inside were more than fifty chairs like those in a dentist's office. Roughly half were filled with people staring at screens above their faces. The screens were designed much like the lights that dentists shined in their patient's mouths. Everyone wore gray gloves and typed on air.

Weird.

Neil spotted Jarl in a chair, typing away at a nonexistent keyboard. Neil didn't want to interrupt, so he crossed the room to a chair near the back. Gray gloves hung on a hook beside the chair. He reached to remove his wrist-comp and realized the holder strapped to his left arm was empty. He'd forgotten the wrist-comp back in his room. He debated heading back to the dorm to retrieve it, but he doubted he'd hear anything from Maellyn or Riagan for several hours.

He removed the wrist-comp holder from his arm and slipped it into a pocket in his jeans before donning the gloves. They gave his fingers a small electrical shock, and the screen lowered, forcing him to recline.

An enormous white wall filled his entire field of view, as if he were suddenly inside a blank sim. The words *Space City DUN* hovered in the air in large black letters. A log-in line requested his last name and student/instructor ID number.

How to input the information?

He thought for a minute. Others in the room held their hands in the air, fingers typing on invisible keys. He raised his hands and a keyboard appeared at the bottom of the white screen. It was awkward typing at first, but after a couple of mistyped letters, he successfully inputted his last name. Next his student ID number. Enter.

Welcome, Neil Ericson.

Search and *Browse* buttons appeared on the blank screen. He tapped the search button and a box appeared on-screen. He typed in CME. A series of articles appeared at the top with the words Coronal

Mass Ejection and CME in the titles—more than five hundred results. This would take him all day!

Below the articles were videos and pictures of the sun spewing out solar flares. Neil tapped on the first video. Onscreen the sun discharged a massive, lava-like energy burst out into space.

A narrator explained the phenomenon. "A Coronal Mass Ejection is an eruption on the sun caused by a solar flare. The solar flare hurls radioactive plasma out into space. The ejection is hurled at more than eight million miles per hour and may be larger than a mountain. A mass hurled at the Earth can reach it in less than a day, knock out electrical systems, and even cause hurricane-like damage upon the planet."

The yellow blast of energy onscreen hurtled toward Earth, which was surrounded by blue lines that represented the planet's magnetic field. Neil had never seen anything like the energy blast passing by the Earth. How did it differ from regular sunlight?

"Most of a coronal mass ejection's energy is deflected by the Earth's magnetic field. If not, every ejection that struck Earth would tear at the atmosphere until it eventually wore away."

The video described solar flares in more detail, as well as coronal quakes and tsunamis. Was the CME device based off a solar flare?

He exited the video, selected the first article on the list, and started to read. The article provided similar information. The next article and the following ten all related to this natural phenomenon, as opposed to a device. This was getting him nowhere.

What had Maellyn called the device? He thought back to that day in the jungle on Niveum as they hiked to see the Apidium. He had only half paid attention to her explanation while hacking away at the foliage blocking their path. Coronal... Mass... Ejection... Ejected... Ejector. Coronal Mass Ejector.

He typed the words into the search box and received zero search items. He punched the air in frustration, which activated another video on the sun. He tried word variations without success. The search broadened his knowledge about sunspots and the elements comprising the sun, but yielded nothing about the device.

Finally, he discovered one article in which a research team proposed a device which mimicked a coronal mass ejection, but the article offered only a theory about a power generator. It lacked concrete details.

Frustrated, he considered wandering the hallways questioning everyone until he found the team working on the CME. That would likely just get him in trouble. Dr. Trevena had made it clear that access to the details and the device were restricted.

Maybe he didn't need to know exactly what the device did, though. If the CME worked in a similar manner as a coronal mass ejection, then... it must discharge massive amounts of radioactive plasma at very high speeds. According to the videos, the Earth's magnetic fields protected it from the brunt of a CME. Space City's engineers must have created a magnetic field around the ship to protect it and everyone onboard from solar radiation, yet that was based upon their distance from the sun. Would the ship's protection be designed to handle a direct, close range strike from a newly-created CME device?

He searched through the remaining articles, but found nothing else about the proposed device. Hundreds of articles and he had nothing more than one theory.

Exhausted, he yanked off the gloves and the screen disappeared. Sitting up in the chair, he noticed that Rois was in the chair next to him, doing her own research. How long had he been here?

A large digital clock on the wall at the front of the room read 22:30. He had searched all day, missing lunch and dinner. His stomach rumbled in complaint.

The research room was empty except for the two of them. Should he say something to Rois? Deciding she might be working on something important, he rose quietly from the chair and started for the exit.

"Studying during winter break?" Rois asked. "I'm surprised at ya, Neil."

Caught!

He turned back to find Rois sitting up in her research chair, removing the typing gloves and replacing them on the hook. He faked a smile, hoping to hide his nervousness. Riagan would kill him if he told her about what he was researching and why.

Then what he hoped was a good excuse hit him. "I'm worried about my Astrobiology grade. Sergeant Terror's midterm exam was rough and I don't want to fail for team captain because of it. Don't tell Riagan."

She winked at him and smiled. "Honestly, Riagan should study a little more, but you know how he is."

"I'm going to swing by the mess hall," he said, relaxing but wanting to change the subject. "Care to join me?"

She placed her hands on her belly and puffed out her cheeks like a blowfish. "I amn't hungry. Still stuffed from dinner. I'll walk out with ya, though."

She shared details of her trip into the city with Maellyn as they exited out into the main hallway. At the far end of the long main corridor stood a Dahaka, its back to them.

They both froze in shock.

A good deal taller and larger than either of them, the Dahaka wore the familiar obsidian armor.

Terrified the Dahaka would turn back and find them, Neil pushed Rois back into the research room, his skin tingling. Why was a Dahaka in the science labs?

Her eyes were wide in shock.

Neil risked a glance out into the hallway. The Dahaka opened the exit door, but as it did so it shrunk to normal human height. At the same time its obsidian armor became a gray Space City suit. A second later, the Dahaka had completely transformed into a normal-looking human citizen. It donned a cap and stepped outside.

"Right, what's it doing?" she managed to whisper, half hysterical.

"It changed," he replied, staring at the exit door. What had he just seen?

"Changed how?"

He put his hands on her shoulders, hoping that would calm her a little, or maybe himself. Was he going crazy? "The Dahaka changed, and… looks like an ordinary human." He hadn't imagined the Dahaka. She had seen it, too.

She didn't ask how such a thing had happened, or even give any indication that what he had just said was impossible. Mouth wide, she stared at the open door as if expecting the Dahaka to come through it at any second. "Is it still out there?"

He shook his head.

"What do we do?"

What could they do? Report it to Dardanos? That had accomplished nothing so far. If he followed the Dahaka he might observe another meeting with the traitor, but that was risky. He might be seen this time.

He grabbed his grandfather's coin from his pocket. This surely qualified as a difficult choice to make.

She frowned at the coin.

"If it's heads I'll go straight to Headmaster Dardanos," he said. "Tails, I'll follow the Dahaka."

"No, we will," she replied, nodding.

He shook his head. "I can't put you in harm's way. Riagan would kill me."

She put her hands on her hips and gave him her best *do-you-really-want-to-challenge-me* stare. "It's not ya job to keep me safe. Riagan's either."

Glancing at the coin, he wished he had never come to the research room. But if he hadn't, she would be dealing with this on her own.

He started to flip the coin, but hesitated. Would his grandfather have let the coin decide in a case like this? Neil remembered all the stories his mother had ever told him about his grandfather's heroics. He doubted his grandfather had flipped a coin in those cases. Nor would his grandfather have stood by while innocent lives were threatened. They needed evidence, a lead to pursue, and he could get it if he just had the courage to follow the Dahaka. He wasn't his grandfather, though.

Won't become him either if you do nothing now, he thought.

His grandfather had been a hero because he had acted when others were in danger. He hadn't hid behind the randomness of a coin flip or made excuses. Neil realized in that moment that his grandfather had given him that coin when he was an innocent child unready for life's difficult choices. But he was a child no longer.

He slipped the coin back in his pocket.

The decision made, Rois stepped past him through the door. "After it."

"Wait." He grabbed her arm, stopping her. "One of us should go alert Dardanos. Get backup."

"You tell him then." She ran down the main corridor, forcing him to keep pace with her.

He didn't want to put her in danger, but there was nothing he could do to stop her. He hoped that Riagan would not have a reason to be pissed at him when this was all over. If he found out at all, he was going to be furious.

Rois only slowed when she reached the exit to the facility. She eased the door open. The street was empty. He stepped outside first, checking toward the quad. No sign of the Dahaka.

"Is that him?" She pointed in the opposite direction toward the city.

The Dahaka, moving swiftly toward the edge of campus, still resembled a normal person. Positive that they were making a terrible mistake, Neil nodded and they pursued.

They stuck close to the shadows, until, at the edge of campus the Dahaka broke into a run. Neil abandoned caution and gave chase, but the Dahaka's fast, powerful strides soon carried it through the mostly open field between the city and campus. Upon reaching the city outskirts, the Dahaka quickly disappeared. Nevertheless, neither Neil nor Rois spoke as they gave chase. Twenty anxious minutes passed before they reached the city.

At night, the trees lining the streets glowed, lighting the walkways like streetlights. Normally, Neil might have marveled at such a sight, but with a Dahaka on the loose, they seemed more like lights on a ghost ship. A fair number of people roamed the streets, but few paid much attention to those around them. Plus, the Dahaka was in disguise, so why would they notice? How had it transformed like that? How many others might be lurking onboard? The possibility made him shiver.

He studied the nearest buildings and moving walkways; a mouse searching for a cat in a maze, but without the ability to smell.

"Right, what now?" Rois asked, her whole body tense.

"I don't know."

They boarded the moving walkway and searched side streets. He listened for screams of terror, but everyone milled about in oblivious silence. A black widow roamed undetected through the glass spider web.

He was about ready to give up the search in defeat when he spotted a cap overhead on the monorail platform. Many people in the city wore the Space City suits, but only the instructors ever wore those caps; the Dahaka had one, too. It slipped back into the shadows.

Neil pointed to the platform. "It's up there."

Right then the monorail pulled into the stop. Rois raced for the stairs leading to the platform, leaving him to hurry after her. Their feet clanged up the three flights of aluminum steps, but trying to catch a rail before it departed wasn't an uncommon occurrence. When they reached the top, the only people in sight were headed for the stairs. Neil and Rois rushed onto the closest car where a half dozen people sat, waiting for the monorail to carry them to their stops. None of them was the Dahaka; Rois eyed each warily.

"See it?" she asked, a little worry in her voice.

He looked through the glass doors at both ends, searching the other cars for the Dahaka. "It's here somewhere." It had to be. Where else could it have gone?

At each stop, people trickled off. None of them the Dahaka. Once only two people remained in their car, and a couple of others in neighboring compartments, Neil feared they had made a mistake. Rois chewed her nails, continually scanning the cars ahead and behind them.

At a residential stop, the two remaining passengers rose to get off. Neil moved to the door, Rois close beside him. Searching the crowd, he spotted the instructor's cap. The disguised Dahaka swiftly walked to the steps and started down toward the street.

Neil and Rois rushed off the monorail, but got stuck descending the stairs behind a couple taking their leisure, arm-in-arm. Neil exchanged a frustrated glance with Rois, but there was little they could do. By the time they reached the street, the Dahaka was a good distance east along the moving walkway. If they lost the Dahaka here, they would never catch it. Jumping on the walkway, they broke into a jog to close the distance between them. Fortunately, enough people still milled about the walkways and side streets to disguise them.

Windows throughout the neighborhood were filled with lit luminaria. Intended as a winter holidays decoration, they reminded Neil right now of a candlelight vigil. He hoped they were not an omen. How many people might die if the Dahaka succeeded with its plan?

The people riding the walkways had thinned, leaving them alone following it. Neil and Rois slowed their pace, so as to not draw its attention.

"Put ya arm around my shoulder," Rois said.

"What?" Neil asked.

She grabbed his arm and placed it over her shoulders. She turned to face him. Her mouth was drawn in a thin line, clearly uncomfortable turning her back to the Dahaka.

Neil glanced nervously from her to it. Where was it headed?

"Just keep an eye on it," Rois told him.

The Dahaka turned right at an intersection. When they neared the intersection, Neil led Rois off onto the sidewalk. If only he had his wrist-comp. He could've taken a picture and sent a message to the instructors. In its present disguise would anyone believe him, though?

They eased over to the nearest building, and at the corner, peeked around. The Dahaka entered the building across the street and a chill ran through Neil.

"That's Maellyn's building," Rois said, worry clear in her voice.

"Is Maellyn back on campus?" Neil asked, his every instinct screaming at him to rush to her aid if she were here. The Dahaka had to be headed for Dr. Trevena. As lead scientist, he likely had access to the CME. Maellyn would be the perfect bargaining chip to get her father's cooperation.

"She is," Rois said. "She got an urgent message from Instructor Fintan. Said she had to meet him."

Neil exhaled in relief. At least she was safe, for now. Her father was probably a different matter. He tried to tell himself that the Dahaka might be here for someone else, but the coincidence seemed too great.

Crossing the walkway, they rushed into the bottom floor of the building. There was no sign of the Dahaka, but the elevator was climbing.

"This way," Neil said, dashing up the stairs.

They ran hard up to the thirteenth floor and exited out into the hall, Neil wondering what they should do if the Dahaka went for Dr. Trevena. He remembered the video Instructor Aldrin had shown them their first day in history class, a Dahaka stabbing an Azzaro with the tusk on its armor. He and Rois lacked the training of the Azzaro soldiers. Could they really save Dr. Trevena if it came to that?

Neil dropped to a crouch to peek around the corner. Sure enough, the Dahaka waited in the hallway before the door to Maellyn's place.

A second later the door opened.

"How did it go?" Dr. Trevena asked, stepping aside to allow the Dahaka to enter.

*****

"What is Dr. Trevena doing?" Rois asked as they exited back out to the street.

Neil was too stunned to respond. He had been debating what he could do to help Dr. Trevena. Now it appeared that Dr. Trevena was the traitor he had overheard months ago, but he couldn't make himself voice that realization. But what should he do? He didn't exactly have any proof. It would be his word against Dr. Trevena's. How would his grandfather have exposed a traitor in the Air Force?

Rois grabbed his arm, pulling him from his thoughts. Her eyes teared up. "What now?"

"No idea." His own eyes stung.

Dardanos had said that they had discovered problems with temp badges at the labs. And Dr. Trevena controlled the labs. He was in the best position to cover up any moves that he made. Neil needed irrefutable evidence.

How would Maellyn handle discovering that her father was a traitor?

"What are they after?" Rois asked.

"CME," he replied without thinking.

"A CME?"

He closed his eyes, mentally kicking himself.

"How do ya know?" She let go of his arm and turned to study his face.

"I've seen the Dahaka before."

He proceeded to tell her everything, including Riagan's participation. She grew angry when she learned that Riagan had refused to help him at all, especially since he had used her safety as an excuse for doing nothing.

"Right," she said, hands on hips. "If he wants to hide in the dark, let him. I'll help."

Neil felt grateful for the offer. It was nice to have someone to share this with. But a little voice in the back of his mind said Riagan would kill him when he found out. Neil decided to tune that voice out.

208

They discussed everything in detail on the monorail. Rois questioned him carefully about everything he had seen of the Dahaka that first time, the visit to Dardanos' office, and everything he had learned earlier today in his research. It took them the entire ride back. They both worried how to tell Maellyn and what to do now.

As they departed the monorail and headed down to the street, Neil found he was reluctant to return to campus. Once they reached campus, they had to decide what to do next, and nothing seemed like a good option.

"What are you doing off campus at night?" a familiar voice asked.

Across the moving walkway, Dardanos glared at them. Rois gasped in shock, and Neil's heart thudded in his chest.

"You're breaking curfew. What're you doing here?"

Before Neil could respond, Rois blurted out. "Following a Dahaka."

"You what?" Dardanos' eyes widened.

Neil closed his eyes and groaned. He had not wanted to reveal this yet. Accusing Dr. Trevena of being a traitor would draw his attention to them. Too late to take it back now, though.

Rois continued as they crossed the moving walkway. "We found a Dahaka in the science labs and followed it."

Dardanos frowned. "In the labs? That's ridiculous. Followed it where?"

Neil hesitated. This was going to hurt Maellyn bad. He hated to be the one responsible. He was also afraid what would happen next.

"Followed it where?" Dardanos repeated.

"Dr. Trevena's apartment," Neil said, unable to think of a lie on the fly, especially without being able to corroborate it with Rois.

A dangerous glare entered Dardanos' eyes. "That's a serious accusation."

Neil offered no reply. He wanted to be wrong.

Dardanos looked to Rois for confirmation. "Are you sure what you witnessed? Maybe you got confused in the dark?"

Rois trembled at Neil's side, but she kept her voice steady. "Too tall to be human… at first. And the labs are well lit. We followed it to Dr. Trevena's place. Neil's not making it up."

Dardanos' face turned compassionate. "I can tell from both your faces that he's not."

Neil felt sick to his stomach. Under what circumstances would he next see Maellyn?

Dardanos turned his wheelchair back toward campus. "I can review the labs' security camera footage from my office."

That revelation stunned Neil. Why hadn't he thought about the labs having security cameras? Made sense and gave them proof before Dr. Trevena could cover it up. That only made him feel slightly better. The harm to Maellyn remained.

Dardanos questioned them on their way back to campus. Neil answered everything as best he could, but his thoughts were all on Maellyn. What did this mean for her? She would be crushed by the news. Would she hate him when she found out that he had snitched on her father? He had not had a choice. Space City was in danger if the Dahaka got a CME. He had done the right thing, his duty, or devoir, as Instructor Tereshkova liked to say.

Would Maellyn agree… or understand?

Those questions haunted him the entire night.

Chapter 25

Neil Faces a Tempest

Neil picked at his beef stew during lunch the next day as his mind raced like a runaway roller coaster. He worried about what to tell Maellyn and how she would handle the news. Riagan and Jaya debated who would win the racing championship, but Neil barely registered what they said. Rois also ate in silence, occasionally exchanging uncomfortable glances with him.

Maellyn had not returned to the dorm last night. Rois guessed that Maellyn had remained tied up with whatever emergency Instructor Fintan had contacted her about, but Neil worried nonetheless. She could have returned home without their knowing.

He had risen early and dressed, before heading to help Instructor Tereshkova feed the newborn sea scorpions. He had taken care to avoid the spikes on their arms, but the mother still stung him when he tried feeding a baby too close to her. The pain from the sting had been excruciating until Tereshkova applied a salve from lepteer roots. After the feeding, Neil had nudged the sea scorpions into a spare tank and cleaned their main one. The animal shelters that Tereshkova needed cleaned were never-ending.

When he had finished with the tanks, he had grabbed a quick shower before Riagan and Jaya dragged him to lunch. He had little desire to eat, though.

"Where have ya been?" Riagan asked as Maellyn stumbled into a chair beside them.

Neil and Rois exchanged relieved glances.

Maellyn wore a wrinkled pink t-shirt, her hair tied back in a ponytail. Her eyes were red and they flashed between anger and despair. Slumping in the chair, she said, "Some brainless fool falsely accused my father of housing a Dahaka."

Her sudden scowl made Neil think she might slap a serpent hawk right now. It made him want to simultaneously comfort her and run for hiding.

Jaya and Riagan gaped.

"Ya father is aiding a Dahaka?" Riagan asked.

Maellyn gave him a withering glare. "Do you have a skunk sack for a brain? Of course not."

Neil bit his lip. Things were about to go badly, but like a garden hose in the face of a forest fire, he was powerless to stop it.

Overcoming his initial shock, Jaya asked, "Why would someone lie about your father?"

"Claimed they followed the Dahaka from the labs to our home," Maellyn said.

Neil was unable to meet Maellyn's gaze for fear she would read his guilt in his eyes. He looked at Rois, but she focused on her plate, though she didn't touch her food.

"A lab tech?" Riagan guessed.

"Even the dumbest lab tech wouldn't make a mistake like that," Maellyn said. "My father is working a project that allows an officer to transform his suit to imitate others. An assistant had been conducting a demonstration."

Rois gasped, her face reflecting the shock that Neil felt.

Suddenly hopeful, he asked, "The person who reported it made a mistake?"

"Yes, but it led to a full scale inspection of our home, as well as the labs." Maellyn rubbed her eyes, clearly exhausted. "I had to return home early this morning so Dad could join inspectors at the lab."

Neil gave Rois a tiny smile. She met his gaze for a second. Things would be ok. Maellyn's father wasn't a traitor.

Rois placed a hand on Maellyn's arm. "I'm so sorry, Maellyn."

Maellyn grimaced. "I'm already dealing with a setback in the Apidium experiment. This was the last thing I needed."

Neil's buoyancy evaporated, and he wished that he could comfort her. So that was Instructor Fintan's emergency. "What happened?"

"Seems the disease adapted, jumping from the mosquitoes to the moths, which would render our spheres useless."

"What're ya going to do?" Rois asked, face pained. "Can we help?"

Maellyn threw up her hands. "I don't know. Fintan and I worked on it late into the night until Dad called me and I rushed home."

"A Dahaka wandering the labs would've been shocking," Riagan mused. "Did ya see it?"

Neil waited for Maellyn's answer until he realized Riagan had spoken to him. "What?"

"Did ya see the Dahaka?" Riagan asked.

"How would I?"

Riagan shrugged. "Ya went to the labs. Thought ya might've seen the disguise."

Neil's first instinct was to deny it, create an excuse to avoid adding to Maellyn's stress. Would Rois go along with it? Yet as a lie stained his tongue, he knew it was only a matter of time before she learned it was Rois and him. The news would come out soon enough, the lie revealed, a nail in the coffin.

"I did." With his eyes, Neil implored Maellyn to forgive him. "It was me."

"Me, too," Rois added.

Thunderstruck, Maellyn, Jaya, and Riagan stared at the two of them. Maellyn's nostrils flared. "You reported my father?"

Neil tried to explain, "It was an accident. We were in the research room and when we left, the Dahaka was standing by the exit. We had to do something."

"My father is the lead scientist. You accused him of aiding the Dahaka," she screamed at him, then turned to include Rois in her fury. "My father!"

The whole lunchroom had gone silent, and everyone listened to them.

"I'm sorry." Neil wanted to reach out and touch her, but didn't dare move. "I didn't know what to do."

"Ya took Rois with ya after what ya thought was a Dahaka?" Riagan asked, eyes now blazing to match Maellyn's. "What were ya thinking?"

Rois jumped to her feet. "It wasn't his decision. Nor yours. And I don't need ya to protect me!" She opened her mouth to say something else, appeared to notice the other students in the lunch room, and kept whatever she had been about to add to herself.

Maellyn's eyes, hurt and accusing, shifted between them. Neil wondered what he could say to make this better.

"We made a mistake," Rois added, tone still angry.

"You should've trusted my father!" Maellyn stormed from the mess hall.

She passed by Patrick on her way. After she left, he grinned in satisfaction at Neil. At that moment, if Patrick had said anything, Neil thought he might've attacked him. For once, Patrick said nothing. The moment passed.

Neil had tried to do what was right. Both he and Rois. They hadn't wanted to believe ill of Dr. Trevena. Surely Maellyn would realize that. Her father hadn't suffered more than minor inconveniences. If he had kept his mouth shut, however, Maellyn wouldn't be infuriated with him right now.

Everyone insisted Space City's security measures were impenetrable. The Dahaka weren't advanced enough technologically. Why hadn't he listened? He should've known the Dahaka couldn't waltz into the labs. If he and Rois had minded their own business and let others worry about the infiltration plot, like Mr. Chapman, who had gone to handle it, Maellyn wouldn't be angry with him.

Instead of being a hero like his grandfather, he had stuck his nose where it didn't belong and now he was paying for it. But how could he have known that?

With nothing to release his anger on, he shoved his tray away and left.

Chapter 26

Riagan's Decapitation Simulation

"Enough moping. We've got us a team captain certification to pass." Riagan kicked the foot of Neil's bed.

Neil lay sprawled on it, an all too common occurrence these days. A candy moat surrounded him and the empty wrappers overflowed and spilled onto the floor. Since his fight with Maellyn two months ago, he had spent all of his free time dwelling in self-pity.

"I've got homework to finish." Neil rolled over on his side, facing the wall.

Riagan grabbed his runners and threw one at Neil's back. "General Stribog booked us in the sim facility today. If we don't pass, kiss a team captain position goodbye. We're done."

Neil rolled to a sitting position, grabbed the runner and tossed it back, but Riagan ducked.

"I don't want to be a team captain anymore," Neil said petulantly.

Riagan rolled his eyes as he retrieved the runner from his bed and started to pull the pair on his feet. All this pining after a girl. "If we don't become team captains, that makes it easier on Patrick. What if you get assigned under him?"

He grabbed Neil's wrist-comp from the night stand and tossed it on his bed. Rois had tried to reason with Maellyn. After all it was a simple mistake. Maellyn's response was that she couldn't deal with it right now. She had the Apidium monkeys to worry about. These days, Maellyn rose early, returned to the room late, if at all, and rarely spoke much to Rois either. Riagan understood where Maellyn was coming from. Neil couldn't leave well enough alone.

"We've gunned for team captains all year," Riagan said. "Don't leave me like an awkward turtle spinning on its back."

Neil finally rose, grabbing his wrist-comp. "Fine. But only 'cause Instructor Glenn said you need the help."

First step—get Neil up. Second, get Nico to cut off his candy supply. Neil's daily health scans showed a slight blip from all the sugar he'd been consuming; poor discipline played a role in team captain selection. Team Captain Gilbright assured him it took a lot of sweets to register, but Neil didn't need to push it.

As they passed by Jaya's room, Riagan spotted him curled up with Rois on his bed watching a rock concert on his mini 3D TV. The band floated in the air above them, jamming away. A twinge of discomfort lanced through Riagan at seeing his sister with a guy—an alien at that—but he liked Jaya, knew he was a good guy, so he let it go.

"We've got General Stribog's Team Captain certification mission," Riagan told Jaya. "Ya took it already?"

Jaya removed his arm from around Rois and sat up, muting the show as he did so. He looked past Riagan at Neil, giving him an appraising stare. "About time you got training again."

Neil didn't respond.

"Any tips?" Riagan asked.

"Sure. Hope you've been practicing with the drones and be ready to run. A lot."

"Thanks," Riagan said, hoping Neil's recent trend wouldn't cost them.

"Also," Jaya began, as if remembering something else, "be prepared for the unusual. There will likely be a surprise of some sort."

They hurried to the sim facility, donned their gray suits and added helmets and mini oxygen tanks. After climbing into cages, Riagan called up General Stribog's certification sim and hesitated. Once they started, it was pass or fail. No second chances. They either completed the tasks the general had assigned or they were out of the running to be team captains.

Knowing he couldn't delay either, he took a deep breath and activated the sim. Darkness enveloped them. They stood on a large, floating metal grate above a dark, cloudy surface. A burst of adrenaline washed through him, same as it did every time he entered a new sim.

He loved it.

The sim was set on the Kali home planet, Erebus, a Neptune-like gas giant that revolved far from its sun and received scant light or heat. Their gel suits provided great insulation, but Riagan still felt the chill. He leaned over the platform rail. Thick gaseous clouds covered a liquid surface more than 200 meters below, so it was safe to assume falling off the grate platform wouldn't help them pass.

"Was Maellyn right?" Neil asked. "I trust her. Shouldn't I trust her father by extension?"

Riagan rolled his eyes, having heard this question countless times over the last two months. "The labs have security cameras. The city is probably filled with them, too. The Council was going to find out regardless." He had also given this same response numerous times.

What Neil didn't seem to grasp was that this was all a result of him borrowing problems. Riagan believed they should defend each other—Rois, Maellyn, and Jaya…the group. If they made team captains, they gained responsibility for their teams. The instructors on the other hand, handled threats to the academy, and the Council dealt with dangers to everyone onboard Space City. The Council and instructors were all in a better position to handle a traitor than either of them.

"If it had really been a Dahaka, though—" Neil said.

"It wasn't! Now can we get on with this sim? We need to activate the drones."

Riagan pulled up the option in the certification folder and a drone appeared in the air just above his head. Instructor Nez had introduced the tech when the spring semester started. The black drones resembled miniature helicopters with five top propellers. Thus far, they'd primarily used the drones as scouts to obtain aerial imagery of a sim. There were several grate paths leading away from the platform in all directions. They'd need the drones to plot out a route for them.

He recalled the map on his wrist-comp. "We need to reach the palisades to the northeast."

"If there are cliffs, why didn't we start there?" Neil asked. "Instead of this platform over nothing?"

Riagan shook his head and switched over to the drone feed. Like much of the planet and the Kali, all life forms on Erebus were composed of gas. A majority of the gaseous forms resembled worms floating through the air in a wide array of sizes from not much more than a swarm of bugs to as large as whales. Random changes in movements showed they possessed some sentience.

As he guided the drone northeast, it mapped out the grate paths, marking them on his map. He and Neil fanned their drones out to maximize the coverage area with minimal overlap to ensure there were no gaps between them. The grate paths multiplied and crisscrossed, creating an increasingly complex web with many dead ends. He activated a route analyzer program to plot out their most direct path to the palisades. With that running, he turned his attention back to studying the drone feed.

In addition to the worm-like forms, there were gaseous balls which pulsed, as if to a beat. Maybe a heartbeat? Still others resembled throwing stars or took on more exotic appearances. Unlike the Kali, whose black-as-coal gaseous forms blended into the dark landscape, the many creatures they found comprised a rainbow of colors. Each one glowed, filling the planet with millions of gliding lights.

Neil set off along one of the grate paths, following the recommended path by the route analyzer program; it hadn't finished running yet, but apparently had covered enough of the distance to set out the first part of their route. The grate paths lacked guard rails and were no more than a couple of feet wide. Riagan's fear of heights kicked in, especially with no discernible bottom below the clouds. One misstep and he'd be done for. Neil wouldn't have time to react and save him. Riagan tried to limit that unease by focusing on the path ahead and staying in the middle.

In the distance, running alongside the dark outline of the cliffs that he could just make out, half a mile up, was an enormous glowing white mass. What was that?

A sensor on Riagan's wrist-comp set off a flashing alarm.

Warning: megacrabs approaching.

Riagan stopped in his tracks and zoomed in the drone feed on two jungle green-colored boulders with long, tubular appendages. He supposed the shape might generally resemble the outline of a crab.

"If those megacrabs reach us, I've got crystallizers." Riagan pulled a pair of softball-sized yellowish cylinders from his pack. The crystallizers would condense the gas to liquid before solidifying them within milliseconds. Once in solid form, gravity would take care of the rest. At present, the megacrabs weren't on their suggested route, but better to be prepared than fail.

Neil shrugged as he continued forward. "Why bother? What are they going to do? Cover us in fumes?"

Riagan fidgeted as he realized he had forgotten to tell Neil about the new setting. "Um... well... General Stribog set the sim... to advanced."

Neil stopped in his tracks, his head doing a 180. "He what? I thought only fourth years could use advanced sims?"

Riagan forced an uneasy smile. "It's a Team Captain cert."

Neil considered this for a moment then shrugged. "It's a sim. Even in advanced mode, what does that really mean?"

"The sims can send false signals to the brain, make it think different parts of your body are wounded. You feel pain to mimic what you'd experience if you were really exploring the planet."

"Ok, but we're on a gaseous planet." Neil raised his arms straight out. "No solids anywhere."

"Yes, but the chemical makeups of the creatures here. Some of them could be toxic to us. The sim will make your body feel like it's been poisoned."

"So? We just end the sim then."

Riagan wanted to shake Neil. "We can't without failing the certification. We've worked all year for this and I for one am not failing. I'm going to be a team captain!"

Neil bit his lip, wrinkling his nose in the process. "Great. Let's get this over and done with then." He resumed the trek once more, taking a right at an intersection per the directions on their map.

Following, Riagan turned his attention back to guiding his drone to the cliffs, which he quickly discovered weren't really cliffs after all. Instead, a mountain-sized grate cube hung suspended in the air. It was clearly artificial, likely added by the sim's programmer just like the platform they were standing on, as well as the paths between there and here.

"Wow. Look at that!" Neil's pace quickened.

Riagan's eyes shot up from his screen and he searched the vaporous landscape for the megacrabs, as he hurried to keep up with Neil. They couldn't have covered the distance that fast. The back of his neck tingled as he searched frantically for them.

Then he realized Neil was staring upward at the glowing white mass. Except now that they were closer, Riagan realized it wasn't one great big light, but a million little ones—a sort of coral reef teaming with life that now looked like a living mosaic. Rois needed to see this.

A coal-colored shadow, the size of a man, moved across the reef.

"Kali," Neil murmured.

Half a dozen more shadows crept over the mosaic. At least a hundred yards separated it from cliffs, so Riagan doubted the Kali had spotted the tiny drones. He hoped the Kali hadn't spotted them yet either.

Fortunately, the route analyzer sent them in another direction where the giant gray cube blocked them from view.

"What are we searching for?" Neil asked.

"A nidus." Riagan accelerated his drone up and over the gray cube, noting with distaste that it would be a long climb up, several stories at least.

"A what?"

"A breeding place of some sort."

"Why?"

"Don't know. But we have to get there."

Above the cliffs, the drone feed showed copper, teal, and amber clouds that darted around in unusual, animal-like patterns. They'd hardly be able to move up there without coming in contact with the various creatures.

"I'll start scanning those with my drone," Neil said. "Figure out which are harmful so we can avoid them. Keep looking for the nidus."

Riagan nodded.

"I wonder how scientists study these creatures?" Neil asked. "Guess there's no dissection in Erebus studies."

Riagan frowned. "That takes the craic out of it." But Rois would be relieved. She always hated dissection.

On top of the cube, about two hundred yards in, a circular depression, twenty feet across, was filled with tiny beads of light. Riagan zoomed in on the bowl. The little beads reminded him of studying bacteria under a microscope. That was surely the nidus.

A shout over the drone audio startled them.

"What was that?" Neil asked.

Had the Kali spotted the drones?

Riagan zoomed back out and rotated his video feed. A bright amber light raced past the drones. Riagan panned toward the source and was surprised to find Cade Martin driving what could best be described as a futuristic go kart across the giant cube.

For a moment Riagan just stared at the feed, trying to figure out why Cade was in their sim. He hadn't been in the sim facility when they'd started up. Had he snuck in just for fun? That was generally heavily frowned upon.

Then he remembered Jaya's advice that they should expect something unusual. A surprise participant was certainly a curve ball. But if that was the case, what was he there for? Was he an opponent meant to stop them from achieving their goal? But Cade was already racing his kart past the nidus, so that didn't seem to be it.

"What's he doing?" Riagan asked.

Neil shook his head. "No idea. There's nothing in our test folder about him."

Then Riagan realized why Cade was in flight. A hundred Kali pursued him.

"Look at this." Riagan showed Neil his feed.

"Are we supposed to rescue him?" Neil asked. "Getting there in time to help would be a challenge."

Riagan bit his lip, thinking back to their midterm exam when Patrick sacrificed teammates and did everything in his power to solve the puzzle. "Perhaps Cade is a distractor. Maybe General Stribog is testing us to see if we'll follow our mission orders, rather than be distracted by one person."

"With that many Kali in pursuit, it would be a death sentence for Cade if we don't help him," Neil argued. "We can't just ignore him."

"It's a sim. He won't die," Riagan argued, watching Cade evade the Kali in the kart. He was faster than they were, but with their numbers, they'd eventually surround him.

"That's not the point and you know it. We have a moral choice to make. Save someone in danger or sacrifice them for the mission."

"What if it's not that simple? What if completing our mission means saving a lot more than one life? What if by choosing Cade, we doom others?"

Neil punched Riagan's shoulder, drawing his attention. "We can't assume anything about the mission. All we can do is make a decision with the information before us. And I say Cade's life is more important than anything we'll find in that nidus."

Riagan hesitated.

"What if it was Maellyn or Jaya?" Neil asked, picking up on Riagan's doubt. "Or Rois? What would you do if it was her up there?"

Riagan sighed. "You're right. Helping is the right thing to do."

"That's right." Neil waved for Riagan to follow. After a few feet, they broke into a jog. They weren't that far from the cliffs at this point, but it would be a long climb up. He hoped Cade would hang on in the meantime.

"Uh, Riagan, we have a problem," Neil said. "The megacrabs just registered on short range radar."

Riagan risked a glance at his wrist-comp, though it made him uncomfortable taking his eyes off the path for even a second. Sure enough, two dots representing the crabs blocked their present route.

"I've still got those two crystallizers," he replied. "That should take care of them."

"Too dangerous." Neil typed away on his wrist-comp as he ran. "We'd have to get within range of their arms to throw the crystallizers. Our best bet is to avoid them."

Neil darted right at an intersection, diverging from the recommended route. Riagan shrugged off his pack as he ran and dug out a crystallizer. He didn't want to be empty-handed. The megacrabs would likely pursue them. Or some other creature may hinder them. And if he was honest, he really wanted an opportunity to use one.

The highlighted path on his wrist-comp changed based upon the new route Neil had taken. It ended at the cliffs a little to the east of the original location, putting them further away from Cade, but it was that or go through the crabs. Riagan switched back to the drone feed. Cade still fled the Kali. As far as Riagan could tell, Cade didn't have any particular destination, just stayed out of reach.

The wrist-comp beeped shrilly, an icon for the map function flashing red. Riagan switched back over. The megacrabs were in pursuit, coming straight at them across open sky.

"Almost there," Neil shouted as they cut left. It was now a straight shot to the cliffs. And there were no other side paths for them to take.

A whistle of air picked up around them, so loud it drowned out all else, but wasn't accompanied by the feel of wind buffeting him. It took Riagan a minute to realize the sound came from the megacrabs bearing down on them. Despite the name, he hadn't anticipated the size. Tall as a mature oak, they resembled hills instead of boulders. Their arms resembled concrete drainage pipes. The fact that they were composed of a gray-green smoke didn't lessen the cold anxiety welling through him as they closed in.

Neil reached the cube cliffs and started to climb. The cube was made from the same grate substance as the path they had run along, leaving plenty of hand and footholds. But Riagan knew they wouldn't make it a quarter of the way up the cube before the crabs reached them. He wheeled around, pressing his back against the cube wall, crystallizer raised. He waited as the crabs drifted closer, fighting the instinct to run. The whistling grew until Riagan wanted to cover his ears.

When the first of the creatures had closed to within fifteen feet or so, it raised one arm, preparing to strike. Riagan threw the crystallizer, hoping this would work. The crystallizer hit the bulk of the crab and burst, shooting out a bluish stream which rapidly consumed the creature. It had no time to respond before transforming to a water ball. The second crab hit the first, and began its own transformation while the first hardened to ice and dropped. The second crab tipped forward as it became water itself, froze, and plummeted after the first toward the clouds below. The whistling vanished, a welcome relief to his ears.

Riagan exhaled. He'd done it! Taken the crabs out and with just one shot. He hadn't planned it that way. Just lucky.

Knowing he had no time to waste, he turned back to the cube and started climbing after Neil, who was a good fifteen to twenty feet up, maybe a tenth of the way. The cube was cold, like grasping ice, but not slippery at all. In fact, the handholds were sharp enough that he had to grip lightly so as to avoid cutting himself. His heart continued to beat rapidly, and he risked a couple of glances to make sure the crabs hadn't somehow returned. Confirm they were truly gone.

The climb took awhile, Riagan's arms cramping about a quarter of the way because he couldn't fully extend them. They found a narrow ledge about halfway up where they could sit, dangling their legs off the side for a brief moment. Riagan shook out his arms to alleviate the cramping. He was thirsty, but didn't want to fidget around with his pack and risk knocking himself off the ledge.

Neil pulled up his drone feed to check on Cade. He remained well and fleeing in his kart. How much fuel did he have left? They needed to get to the top.

Groaning, Riagan pulled himself to his feet and they resumed their climb. Before long he wished for another ledge to rest on, but there were none. He forced himself to keep climbing, reaching up with one arm after another, pulling himself up one foot at a time until he could see the top. Fifteen feet. Ten. Five. And then he hauled himself up onto the cube.

Up here, there were gas creatures everywhere in a host of colors. The buzz of the kart's engine drifted toward them, but Riagan couldn't spot it through all the creatures. They'd have to wade through slowly, trying to avoid touching anything. Who knows what harm might come from brushing any of these creatures. Any one of them might carry a chemical concoction to cause great pain or other harm.

He fished the last crystallizer out of his pack. Neil eyed it, but said nothing. They'd have to save it for a desperate moment.

They strode forward, weaving their way among the creatures, one moment walking, the next inching sideways with breath held as they attempted to shrink inward to avoid touching anything. Riagan wanted to scan the creatures to get information on which ones might cause harm, but there were too many varieties and they didn't have the time.

With each step their boots clanged loudly on the cube surface. Riagan winced, but there was nothing they could do about it. They'd lose the element of surprise long before they got into range to attack the Kali. But fortunately, none of the creatures around them seem to take any notice. As long as they took care they were fine, though keeping their eyes on all the creatures surrounding them was a challenge.

The light from the nidus flared brightly. It wasn't until that moment that Riagan realized he'd forgotten it. The creatures ahead were drawn toward it, opening up a space where he and Neil could move more quickly.

The nidus was a large, golden depression in the ground and it teemed with small creatures. The larger creatures surrounding it pulsed in a dance around it. The air around it hummed and there was a warmth emanating from it.

Riagan pressed forward, wanting to see it more closely, but also wondering if that was safe.

"Look." Neil pointed past the nidus where a figure was zooming toward it.

Cade, on his kart, the Kali almost within reach now. The Kali army roared in fury. Cade was headed straight for the nidus, which stirred up a panic in Riagan. He sensed that if Cade drove his kart into it, he would cause great harm. He opened his mouth to warn Cade away, but knew it would be futile. Cade would never hear him over the Kali. And it was too late to summon the drones. Not enough time to guide them over to warn Cade away.

All they could do was watch helplessly as Cade neared the golden depression. Riagan tensed, bracing himself. Several feet before Cade reached the depression, one of the Kali dove in front of the kart and it flipped, sending Cade flying. Riagan gaped as Cade flew up and over the nidus. His arms and legs wind-milled as he cleared the creatures in it. A few of those dancing around the nidus darted out of Cade's flight path. He struck the ground.

Riagan cringed. When Cade didn't rise, Neil ran forward, Riagan following after a brief hesitation.

"Cade, are you all right?" Neil reached him and dropped to his knees. He grabbed Cade's shoulder and shook him. "Cade."

Riagan stood there, a sick feeling in his stomach. It had been a nasty landing. Then logic kicked in. This was a sim. The crash wasn't real. Was he faking for the purposes of their test? Or was there really a way for the sim to knock him out?

Movement around him drew his attention. The Kali. They'd gone quiet, but were surrounding them.

"Uh, Neil," Riagan said. There was no means of retreat.

"He's not waking up," Neil said.

"And we have no means of escape."

"Can you clear a way with the crystallizer?"

Riagan held up the crystallizer threateningly and the Kali paused. It wouldn't be enough, however. No matter which direction he chucked it, the crystallizer wouldn't take out enough Kali to open up an escape. He briefly considered throwing it at the nidus instead. That might buy them some time, but he instantly regretted the thought. While he didn't know how, he knew it was the place that life emerged from on the planet. Or at least one of them. Attacking that would be like committing mass genocide. He couldn't do that in good conscience.

The only option was surrender. Riagan tried to rack his brain for another option. That had to mean they'd failed the test. But what could he do? He set the crystallizer on the ground slowly where all the Kali could see it. Rather than wait to see how they would respond, he placed a hand on Neil and ended the sim for all three of them.

A heartbeat later he cowered inside the cylindrical cage in the sims facility. He stomped a foot, angry that the test had ended that way. What could they have done differently? Perhaps they should've started toward the cube from the start? Or maybe they should've alerted Cade to their presence sooner?

"Cade!" Neil jumped out of his sim cage and ran toward another.

As Riagan opened his own, he spotted Cade collapsed inside one. He frowned. There was no way anything inside the sim should have any effect on him now that it was ended.

Was he still inside the sim? He shouldn't be. Since they'd been connected by touch, when Riagan had ended the sim it should've ended for all three of them.

Neil reached the cage and tore open the door. Riagan hurried over as Neil shook Cade's unconscious form.

"Cade, can you hear me?" Neil asked. "Cade. Cade."

After several desperate moments, Cade's eyes fluttered open to Riagan's relief.

"Are you all right? How do you feel?" Neil asked.

"General Stribog hid it well," Cade said weakly. "I... found it... anyway."

Riagan frowned. "Found what?"

"He won't like it." Cade passed out.

"Cade. Cade wake up." Riagan stepped into the cage as Neil shook Cade's shoulders once more. Riagan checked Cade's pulse. Weak. His breath was shallow and his face pale. It made no sense.

"What should we do?" Riagan asked. Should they carry him to medical?

Neil activated the emergency button on his wrist-comp. "Wait for help."

Within minutes, medics surged into the facility, followed by Headmaster Dardanos and General Stribog. The medics crowded around Cade, forcing Neil and Riagan out of the cage, while they checked his pulse and vitals with their instruments.

Riagan cast sidelong glances at General Stribog. What did Cade's last words mean? What had the general hidden? What was wrong with Cade?

While the medics worked, Dardanos questioned them. Neil recounted everything they had witnessed, but looked strangely uncomfortable as he talked to Dardanos. Riagan offered bits and pieces, but mostly he studied Cade, wondering what was going on. He'd never heard of anyone actually getting hurt in a sim. How was this possible?

The medics finally placed Cade on a stretcher and carried him from the room. They had been unable to wake him, leaving Riagan sick with guilt.

When Dardanos finished questioning them, he turned to the General. "What was Cade after? What did you hide in there?"

"The grand beacon alone," the General said.

"Surely not," Dardanos said in disbelief. "No way a first year reached the beacon. Especially not one with a disabled leg."

General Stribog billowed. "It should be beyond reach of all but fourth year students."

Riagan shook his head. What was a grand beacon, and why was it impossible for Cade to be after finding it? "Cade had sounded scared. He must've found something."

"Cade was hurt and likely disoriented," General Stribog said. "We can't guess what he was saying. Might have been nothing."

"How was he hurt?" Riagan asked. None of this made sense.

"We'll have to wait for a doctor's assessment," Dardanos said. "Until then we have no idea, but it's nothing in the general's sim. It's run perfectly for ten years."

Riagan didn't argue. Cade must've entered the sim on his own. It wasn't unheard of for a student to try to sneak into someone else's sim and try to beat them in completing their tasks. It was known as stealing the sim. But it sounded like Cade had been there for another reason altogether and somehow endured real harm from it. His last words had been that General Stribog wouldn't be happy with whatever Cade had done. Was there something the general was hiding? If so, they wouldn't get any answers until Cade awoke.

Chapter 27

Neil's Championship

Forty thousand fans on their feet exuberantly waved team flags and hand painted signs. The Academy Games championship had arrived—Ursa vs. Taurus.

The school year was winding to a close, and the championship presented Neil's last chance to prove he deserved to be a team captain for the final exam on Mars. While they hadn't completed the Team Captain certification that General Stribog had given them, they were given a pass for rescuing Cade. Hardin had designated him as a sub-captain today to give him one last chance to demonstrate leadership. Bragging rights over Riagan wouldn't hurt either. Riagan had spent all week trash talking about how Taurus would drub Ursa, largely due to his own heroics. His boasting had gotten so over the top that Rois had confided to Neil that she was pulling for him.

Neil accessed the Ursa app on his wrist-comp, which was in a Velcro holder on his arm. The app tracked eggs captured and lost as well as teammate positions. Anand and Devika guarded the bowl, while Jack Johnson, Hanna Jensen, and Jiro Takeda hid up in the rocks to defend their base. The app didn't track opponents; the instructors blocked that option.

Satisfied that the app worked, Neil led Eris and Dirk into the forest, searching for the patrol led by Team Captain Gilbright, designated T1. About halfway in, he motioned for them to hunker down behind several boulders. Eris frowned, but didn't question him.

Neil searched for the enemy patrol.

"What do you see?" Eris whispered.

Neil put a finger to his lips.

He waited.

As planned, Hardin and Trini jogged past. Seconds later, a pair of Taurus defenders, T6 and T7, slipped out from behind oaks and pursued the two. Neil smiled and they marched onward. So far their plan was working to perfection and he led his group to the Taurus' base unchallenged.

The pits, which he had leapt across to win his first match, were now filled with water. Crocodiles floated on the water's surface, their snouts hooked downward. He shook his head in consternation. No more heroic leaps.

Before the year had started, he'd have thought the academy instructors mad for using crocodiles in a student game. Now he just scanned a croc with his wrist-comp and discovered it was a breed known as Terocrocuses that were native to Gleeson, the Malsain home planet. The academy didn't shy away from preparing students for the dangers that awaited them on other planets, albeit with some controls.

With the pits impassible, the lone way into the Taurus base was through the center path, which meant a fire fight. Hardin had discussed their opening attack plans that morning. Everyone knew their responsibilities.

A few minutes remained before the roaming Taurus patrol should pass through the area. Neil took a calm, relaxing breath. He darted out from cover and charged down the center path, hunched over slightly to make his chest target harder to hit. Enemy fire flew past his shoulders from the base, so he dropped to his belly. T9 and T10 hid behind bushes on either side of the path. Neil fired at T10, but the guard ducked. Eris dropped down next to him and took out T9 with one shot. She never missed.

Following them, Dirk shot T10's right arm, immobilizing it before Neil's second shot lit up the guard's chest target.

All clear.

They scrambled to their feet. Neil and Dirk sprinted past the indignant guards into the base. Eris remained out front, ready to provide cover fire. Too good of a shot with either arm, she never carried an egg unless absolutely necessary.

Unlike their previous matchups, there wasn't an unlocked box from which to swipe a bronze egg. For the championship, they had to unlock the five boxes to retrieve each egg, and every lock worked differently. Neil studied the silver boxes. The one on the far left had a keyhole in the top. Removing his wrist-comp, he scanned the keyhole.

"Get your printer ready," he said.

Once he had the keyhole scanned, he ran a quick program to create a diagram of the key needed to open the lock. While he worked, Dirk pulled out his 3D printer.

"What's taking so long?" Eris called from out front.

"Almost done," Neil yelled over his shoulder.

"Make it quick," Eris hollered back. "The Taurus defenders will soon know their guards are missing."

"Here I was hoping we'd have time for a barbeque," Neil muttered as he sent the print command for the key.

Dirk's printer floated a few feet above the ground and started to print the key on the print cloth he had laid out.

"Do you want BBQ sauce or Jamaican jerk on your chicken?" Neil asked.

Dirk scrunched his nose in distaste. "I'd prefer brats."

"Eris, you in the mood for chicken or brats?" Neil asked.

"What?" Eris stormed into the base, face flushed in annoyance.

Neil sighed. "The key will be printed in a second."

The key actually took two minutes to print, but fit the keyhole perfectly. Neil unlocked the lid and retrieved the bronze egg and handed it to Dirk since he was fastest, in case they needed to sprint.

Before leaving, Neil pulled back up the Ursa app. Hardin and Trini were still on the move on the left, hopefully distracting the patrol.

As they departed the base, they found one croc at the edge of the right pool, studying them. Inching over to the far left side of the path, they hurried past. When they were halfway down the path, the croc leapt up from the pool, jaws snapping mere inches away. The lunging croc gave Neil such a shock that he nearly fell into the water on the left, but just managed to keep his feet and sprint free of the pools.

Having missed them, the croc slid back underwater.

Expecting the guards to be running back by the shortest possible route, Neil led his group away from medical. He kept a wary eye on the crocs until they were well past, safe among the trees. From there, the run back to home base would be easy. They quickly jogged back through the forest, but the moment they crossed midfield, laser fire rained down on them from the rocks. One shot struck Dirk's arm and he dropped the egg. Neil cried out as another shot hit his right leg. His leg locked and he stumbled, dropping to his knees.

He lurched upright and found T3 and T4 emerging with chest targets flashing. Eris had already shot them. Their mistake not aiming for her first.

Dirk whistled appreciatively, then retrieved the egg from the ground with his good arm while Neil climbed to his feet.

"You boys going to live?" Smiling, Eris eyed Neil's leg. "Want me to help you?"

Annoyed at her *pleased-with-herself* smile, Neil waved her away. "I'll limp until I can reach medical. Let's get the egg home first. Dirk?"

Dirk held the egg with his left hand. "Can't shoot, but first thing first."

They didn't cross any other Taurus players on their way to the bowl. Inside, sudden movement to his right caused Neil to jump. He nearly toppled over his bum leg. When he checked again, he swore.

Eight-foot-long, centipede-like creatures crawled on the walls. Twice as wide as a man, the centipedes possessed brick red plates which covered their bodies. Bony pincers, about as thick as Neil's arms, poked out on either side of the creatures' mouths. Though Neil couldn't say why, these enormous centipedes freaked him out worse than the terocrocuses. He was half tempted to avoid the bowl altogether, but would never hear the end of it from Riagan. Besides, what team captain sent his people somewhere he refused to go?

As Dirk placed the egg in one of the silver boxes in the row, Neil noticed one of their eggs had been captured already. And Devika stood guard alone.

"Where's Anand?" Neil asked.

A surly expression crossed Devika's face. "Too interested in overgrown bugs only. I told him to focus. He didn't listen. Got shot in the back."

"Were you the one who shot him?" Neil asked, hoping Devika would not risk the championship game to prove a point to her brother.

Devika smirked. "The thought crossed my mind."

How did Hardin manage to handle the twins?

The captured egg safe, Neil led his group to medical, which was like a dugout along the right side of midfield. There, an older boy pointed a device at Neil's leg, pressed a button, and the suit unlocked. Another boy unlocked Dirk's arm, and they were on their way back into the forest.

"Hardin, we're on the attack from medical," Neil said over the tradutor.

"Copy," Hardin said. Neil thought that was all he was going to get, but after ten seconds, Hardin added, "In a firefight with the patrol in the back-left corner. You're clear."

Neil, Eris, and Dirk wasted no time running to the Taurus base. They closed in, preparing to attack the guards, when lasers shots flew over their heads from behind. Neil swung around in surprise to find Dirk standing still, his chest target flashing. A pair of Taurus offensive players were charging after them. Neil stepped forward and pulled Dirk into an embrace, feeling awkward doing so, but it allowed him to use Dirk's body as a shield. The Taurus players shot Dirk a couple of more times in the back while Neil lined up a chest shot and took one out. Using a tree as a shield, Eris took out the second.

Neil immediately let Dirk go and stepped back. "Sorry."

"Heck no. That was quick thinking," Dirk said in admiration before jogging off for medical.

Neil and Eris pressed on to the base, taking cover behind oaks not far from the pools. The Taurus guards hid in their same spots in the bushes to either side of the central path into their base. But this time, before Neil could direct Eris, she aimed, took two shots, and the base guards were eliminated.

Neil's jaw dropped, unable to believe she had shot them from this distance. He could tell from the guards shocked expressions that they couldn't believe it either.

More of the crocs had closed in on the central path, but none attacked as Neil entered the base.

The next box didn't have a keyhole. Using his wrist-comp to run an analysis, he discovered the box lid was made of a substance that dissolved in water. Unfortunately, the only water was in the pits with the terocrocuses.

Eris was standing guard at the base entrance, so he snuck out the left rear entrance to the base and dropped down to scoop up some water. Ten feet away, a croc turned and swam toward him. Heart hammering in his chest, he jumped back to his feet, trying not to spill all the water as he ran back inside to unlock the second egg.

Knowing the crocs were crowding the path and probably wouldn't ignore them on the way back out, he searched the base for another weapon. Would laser fire be enough to hold them off?

An idea popped into his head. He grabbed an empty box and headed out of the base, Eris following. One croc crowded the left side, while two rested their snouts on the right edge.

He broke out in a cold sweat and he wanted to stay inside the base. This was crazy to sneak past three crocs.

He closed his eyes, took a deep breath, and charged the lone croc in the left pool. He screamed as he ran and threw the box at the croc. It jumped up, caught the box in its mouth, and dove below the surface. Meanwhile, Eris fired at both crocs on her side. They dove underwater, allowing Neil and Eris an open path.

They rendezvoused with Dirk back near midfield and delivered the egg to base unobserved where they discovered the Taurus had also managed to swipe a second egg.

On their third trip into enemy territory, an ambush set by T1 surprised them. All three of them were shot in the chest. Neil berated himself for carelessness; a good team captain would expect the enemy to change tactics. That trek to medical had been humiliating. Thankfully, neither Eris nor Dirk said anything.

While the nurse was turning off their chest targets, Neil pulled up the Ursa map to see two teammates fleeing the Taurus base. Had to be Hardin and Trini.

"Hardin, do you need assistance?" Neil asked over the tradutor.

"Negative. Keep on the attack."

"Let's go," Neil told his group, determined not to be caught off guard again.

A fourth bronze egg was obtained by Trini when she correctly guessed the password for a box keypad. She'd come up with *Devils* in honor of the team that won the Space City Games championship. Taurus quickly struck back, stealing a fourth egg from them.

The championship was on the line.

Neil led Eris and Dirk back into enemy territory. With each step, Neil felt a growing weight and excitement. Everything he'd worked for this year was coming to this point.

The championship.

A team captain spot for the finals.

It all came down to this.

Approaching the Taurus base, they found five guards ringing the pools—two up in trees and a trio in trenches—not to mention the pair inside. Too many to take on.

"Hardin, can you send me an egg?" Neil asked over his tradutor, formulating an idea.

"We're down to our last one. What for?" Hardin replied back.

"We've got to gamble. Lend me one, make sure you're not seen on your way here, and I can deep-six 'em."

While Hardin considered, Neil studied the Taurus defensemen. They were interspersed well. Taking them out without heavy losses would take too long. They needed to thin the herd.

Hardin came back on the tradutor and agreed to send the egg with Jiro Takeda. Normally a defenseman, Jiro had better speed than anyone else on the team. Early on Neil had wondered why Hardin didn't take advantage of Jiro's speed on offense, until he learned that Jiro just wanted to play defense. Hardin hadn't pushed him.

Neil led his team back near midfield to wait for Jiro and fourth year student Hanna Jensen to join them. Hardin arrived to help guard Jiro.

"Five guards protect the path into the Taurus base," Neil said. "Give us five minutes, then charge past with the egg."

Hardin nodded.

Neil, Dirk, and Eris circled wide left of the base, coming in behind the trenches. Neil felt confident that this plan would work.

After five minutes Jiro charged past the Taurus defenders, bellowing like a madman. Hardin and Hanna tailed him, ducking fire from several defensemen. Hardin was hit in the arm, Hanna the shoulder. Jiro zipped past unscathed and they fled.

As Neil had hoped, several defensemen tried to play hero. The guards in the trees dropped to the ground and pursued Jiro. To Neil's delight, T9 from the trench also gave chase, greatly reducing the defenseman they had to get past for the final egg.

Neil motioned to Eris to take out the two guards remaining in the trenches. She slipped away. He and Dirk would retrieve the final egg.

They jogged over to the water-filled pits and followed those around to the center path. Neil kept an uneasy eye on the terocrocuses, which swam lazily, unconcerned with the commotion. Very strange for animal defenders. Typically, they all went berserk as the number of eggs dwindled.

"Give me some cover fire," Neil said.

Dirk fired into the base, and Neil darted up the path, hunched low. The base guards returned fire. Neil was only three steps up the path when a terocrocus lunged up from the water. Instinctively, he dove forward. Jaws clapped shut like a bear trap behind him. He landed hard, but scrambled forward on hands and knees, desperate to get into the base and not daring to glance back.

T7 stood stunned, staring at the terocrocus that had lunged at Neil. T10 shot Neil's right arm, so Neil shot him with his left hand. Dirk took out T7.

The base clear, Neil spun around, half expecting the croc to come barreling at him. The croc flexed in the middle of the path, wildly waving its tail, blocking Dirk outside. Neil's heart hammered in his throat. He was tense and ready to run, but the croc didn't advance into the base.

After a few more seconds without the croc attacking, Neil decided he was safe enough for now. He focused on the last box, which was completely smooth. No obvious locks. He tried removing the lid to make sure it was locked. It was. He picked the box up, lifting it off of two short, thin metal rods in the ground. He examined the sides, but they didn't move or separate. Turning the box over, he discovered two holes in the bottom that the metal rods had been poked through. They didn't look like keyholes, but he scanned them anyway with his wrist-comp.

Time was running short. He needed to figure out this lock soon.

The scan revealed nothing; the two holes in the box were just that. He tried to remove the bottom, but it was as secure as the rest of the box. He was at a loss.

"Neil, hurry up in there," Dirk shouted.

Neil slammed the box back on the metal rods. What was the locking mechanism? He decided to scan the top for other clues, but that turned up nothing either.

Fans in the stands started to boo.

Embarrassed, he nudged the box with his toe and this time it slid backward a little, but the bottom stayed in place. Kneeling, he pushed the box and it slid clear of the base. He picked it up and the final bronze egg lay on the ground. Excitement bubbled through him as he grabbed the egg.

The championship was in his hands.

Rising, he turned to leave, already trying to develop a plan to get rid of the croc, when his chest lit up. He stared in shock at his flashing chest target.

He was dead.

Two Taurus defenders raced past the croc into the base as it slid back into the pool. Outside, Dirk had turned with slumped shoulders to head to medical, his back target flashing.

"I'll take that," T5 said, retrieving the bronze egg.

Still in shock, Neil ran for medical. They had no time to waste.

The crocs ignored him since his chest target was flashing. He didn't make it far before Riagan came charging out of the forest, headed for the Taurus base with the last bronze egg.

That made five.

Hardin and Trini gave chase, but they were too far back to catch Riagan.

Heart sinking like an anchor, Neil watched in agony as Riagan carried the egg into the Taurus base and a trumpet sounded, signaling the end of the match. Taurus had won the championship.

Riagan was the hero.

At midfield, Taurus players celebrated. Their fans cheered in the stands as their team lined up.

Neil stared desolately as Instructor Glenn rumbled toward Taurus, followed by three students with bundles in their hands. One student handed Glenn a laurel crown. It was fragile as a twig in the instructor's massive hands. He placed the crown upon Team Captain Gilbright's head, followed by identical ones on each Taurus' players head.

Neil wanted to stalk off the field, but that was being a poor sport. Riagan had beaten him. Riagan deserved the crown and to be named a team captain. Neil owed it to Riagan as his friend to congratulate him on the victory, no matter how much it hurt.

A student handed Glenn a large crystal sphere with an amber glowing ball inside. Glenn handed the sphere to Gilbright, who held it aloft. The amber ball was a miniature sun, an imitation captured within the sphere—the Sun trophy. Taurus' fans cheered even louder.

"Thought you won the championship for us with that gamble," Eris said as she caught up with Neil.

Dirk was with her.

"Thought so, too," Neil said, tired enough to collapse there on the ground now that his adrenaline was draining away. "Can't believe we lost."

"Everything has an end. Only the sausage has two," Dirk said sagely.

Neil scowled. "What?"

"The season is over," Dirk said, as if that explained everything.

"They'll still make you a team captain, Neil," Eris said. "You're the best leader we had besides Hardin."

Not in the mood for comfort, Neil snapped. "We lost! Riagan will get it."

"Better believe it. Space Ace," Riagan said as he thumbed his chest and strutted like a rooster over to them. "They're going to announce team captains at the Academy Formal. I'd say that performance locked it up for me."

Neil gritted his teeth and clenched his fists to control his frustration, but congratulated Riagan.

"Don't worry, I'll choose ya as my second," Riagan promised, eyes glowing.

Neil wanted to knock the laurel crown from Riagan's head, but restrained himself.

"Speaking of the formal, would you go with me?" Eris asked Neil. She wore an impish grin.

"I don't know," Neil said.

The last thing he wanted to do was attend the formal. Maellyn still refused to talk to him, even now after apparently solving the Apidium problem. Now that he wouldn't become a team captain the formal would just be adding insult to injury.

"Sure he will," Riagan said. "Ya have to go. I'll find a date and we'll all go together. I shouldn't have trouble finding a date myself, seeing as I won the championship for us. I'm nonpareil."

Eris nodded. "I know several girls that would go if you asked."

"Problem solved." Riagan grinned broadly.

"Great," Neil muttered.

Mars loomed in the sky. The final exam was days away. He had spent the entire year hoping to lead a team during his first trip to Mars, but that had become a remote possibility. The instructors had told them how close they were and how the championship was their last showcase. How could he expect to get a team captain spot after failing?

He wanted to crawl back into bed and bury himself in candy.

Chapter 28

Neil Breaks into the Science Lab

Neil and Riagan, in their dress blues, marched up the steps to the academy lounge with Eris and Devika, passing by the red roses growing on the step rails. Neil had already seen one guy stopped and searched by the guards at the door for alcohol when the roses turned white, but they remained red at their passing.

As they entered the lounge, Riagan was puffed up like a conquering hero. He had been insufferable since the championship game. Only their need to cram the last two days for final exams had kept him tolerable.

Eris also wore a triumphant beam, her arm hooked through Neil's, as they entered the academy lounge. She wore a maroon dress and an Ursa pin in her hair. He wasn't sure why she was so happy. After all, she'd been on the losing team in the championship, but by the look on her face you'd think she had won everything.

Students crowded the lounge, filling up on purple melon punch and hors d'oeuvres. A dance floor at the center of the lounge was widely avoided by all the guys. A few of them actually circled around the dance floor as if it spelled their doom.

"There's Taurus." Riagan pointed out his teammates and pulled a glowing Devika off with him toward the group. Neil was sure this was the first time he had seen her without Anand.

"Ericson, can I speak with you?" Instructor Nez asked, approaching.

"Oh. Sure." Neil gave Eris an awkward glance.

"I'll get us some punch," she offered.

"Thanks."

Neil followed Nez over to a corner, wondering what this was about. Had he done something wrong?

"You've earned a team captain spot for tomorrow's exam," Nez said, a hint of a smile on his face.

Neil blinked, unsure he had heard Nez right. But there was no mistaking the congratulations on Nez's face. Neil almost jumped in the air. He wanted to race over to Riagan and tell him the good news. "I thought I'd lost."

"Riagan will be your number two," Nez added.

"Oh." Neil's elation plummeted. "When will you tell him?" Now Riagan was going to be intolerable to live with for a completely different reason.

"It's customary for the team captains to inform their number two."

"I… Ok." Neil stared across the room at Riagan, who talked animatedly with his teammates. This was going to go horribly.

Nez held out his hand. "Congratulations on your assignment. You've demonstrated great leadership qualities this year. I expect you'll do well."

"Thank you." Still in shock, Neil shook his hand.

The thrill of his selection was gone. After coveting a team captain all year long, he suddenly wished the instructors had chosen someone else. The last thing he wanted to do was tell Riagan that he'd been passed on. Why did they make him do it? He had hoped to celebrate with Riagan, but now a part of him feared his friend might blame him for this.

Eris re-emerged from the crowd and handed Neil a glass of purple melon punch. "What did Nez want?"

"I got team captain," Neil said glumly.

"That's wonderful!" Eris said. "You totally deserve it. Who's your number two?"

"Riagan."

Eris chortled. "That's awesome. After he ribbed you at the championship? Can I be there when you tell him?"

He resented her enjoyment. He knew how Riagan would take the news and had no desire to humiliate him on top of it. Rois needed to be the one with them when he told Riagan. No one else. She could keep him from overreacting.

"Will you dance with me?" Eris asked, setting her glass aside.

"No one's on the dance floor." He didn't want to dance, especially not first.

"You're a captain now. If you go, others will, too."

"Eris, I really don't—"

She grabbed the drink from his hand and placed it beside her own, then pulled him out onto the dance floor. "Every girl wants to dance. I saved you the trouble of asking. Don't embarrass me by refusing."

Other students had already taken notice. A few girls jealously regarded Eris. If he declined now, he really would embarrass her. But he had no idea how to dance. Why was all of this happening to him?

She took his left hand and placed her other on his shoulder. He placed his free hand on her waist. Was that right? He moved it toward her back, which felt awkward so he moved it back to her side. Why had he let her drag him out here? He stared at her beaming face, not daring to glance around to see who was watching.

Probably everyone. Gawking and laughing.

"I'm glad you came with me," she said as they shifted from one foot to the other.

He smiled, not sure how to respond. He had never danced with a girl before, except his mom when he was little. All his focus was trained on not stepping on her feet or tripping. How obvious was it to everyone that he couldn't dance?

After a minute, a few other couples surrounded them. Relief washed through him. Now if he made a mistake it might go unnoticed. He risked a glance into the crowd and spotted Maellyn on a couch in an amethyst dress. Her resplendence made him yearn to talk to her. He wished she were here dancing with him instead of Eris. But when she noticed him, her eyes flashed angrily, lips pursed. She rose and stalked away.

Just great. This formal was turning out to be every bit the nightmare he'd feared.

He had hoped Maellyn might eventually forgive him, yet every time he tried to apologize she stormed off. He had made a simple mistake. Anyone might have made it. How was he to know about her father's secret project? He had tried to do the right thing. Would she hold it against him forever?

The song ended and he quickly pulled away from Eris' grasp. "I need to talk to Riagan about being my number two," he said as an excuse to get off the dance floor.

"Can't you do that later?" she asked, flushing.

"I need to get it out of the way." He slipped away before she could argue further. He pushed past the other dancers until he was clear of the dance floor, then rushed over to where Riagan cut up with his teammates.

"My number two," Riagan announced, clapping Neil on the shoulders.

Neil winced at his words.

"Ya rocked on the dance floor. Cheers." Riagan held up a glass of punch as if toasting. "Keep it up and all the girls will fight over ya. Even made your one jealous."

Neil scowled, not wanting to discuss Maellyn. He doubted that jealousy was the reason for her departure, but Eris certainly hadn't helped by drawing attention to them coming to the formal together.

As if sensing Neil's frustration, Riagan gestured toward the balcony at the back of the lounge. "Come on, I've got something that'll cheer ya up." Riagan led the way, Devika still on his arm. Neil followed reluctantly.

"Where are we headed?" Eris asked as she joined them.

Neil wanted to groan. He hoped she didn't spill the beans about him getting team captain instead of Riagan. Neil debated telling her the truth—he'd only agreed to come with her because she and Riagan had pressured him into it—in order to get rid of her. Instead, he pressed his lips together to hold his tongue. He wouldn't humiliate her in front of Devika and Riagan.

They stepped out back onto the lounge balcony where Mars dominated the view, covering most of the sky as the moon had his first night here. Tomorrow he would set foot on a new planet for the first time. The thought sent a chill of anticipation through him, brightening his mood slightly. He just had to endure this for a couple more hours.

Riagan pulled a flask from his pocket. "To our last night of the school year." He took a drink. He raised the flask again. "To me on winning the championship."

He drank again, then offered the flask to Devika. She took a swallow and started coughing.

Neil scanned the balcony for instructors or lounge staff. "How did you manage to get that past the rose detectors?"

"A team captain must keep secrets to himself, even from his number two." Riagan grinned as if he'd told a great joke.

Eris snorted, but didn't comment. She gave Neil a knowing glance, which he ignored. She was *too* happy at learning Riagan wouldn't be a team captain.

Devika took a second swig and handed the flask to Eris, who drank. She offered it to Neil.

"I'm ok." Neil waved her hand away.

Riagan grabbed the flask and shoved it in Neil's face. "Ya can't turn down whiskey."

Neil took a step back. He didn't want any. Truthfully, he didn't want to be here at all. He was not in a celebratory mood, what with Maellyn still angry at him and Riagan soon to be.

"Tomorrow's the final exam," he protested, hoping that got them to back off.

Riagan frowned. "Oh, please. A couple of swallows won't kill ya."

"You go ahead." Neil pushed the flask away.

Devika's upper lip curled. "Maybe the whiskey is too tough? We could probably find him a wine cooler."

He flushed. His wrist-comp started vibrating. He reached into his jacket pocket and pulled it out, hoping it would be Maellyn.

One new message from Rois. The subject line read *Urgent: I Found Something*.

"I need to go," Neil said, starting back inside.

"C'mere," Riagan called. "Ya can't go."

Neil hurried through the lounge and headed for the exit. He and Rois had been secretly discussing for weeks how they might discover the actual traitor. She excelled at digging for more information. She had discovered that the CME was actually a power generator for outposts on Mars, confirming what Dr. Trevena had told him previously. He felt another twinge of guilt that he had suspected Maellyn's father of being a traitor. The confirmation also surprised him because he had expected the Dahaka to be after a weapon.

Hurrying down the front steps of the lounge, Neil pulled up the message from Rois.

I know what happened to Cade. It was the traitor. Meet me in the sim's facility in an hour and I'll show you. Rois.

As he reached the Space City U campus, movement by the science labs caught Neil's attention. General Stribog was approaching the labs. He opened the door and slipped inside, a wisp of smoke billowing behind him.

Suddenly, the spark of a memory stirred in Neil's mind. That day he had seen the Dahaka in the window. The traitor had been completely out of view, except… there had been smoke. At the time he had thought that the traitor was smoking. Could it have been the general instead?

Neil read the message a second time.

I know what happened to Cade.

Cade hadn't woken from his coma since General Stribog's sim. The doctors were baffled.

It was the traitor.

Headmaster Dardanos and the instructors had repeatedly explored the sim to search for what had gone wrong, but found nothing. What had Rois discovered that they had missed?

Meet me in the sim's facility in an hour—

Neil wanted to talk to her right away, but where was she? He hadn't seen her or Jaya at the formal.

Cade's final words drifted into memory.

General Stribog hid it well. I found it. He won't like it.

The General had suggested that Cade had referred to the grand beacon. Had it been a cover? And now he was sneaking into the science labs on a night when everyone else was attending the formal. Instinctively, Neil reached into his pocket and grasped his grandfather's coin, but didn't pull it out. Touching it gave him some small comfort, but he knew he could no longer let it make his decisions for him. A team captain had to make decisions.

What had his efforts gained thus far? He had lost Maellyn when he falsely accused her father of being the traitor. If he was wrong again, people would think he was crying wolf. Maybe he should wait and see what Rois had discovered.

What if an hour was too late?

Despite learning that the CME was supposedly a power generator, he was still worried about what the Dahaka would do if they got their hands on it. If the general was smuggling the CME to the Dahaka, who else might be hurt in the process?

He let go of his grandfather's coin. He needed to know what the general was up to, even if it turned out to be nothing. He hoped it was nothing.

Hurrying into the science lab, he found the main hallway deserted. He scanned the labs around him as he cautiously made his way toward the first side corridor. He strained for any sound of danger. All the doors were shut and only a few lights were on. General Stribog might be in any of them. What if he came out and found Neil lurking in the hallways? That made the hairs on Neil's arms stand up. He had no weapons.

In his head, he heard Riagan's voice, a devil on his shoulder, hissing at him to leave. The security cameras in the labs would capture everything.

What good were the security cameras if the general got away with the CME before anyone saw the footage? Or worse, he might encounter someone while trying to move the CME off the ship. He couldn't live with himself if he slunk away now and an innocent was harmed.

The general could come from any direction, and possessed a lot more stealth training. Neil might have only one chance to act. Ice ran up his spine as he eased along the middle corridor. Each step was like wading through quicksand. He was terrified, and wondered if his grandfather had felt a similar fear during the war.

Neil forced himself to step around the corner to the second corridor. He flinched in shock. Jarl stood before a lab door with its keypad hanging halfway off. The hallway beyond Jaya's father was empty. Same back the other way. No sign of General Stribog.

"What are you doing here?" Neil asked in confusion.

Jarl jumped, inhaling sharply, before recognizing him. The Azzaro smiled. "I'm surprised to see you. Why aren't you at the formal?"

"I needed some air," Neil said. "Have you seen anyone else around here?"

"Only me, trying to repair the keypad on my lab."

"This is your lab?"

"It is," Jarl confirmed. He turned back to his work. "They gave me one with a lousy keypad. It works only half the time. I guess that's why I got it. No one else wanted it. Can you give me a hand?"

Neil checked the hall again. Empty except for the two of them. Had the general gone into a lab on the first corridor?

As Neil stood there with Jarl, his anxiety felt foolish. Just because he had a memory of smoke when he'd seen the Dahaka, didn't mean the general had been there or was the traitor. He was an instructor after all, and probably had a completely normal reason for being in the labs. He might have his own lab as well. Neil had let Rois' cryptic message and his imagination concoct a crazy conspiracy.

"Sure." Neil hurried over to Jarl.

"I'm having trouble reaching that screw." Jarl pointed at the small screw in the bottom of the keypad box and handed Neil a slender screwdriver. "My hands are too big. Can you get it?"

Neil stuck the screwdriver carefully in the box. He had to hold the tool with his fingertips in order to reach the screw. It took him a couple of seconds of fiddling with the screwdriver before he lined it up with the screw. A few slow turns and the screw loosened.

"I've got it."

The screw came free of its hole and Neil turned the keypad over to dump it into his fist.

A tiny prick stung his neck.

Alarmed, Neil dropped the screwdriver and keypad and jumped back. Feeling his neck, he stared at Jarl as a wave of dizziness hit him. Jarl held a needle in one hand.

"What was…" The words slurred in his mouth.

"Easy now," Jarl said. "Lean back against the wall."

Dread slammed into Neil. The world swam and he stuck out his hands to steady himself. "What did you do?"

"It's ok. You won't remember this. Try to relax."

Neil fell back against the wall, staring at the Azzaro in shock. His vision blurred and he shivered uncontrollably.

"Breathe," Jarl urged. "The chemical hypnosis heightens emotional centers in the brain. You can calm yourself by breathing."

"Why?" Neil asked. "You're Jaya's father."

"You won't remember when you awake anyway."

Neil knew he couldn't run. He felt in his pocket for his wrist-comp, thinking maybe he could somehow send a message, but it fell from his weakening grasp. It thudded on the ground. Jarl retrieved it, while Neil blinked to try to clear his vision. The room was teetering.

"Guess I'll be visiting Rois next," Jarl said grimly.

Rois! Neil had to get to her, to warn her. He fought to stand, to clear his head, but a weight dragged him down into darkness.

*****

"Ya left too early," Riagan said as a light burst on.

Neil lurched up in bed, head foggy. Disoriented from sleep, it took him a minute to realize that he was in his own bed.

Riagan stared at him, then shook his head. "Why did ya leave?"

Neil considered this. How had he gotten here? "Leave what?"

"The formal. Ya missed Eris clobber Patrick with a butternell. Turns out he's allergic." Riagan looked like the cat who'd got the cream, as if it had been his own doing.

"Wish I had seen that," Neil admitted, blinking his eyes. He was exhausted, and wanted nothing more than to go back to sleep. The last thing he remembered was dancing with Eris. Maellyn had seen them and stormed out. He couldn't remember the rest of the party, coming to bed, or anything in between.

"Can't believe they haven't announced team captains," Riagan said.

Neil bit his lower lip and groaned. He had forgotten about talking to Riagan. He didn't want to tell him, but had to at some point. Was it too late to get Rois now?

He fumbled on his nightstand for his wrist-comp so he could send Rois a message. Something he couldn't quite recall tugged at his memory as he checked his messages. It was empty. He must've cleared out his messages before going to sleep. Why couldn't he remember how he got there?

Riagan sat on his own bed. "Guess they'll announce before the exam starts."

Neil sighed and set his wrist-comp aside. He couldn't put this off any longer. "Actually, Instructor Nez told me I made team captain." He hesitated a second. "I'm supposed to tell you that you're my second."

Riagan stared at him, dumbstruck, his good humor evaporating. "I won the championship. That was the final test."

Neil pressed his hands to his face in an effort to clear the fog from his mind. "Apparently there was more to it than that. I don't know. Instructor Nez didn't tell me." Neil wanted to go back to sleep. Why couldn't he remember leaving the party?

"Hey Riagan, did anything happen at the formal?" he asked.

No answer. He glanced up, but Riagan had left the room. Neil debated going after him, but thought better of it.

Riagan might want to be alone right now.

He would.

Chapter 29

Riagan's Fall

A hallway alarm woke Riagan the next morning. Head throbbing from only getting a couple hours of sleep, he wanted to roll back over and wait for the alarm to silence. Instead, he pushed back his covers and rose to his feet, his training kicking in. Neil blinked sleep from his eyes as he rose and they silently dressed in their explorer suits.

Boys in adjoining rooms and out in the halls started to shout "Landing Day" and "Can't wait to walk on Mars."

Instructor Nez shouted orders. "Out of bed! Collect your gear! Assemble in the courtyard in fifteen minutes!"

Despite his exhaustion, a surge of energy washed through Riagan. He had waited all year for this. Not the final exam, but the exploring Mars. Before his recruitment, he'd never dreamt of one day visiting the red planet, but now that it was a reality, they couldn't reach the surface fast enough.

After inserting his tradutor, Riagan grabbed his helmet and the two of them pressed through the mass confusion in the dorm hallway. Out in the courtyard, instructors separated everyone by class year.

Nez, in charge of the first-years, strode in front of them. "Your team assignments are on your wrist-comps. Review them and file in with your team captain."

Riagan moved over beside Neil as he pulled up the final exam assignments. They were joined by Eris, Nico, and Fran Snelling, but not Rois. Riagan blinked twice, unable to believe she wasn't on their team.

He searched the courtyard and spotted her grouped with Maellyn, Jiro Takeda, Jaya, and Patrick and Caleb. Patrick's face was still red and slightly swollen, like a boxer after a fight, from Eris hitting him with a butternell at the formal. Patrick's condition only gave Riagan a second's satisfaction, before he clenched his fists. This was not happening! Why had Nez put Patrick and Rois together? He had seen firsthand what Patrick had done to her.

"We need to change assignments," Riagan said, starting toward Nez.

"Get in line," the instructor snapped, face darkening.

"Ya can't—" Riagan began.

Neil put a hand on his chest, stopping him. "Let me handle it. I'm *team captain* and this is our final exam."

Riagan ground his teeth at the reminder. Another slight from the instructors, but he nodded.

"They teamed your sister with Patrick?" Nico asked, typing away on his wrist-comp. "That's not right."

Riagan ignored him and watched Neil approach Nez. The instructor listened impassively. Forcing Rois to team with Patrick after how he had humiliated her was a slap in her face.

Riagan's wrist-comp alerted him to a message from Rois. He pulled it up.

Don't worry about me. I can handle it.

He met her eyes, and shook his head. He wanted to talk with her on the tradutors, but each team had their own frequency for the exam.

Rois started typing on her wrist-comp again.

Patrick isn't going anywhere. Going to be teamed with him sometimes whether we like it or not. He can't hurt me. I've got Jaya and Maellyn with me today. You should appreciate that Patrick has to take orders from Jaya.

Another time it might've amused him, but today it wasn't enough to restore his mood. Surely, they could swap Fran for Rois.

But Neil returned, grinding his teeth. "Nez insisted the teams were carefully chosen. We take the exam as assigned or fail." He cast a pained look at Rois.

Riagan almost threw his wrist-comp. He would rather fail. Rois glared at him, Jaya and Maellyn at her side. He knew what she would say. She had made her arguments before when he had wanted to get even with Patrick. Rois believed that Space City offered a better future for them and she wanted to stick it out. If he failed, they would be separated. But he hated doing nothing.

Only the knowledge that Jaya was in charge of her group diminished Riagan's frustration. Jaya would look after her. If anyone in their year was a good choice for team captain, it was him. Riagan wondered how long Jaya had known he'd been named a team captain. Neil hadn't known before last night. Instructor Nez must've informed him at the formal. Except as Riagan thought about it, he couldn't remember seeing Jaya at the formal last night. Or Rois for that matter. They'd planned to come. She'd even gotten a new dress for it. And Maellyn had been there. At least briefly.

He pulled out his wrist-comp to message Rois.

I didn't see you at the formal last night.

I guess I fell asleep. Jaya had been summoned by General Stribog, who informed him that he'd made team captain. On his way to pick me up, he said I messaged him that I would be late. I don't remember that or why I sent it, but I checked my messages. It was there. So he went back to his dorm to wait for me. When I didn't message him back, he came looking for me. Found me asleep in bed. I've been studying so much lately for exams, I guess the lack of sleep just caught up with me.

Riagan couldn't say he was surprised. She had always overstudied in school, terrified she was going to fail. But it was strange that she couldn't remember going to sleep, just like Neil.

He didn't have time to think more on it. For the next hour everyone ensured their packs had the required supplies, reviewed the exam maps, and scanned themselves. Adrien Laroque failed his health screen—the doctors wouldn't take a chance with his health—and he was removed from the exam. Too bad it wasn't Patrick.

After they completed preparations, Nez led the first years toward the spaceport. They soon reached a large gray ship where General

Stribog ordered them to their assigned seats along one side of the hull or the other. Despite Riagan's frustration, his excitement returned as he took his seat between Neil and Fran Snelling.

"Do we know anything about the exam?" Fran asked, looking over Riagan's shoulders at Neil.

Neil raised his palms upward. "Nez and General Stribog have kept things quiet. I asked both Dirk and Hardin about their exams, but supposedly it changes every year."

And then the roar of the ship taking off, like an irritable bear waking from hibernation, silenced all discussion. By the time it quieted, once they were beyond Space City's artificial atmosphere, everyone was staring at their wrist-comps or lost in silent contemplation.

Riagan wondered what it would finally be like to stand on Mars. He knew details. It would be cold. Absolutely freezing. And the atmospheric pressure would be much lower than what they were accustomed to on the ship, which was in line with the Earth's. But those were just technical details. That's why they wore their explorer suits and helmets, which regulated their body temperatures and provided appropriate pressure. None of that told him what it would feel like to be there.

A short time later the ship shook from turbulence as it entered Mars own atmosphere. The shaking rattled his teeth and the seat straps were all that prevented any of them from being thrown about.

When they finally landed and the ship powered down, there were murmurs of excitement from everyone. Riagan unbuckled himself and rose, legs feeling a little wobbly after the flight, but it only took a moment for them to steady.

Nez and General Stribog handed out pairs of drone rockets to each team, while ordering them to don their helmets! Drop their face shields! Activate their suits oxygen system! Verify their suits' pressure regulators operated correctly! And pair the wrist-comps with their face shields! Seeing exam data on their face shields as needed, rather than constantly checking their wrist-comps, would be imperative to passing. They had no time to waste.

Riagan completed the routine safety checks, all the while suppressing the desire to shout for Nez or General Stribog to open the ship's bay door and let them loose. And then Nez hit a button and the door lowered to the ground and they raced out onto Mars' surface.

A reddish desert streaked with angular dark gray rocks and sand dunes—devoid of any plant life, automatically giving it an alien feel—as far as the eye could see in any direction. The color of the surface came from the oxidized iron dust that covered the planet. The air was presently filled with that dust, giving everything a hazy brownish quality.

In the distance, an enormous sandstorm raged over Hellas Basin, which was the biggest hole in the ground in the solar system, caused when an asteroid hit Mars' surface in the ancient past. Repeated lightning illuminated the storm, revealing two copper-colored funnel clouds deep in its heart. Of course, the Hellas Basin was over two thousand kilometers in diameter. Those funnel clouds were hundreds of miles away at least. Much farther away than they'd have time to travel for today's exam.

As he took his first steps onto the Martian surface, the hairs on his arms rose, and not from the cold, which the suit was quickly adjusting to. He knew he would remember this moment for the rest of his life. Reverently picking up a handful of red dirt, Riagan let it spill through his gloved fingers. He wished he could remove the gloves and touch the dirt with his bare hands. Would it feel any different from Earth?

A few classmates stepped about gingerly as if they feared falling through the ground. Others ran wild like pent-up hare dogs suddenly freed. A few jumped impossibly high, their feet reaching above his head before landing, as if some invisible force momentarily lifted them up before gravity kicked in.

Riagan soaked it all in. He wanted to explore the entire planet, and he promised himself that this wouldn't be the last new world that he visited. He wanted to see another, and a third after that. A hundred. No, a thousand alien planets.

After granting a couple of minutes to enjoy the novelty, General Stribog reigned everyone in. "Your exam's started."

Riagan scowled, not ready for business, but the instructors were in no-nonsense mode.

"Riagan, scout ahead," Neil said, handing him one of the drone rockets.

The drone rockets resembled short black bazookas. They were necessary because regular drones wouldn't fly on Mars, where the atmospheric pressure was much too low to accommodate traditional aerial spacecraft. Each rocket came with a case that held a dozen golf ball-sized drone cubes. Riagan removed a cube from the case and stuffed it into the rocket. The rest he slipped into his pack for the time being.

"Into the wolf's mouth," Nico said cheerfully.

"Probably a lot of traps," Riagan agreed.

Nico laughed. "No. Into the wolf's mouth means good luck without saying it."

"Oh."

Riagan set off in a jog, feeling lighter than normal so that he covered a little more distance than usual. A dot on his map, displayed on the right side of his face shield, showed their first destination. He shrunk the map down to a size on his face shield where he felt comfortable that it wouldn't hinder his view too much. He decided to hold off on firing his drone rocket for the time being. At the moment everything was open and clear. They were headed straight into the dust storm surrounding the Hellas Basin.

Before Riagan got far, the wind started to wail like a banshee, whipping up the dust clouds until they became like a dense fog. The dust coated his helmet, restricting his view. So he raised the drone rocket about forty-five degrees upward and fired. There was a loud pop and the drone cube shot into the air, quickly lost from sight.

The drone cube was made up of several mini drones that separated upon firing, much the way shotgun shells sprayed pellets. The mini drones arched through the air and landed roughly ten miles away. Each mini drone possessed its own camera feed, which was transmitted back to a central computer on the ship they'd landed in. The computer combined the overlapping feeds into one larger view that Riagan could tap into with his wrist-comp and display on his face shield, which he did so now. He was thankful the face shield showed the feed, because he wasn't sure he'd be able to see anything on the wrist-comp.

The feed showed more open desert and the beginning of Hellas Basin, though the picture quality wasn't great due to the dust. Still, it provided more than he could see on his own.

By the time he reached the basin's edge, the wind buffeted him about, nearly toppling him several times and severely slowing his progress. He felt isolated from the team, with only Neil's faint commands over the tradutor to keep him company. Brushing dust from his helmet, Riagan decided to fire off a second drone cube to see what awaited below and hopefully get an actual visual of their first destination. While he waited for the drones to land, he started his descent. The slope was pretty steep, forcing him to take his time. A short time later, the new drone feed appeared on his face shield. About thirty seconds into the feed, three red blobs appeared on the far left of the screen. He froze, pausing the feed and expanding the view to identify what he was seeing.

Traga. Three of them lying in ambush. Probably thirty yards to his left, but further down into the basin.

He started to report the sighting when a rock slid out from underfoot. He fell backward, landing hard, and slid down the slope. He clawed at the ground for purchase, finding nothing but dirt. Finally, spreading arms and legs wide as if to create a snow angel, he skidded to a halt on a somewhat flat patch.

Gasping, Riagan felt a few bruises, but nothing worse. He lurched to a sitting position and searched for the Traga ambush. No sign of them through the dust clouds. He searched for his wrist-comp. It lay a few yards back up the basin, its screen broken. He retrieved it, but found he could do nothing with it. The drone feed remained on his face shield, but he could no longer control it. Nor switch to a new feed if he fired another drone cube, rendering the rest in his pack useless.

He punched the ground. What lousy luck!

"Neil, come in," Riagan said as he dumped the wrist-comp into his pack. "I've spotted an ambush, nine o'clock."

Nothing over the screaming dust storm.

"Do ya want me to engage?" Riagan asked, wondering if he could find them now on his own. He'd slid a good way down the basin slope and now had no idea if they were above or below his present position. He certainly couldn't see them.

This time Neil responded. "Negative. We'll circle. Press... to... supply—"

"Affirmative." Riagan rose to a crouch and crept downward, now wary of loose rocks. Fortunately, he was able to shrink the drone feed to the corner of his face shield again and since there wasn't much new to see on it, he switched back to his map. He took measured steps and kept watch for the Traga so they wouldn't surprise him. What else awaited them in the storm? Without the drones, he was blind.

Fifteen uneventful minutes dragged along until he spotted a lone building, little more than a hut, up ahead. From outside, it resembled a temporary shelter, a ten-by-ten-foot room which could self-assemble itself in five minutes. The shelter was standard issue for any explorer team, as long as they had a vehicle to carry it in. It was a little too large for a pack. He picked up his pace, anxious for a reprieve from the pummeling winds.

As he neared the entrance, the ground exploded a few feet before the door. Riagan's breath caught in his throat. He studied the ground. Were there landmines?

After a few cautious steps forward, he spotted a mini drone, half buried in the dirt. Someone on the team had fired their own drone cube. Thankfully, it hadn't hit him. He hoped whoever it was got docked on their grade. Everyone knew not to fire a cube if there was someone ahead.

He didn't bother retrieving it. The instructors would send out a drone collector later. All the mini drones were magnetic. The collector was a supersonic craft—its speed necessary to fly in Mars thin air—which collected the minis. Unfortunately, it couldn't be used to collect visual data like the minis, because it was traveling too fast. But it certainly helped with collecting the minis.

Now to get out of this storm.

Protocol dictated that he wait for the rest of the team before entering the shelter, but he was tired of the pounding wind and dust. He opened the door and stepped into the shelter. Before he could take a second, a laser struck him in the chest, lighting up the suit's target. He halted midstride and stared at his flashing target, dumbfounded.

He had been shot.

Searching for the shooter, he spotted an automatic gun hanging from the ceiling in the corner.

"You're down," Nez said over the tradutor, obviously monitoring the situation on a video feed back on the ship.

Riagan remembered Gilbright's warning to them on their first day of Battle Tactics. They were always being tested. He had lowered his guard too easily, thinking of this place as nothing more than a safe bunker. Little wonder the instructors had named Neil team captain over him.

Like in the Academy Games, Riagan was 'dead' until he returned to the ship, which put his team at a disadvantage. He would also lose points on his grade. Hopefully he wouldn't fail altogether. Berating himself, he turned to march back outside.

"Stop," Nez ordered. "You'll wait until after your team comes. Remain out of view."

Riagan gritted his teeth and did as directed. He couldn't talk or warn them, but passing them on his return to the ship would have alerted them to trouble. Now he had to hope that Neil and the rest were more cautious than he'd been.

Leaning against a wall, he studied the shelter. Spread out on a table on the back wall were five skunk sack eggs. What did they need them for?

He grinned as he recalled the sulfurous stench that the rotten liquid left all over Caleb's bed last fall. That had been a good prank. He might need to do an encore for Patrick if he hurt Rois in any way during the exam.

"Riagan, report," Neil said over the tradutor. "Have you reached the shelter?"

Riagan clamped his mouth shut and focused on the eggs. What had Sergeant Terror said they warded away?

"Riagan, what's your status?" Neil asked. "Are you in the shelter?"

Tereshkova had said the stench warded away predators, specifically… the Hyaenodon. Were the beasts on the loose in the basin? As cold as it was outside, the Hyaenodon couldn't possibly survive. But what about their next destination?

Voices outside caused him to tense. The gun in the corner fired again. A pack poked into the room. The gun fired a second time at the pack, which Neil held like a shield before him as he entered. He shot a target at the base of the gun and it stopped firing.

Riagan grinned in relief.

Neil turned to him, a cocky smile on his face. "Guess we're down a man. When you didn't respond, I figured you got caught by another ambush."

Riagan debated shooting him in the chest for that comment, but knew that would definitely earn him a failing grade for the exam.

The team joined them in the shelter and Riagan decided to wait and hear what they discovered about the eggs and their next destination before he returned to the ship. Nez had ordered him to wait, and hadn't said for how long.

"I can't believe you got taken out." Nico shook his head.

Riagan colored in embarrassment, unable to believe it himself. "Me neither."

Neil focused them on the task at hand. "Skunk sack eggs. We'll encounter Hyaenodon ahead. They'll have to be inside to survive, so we need to send the drones in search of large structures in the area."

Eris eyed the eggs with a distasteful expression on her face. "I've got no room in my pack."

"We can't carry them," Neil said. "All we need is the juice. We'll cut them open."

Everyone grumbled. Riagan knew where this was going and he didn't like it. Granted, thanks to their suits and sealed air systems, they wouldn't have to endure the stench, but still...

"What do we carry the juice in?" Fran wrinkled her nose in disgust, not catching on.

"We'll smear the juice on our suits." Neil retrieved a knife and cut open one of the eggs. "It's the simplest solution. We should also take the leaves in case of injuries."

"This is disgusting," Fran said, pouting as she dipped her gloved hand in the skunk sack juices.

Nico smeared them on his arms. "You'll be thankful when we come across Hyaenodon."

Riagan had to agree.

Once Neil finished coating himself, he cut open the last skunk sack. He picked it up and approached Riagan.

"Cheers," Riagan said dryly.

Neil scooped out the juice and smeared it all over him. "After returning to the ship, you can come straight to meet us."

Once he was finished, Neil, alerted by a new message on his wrist-comp, studied it for a moment before speaking. "We're headed deeper into the basin. I've just distributed the latest instructions."

Riagan groaned. Would they give him a new wrist-comp when he got back to the ship? It would be difficult to catch up if he was flying blind.

"Let's head out," Neil said.

The others bemoaned having to brave the storm again so soon. Riagan kept his mouth shut. He had let his team down. He couldn't leave them undermanned for long, so he led the way outside, wondering if he would be able to catch up. Determined to not be MIA for the rest of the exam, he started back up the slope toward their ship.

"We've got in-coming," Eris warned, pointing toward a figure approaching from the east. "Maybe another ambush?"

Riagan turned back to find a figure limping toward them alone, but appeared to be wearing one of their explorer suits. He had a hard time recognizing who it could be through the dust.

"We'll check them out, but remain alert," Neil said.

Everyone was tense, scouring the area nearby and taking measured steps. Riagan was torn between watching to see who the figure was and hurrying back to the ship so he could return.

Suddenly, Neil broke into a run toward the hobbling figure, leaving everyone else behind. After a second look, Riagan realized who it was in the storm.

Maellyn!

Blood covered her arms and sides.

Riagan raced after them.

Neil reached her first and threw an arm about her shoulders. She slumped into him.

"Are you all right?" Neil asked, terror in his voice. "What happened?"

Aghast, Riagan searched the storm for Rois. Why were they separated?

"Dahaka." Maellyn shook. Her face was ashen. Or did it just look that way from the dust covering her helmet? "They attacked us." She started to cry.

A chill enveloped Riagan, freezing his bones. What were the Dahaka doing here? And where was Rois?

"Instructor Nez, come in," Neil shouted. "Sergeant Nez. We're under attack."

Silence from the tradutors.

"Where's Rois?" Riagan wanted to grab Maellyn and shake her for answers. Whose blood was that on her suit? He didn't see any rips in it.

Maellyn stared at him desperately.

"Where?" he whispered.

She pointed east, the way she had come.

Riagan ran. Neil shouted at him to wait. Let them fire off some drone cubes to get a visual. But he had no time to waste.

The basin's incline made running difficult. The storm blocked so much from view, but he charged forward, his sole concern finding Rois. His head swiveled left and right, searching. He hoped she would hobble out of the storm like Maellyn. He would've settled for Jaya or even Patrick if only to give him a better idea of where to find her. Even seeing the Dahaka would help. But the storm hid everything. He wanted to scream, as if his fury might part the red dust. He remembered the tradutors had an emergency frequency and switched to it.

"Rois. Rois, can ya hear me? Rois. Where are you? Rois."

And then he saw them, a wreckage on the ground. Patrick. Jiro. Caleb. All lay crumpled on the ground, unmoving. Jaya lay, sprawled out, a few feet away.

Rois.

He zeroed in on her, desperate to get to her side.

"Rois. Rois, wake up." Riagan scooped her up in his arms. Blood was smeared around what resembled a scar in the side of her suit. Nanobots in the suit's material had already sealed up the suit to prevent loss of air and exposure, but also concealed the severity of her injuries. "Rois. Wake up. Ya going to be ok. I'll get ya to the ship."

He tried to lift her and she screamed and lurched.

"No. Not yet," she gasped.

He slackened his grip to avoid causing her further pain than necessary. "I need to get ya to the ship."

"Not yet. I can't go." Her pupils were wide with terror.

"Ya hurt. Ya need medical attention." He remembered the skunk sack leaves, but he didn't have any.

"Not yet. I can't go. Where's Jaya?" she craned her neck, searching for him. "I can't go. Not yet. He promised to take me to Sundara."

She seemed delirious. He needed to get her back to the ship before it was too late.

"Rois, I've got to carry ya." He started to lift her and she screamed again. He had to get her back, but his efforts only seemed to make things worse.

"Ya have to—" Rois gasped and clutched his arm weakly. "Ya have to… take care of me. Mom and dad depend on ya."

"I know." Tears blurred his vision.

They had to go now, period. He lifted her, this time ignoring her scream of pain as he surged to his feet.

"Not yet," she cried. "It hurts. I can't go."

"We've got to go." He started to carry her away, guessing at the direction of the ship.

"Jaya. Jaya," she called. "Not yet... I... don't let me…" Her words trailed away.

"Rois. Rois."

Her head had fallen back.

"Rois, I'm getting you help. Hold on."

But her eyes stared at nothing. He cradled her head, but she looked through him, no longer seeing.

"C'mere." His knees crumpled beneath him and he fell to the ground. He kept a tight hold on her. "Rois, c'mere."

She hung limply against his chest. In that moment he saw their mother's eyes in hers; they both hung lifeless in his arms. This vision of the two of them would haunt his nightmares forever.

Despair froze to madness, turning him into a blizzard.

"Riagan, I'm sorry." Neil set an apologetic hand on his shoulder.

He stiffened. He hadn't even heard them approach.

"Where did they come from?" He eased Rois down, his thoughts slow and jumbled.

He rose and turned toward Maellyn. She gestured into the storm. He followed the line of her fingers and something inside him cut hard.

Chapter 30

Neil Tracks Riagan

Neil stood trapped between Rois' dead body and Riagan's fleeing form. How could Rois be dead? He had argued with Instructor Nez to switch Rois to his team only an hour ago, and now she was gone.

Riagan ran alone, half mad with grief, into the Martian landscape. Likely toward an encounter with the Dahaka. Meanwhile Space City, everyone onboard, and all the students down on the surface for final exams, had no idea about the Dahaka that threatened them. How many Dahaka hid here in the storm planning some sort of attack?

Neil knew he needed to sound the alarm.

"Instructor Nez, come in," Neil yelled over the emergency band. "General Stribog. Headmaster Dardanos. Instructor Tereshkova. Anyone. The Dahaka… they're attacking."

Silence.

"Now the emergency frequency is inoperable!" Neil told his team.

Fran, Eris, and Nico were checking on the rest of Rois' team to see if anyone else was alive.

"Impossible." Nico knelt next to Jaya's prostrate body. "The tradutors connect with the satellites in Mars' orbit, providing ultra-high-frequency communications coverage. Severe weather isn't supposed to affect them."

"Something's jammed the tradutors," Neil replied.

Nico checked Jaya's suit health monitor. He shook his head.

Neil closed his eyes for a brief second. They needed to reach someone. They needed help.

A few feet away, Patrick stirred. Blood covered his suit, which possessed a scar similar to Rois' own, where nanobots had resealed it.

Despite Patrick's cruel attacks, he didn't deserve to die. Neil knew he had to do something fast.

"Fran, I need an emergency shelter." He removed a knife from his pack and knelt down at Patrick's side.

Fran approached, pulling a clear emergency shelter, which looked like a folded sheet, from her pack. She grabbed one end and flung it out over Neil, Nico, and Patrick. As the shelter descended over them, she quickly ducked underneath. It curved and stiffened, forming a dome over them. A chemical compound lining the perimeter of the shelter rapidly formed a bond with the ground to create a seal. Fran followed that with a miniaturized "space heater" which rapidly warmed the air inside the shelter to an endurable temperature. Certainly not a pleasant level, but enough that they could open up Patrick's suit to treat his injuries. And the shelter's substance allowed it to trap the heat for as long as it remained in place.

Neil quickly cut the "scar" in Patrick's suit, opening up a hole which he pried apart to prevent the nanobots from resealing. "Fran, hold this for me."

She swallowed, face pale as she stared at the ugly gash in Patrick's side. Blood covered his torso and the inside of his suit. But she bent and took the flaps from Neil.

He pulled skunk sack leaves from his pack and wiped some of the blood away. "Patrick, can you hear me?" he asked.

Patrick moaned. He opened his eyes. There was confusion in his gaze.

"How do you feel?" Fran asked him.

Patrick blinked slowly as if about to fall asleep. He sucked in air as Neil dabbed at the wound.

"I think he's got a concussion." Neil noted that Patrick's eyes lacked focus. "We need to keep him awake."

Outside the shelter, Jiro surged to a sitting position, suddenly waking and blinking.

Eris bent down beside him. "How do you feel?" Neil heard her words over the emergency band.

"I'm…" Jiro swayed. "I don't know."

Neil chewed a couple of skunk sack leaves to make a paste. The leaves created a cooling, winterminty affect in his mouth and tasted a bit like aloe. Neil applied the paste to Patrick's wounds. It would help fight infection and promote clotting.

"Do you have any liquid stitches?" Neil asked. Fran nodded at her pack.

He fished around until he found a white tube. He removed the cap and squeezed a large line over Patrick's wound, then dabbed the liquid stitches with the remaining skunk sack leaves to cover the wound as best he could. It should prevent further blood loss, but Patrick needed a doctor. They needed to get him and the rest back to the ship immediately.

"Let's seal it up," Neil said, capping the liquid stitches tube and depositing it back in Fran's pack. She pressed Patrick's suit flaps together so the nanobots could reseal the tear. Neil waited for a thirty second count before lifting the emergency shelter, breaking its bond, and tossing it off to the side.

Maellyn knelt beside Rois and stared at her immobile figure. Rois' vacant eyes stared past her. Neil stood, wishing he could close them, but didn't want to remove her helmet here. Leaving her like this wasn't fair. Yet the moment he moved over and stooped to pick her up, he heard her voice in his head, as if speaking to him from death.

Look after Riagan. He needs your help more than I do.

Neil ran his hand over her helmet, imagining that he brushed back her hair. He wished he had a last chance to say goodbye. Instead, he said, "Get them back to the ship and warn the instructors. I'm going after Riagan."

"I'm coming." Maellyn climbed to her feet as if she had also heard Rois.

He shook his head. "You need to help get Rois back to the ship. You're in no shape to fight Dahaka."

"I won't let you face them alone." Maellyn walked past him after Riagan, doing her best to hide her pain and exhaustion.

"Academy regs dictate that I'm your commanding officer," Neil called after her. "I can order you back if necessary."

She kept on as if he'd said nothing.

Eris took a step after her. "I'm your best shot."

If Neil didn't take control now, he would never have it. He would have to stop the others, too.

Neil blocked Eris and gestured toward Patrick, who had started moaning again. "Patrick needs a doctor. The leaves helped, but he needs real medical treatment. You three must get him and Jiro back to the ship and sound the alert. A bigger attack is coming." He felt certain of that fact.

Eris, Nico, and Fran all started to argue.

He clenched his fists and glared. He had no trouble showing his anger. Not with Rois and Jaya dead at his feet. "I'm ordering you to get them back to the ship. We need to be the ones who sound the alarm for everyone's protection. We must be space aces."

The three stood straighter at this, nodding as if realizing the wisdom in his demands. They set to work getting Patrick and Jiro to their feet.

Neil hated to leave Rois and Jaya, but for now he had no choice. Turning his back on them felt like another betrayal they didn't deserve, but he heard Rois in his head again.

Help Riagan. That's what you can do for me.

*****

Neil caught up with Maellyn and handed her a skunk sack leaf. "Can you jog?"

"Set the pace." She bit off some of the leaf. Chewing would provide marginal relief.

He had abandoned the idea of ordering her back. Her determined march convinced him that any commands from him would fall on deaf ears. He could try to fight her back to the ship, or they could go together to find Riagan. Not both. And he knew how she would respond if he tried to force her to turn around. Did that make him a bad team captain or a practical one?

They jogged deeper into the basin. He set a slower pace to avoid overtaxing her. He wished she would've returned to the ship, not only because he worried about her, but because he could track Riagan faster on his own. But a part of him knew that she had to come just as much as he did.

"How many attacked you?" he asked, hoping for one or two.

"Four. Upon us fast. I scarcely noticed before one knocked me out."

His hope withered. Were those four alone, or part of a larger force? Riagan had run off frenzied. Would he attempt to take them all on alone?

"Glad you weren't hurt worse," Neil said.

For a response, she jogged faster, as if to prove that she was all right.

Ten minutes later they reached what appeared to be an outpost. It was made up of four white metal buildings, one of which was three stories tall and surrounded by the other three that were half its size. It had to have been here some time, and looked like a typical field structure. How was it kept hidden from everyone back on Earth? He knew that Space City was cloaked. They must do something similar to hide their activities on Mars.

He half hoped they'd be lucky enough to find someone that could contact the ship. That hope died when they found Riagan behind the closest building. He fired his laser through an open doorway into the large central building. Were the Dahaka inside?

Neil switched his suit laser over to full power. Normally, their suit lasers were restricted to training mode for all school functions, but Nico had found a way around that and shared it. He never mentioned how he learned about it.

Hurrying to join Riagan, Neil was glad they weren't too late. *I found him, Rois.* Finding no one in the open door of the middle structure, he asked, "Are you ok?"

Riagan fired again. "Four inside." He seemed normal and collected again.

"We need to retreat and get help," Neil said, feeling that his words lacked command.

Riagan shook his head. "They killed Rois. I'm going to return the favor."

Trying to force command back into his voice, he said "Maellyn said there were at least four. Could be more. We need backup."

"Go back then!" Riagan snapped. "Run if ya scared. They're going to pay."

Neil shook his head. He tried the emergency band once more. "Instructor Nez, come in." Someone had to be listening. "Glenn. Tereshkova, come in. Can anyone hear me? We tracked Dahaka to four buildings southeast of the ship. We need backup." He waited, screaming in his head for someone to respond. "Nez. Can anyone here me?"

What had happened to their communications? The longer Space City and the instructors remained out of contact, the greater the danger they were all in from whatever the Dahaka had planned. He did not want to face the Dahaka, but his choices were to either help Riagan or abandon him. He'd already lost Rois, whom he thought of as a sister. Losing Jaya hurt, too. He was not going to lose his best friend on top of it.

He rose and took a step forward. "Cover me. I'll check it out."

Riagan opened his mouth to argue, but Neil sprinted forward before he could respond. A part of him hoped they wouldn't find the Dahaka, that Riagan had just lost it.

The cover fire wasn't returned, allowing Neil to safely reach the doorway to the central building and duck down beside it. A glass door ten feet in sealed the entrance. Beyond the door, an empty hallway ran a good fifty feet before ending in a bunker filled with crates.

He waved Riagan and Maellyn over and they slipped inside. Riagan pulled the exterior door shut behind them. Air filled the space, pressurizing the area, and the interior door slid open.

"Those better be automatic doors," Neil said.

Maellyn nodded, eyes worried. Riagan just stared ahead, focused on his mission.

Neil felt like prey being lured into an ambush. According to the environmental readings on his wrist-comp, the room held breathable air so he removed the helmet. Riagan and Maellyn followed his lead.

They proceeded through the empty corridor, ready to shoot at the slightest movement. Neil's insides were ice. Each step forward took tremendous effort. They were unprepared to face Dahaka. He wanted to flee, but then saw Rois' sightless eyes judging him for his cowardice. How many others might also die if he turned back now? They had no guarantee help would arrive in time, so it was up to them.

They reached the open bunker. Three Dahaka in obsidian bone armor stepped out of a doorway on the far side of the room. They held the leashes of two large gray beasts. Reptilian skin covered wolf-like, horse-sized bodies. The beasts flashed sharp teeth and growled a warning. The Dahakas' crimson eyes grinned viciously at them. Silently, the Dahaka released the beasts, which stalked forward.

Neil broke out in a cold sweat and his instincts screamed for him to run. If the beasts caught them, they would be ripped to shreds in seconds.

The beasts sniffed the air and one pawed his nose, as if trying to rid itself of something. Were the skunk sack juices deterring the beasts?

Maybe they could use that to make an escape.

"You guys prepare to run," Neil said.

He forced his arm to steady as he took aim and fired at the creature on the right. At the last second his fingers shook and his shot struck the beast in the shoulder. The alien predator roared in fury, shaking the walls, but it stopped coming.

Rather than use his shots as a diversion to help them escape, Riagan and Maellyn also fired. Their shots aggravated the creatures, but caused little obvious harm.

The Dahaka laughed and jeered at this great game.

Neil considered shooting them, but their armor left little exposed. It seemed to him that the beasts posed a bigger immediate threat anyway.

"Ideas?" Maellyn's voice trembled.

"Just this." Riagan removed a light grenade from his pack.

"Where did you get that?" Neil asked.

"Printed it last night. Couldn't sleep after you told me about team captain, so thought I'd make use of the time. Thought this might prove useful today."

"You'll kill us all," Neil protested. The grenade might bring the building down upon all their heads.

For answer, Riagan pressed his three middle fingers into ridges in the cylinder and tossed the grenade at one of the creatures. The beast caught it in its mouth. It dropped the grenade on the ground and pawed at it.

"Get back." Neil pulled Maellyn back into the hallway, desperately trying to shield her.

I'm sorry, Rois. I failed again, he thought.

Riagan dropped to their sides as light rocked the bunker. The building shook as the ceiling collapsed behind them. The force of the explosion threw Neil further down the hallway and he landed hard on his pack and life support system. He scrambled to his feet, ready to carry Maellyn to safety if need be before they were buried, but the building stopped shaking. The bunker was filled from the cave in, burying the beasts. Hopefully the Dahaka, too. But the rest of the building, including the hallway, appeared stable.

"Blimey!" Maellyn said.

Riagan climbed to his feet, brushing off debris.

Neil took measured steps toward the bunker, searching for the creatures or the Dahaka, but there was no movement inside. Unnoticed when they'd entered, a staircase along the right wall led upward past the shattered second floor of the bunker, which made sense. The building had been a few stories tall.

He gestured upward. "Any bets what's up there?"

"There's at least one more Dahaka unaccounted for," Maellyn said.

Riagan moved toward the stairs, but Neil grabbed his arm. "Lasers won't damage Dahaka armor."

"I only printed one light grenade," Riagan said. "The lasers are all we've got."

A shiver swept through Neil at the thought of using another light grenade in here, considering the damage the last one caused, but he knew it might be their only hope of stopping the Dahaka. "I've got supplies in my pack."

He slipped the pack off his shoulders and found busted containers with compounds spilt everywhere. He turned to Maellyn. "What about you?"

She shook her head. "Lost mine during the attack."

Riagan searched his pack, removing broken containers, too. Only a small amount of his supplies remained. Neil examined his own more closely. A little bit of CO_2 remained in one container. Between that and what they could salvage from Riagan's, they might have enough to make one golf ball-sized grenade.

"Give me your wrist-comp," Riagan said. "Mine's broken."

After handing him the device, Neil grabbed his 3D printer and poured the contents into the supply slot. He was no mixer like Rois, but it would have to do.

"Ready?" Riagan asked.

Neil nodded. He set the printer down. Riagan gave the command. The printer rose into the air and started building a tiny light grenade.

Casting anxious glances up the stairwell, Neil wondered if the last Dahaka definitely lurked somewhere overhead. It seemed likely. And if so, what was he planning and how much time did they have left?

The printer laid thin layer upon layer in rapid progression, so that the grenade seemed to be growing right there in front of their eyes. Despite the speed, it would take several minutes to finish. It felt like hours.

Riagan's eyes studied the growing grenade almost greedily. Whoever faced the Dahaka would likely not make it through another explosion. Neil could not let Maellyn die today. Riagan either. Could he convince them to let him go on alone? He wasn't anxious to die himself, but it was better than either of them dying. And if things indeed went wrong, at least he had avoided becoming a ghost like his uncle.

The printer completed its job and lowered to the ground. Before he could grab it, Riagan seized the small light grenade and charged up the stairs, as if he had suspected that Neil would try to take it away from him. Maellyn and Neil chased after him.

Neil wanted to shout at Riagan to stop, to let him go up alone with the grenade. No reason for all three of them to put their lives in danger. But the words stuck in his throat. What right did he have to try to stop them? They had as much right as he to fight, regardless the cost. He wanted to protect them, but it was their choice to make.

"Attack the moment you see it," Neil said as they neared the third-floor doorway.

Riagan reached the top step, already raising his arm to throw the light grenade, but as he burst into the room he plunged face first onto the floor. The light grenade struck the ground, jarred free from his grasp, and bounced off to the side.

Neil skidded to a halt, shocked at how quickly their plan had disintegrated. A wire, shot from a square device at floor level just inside the door, was wrapped around Riagan's leg.

Across the room, an obsidian-armored Dahaka leaned over what resembled a futuristic silver cannon, a good eight feet long. The cannon pointed out a window in the general direction of where Space City was in orbit. Seeing it, Neil had a hard time imagining the cannon could do any significant damage to the ship. Maybe they should've waited for backup after all.

The Dahaka bellowed at their intrusion and typed on a panel on the cannon's side.

Neil bent to help Riagan unwind the wire from his ankle. Riagan pushed him away. "Get the grenade."

"Ok." Neil took a step toward the grenade, but the Dahaka had finished, slammed the panel cover closed, and rounded on them. Neil froze under that murderous crimson gaze.

They were dead.

"The Council regards us so little, they send children to face Angra Mainyu?" The Dahaka leader raised the shield on his obsidian bone helmet to reveal his pale white skin that only accentuated his manic red eyes. Mainyu was larger than other Dahaka they had seen, like an armored polar bear. "Your comrades will soon learn respect."

Terrified, but resolved to at least delay Mainyu, Neil pointed at the cannon. "Is that how you hope to get on the ship and steal the CME?"

The Dahaka growled. "The Council is so confident in its superiority. This *is* the weapon. One shot from it will douse the ship in a deadly amount of radiation. No one onboard will survive."

Neil felt sick. How had they smuggled the CME off the ship? He'd been told it was impossible to steal it, and yet here it stood.

"I don't care about the CME," Riagan yelled, firing at Mainyu's face. "Ya killed my sister. I'm going to destroy ya."

The moment Riagan attacked, Neil saw his chance and bolted for the light grenade. Mainyu ducked Riagan's laser fire, but one beam grazed his cheek. He dropped his facemask and barreled over to cut Neil off. The three of them were no match for the Dahaka. He was too big and fast. Too strong.

"You're a fragile race who leached your technology from others in order to gain dominance." Mainyu fingered the tusk on his right forearm, as if contemplating stabbing them with it. "Once I radiate your ship, you will all be gone and I'll have access to all of its resources. How long do you think your unsuspecting Earth will hold against an invasion?"

If the CME came even close to generating the power of one solar flare from the sun, Earth didn't have a single weapon to counter it beyond its magnetic field. The Dahaka had snuck onboard a Space City on full alert. How would Earth fight a threat it didn't know existed? At that moment, Space City's secrecy from Earth seemed a cruel shield.

"Who was the traitor?" Neil asked, suddenly furious. He had to know who had consigned them all to death. "Who helped you obtain the CME?"

The Dahaka grinned ghoulishly. "They'll be dealt with when the cannon destroys your ship."

They? Neil's tongue stuck in his throat.

"You pervert my father's work!" Maellyn fired at the CME, but the shot bounced harmlessly off the silver cannon. "Why do you anticipate everything, Dad?"

The reminder that Maellyn's father had made the CME boosted Neil's confidence.

"Less than a year ago, I was one of the unsuspecting people on Earth," he said. "Once we were all ignorant. But the moment we made contact with the Azzaro, we started working *together* to form alliances and quickly advanced."

"How will that power help when your enemy has all your weapons?" The Dahaka measured everything in terms of power. Nothing else mattered to them.

"I don't know, but we are here," Neil replied. "And that matters." It didn't matter that they were three teenagers without the proper training to fight a Dahaka. They had come, all three of them, knowing the danger they faced. Knowing they were risking their lives. But some things were more important than that. Some things required them to come together. Required sacrifice to protect the world they loved. They weren't here because they wanted to be. They had to be. So that no one else aboard Space City would have their time cut short like Rois.

Mainyu sneered. "You share the same blind arrogance all humans possess. Unfortunately, you'll never know that your confidence is foolish."

"Riagan, get the light grenade," Neil ordered. "Maellyn, find a way to stop your father's CME."

He fired with both arms at Mainyu and charged, trying to keep the Dahaka focused on him. Each shot rebounded off the obsidian armor, except for one to Mainyu's left hand, which caused the Dahaka to shout in pain. What Neil had taken as an extension of the armor turned out to be plain black gloves.

Neil diverted his aim at the Dahaka's hands and kept firing. Furious, Mainyu burst forward like a panther. He slashed at Neil's neck with the tusk on his right arm. Neil ducked. He fired upward at Mainyu's neck, desperate for an opening. The shots struck the chest armor as Mainyu stabbed downward with his left arm.

The tusk plunged past Neil's face. He barely had time to think that this was madness, before a kick from Mainyu sent him sprawling onto his back. Before he could roll away, Mainyu seized him by the throat and lifted him into the air, squeezing. Neil raised his arm to shoot, but the Dahaka knocked it away and head-butted him. Blinding pain surged through his skull. Everything blurred. His nose ran and he hit the ground hard.

"Neil!"

He blinked, trying to clear his vision. Who had called him? His head throbbed. He wanted to sleep.

"Neil!"

This time he realized that Maellyn was shouting at him in alarm. She grabbed his arm, trying to pull him up, but he lacked any strength to rise. He wanted to calm her, but was unable to focus.

She screamed and let him go. The terror in her voice drew him back. He opened his eyes. Blood oozed down his cheek. His vision swam, but he caught a blurry Maellyn dodging an attacker. He struggled to sit up. Horror crashed over him like a tidal wave.

Across the room, Maellyn dodged Mainyu's attacks, firing back, but her shots bounced harmlessly off his armor. The Dahaka pursued her slowly, almost casually, stalking her. He wanted to enjoy this.

A few feet away, Riagan lay collapsed. Barely conscious, his head turned toward Neil. He pushed something forward. The light grenade rolled across the floor and bumped Neil's leg.

For a moment he stared at it, unsure how to attack. If he tossed it at Mainyu, he risked hurting Maellyn in the process. He couldn't do that. Yet what else could he do to stop Mainyu? He wasn't strong enough on his own.

But he didn't have to be strong enough to beat Mainyu. He just had to draw the Dahaka to himself, away from Maellyn and Riagan.

Neil had always been in awe of his grandfather's bravery. Yet his grandfather couldn't have known he could pull off his heroic feats. He had simply cared enough about the people he was fighting for to put himself on the line.

Maellyn tripped and fell backward as Mainyu closed in on her.

Pushing back the fogginess threatening to overwhelm him again, Neil grabbed the grenade. He struggled to his feet and stumbled forward. "Mainyu!"

He raised his left arm and fired. And scored the side of Mainyu's neck.

The Dahaka spun around and charged like a bull that had spotted a red flag. Neil fired again, while pressing the slots in the mini grenade. Mainyu raised his arm to impale Neil with the tusk. Instead of falling back, Neil lunged at Mainyu and the Dahaka's arm pounded the side of his head. A second later Mainyu's body slammed into him.

The cold armor knocked out Neil's breath. He wanted to crumple to the ground, but knew he couldn't.

Instinctively, he jammed the grenade into the gap between Mainyu's armor and helmet. It caught and held. Neil wanted to hold on, to keep them pinned together so Mainyu couldn't knock away the grenade. But what strength he had evaporated and a second punch from Mainyu sent him flying into the wall with a sickening thud. He collapsed on the ground. A bright light shot through the room, followed by an explosion that shook the walls. He braced for the ceiling to collapse, or the floor, but nothing else happened.

He risked a glance up. Mainyu was gone and the only trace of him was painted on the walls and ceiling.

I'm alive! Neil thought, unable to believe it.

Maellyn rushed to his side. "Are you all right?"

He groaned as he pushed himself to a sitting position. She helped him to his feet. His nose bled and his whole body protested, but he was well enough.

Riagan.

Neil hobbled over to Riagan, who remained flat on his back, eyes unfocused. Neil knelt and placed a hand on Riagan's shoulder. "Riagan, are you ok?"

Riagan's eyes slowly latched onto him. "Is it over?"

Neil smiled in relief. They were safe.

Maellyn interrupted. "I couldn't get the CME panel cover open."

For a moment he was lost, unsure what she was referring to, but his relief was draining away at the urgency in her voice. Then he realized that she was talking about the CME. She'd been unable to deactivate it. He stared at the cannon, unable to believe that they had actually beaten Mainyu, but it might be for nothing. They were alive. For how long?

"Help me up," Riagan said.

Neil and Maellyn lifted Riagan to his feet, helping to steady him for a moment. Then Neil hobbled over to the CME, his right knee throbbing. He tried to pry open the battered panel cover, but it didn't budge. A smooth, silver shell covered the CME, providing no other openings to exploit. They could not turn it off.

He stepped back from the device, wondering how long before it would fire, doubting they had any time to wait for help. It was on them to do something to stop it from killing everyone on Space City.

Moving to the front of the CME, he placed both hands on the silver tube. He shoved and gasped from the exertion. The CME weighed a ton. How had anyone gotten it off the ship unnoticed?

"Give me a hand," he said.

Riagan and Maellyn move to his side.

"One. Two. Three."

Neil pushed hard, straining. With their help the CME shifted slightly.

"Release."

Any moment the cannon could fire, destroying the ship and leaving them stranded on Mars until they died. What would Earth think when they sent their next rover here and discovered their remains? He started to laugh deliriously.

"Neil?" Maellyn asked.

He sobered and shook his head, not wanting to share his thoughts. "On three." They could do this together. "One. Two. Three. Puuuusshh. Release. One. Two. Three. Puuusshh. Release."

They kept pushing, releasing, and pushing again. Inch by inch the CME shifted until it pointed at the wall. That had to be enough.

"Let's go."

Neil grabbed Riagan's right arm and Maellyn grabbed the other. They staggered across the room, supporting each other, and descended the stairs. Halfway down, they ran into General Stribog on his way up. Panicked, Neil raised his arm to shoot.

"You're safe." The general waved for them to hurry down.

"How did ya find us?" Riagan asked.

"Your team warned us."

Enough time had passed for that, Neil decided, but had only the general come? Or had he already been here?

Overhead, an explosion rocked the building. Neil darted a fearful glance upward. Smoke enveloped him. The general wrapped them in a tight but insubstantial embrace.

Neil choked, having trouble breathing as he fought to escape. Then they flew. He hoped toward safety, but what if they weren't? Mainyu's words echoed through his head. *They'll be dealt with…* More than one traitor? Was the general really here to save them?

He gasped for air. As he drifted toward unconsciousness, he fought harder to escape, lungs burning, but both efforts were futile.

If the general killed them now, at least they'd saved Space City. The CME was destroying this place and hopefully burying itself. His grandfather would be proud. This thought drained with him into blackness.

Chapter 31

Riagan's Mourning Revelation

Riagan slumped over Rois' open coffin in a room at the back of the Academy infirmary. He wanted to lie next to her and die as well for his failure. Why had he let the instructors separate them?

After they had defeated Mainyu two days earlier, he had returned to the ship, found Rois' body, and sat with her for hours, begging himself for an answer as to why he hadn't done more to ensure her safety. Around dawn, he had admitted the answer, and it cut him deep.

He had wanted to win.

Teaming up with Neil had given him the best chance to win the exam. He had believed they were unbeatable together. Nor would Rois have changed teams even if the instructors had allowed it. She had wanted to remain with Jaya. She had insisted that he would protect her in Riagan's stead. But Jaya lay in another coffin a few feet away.

Riagan had placed his desire to win above his concern for her, and thereby lost her forever. He had chastised Neil and Jaya bitterly for doing nothing when Patrick had attacked her last fall. He had accused Neil and Jaya of betraying them through inaction. Now he had betrayed her in kind, but the cost had been far worse.

Neil stepped up and placed a hand on Riagan's shoulder. For a moment they stared quietly at Rois' pale form, a sacrificial statue.

"You couldn't have known," Neil said. "We never suspected the Dahaka were hiding in the storm. No one had any clue."

"I never helped ya," Riagan said, the admission scalding him.

"You helped me to the end. We defeated the Dahaka. We avenged Rois."

Riagan quivered. "I told you to let it go. I ignored the problem. I refused to help when doing so could've made a difference."

Neil gave his shoulder a light squeeze. It was meant to be comforting, but only served as another reminder of his failings.

"I told Headmaster Dardanos everything," Neil said. "He investigated. What could we have found that he missed? If you blame yourself… blame me, too. I failed her."

Hot tears filled Riagan's eyes. "Failure? I never tried. I refused to worry about the Dahaka or the traitor. Even after what happened to Cade, I turned my back because it was easier. Rois is dead because of my cowardice."

"The Council found nothing," Neil said. "This was beyond us."

The council had not spoken in the aftermath of the attack. How the Dahaka had stolen the CME wasn't revealed, if known. He and Neil suspected General Stribog, but the council confirmed nothing. They didn't have to. Cade's prolonged coma seemed proof enough to Riagan. But Mainyu's claim of more than one traitor was troubling. And if General Stribog was a traitor, why had he rescued them? They had too few answers.

The cries from a mourning woman drew their attention. Entering the room, a short and thin Azzaro woman sobbed on Jarl's shoulder. Three other Azzaro men that Riagan didn't recognize followed them. They approached Jaya's coffin. Jarl had one arm wrapped around the woman, must be Jaya's mother, and his own cheeks were wet. When they reached the coffin, the woman threw herself onto Jaya's body. "Jaya. Jaya." Her body wracked by sobs, she clung to him as if she never intended to let go. She wailed as if someone were literally ripping her heart from her chest.

Jaya had tried to save Rois. He had fought for her in their last moments. Wherever Jaya and Rois had gone after death—Riagan wasn't sure what he believed about life after death—he hoped fervently that they found each other. They deserved peace together.

Jarl pulled his wife off their son, and whispered to her, though in the quiet room they could hear his words.

"Juna, It's time to take him back home."

She stepped aside, shaking and her eyes were red. The other three Azzaros moved to separate corners of Jaya's coffin, one lowering the lid as he did so. Jarl attended to his wife for a couple of more minutes before moving toward the last corner on the coffin. At that moment, two Space City officers entered.

"Jarl, will you come with us?" one officer asked.

"What? No." Jarl glared and gestured at the closed coffin. "I'm preparing to return my son home. Whatever it is, it can wait."

"I'm afraid not, sir," the officer said darting an uncomfortable glance toward Juna. "We have our orders."

Jarl clenched his fists firmly at his side and strode right up to the officer. "This is outrageous. I'm going to lay my son to rest on Sundara."

Rather than argue the point further, the officer grabbed one of Jarl's arms, motioning as he did so for the second officer to help him.

"Jarl, what is this about?" Juna's fearful eyes darted between the men constraining her husband and the coffin. The three Azzaro surrounding the coffin watched with mouths wide, seemingly paralyzed by the scene.

"Unhand me," Jarl demanded, struggling to get free as the officers cuffed his wrists.

For a reply, the officer clapped him across the back of the head. "After what you did, betraying us all… the Council will deal with you."

"What?" Jarl paused, eyes widening. "I've done nothing wrong."

The Azzaro who had closed Jaya's coffin took one step forward, but the first officer raised a hand in warning.

"Don't interfere. This is an official Space City investigation."

The Azzaro immediately stopped. Then the officers pulled Jarl toward the door.

"Jarl, why are they doing this?" Juna swayed as if she might faint.

"Please, my son," Jarl pleaded. "I will return as soon as he's laid to rest. Surely whatever it is the Council thinks I've done, they can wait that long."

But the officers ignored him. Jarl began to shout once they had him out of the room.

Riagan just stared in stunned silence. What had Jarl done that they would stop his son's funeral? The officers had said he'd betrayed everyone. Had he been the traitor? It seemed unbelievable.

The Azzaro who had tried to intervene now approached Juna, who broke down, burying her head in his chest. "It's ok," he soothed. "We'll figure this out."

The other pair fidgeted by the coffin, clearly unsure what to do.

Holding Juna to him, the Azzaro looked over at Riagan and Neil. "Would one of you stand in for Jarl and help us deliver Jaya home? We don't have time to summon another."

Juna's sobs grew louder.

Riagan's heart broke at her cries. Rois would want Jaya treated properly. If Jaya wasn't, maybe the two of them would never find each other in the afterlife. Riagan took a step forward, but Neil placed a hand on his arm to hold him back.

"I'll go," Neil said. "You should stay with Rois." He stepped over to the corner that Jarl had been headed for when he was arrested.

"Bless you," the Azzaro said, letting Juna go and stepping toward his own corner.

Juna wiped the tears from her eyes, doing her best to compose herself. "Bless you. Bless you." She gave Neil a smile of gratitude, though her eyes remained dull.

Neil and the Azzaros lifted the coffin, grunting a little as they lifted it up onto their shoulders. They made it a few steps toward the door when two more Space City officers entered.

"Neil Ericson, will you come with us?" one asked.

"What for?" Neil looked unsure whether he should keep holding the coffin or try to set it down.

"There's evidence Jarl chemically hypnotized you," the officer said.

Juna gasped and the other Azzaros' eyes widened in alarm.

Neil gaped. "What does that mean?"

Riagan looked at Neil, half expecting to see heretofore unnoticed signs of the hypnotism. Surely the officers were confused. When could Jarl have done this?

"If you'll come with us," the officer said, "—that will be explained. This is for your protection."

"Can this wait?" Neil's face was pale. "I need to help escort my friend's remains."

"Of course," the officer agreed, clearly willing to accommodate the hero who thwarted the Dahaka on Mars. "But for your own safety, we need to accompany you."

Neil nodded then looked at Riagan. "I'll come back after we get Jaya to Sundara."

Riagan pursed his lips, feeling a surge of gratefulness for that, which overwhelmed his ability to speak.

After turning back to Rois, a couple of tears leaked from his eyes. He wished she were just sleeping. And that triggered a memory. Neil in bed after the formal. He'd been surprised to find Neil already asleep. And Neil had been confused how he'd gotten there. Had that been the night Jarl had hypnotized him? That had to be it. What else made sense? And Rois. She hadn't remembered going to bed that night either. Had she been hypnotized as well? They must've learned what Jarl had been up to, and he hypnotized them to cover up stealing the CME. The pieces fit.

His guilt reignited at the realization. If he hadn't ignored Neil, if he had just helped him, maybe they could've prevented all of this before they ever set foot on Mars. He leaned on the edge of Rois' coffin, needing the support.

It all led back to him. She lay here because of him. He tried to imagine her looking up at him, but all he could recall was her empty eyes. Their mother's unseeing eyes. He had failed them both.

After some indeterminate amount of time, Neil returned with four officers in tow.

"It's time to send her," Neil said softly.

Riagan fought the urge to yell, to tell them to go away. He just nodded and the four officers surrounded the coffin and picked it up. They carried it toward the Spaceport, where it was loaded onto a specialized rocket that would carry her toward the Sun, where she would be cremated. He'd been given the option to take her back to Earth for burial, but he had no desire to return. Neither of them had left behind anything worthwhile, and after everything, he couldn't bear to send her back.

He'd also had the option to launch her in any direction into space. Toward a favorite point. But he hadn't liked the idea of her floating forever in space. What if someone found her and examined her? No. The sun would take care of her.

The officers gave him and Neil some space as they stood around the rocket. Riagan tried to work up the courage to actually say goodbye and send her on her way. Throughout the rest of the day and into the night, Neil shared different moments with Rois over the course of the last year. Riagan recounted some of their best memories of growing up, few though they were. At times he choked up too much to continue, so they'd stand in silence for a time.

Eventually, he decided it was time or he'd never be able to send her off. He typed in the simple code for the rocket's keypad and they retreated back to a safe zone to watch the rocket launch into space. Long after the rocket had dwindled from view, he still lacked parting words for her.

Chapter 32

Neil's Fireworks

Neil waded through students on the academy quad. Tonight was his first bit of freedom since the Council had summoned him. The revelation that Jarl had chemically hypnotized him had left him confused and scared. Spending a week with the academy doctors undergoing tests and observation, about which they offered little explanation, had offered no relief.

"I've brought someone to visit you."

Neil spun around to find Maellyn approaching with her father; Petey perched on her shoulder.

"Petey!" Neil said. "He's gotten so big."

The teinyosaurus had doubled in size, his wingspan roughly a foot wide now. Neil pulled out a pyrn bite and offered it to him. Petey gobbled it up.

"Nearly as big as his mama." Maellyn's yellow daisy earrings reflected the setting sun and seemed to highlight her smile. "How are you feeling?"

Neil took Petey from Maellyn's arm. Looking from her to her father, Neil felt a little uneasy. It was his first encounter with her father since accusing him of being the traitor. "A little shook up. They're saying I was chemically hypnotized by Jarl twice. First time when I overheard him talking with the Dahaka, Ormazd. The second in the science labs after the formal. I can't believe he's the traitor."

"What does that mean for you?" Maellyn's concern clouded her face, hiding the smile he wished would return.

He shrugged. "I can't remember either attack. But I don't feel any different."

"A lot of people are surprised that Jarl was the traitor," Dr. Trevena said.

Neil felt his cheeks reddening and he grimaced. "I apologize for suspecting you."

Dr. Trevena firmly shook his head. "No one can fault your actions. You did your duty. I'm especially proud you did so considering your affection for my daughter. You didn't allow personal feelings to prevent you from doing the right thing."

Maellyn blushed at that.

"But I knew you and your daughter," Neil said. "You welcomed me into your home. I should've trusted you."

"You can't trust blindly," Dr. Trevena said. "Just because you care about someone doesn't mean they're incapable of wrongdoing. Never ignore criminal behavior, no matter who it is. Good people, those with integrity, choose to do what's right, always."

A weight fell off Neil at Dr. Trevena's words. He hoped that meant Maellyn had also forgiven him. Petey stepped along Neil's arm to his hand, searching for more pyrns. Neil fished out another for him.

Dr. Trevena continued. "I'm also thankful for your leadership during the attack. Your actions saved Maellyn's life, as well as Patrick's and a great many others."

Neil focused on scratching the back of Petey's neck, too embarrassed to meet their eyes. "Jaya was so committed to Space City. His father, too, I thought."

"Often the people we know the best are the ones we are the blindest toward." An anguished look entered Dr. Trevena's eyes.

Neil wondered if the doctor felt partly responsible because he must've given Jarl his lab.

"In this case, Jarl fooled everyone," Dr. Trevena added. "Maybe his wife and son the most."

"How was he discovered?" Neil asked.

Rumors had spread rapidly after Jarl's arrest, and varied widely. Even confined to the hospital, Neil had heard most of them.

Dr. Trevena brightened at the question. "Cade finally woke up."

"He's recovered?" Neil asked, surprised and relieved. How had he not heard about Cade waking up?

Dr. Trevena nodded. "Told the instructors that Jarl attacked when Cade stumbled upon him arranging delivery of the CME with

Ormazd. The Council started investigating and that's when they discovered what happened to you."

Neil would have to thank Cade later for his discovery. Maybe take him a small stash from Colombo Caramella as well.

"The Council moved Cade to its headquarters for safeguarding," Dr. Trevena added. "I've spoken with him a couple times. He is recovering nicely."

Why was Cade being safeguarded with Jarl imprisoned? Neil heard Mainyu's words again. *They'll be dealt with.* Someone else was involved.

"General Stribog is completely innocent?" Neil asked. "What about Cade's words after his collapse? And Mainyu claimed there are multiple traitors."

"Delirium on Cade's part, I expect," Dr. Trevena replied. "The general wasn't in the sim. That's certain. As for multiple traitors, the Council is thoroughly investigating the matter, but all signs point to Jarl working alone. Mainyu probably lied to you. Either way, I assure you Stribog is on our side, no matter what gossip students still spread after all these years."

"Are you sure you're not blind toward him?" Neil asked.

Dr. Trevena chuckled. "I'm confident I'm right. The instructors would all vouch for him as well."

None of it made sense. General Stribog was loyal despite the common association between Kali and Dahaka. Jaya had worked so hard to become a team captain and had loved Rois. He had been committed to this place. Yet Jarl's betrayal had led to both Rois and Jaya's deaths. Why would an Azzaro sacrifice so much to help the Dahaka? At least he had failed.

"What are your plans for the summer holidays?" Maellyn asked.

Before Neil could respond, a familiar gruff voice spoke from behind him. "Hopefully he'll stay with me."

Neil turned, trying to place the familiar voice. He nearly dropped Petey on the ground. The teinyosaurus complained at getting jostled. Neil moved the little guy to his shoulder, desperately trying to process the man before him.

"Hello Neil," his grandfather said, standing next to Mr. Chapman. "You can't know how happy I am that you're here."

While older and with a few more wrinkles, Neil's grandfather still resembled an Air Force officer. He was strong. All the short red hair Neil remembered had grayed. And Mr. Chapman was back from his assignment, too. Had Mr. Chapman returned with his Grandfather?

"Grandpa." Neil tried vainly to make sense of this. "When mom said you disappeared… I never imagined… you're here?"

His grandfather beamed proudly. "Harold informed me that he recruited you." His grandfather reached out and squeezed Mr. Chapman's shoulder. "I've been with the Azzaros a long time. Since the war with the Dahaka. I only returned today."

Half formed questions and conflicting emotions erupted through Neil.

"I'm sorry to hear about your mother. I just learned about that as well." A deep sadness, like a bottomless pool, filled his grandfather's eyes.

Neil fought back tears at the mention of his mother.

"I hope we'll have time to talk," his grandfather said. "Back at home if you agree."

Home.

Neil wanted that very much. He had expected to stay in the dorms over the summer, one of the few kids with nowhere else to go. Now he had his grandfather back. He could hardly believe how far he had come since last summer when Mr. Chapman had stopped him outside the recruiter's office. The old man had taken his grandfather's coin and—

"You knew." Neil looked to Mr. Chapman for confirmation. "You knew my grandfather was a part of Space City. You brought me here because of him."

Mr. Chapman smiled. "I knew, but I had made up my mind even before you told me. I had a feeling about you. My intuition was correct. We might have returned to find our home gone if not for you."

Fortunately, fireworks shot up into the air, diverting everyone's attention as Neil blushed again. First the usual flower and star fireworks lit the darkening sky with reds, greens, blues, and whites. That was followed by coordinated fireworks which created a grandiose figure. Neil gaped in recognition.

"Is that you?" Maellyn asked.

"I can't believe it." Neil was amazed at the detail—his red hair and an explorer suit.

"You did more than anyone to thwart the Dahaka attack," his grandfather said. "The fireworks are a tribute."

More fireworks shot into the sky, emblazoning the figures of Maellyn and Riagan in a slightly smaller scale.

"We should've all been together for this." Neil didn't like that their figures were smaller, or came after his. "They did as much to stop the Dahaka as I did."

"You led them," Dr. Trevena corrected. "You actually killed Mainyu."

"Still can't believe it," his grandfather said, awe in his voice.

The esteem from his grandfather felt good, but he didn't deserve all the credit. He wished Riagan was here, too. He deserved this as much as they did. He needed it more.

"Maellyn, would you want to take Petey out to the spaceport?" Neil asked. "Check on Riagan?"

"Sure." Her face shone in the light from the continued fireworks.

"Grandpa, can I find you later?"

His grandfather nodded. "Meet me at the edge of campus at midnight. We'll talk on our way to the city."

"Great!"

Neil and Maellyn slipped away through the crowd out toward the spaceport. He was glad to spend time with her on good terms for the first time in a while.

"My father was right," she said as they approached the garden. "You always did what was right."

"You're finally apologizing," he teased.

Her cheeks reddened like hot coals in a fire.

"I'm kidding." He hoped she didn't take offence. "I'm just glad you're not mad at me anymore."

"It was difficult for a while," she admitted. "Rois tried to reason with me. She made a lot of good points. Even my father suggested I was wrong to hold a grudge, but the setback with the Apidium… it was too much to handle. Focusing on the Apidium seemed critical and… also somehow easier to handle."

"I heard you found a solution?" he asked, wanting to hear her talk about it because she took so much pleasure in the Apidium. It would make her smile.

She nodded, and her face took on the expected glow. "We feared the disease the mosquitoes carried had mutated and jumped to the moths, which would've rendered our spheres useless. After investigating more, we discovered it was actually a similar, yet less virulent strain. It will help the Apidiums' immune system fight it off."

"That's great! So you can take the spheres to Niveum, now?"

"We'll start week after next," she confirmed. "I'll be gone for the whole summer."

"Oh," he said, feeling like a parade balloon that had been pricked.

For a few seconds they walked in silence. They followed the road into the garden, where the trees were glowing like massive fireflies. Their light reflected off the flowers in the beds surrounding them so that the flowers sparkled.

"What makes the trees glow?" he asked, remembering first seeing them in her neighborhood the night he'd followed the man he'd believed was a Dahaka. The trees had seemed more sinister at the time.

"They're bioluminescent," she replied. "They've had genes added to make them glow."

The firefly trees provided a far more natural light, like moonlight, than any streetlamp.

They walked in silence, enjoying the faint glow of nature, until she finally spoke up. "After the Dahaka attacked, I thought I was dead. And all I could think of was to find you. I had to find you and apologize."

Tears filled her eyes. He wanted to brush them away, but he was afraid to act so boldly. "There's nothing to apologize for."

She brushed away her own tears and he lamented the missed opportunity. She reached out gingerly for his hand. Her touch wiped away all the pain and frustration of the last several months. She was here now.

"I'm just glad you found me," he said.

Instinctively, though he couldn't guess why he had felt such a strong compulsion later, he leaned forward. Her eyes drifted shut as if falling asleep and her chin lifted slightly. Their lips met, brushing gently. They paused. Her breath tickled his lips. Then compulsion took over again and he pressed his lips to hers once more. He lost track of time for a while, and when they finally stopped to breathe, he was thrilled to see her smile had grown like a quarter moon.

"I've been waiting for that," she whispered.

He touched her cheek. Her skin was incredibly soft. He wanted to kiss her again.

"Don't make me wait too long before you do that again," she said.

"I promise."

And he did kiss her again. He never wanted to stop. Their kisses grew more eager.

"Congratulations on your ensky, Neil."

They broke apart, whipping around. Instructor Tereshkova approached from the spaceport. She smiled knowingly at them.

His face burned. Maellyn had taken a step away from him as if an invisible wall suddenly separated them. He wanted to pull her back close.

"You'll make excellent team captain," Tereshkova added.

Neil had to fight through cloudy thoughts to process her words. "Ensky?"

Tereshkova laughed. "A rise in rank. You were an exemplary team captain in exam, so you'll be one for year two. Enjoy your summer."

"Thank you! You, too."

Tereshkova headed back toward campus, leaving him and Maellyn alone once more. He reached for Maellyn's hand and grinned. A good summer awaited. The first summer he had anticipated in years.

Epilogue

"Who did you lose?"

Startled, Riagan turned to find a frail old man shuffling over, his weight supported by a staff. The hand gripping the staff was all knuckles. Thin strips of white hair hung halfway down his back. It took Riagan a moment to recognize the man—the gardener who tended the flowerbeds and orchestrated the robots in the garden out front of the spaceport.

Annoyance at the intrusion filled Riagan's voice. "My sister was killed in the Dahaka attack."

The man's eyes softened. "I'm sorry to hear she's dead. Were you on the planet as well when it happened?"

Riagan didn't answer. He wanted the man to leave, return to his garden. He had come out here to be alone.

"The Azzaro didn't act alone, you know."

Riagan bristled, especially not wanting to discuss anything about Jarl.

The old man studied the sky, Mars resembling nothing more than a large star now. "The Azzaro was a pawn of others."

Riagan frowned. "How do you know? You're a gardener."

"Space City is littered with corrupt men, willing to do anything for more power and wealth."

Riagan balled his hands into fists. The two things helping him deal with Rois' death were that he had beaten Mainyu, and that Jarl, the traitor, had been caught. Yet, if the old man was correct, at least one of Rois' killers remained free. The possibility burned his heart. "Why are you telling me this?"

The old man adjusted his grip on the staff, trying to straighten himself a little, but he only succeeded in drawing focus to his stooped form. "One, because you deserve the truth. Second, I need more sources."

"A source for what?" Riagan wondered if the man had lost his mind.

"If you'll act as a trusted source, you'll have a chance to root out those that killed your sister."

The old man's placidity irritated Riagan.

"Mainyu killed my sister and I got him."

Nodding, the old man agreed. "You did. But those that helped the Dahaka are as responsible for her death as any."

Riagan couldn't argue. He had spent the days since Jarl's arrest furious at the betrayal, and uncertain if maybe Jaya was involved as well; he found that difficult to believe. But if the gardener was correct, others still roamed free. That wasn't something he could tolerate.

"What do you need me to do?" he asked.

"Our first job is to figure out what Mainyu was after." The old man placed his left hand on Riagan's shoulder and pressed to turn him around.

"He was after the CME," Riagan replied. Surely the old man knew as much. If not, this whole conversation was pointless. "He stole it to destroy Space City and Earth."

"That was a distraction." The old man hobbled forward. "I believe it served as a cover for a darker purpose. I think there are other traitors onboard still working toward that purpose."

Hatred surged through Riagan, the same as when he held Rois' bloody remains in his arms. If anyone involved remained free, he owed it to her to find them. He would spend his life, if he had to, finding those who had betrayed her.

"Will you help me?" the old man asked.

Riagan felt Rois' shou necklace which now dangled from his neck. Their parents' last gift to her. All he had left of any of them was that necklace. All his family was gone, except for in his nightmares. He had turned his back and refused to help Neil find the traitors before.

He would not do so again.

About the Author:

Jared Austin is a young adult science fiction author who lives in the Rocket City—Huntsville, Alabama. With Space City and the books in the series to follow, he hopes to show and inspire his daughter and son, as well as all of his readers, that science and technology are not dull subjects, but gateways to a brighter, exciting future.

If you would like to learn more about the series and future novels, visit: https://jareddanielaustin.com

Books in Series:
Space City
Escape
Space City Outbreak
Contact Not Found

Follow me on social media:
Facebook Author Page: www.facebook.com/jareddanielaustin
Instagram: jared_austin1981
Twitter: @JaredAustin1981

Thank you for reading my book! If you enjoyed it, please consider leaving a review. Even just a few words would help others decide if the book is right for them. Best regards and thank you in advance!

www.ingramcontent.com/pod-product-compliance
Lightning Source LLC
Chambersburg PA
CBHW072056190726
48294CB00005B/1559